MALICIOUS INTENT

A Hollywood Fable

MALICIOUS INTENT

A Hollywood Fable

MIKE WALKER

BALTIMORE
1999

Published by Bancroft Press
"books that enlighten."
PO Box 65360, Baltimore, MD 21209

ISBN 1-890862-05-3

Printed in the United States of America

Jacket design: Steven Parke for What?design
Book design: Susan Mangan

Distributed to the trade by
National Book Network, Lanham, MD

To Sloane Sophia

For encouragement above and beyond the call, and for simply putting up with me: my wife, Tomi; my children, Justin and Wendy; Deborah Hughes; Jim Meyers; my agent, Caron K; Michael Viner; Deborah Raffin; Ms. Geary; David Wyler; Catherine Wyler; Dennis Bogorad; and, of course, the indispensable Brunhilde Frappe.

And heartfelt thanks to my editor, Sarah Azizi, whose every suggestion revealed an unerring sense of tone and structure.

"Two things are certain: death and tabloids!"

—Burt Reynolds after collapsing from stress in 1994

TINSELTOWN FOLLIES

CHAPTER 1

9:31 A.M.
"E!" TV STUDIOS
LOS ANGELES

BACKSTAGE in the makeup department at "E!" TV on Wilshire Boulevard, Joan Rivers fired raunchy one-liners at a pack of paparazzi; had them laughing so hard the spare cameras dangling from their necks kept banging together. Vita Nelson, the buxom thirtyish makeup lady on duty that morning, couldn't stop giggling. Joan was SO goddamn funny. Vita prayed she wouldn't pee her pants.

Three of the photographers were standard-issue freelancers who worked the tabloid market. The other was Hollywood celebrity lensman Dieter Boursin, on assignment for Cameron Tull's gossip page in *The National Revealer.*

It was time to feed the world's insatiable appetite for show biz gossip.

Snorting explosively at Joan's jokes, the four men circled her and her adorable little dog Spike, peering through their Nikons. Pooch and star sat in makeup chairs, swathed to the neck in protective cloths as Vita pretended to pat at them with a big powder puff. The photogs were going for that time-honored staple of the newspaper and magazine trade known as the "celebrity gag shot."

The headline would read something like this:

"Joan's Doggie Demands Equal Time!"

Then there'd be a chock-full-of-chuckles caption, something like:

"Just make sure your readers know I'm not the dog!" joked Joan Rivers, as the comedienne and pet pooch Spike got equal star treatment at The "E!" makeup department. It was the first taping of a new fashion special Joan was hosting on the cable channel...etc.

Shutters clicked. Flashes fired. Vita mugged for the cameras and waved a powder puff at Spike. The dog barked furiously. Joan made a comical leer at the makeup lady's eye-popping cleavage and cracked:

"That's some set you've got there, Vita. You've got Spike in heat—and he's FIXED!" Everyone cracked up; Vita was laughing so hard she felt her bladder contract. "Oh, Joan, stop!" she gasped. "I'll pee my pants right in front of these guys!"

"Oh, yeah? Upstage me and you're dead, bitch!"

The photogs roared at Joan's comeback, then settled down like good professionals for the shoot. Joan struck poses. Spike mugged. Camera motors chattered like silenced machine pistols. Boursin and one of the freelancers, a scruffy British kid, had their shots in five minutes, then chatted as the other photogs tried for something different with Joan.

Vita unhooked Spike's makeup cloth and plopped him on the floor. She made a show of busying herself with her makeup pots and brushes, listening attentively as Boursin and the Brit traded tabloid industry gossip. Over the years in Hollywood, Vita had learned that keeping her ears open could help pay the mortgage on the Encino house she and her husband Fred couldn't quite afford. Fred, an in-demand lighting tech who worked the major studios, heard a lot of things, too.

In one particularly good year, Vita and Fred had made themselves an extra $43,000 selling gossip items and stories to *The Enquirer, The Star, People, The National Revealer,* and even British and Italian tabloids. Big tits earn big bucks in Hollywood, but so do big ears, Vita had learned. Knowledge was power. The town ran on gossip, hype, and figuring shit out five minutes before the next guy.

Earlier that morning, before the arrival of the photographers, Vita had eavesdropped discreetly as Joan Rivers gossiped with a pal on the phone about Fabio and some Hollywood wife. After Joan got off the phone, she told Vita the wife's name. Vita gasped. "But isn't she married to that new creative hotshot at Warner Bros.?" Joan nodded. "Yes, but they're separated. So no big deal. If it's even true," she added. "But my source on this is pretty good."

Dollar signs danced in Vita's head. She'd have that item sold before lunch. It was sure-fire for Cameron Tull at *The Revealer*. And if he didn't bite, *The Enquirer's* gossip columnist would sit up and beg for it. He'd been her favorite until the time she'd been assigned to do his makeup for a TV appearance and he'd complained that she'd used a shade too light for his skin. Pompous asshole. She'd never said anything to him, of course. He was too big a gossip market to piss off.

As Vita listened to the paparazzi gossip, she heard Boursin mention that one of *The Revealer's* top editors, Steve Bellini, had gone "in the tank" at the Camino Rio Hotel. Vita didn't understand the term. Boursin was explaining it to the Brit.

"At *The Revealer*, when you're dry on ideas, or you're working on a story so big you need total concentration, the editor-in-chief sends you to a luxury hotel. You can pig out on all the room service you can eat and drink, but the catch is you can't leave the room. You stay 'in the tank' until you've nailed the story. Sort of like force-feeding a goose to get paté."

Interesting, Vita thought. But I can't sell that anywhere. She knew Bellini. He was one of *The Revealer's* top editors. She'd even sold items to him. But no one's going to pay for an item saying that Steve Bellini's "in the tank," Vita told herself. It's just inside trade stuff. Vita had trained herself to evaluate every piece of information she heard, no matter how trivial, and to determine what market might pay hard cash for it. In the past ten years, she'd turned into a competent freelance journalist, although she never thought of herself that way. Vita knew she was nothing more than a slightly over-the-hill lady who'd long ago given up her dreams of making it as an actress. But it was okay. She'd turned into a darned good makeup person and member in good standing of the show biz world she loved.

Then the Brit said something that got Vita's full attention: "Yeah, I've heard Bellini's in a bit of trouble over a $50 million libel lawsuit Charmain Burns filed against him over those pictures of her beating the shit out of a horse."

"Ya, I've heard that too," said Boursin in his chocolate-y Swiss-German accent. "Some of Bellini's enemies on his own paper are putting out the story that he's in the tank at the Camino Rio because he's working on their defense for the lawsuit. But I don't believe that shit. First of all, anybody on a tabloid will tell you that libel suits aren't fun, but they're the best job insurance you can get. The paper can't afford to fire you because they need you on the witness stand if it goes to court. And these fucking lawsuits can drag on for years, ya?"

Vita breathed a happy sigh. What a great day this was turning out to be. She had a hot Fabio story to sell for cash. But even better, she had another bit of gossip that could help her career after she whispered it into certain important ears.

Tomorrow she was scheduled to fill in for a vacationing makeup artist on the super-successful *BevHills High* series. Vita happened to know that they were looking for someone to head the show's makeup department. The producer, a lesbian named Billie Craine, loved getting inside info she could whisper into the eager ears of studio bosses. Billie Craine would just love to hear that Steve Bellini might be in trouble at *The National Revealer.* And Billie could give Vita that job. Makeup department head. Wow! She'd be making more than Fred.

Dieter Boursin glanced over at Vita and gave her one of his trademark kewpie-doll smiles.

"What are you looking so happy about?" he rasped.

Vita grinned back. "Honey, sometimes I just love this town, don't you?"

CHAPTER 2

10:06 A.M.
CAMINO RIO HOTEL
BEVERLY HILLS

"...YOU'RE listening to KFWB NEWS RADIO. It's six past the hour... Hope all you Angelenos are enjoying the bright sunshine on this rare, smog-free morning...More on today's weather from meteorologist Bill Dudley...Bill?..."

—

Two miles down the road from "E!," on the swankier end of Wilshire, the bearded, heavy-set man in the $3,000 Armani jacket and Levis whirled like a dervish as he spoke, windmilling his arms, furiously pacing the seventh floor balcony terrace of the $2,100-a-day Humphrey Bogart Suite. The man, a producer, was delivering a Hollywood stroke job, spewing honeyed phrases out into the fresh, golden air.

"YOU are the most finely-tuned acting instrument walking this earth today...

"You are more than a STAR, Miss Meryl Olivier! You are the mirror in which women see their hopes and dreams...

"But more than all THAT, Miss Olivier...

"You're a great, great artist. I know you care nothing about my offer to pay DOUBLE what you made on your last picture—and forgive me for even bringing it up because this is petty garbage that should only be for your agent and me to talk. But God knows you deserve REWARD for your great art! And I want to be the first producer, in this schlock town that cares nothing for great art, who finally gives you what YOU, Miss Olivier, truly deserve..."

The mega-barrage of hype was aimed at a blonde woman who sat rigidly upright on a chaise lounge. She was wearing sunglasses, which she suddenly took off. She'd seen...something. What? She squinted against the light. Ah! There it was again! When he made the hard "s" sound in the word "deserve."

No quirk of human behavior was too subtle to escape the notice of Meryl Olivier, often called America's Greatest Actress. During every waking moment, she constantly watched for the tiniest details of human expression, speech, and action, storing them away for that precise dramatic moment when she'd need them. On this morning, Miss Olivier was at the Camino Rio to hear Noel Gold, the notorious wunderkind producer of eight straight monster-grossing action movies, hit her with a high-voltage pitch to star in his next flick, *Die Faster 5*.

And she *was* listening. Intently. Yet she was repelled and fascinated to observe that at certain angles, the bright sunlight sharply defined a frothy cloud of spittle that sprayed from the producer's fleshy, liver-colored lips.

Totally disgusting, she thought. But what a FABULOUS effect. Of course, it would require a genius lighting man to get it just right on film. But, oh, the Cahiers Du Cinema critics, maybe even Roger Ebert, would rhapsodize about it in their reviews.

"...and you must listen to me now as you have NEVER listened to anyone, Miss Olivier. Because I truly believe I'm delivering the MOST IMPORTANT message you've ever heard in your life. A crucial message that..."

No one in Hollywood delivered "The Pitch," or understood its unique rhythm, better than Noel Gold. Now, he slammed into overdrive. Meryl Olivier's eyes blinked, rapidly, involuntarily. All she could hear, concentrate on, was Noel Gold's voice. It invaded her mind. Her eyes tracked him, fascinated, as he paced, whirled, flung out his arms, shrugged, raised his eyebrows, pursed his lips, smiled, frowned. The mesmerizing barrage of words and motion never let up. God, she thought. Enough already, little toad man! Stop pitching long enough for me to say "maybe."

Noel Gold stared at her unblinking, like some killer bird. Oh yeah, he told himself, you're gonna be mine, baby! I'm "The Gold Man." And the Gold Man never misses. My words are thunderbolts. I have The Power...

He felt it working. The Power! A hot feeling that started pulsing down around his balls. Now it was emanating from his abdomen. A pure energy beam. Like a death ray. What did the Japs call it?...Steven Seagal had told him once...Oh, yeah. *Kihon!* That was it. Power of the spirit!

The Pitch!

It was everything in Hollywood. The lifeblood of deal-making. And Noel Gold was a pitch-meister extraordinaire, a legend. Even his worst enemies—"and that's a cast of thousands," his ex-partner, Lennie Katz used to joke—admitted that if Noel Gold hadn't been born Jewish, he'd have become the television evangelist to watch. The one God Himself would pencil in as a "must-view" in his *TV Guide*.

A Noel Gold pitch? "Bubala, it would melt paint off a whore's fingernails," Lennie Katz used to say, before his pal Noel screwed him into bankruptcy and he ate a shotgun barrel. But even Lennie Katz, who lived for deals, would have loved the way Noel Gold's pitch was bubbling up out of him this morning!

"YOU, Miss Olivier, are the most finely-tuned acting instrument walking this earth today...

"You are MORE than a star! You are the mirror in which women see their hopes and dreams…And men their deepest desires. But more than all that, Miss Olivier, you're a great, great, GREAT artist. A national treasure. Artists like yourself care nothing for money, I know. My offer to pay you DOUBLE what you made on your last picture will not tempt you. That I know also. But as God in Heaven is my witness…"

Noel Gold flung his arms up toward the Hollywood Hills and said it again: "As God is my witness…you will be rewarded, Miss Olivier…"

He paused dramatically, then thundered, "…Let ME be the man who gives you what you truly deserve. It's time for Hollywood to stop turning a cold shoulder to great art, so let ME give you the rewards, the recognition, that are your BIRTHRIGHT!…"

Hollywood bullshit is truly lighter than air. As it spewed out of his mouth, bits of Noel Gold's dreck drifted up...up...up... from the spacious terrace.

Up…up…up…the bullshit rose. Up toward the seductive California sun. And wafted through the open French doors of a suite nine floors above…into ears attuned to hearing Hollywood's faintest whispers…

CHAPTER 3

10:21 A.M.
CAMINO RIO HOTEL
BEVERLY HILLS

HUNCHED over the mahogany desk in his 14th-floor suite, Steve Bellini, senior editor of *The National Revealer,* was pumping a source on the phone and praying he could finally break the hottest Hollywood scandal he'd investigated in months.

It was the kind of story that sounded almost too bad to be true.

"It's *absolutely true*—he's not only HIV-positive, he's got full-blown AIDS," the source on the phone said. "He's already showing symptoms, for God's sake!"

A death sentence. Steve shrugged. Fuck him. Star or no star, the creep deserved to die. He cleared his throat and said carefully, "Does this information come from a new source? And DON'T mention any names!"

The voice on the phone was high-pitched, excited.

"It comes from the same colleague who told me the story originally. But I wanted to make sure. And the best way was to get into his computer records. He's a good friend, and I told him that I'd just installed new computer software at my office that's cutting-edge for keeping records. He knows I'm a computer buff, so when I offered to install it for him free of charge, he jumped at it. The two of us went to his office on the weekend. When I sent him out to bring back lunch, I got a look at the medical rec—"

"Hey, cool it!" Bellini snapped. "You never know who's listening on an open line."

He glanced down at the SP-409 Line Resistance Monitor he'd used for years. It blinked red when anyone tapped in, or yellow if a hotel operator picked up. Now the light glowed green. The line was clean. But it never hurt to keep hammering sources—and reporters, for that matter—about tight security.

"Okay, okay. Sorry," said the source. He rushed on, words spilling out of him. "Look, there's no doubt about my information. I'd stake my professional life on it. You've got a great story here, Steve!"

Bellini snorted. He wanted to say: Yeah, but will you testify for us in court if we get sued? But he didn't. You never, ever mentioned "court" or "lawsuit" to a source.

"Okay," he said. "The AIDS part is a great story. But I've got to nail down the rest of it. Then it's a monster. A fucking blockbuster."

"Yeah, what a headline," enthused the source. "'AIDS Movie Star Infects—"

"Gotta go," Bellini snapped, slamming the phone down.

He shook his head in wonderment.

"What an ASSHOLE!"

"Were you calling me, honey?"

The silky female voice drifted out of the suite's master bedroom. Steve grinned. He rose and quickly checked himself out in the mirror over the desk. He fluffed his thinning reddish hair. Shit. Only twenty-nine years old and I need Rogaine. If this keeps up, no one will recognize me at my next Yale class reunion. He grinned, thinking of the reaction he'd get, introducing himself: "Bellini, Class of '89...I'm in tabloids..."

He took off his horn-rimmed glasses, polishing them on his shirt-sleeve. Staring into the mirror, he checked the whites of his bright blue eyes. Good. Not bloodshot. His strict regimen of two single malt Scotch whiskies per night was working. He patted his waistline. Perfect. That little pot had disappeared.

"Honey?"

Steve walked into the bedroom. And there she was. Just like on TV. Martha St. Clair, second lead on the promising new sitcom *The Smileys.* That perky, girl-next-door face. That body built for sin. His sister Jessica, meeting Martha for the first time, had sighed, "That's how Sandra Bullock would look if God was a sex-crazed teenage boy."

Martha was standing on the snow-white, deep-pile rug wearing heels, stockings with seams, garter belt, and bra. Her panties weren't on yet. She gazed at him, eyes the color of a Rolling Rock bottle held up to the sun. Her lips curled impishly.

"Remember me? I'm the girl you slept with last night." She made a mock pout. "And ignored this morning!"

She turned away from him and bent over to slip on her panties. Oh, that magnificent alabaster ass.

"You little minx," he snapped. "Don't you dare put those panties on until I tell you."

Still bent over, she twisted her head and looked up at him.

"Who are you, Clark Gable?"

He walked over and spanked her sharply. She gasped, then shifted her hip.

"I'm turning the other cheek, big boy," she whispered.

He spanked her again, then pulled her upright and spun her around so her rear faced the bedroom's free-standing full-length mirror.

"Look!" he commanded.

She craned her head over her shoulder and looked at the bright red marks on each cheek.

"Great. My ass has got hand prints like on the sidewalk outside Graumann's Chinese."

"Your ass looks phenomenal," he said, kissing her.

His hand slid down through her pubic hair, fingers moving to separate her.

"Whoa, mister," she shrieked.

She slipped into her panties as she danced away.

"I've got a script reading to get to. So who's the asshole?"

"What?"

"You called someone on the phone an asshole. Rather loudly."

"You know I won't reveal sources. What if you dumped me and started dating some guy at *The Enquirer?*"

"You're right. I've been shacking up with a tabloid guy, so who else would have me—except another tabloid guy? I'm ruined goods. Oh, woe is me."

He grinned sardonically.

"How incredibly witty. You should be in sitcoms."

Martha finished combing her thick brunette hair and reached for her skirt.

"Now, come on. Tell me the name of the star you're after on this AIDS story. You know I never talk. Look at the items I've given you from my show. They'd fire me for that. You owe me."

Steve shook his head. "I won't tell you his name. But I just talked to a source who's helping me nail the story. An interesting guy. A gynecologist with star patients. He loves gossip and intrigue and I guess that's why he tells me stuff. It's certainly not the money I pay him. The guy makes seven figures a year. And if the American Medical Association ever finds out he's my source, he'll never examine vaginas in this town again!"

Martha stared at him, truly surprised. "A *doctor* tipped you off?"

He shrugged. "We have medical sources galore. But, this guy is simply a gossip fanatic. We have sources like that. They get off on knowing they were secretly responsible for a front-page story, or a scandalous column item. People think sources only do it for money. Sometimes it's a power trip. If you know secrets, the urge to tell can be overpowering.

"This guy knows incredible stuff about rich and famous females. He tinkers with their plumbing, delivers their babies, arranges their abortions, stitches them up when they get belted around. Or torn up playing kinky sex games.

"He knows whose husband is cheating with other women—or men.

"He knows which wives cheat with other men—or women. He knows wives who procure women—or men—for their husbands. And he knows husbands who'd be horrified to know they aren't the father of their wife's offspring. The good doctor knows weird shit."

Martha's eyes were wide. "Like what else? Come on!"

Steve Bellini grinned. "Okay. Here's one I love. The doc got an emergency call in the middle of the night from one of his patients, a hot little Brat Pack wanna-be actress who married a studio honcho. After the wedding, she found out that hubby likes to swing both ways. He's very discreet and only does it in the privacy of his own home. But she was cool with it.

"So anyway, one night, the mogul and his new boytoy are playing in his study at the mansion when he phones her on the house intercom. He's frantic, blubbering.

"It turns out that he and Midnight Cowboy have been experimenting with a hand-carved wooden penis he'd bought on a business trip to India. This thing wasn't intended for use as a dildo. It was a joke decoration...a tsotchke. And there was no base at the bottom to prevent it from sliding up the glory hole. So guess what? Up it went—and they couldn't get it out.

"The honcho was panicked. He didn't dare call his own doctor and trust him to keep his mouth shut. So he calls the wife, and she assures him that her guy, the gynecologist to the stars, can keep his mouth shut. I mean, who better for an emergency like this than a guy whose life is orifices?"

Martha was laughing so hard tears were rolling down her cheeks.

"No, wait, wait...It gets better," said Bellini.

"The studio exec wanted the doc to come up to the house. But they had to go to his office because the doc needed his instruments. He put the guy up in the stirrups—which *really* must have made him feel like a girl. Then he started probing for the wooden dildo. But nothing worked! He couldn't get it out. He tried every medical tool—forceps, pliers—everything. They all just slipped off.

"Then the doc gets a brilliant idea. He leaves the humiliated honcho sobbing in the stirrups, goes into his office bar—and gets a corkscrew. He tells the guy to close his eyes, screws the thing in...and POP! Out it shoots like the cork from a bottle of hot champagne."

They collapsed in laughter.

Martha buttoned her blouse and walked over to him. "I've got to go. Listen, nail that creep who's spreading AIDS. If that story's true, it's the most disgusting thing I've ever heard."

Steve grinned. "It's a blockbuster! It'll fly off the supermarket racks quicker than free pantyhose. What a headline! A top Hollywood star discovers he has AIDS—and starts fucking every woman in sight! Worse—he refuses to wear condoms. He rides his unsuspecting victims bareback!"

Martha snarled, "What a piece of shit. Why kill innocent women?"

"Why? This guy is a sex addict. He feels truly alive only when he's got a woman writhing under him. That's when he knows he's a STAR! There's a movie reel that runs non-stop in his thick, narcissistic head. It's a porn flick, and he's the male lead. He can't help it. He's a sicko."

Martha grabbed her bag and walked to the door.

"Don't turn this pig into a victim," she said. "Spare me the psychological caca. He's the kind of asshole who says to himself, 'Hey, some bitch did this to me, so fuck 'em. I die, a few of them die.'"

Steve nodded. "He's probably assuming he got AIDS from a woman. But it could have been a dirty needle. This guy dabbles in cocaine, even heroin. It could even have been a transfusion of tainted blood. Although that's unlikely because these days AIDS screening at blood banks is near foolproof."

Martha had her hand on the doorknob. "Tell me who it is."

Steve shook his head and smiled.

"Can't, baby. Might put your life in danger. But you'll be safe if you don't fuck anybody except me."

"Asshole," she retorted. "Just get the bastard. And think about this. Maybe he got it from a man? Even so-called 'macho' guys experiment! Bye."

She walked out, not quite slamming the door.

Steve pursed his lips, rocked on his heels. He'd thought fleetingly about the bisexuality angle, but...well, let's just consider that scenario again...

The movie star in question was Case Burton, a lounge-lizard handsome Italian from Brooklyn known for his cheesy Mafia wanna-be attitude, gold chains, and lubed hair. Macho. Homophobic. A guy who'd have to send a telegram to get in touch with his feminine side. Bellini had never heard a whisper that Case Burton was bi! But, hey...it's Hollywood. Stars get into weird, kinky scenes. And it's no mystery why. After sampling the usual erotic thrills so available to them, the rich and gorgeous often develop a hunger for things taboo. So they experiment. And because stars are clannish, they often party together. And after a night of drinks and drugs at someone's mansion, the action begins.

Maybe some hot-looking female dances solo to a throbbing stereo. Zotzed males—and females—shout, "Take it off!" She does. They all do. The orgy begins. Inhibitions come crashing down. Bodies coil against each other. The men, more inhibited about same-sex bodily contact, recoil at the warm, rubbery touch of a penis sliding along their skin. Then they think, What the hell! Everybody's a star here. Nobody's gonna talk.

Steve grinned, picturing macho Case Burton taking it up the ass and whimpering like a girl.

Fuckin' ay, *paisan!*

Suddenly, the sound of a man's voice floated in through the open French doors. Steve walked out onto the balcony, looked down at the terrace seven floors below, and recognized Noel Gold instantly. The windmilling arms, the bellowing voice. He heard Noel's voice clearly in the still morning air:

"...And I will IMMORTALIZE Meryl Olivier as a star who can deliver a gross of $200 million a picture..."

Bellini peered down at the woman. Straight, dishwater blonde hair, angular body, the nose prominent, yet elegant. Yeah, it was Meryl Olivier. What was that oft-quoted remark Cameron Tull had written about this woman in his *Reveale*r gossip column?

"…For an actress who so effortlessly creates the illusion of beauty, it's a shock to discover that in real life, she's as homely as your old maid virgin aunt."

Bellini turned and walked swiftly back into his suite. Rummaging in his briefcase, he pulled out a tiny tape recorder. It was fitted with a highly sensitive and directional miniature microphone. The recorder was a special job you never saw in stores. Manufactured by Sony, the "Scoopman" cost about $900 and had digital circuitry that delivered astounding fidelity. Sony had designed it specifically for use by broadcast journalists. It was super-sensitive, easily concealed. It used special postage stamp-sized tapes, far smaller and thinner than micro-cassettes. The whole rig was no bigger than a cigarette pack. Bellini carried it with him constantly. It was perfect for surreptitious eavesdropping across a crowded nightclub when you wanted to hear, say, Madonna and Rosie O'Donnell gossiping about their sex lives.

Bellini took the rig outside. Hunkering down where the balcony to the left of the French doors intersected the building wall, he looped together both recorder and mike using the tape recorder's carrying strap. Then he knotted the strap around the base of the first railing. Standing, he put both hands on the handrail and leaned over cautiously. The device was barely visible. Down below, Noel Gold was bellowing and gesticulating. Meryl Olivier sat silent, unmoving. Bellini checked the rig. Its red light was on, unblinking.

Bellini shrugged. No front page story here. But it could be a terrific exclusive for Cameron Tull's column if the tape captured Meryl Olivier agreeing to star in the next *Die Faster* sequel with Ronnie Foster, the new Bruce Willis smirk-alike. Exclusives made Tull happy. And Tull was invaluable when you needed help—as Steve often had—on a story.

Tull's network of Hollywood sources was legendary. Everybody kissed his ass for contacts. And not just the tabloid world. Reporters from *Time, Newsweek, The New York Times,* NBC, ABC, CBS—all curried Tull's favor. Bellini smiled. The whole fucking world had gone tabloid.

The phone rang. Bellini walked inside and picked up. "Hello?"

"Steve…"

It was Lulu Baines, his senior reporter. "Lulu, all I want to hear from you is three little words."

"If the three little words are, 'I've nailed it,' then this is your lucky day, boss! I finally tracked down one of the girls who's had sex with Case Burton in the past few months. Her name is Vicky Camlin. How I found her is a story in itself. Point is, she was freaked about ratting out Case

Burton. She's a small-time actress and model. Says she's afraid she'll never work again if Case bad-mouths her. Also, she's heard Case is mobbed up back East, and she could get her tits cut off…"

"Tits cut off? Never heard that one. I must be watching the wrong gangster flicks."

Lulu giggled. "Pathetic. Anyway, Vicky has agreed to let me interview her—on tape. I had to promise two things, Steve. Not to use her name in the story. And to give her twenty-five-hundred bucks. She wanted five grand, but I talked her down. I wrote her a personal check. I know I should have called you for approval, but I didn't think you'd want me to wake you up at 4:30 this morning. Is the money a problem?"

"As far as I'm concerned, you DID wake me and I okayed the money. I probably would have gone five grand. Good job, kiddo."

"Thanks. How about our other source? Anything new?"

"Yeah. We now know it's all on the record. You get my drift? We're ready to rock and roll, but listen—ask this woman if she'll file a lawsuit. I'd love the extra protection of getting her charges against Case into the public record by way of court papers."

"I'll ask her, boss."

"Okay, Lulu. File your copy by this afternoon. I need you on a plane to Florida tomorrow to do the Charmain Burns childhood story. Right? You're great, kid. For my money, you beat any guy on the paper."

"I'd rather hear that I still have a really cute ass," said Lulu.

Bellini laughed.

"Trust me, you still have a really cute ass."

Bellini heard a knock on the door. He lowered the phone and yelled, "Just a minute."

"Lulu, somebody's at the door…"

"Okay, I'll call after I file."

Bellini hung up.

"Who is it?" he called.

Again, a knock…a faint voice crying, "Flowers!"

Bellini walked over to the suite's massive paneled door and opened it. A tall, powerful-looking black man stood in the hallway, sporting a wonderfully warm smile.

CHAPTER 4

10:42 A.M.
CAMINO RIO HOTEL
BEVERLY HILLS

OUTSIDE the suite, dangling from the balcony, the electronic spy heard it all.

It picked up the faint cry of "Flowers!"

It faithfully recorded Noel Gold as he approached the huckster's crucial moment: the Big Close—that orgasmic moment when the sucker is about to bite down on the hook.

On the seventh-floor terrace, Meryl Olivier stared in rapt fascination as Noel stroked her closer and closer to surrender.

"…And now the most important point. YOU are the First Lady of the screen and a First Lady should always be daring. I know you've never lent your presence to the great American film genre known as the 'action' movie. But I want you to star in *Die Faster Five* and drive home the message I've tried so hard to make with these films—that we must root out the evils of society for mankind's good. I've tried to make America a better place by promoting that simple, heartfelt theme in the first four *Die Faster* movies. And if I might just mention it, none of them grossed less than 200 million dollars…"

Noel Gold paused for a heartbeat. He thought he'd seen Meryl Olivier's eyes widen, just slightly. Yes, yes, he was sure of it. A subtle shift of mood in her eyes.

Oh yeah baby, you're mine now!

"Let me tell you about the absolutely UNPRECEDENTED financial package of gross points AND merchandising profit sharing I've devised for you. It's a package NO star has ever had in this town, and it's yours if…"

The wind freshened. It whipped snatches of Noel Gold's sugar-coated crap up to the tiny microphone high above. But this time, it didn't reach Steve Bellini's ears. He was standing at the door to the suite, smiling reflexively as the black man in the hall smoothly thrust a bouquet of pink-tipped white roses at him.

Incredibly, Bellini knew they were "Sonia" roses. A florist had suggested them when he'd ordered flowers for a reporter of his named Sonia, who'd just had a baby. Bellini reached out with his right hand to take the bouquet the black man held in his left hand. What a huge hand, Bellini thought. And there's a magnetism about the guy. An aura of coiled power. Like an athlete...

Good reporters have a sixth sense when something's not right. It started to kick in as Bellini, looking puzzled, took the flowers. He asked, "Who sent these?..."

The black man said, "Gators bite hard, man."

The scene suddenly seemed to play in slow motion.

Bellini never sensed the right hand rocketing up at his chin. A piledriver uppercut, textbook perfect. It caught him squarely. Powered by 220 pounds of hard muscle and bone, the punch propelled Bellini's body upward, lifting him onto tip-toes. As he flew back, his feet skittered comically, trying to catch up with his torso.

Then he literally left the floor. He made an upward arc and crashed down onto the room service table that had been wheeled into his suite that morning bearing his favorite Olde English breakfast: porridge and kippers and marmalade. Bellini crashed onto the table, felt slashing pain as glass and crockery cut into his back and shoulders. His head slammed down. He passed out.

At that instant, the black man was striding toward the elevators, mentally high-fiving himself for a job well done. The last thing he'd seen was Bellini's body landing on the room service table.

What he hadn't seen was the table, with Bellini aboard, skidding on its wheels across the smooth tile floor. Picking up speed, it shot out through the French doors and slammed into the balcony railing.

Bellini was catapulted up, out. His body arced up toward the L.A. sun, then plummeted straight down in a shower of glasses, dishes, silverware, food scraps...and an exquisite fluted vase holding a single white rose.

On the huge terrace seven floors below, Noel Gold had a white-hot pitch going. NOW, he told himself, hit her with the killer closing. It was time to dare all, make her react.

"Meryl...you are an extremely beautiful woman. This the world knows. But what they DON'T know, and what Noel Gold is going to make them see for the first time, is the smoldering sexuality you've never allowed yourself to unleash on the screen before. Think of it...Meryl Olivier...the great actress...the new SEX SYMBOL!"

For a split second, Noel Gold thought he'd blown it, that he'd gone too far...but no, no, she was turning her head...she was looking directly into his eyes! America's classiest actress straightened up and...

...my GOD! She'd thrust out her BREASTS at him. He HAD her, he'd DONE it! She'd call her agent, they'd do a deal and...

"SHIT...!"

Crockery, silverware, glass, and food bits suddenly rained out of the sky, followed by Steve Bellini, who was comatose and didn't feel the bone-crushing impact as he slammed into the cement and died.

Noel Gold, momentarily speechless in the shower of smashing dishware, felt something splat onto his beard. He fished it out and recoiled in disgust. It was a chunk of smelly kippered herring.

Meryl Olivier leaped to her feet and screamed hysterically.

"It's a bad omen. I can't do your movie—I just can't! Oh, God, I'm going to HEAVE!"

She snatched up her purse and ran for the john. Noel Gold was suddenly alone. With a corpse.

Flinging his arms wide, he threw back his head and howled, "I don't need this...I DON'T FUCKING NEED THIS!"

Grabbing a phone, he got the hotel manager and launched into one of the trademark screaming fits that had made him a Hollywood legend.

"I'll sue your pile of dump hotel, you slimy-ass, pathetic cocksucker. You motherfucker!"

Throwing a disgusted glance at Bellini's corpse, he shrieked, "Clean up this fucking mess RIGHT NOW, goddamnit! Right fucking NOW!!"

High overhead, hanging from its hiding place, the tiny silent spy listened, unblinking. And heard it all.

CHAPTER 5

11:04 A.M.
CHARMAIN BURNS' MANSION
BEVERLY HILLS

WHAT a bizarre scene, marveled Laddy Burford. The darkened bedroom, dominated by a huge platform bed and mirrored ceiling, was shuttered against the bright Beverly Hills morning. A lamp powered by a white-hot halogen bulb lit up what looked like an emergency room operating table and shed pale light on seven people standing around it in a loose circle.

They all turned, in almost comical unison, as the bathroom door suddenly swung open. Charmain Burns stood in the doorway, framed dramatically in backlighting from the mirrored bathroom. It glowed through her thin silk robe and etched the outline of long, exquisite legs.

Taking a beat, Charmain gazed out at their faces. Laddy Burford grinned and shook his head, admiration warring with disgust. Even in her bedroom, he thought, she's got to make a fucking entrance.

As if on his mental cue, Hollywood's hottest new bad girl strode into the bedroom, shrugged off her robe and stood naked before several of her dearest friends and a couple of total strangers.

The impact of her nudity, heightened somehow by the intimate proximity of these fully dressed voyeurs, hit Laddy like a physical blow. He looked around and knew the others felt the same visceral response to Charmain's sexuality. This is what her TV audiences ate up. They felt the magnetism radiating off the screen from that milky-white skin, those light green eyes and full, pouty lips.

But they'd never experienced the sensual jolt of real-life Charmain standing naked at arm's-length, salacious and ripe with generous young breasts, thighs that hinted power, and a pillowy mons veneris, provocatively shaved of its natural auburn pelt.

"Oh, Charmain, your breasts are wonderful!"

It was Leda Francis, the sweet little British ballerina, speaking in a reverent whisper. "Nipples to die for," blurted Bonnie Farr, the lesbian singer who'd recently come out of the closet—and who, Laddy could personally attest, had a respectable pair of nipples herself.

But Leda was right. Charmain's breasts *were* wonderful. Not overly large, but full, with an ever-so-slight weighty sag, the sure-fire sign of that commodity rare in show business—a natural bosom, unsullied by silicone or saline. In today's Hollywood, heavy-hitters didn't brag that they'd nailed a girl with big tits. They bragged that the breasts were real—"all beef, no filler."

Laddy had once overheard his own father, Ransom Burford, of the department store Burfords, complain to a crony that, "When I squeeze a gal's titties and they aren't real, I tell her to get dressed and go home. If I can't find natural, I'll do without, by God."

Laddy recalled the stab of pain he'd felt at his father's oblique condemnation that sleeping with Laddy's mother amounted to "doing without."

Charmain started giggling.

"God, can't a girl get naked without everybody acting like they're in church? Now come on, this is supposed to be a happy occasion. We're going to have a little party after—that is, if I can still stand up. What do you think, Fiona?"

Charmain directed her question at a tall, striking forty-ish woman Laddy had never met until she'd shown up at the house that morning with a younger man introduced only as "Nicky." Nicky never spoke a word, nodding when introduced. Fiona, who was British, was beautiful in a witchy sort of way, and had a very imperious manner. Laddy disliked her instantly. And he almost laughed out loud when he introduced Fiona to Leda Francis and Bonnie Farr. Leda was cool to her countrywoman, but Bonnie literally bristled. Fiona glared back and the two kept eyeing each other like angry stud horses.

"Darling girl, of course you'll be standing. You'll feel like the most powerful woman in the universe," Fiona replied. "And I think, if I might say so, that it's quite normal for everyone here to act like they're 'in church,' as you put it. They are about to participate with you in 'The Ritual,' and it's a ceremony full of power and reverence."

Laddy almost snorted in annoyance. First Charmain and now this woman—both referring to "The Ritual" as if it should be in capital letters. Christ, he thought, must we sanctify our kinky aberrations? Can't we just admit that this is really weird, but sexy? He almost jumped as the mysterious Nicky suddenly appeared at his elbow and handed him a glass of a greenish liquid.

"It's absinthe," Fiona announced as Nicky passed around the glasses. "The real thing, wine mixed with wormwood, not the imitation stuff they've been making in France since the authorities banned it back in the 30s. It's truly the nectar of the gods, and perfect for this moment."

Raising her glass to Charmain, Fiona intoned:

"I drink to our sister, Charmain, who is about to tune back into the primitive resonance that our modern world has lost. Remember this: the fires of pain forge a link to new powers of sensitivity and lusty appetites for pleasure! Drink, Charmain, and we will witness your baptism in 'The Ritual.'"

Everyone drank, except for the man and woman dressed in white medical garments like a doctor and nurse. As far as Laddy knew, they were strangers to Charmain, recommended by Fiona for the part they were about to play. The woman stepped forward and assisted Charmain up onto the table, then gently pushed her down until she was lying flat.

Everything went quiet again for a moment, and Laddy suddenly remembered his only role in this ceremony. He stepped back quietly and hit the stereo system switch. The opening strains of what was perhaps the only piece of classical music Charmain could identify by name, the *Carmina Burana* by Orff, pulsed through the room.

Charmain loved this magical parable of human life exposed to constant swings of fortune, with its eerily hypnotic choral chants. She often quoted a music critic's summation of the piece: "Man is seen, in a hard, unsentimental light, as the plaything of inscrutable, mysterious forces."

And she'd always add: "That's the story of my fucking life."

On the far side of the bedroom, Laddy saw Fiona and Nicky lighting candles. It made him nervous having them here, but Charmain seemed to trust them. She'd come back from that trip to San Francisco bursting to tell him, and Bonnie and Leda, about a fascinating new power trip that excited her more than any drugs she'd ever taken. She told them about "The Ritual" she'd actually witnessed, and how she was determined to participate herself. And the moment she started talking about her new friends Fiona and Nicky, all three sensed that Charmain had slept with them both. But Charmain never shared that confidence, and Laddy gradually began to sense that her fascination was not with Fiona and Nicky—only with "The Ritual."

Now Fiona and Nicky were back at the operating table. They watched intently with everyone else as the couple in white swiftly laid out metal instruments on sterile cloths. Then the man leaned over and whispered something in Charmain's ear. She shook her head. He straightened up, then touched her left thigh, just near the groin, very gently, and she parted her legs. The act so perfectly evoked the image of an obedient little girl that Laddy caught his breath. Damn, this was an incredible scene. It made him nervous on so many levels that he felt light-headed. He actually heard a roaring sound in his ears. He suddenly imagined a police raid and his father reading about this bizarre scene on the front page of…shit, that's right. It wasn't cops he needed to worry about. How about the fucking *National Revealer,* or *The Enquirer?*

Impulsively, Laddy turned to Bonnie Farr and whispered in her ear, "What if somebody here is a source for the tabloids? Can you imagine *The Revealer* finding out about this?" Bonnie's eyes widened for a moment. Then she grinned as if to say, "Don't be paranoid," and punched his arm. Laddy shook his head and grinned back, weakly.

Yeah, she thinks I'm a wuss, but if she only knew. Had they all forgotten what Charmain's legendary security consultant, Vidal Delaney, had told them, that *The Revealer* almost certainly had an inside source in Charmain's circle?

Oh, Jesus, thought Laddy, looking mistrustfully at everyone in the room. Suddenly, it hit him. All at once, he knew with absolute clarity why the tabloids had such an unbreakable grip on Hollywood, why everyone was constantly looking over their shoulders all the time. Because everyone really DID have shit to hide, goddamnit.

The tabloids had it right. Stars and producers, writers, directors, casting agents—in short, EVERYBODY, or damn close to it—was fucking the wrong wife or husband, doing drugs, having secret gay sex, diddling minors, getting ass-whipped by dominatrix babes, cross-dressing, wearing diapers, or God knows what. And millions of enquiring minds were happy to slap down two bucks every week to read all about it. BECAUSE THE PEOPLE HAVE THE RIGHT TO KNOW, according to the First Amendment of the Bill of Rights.

For one unhappy moment, Laddy wished he was back in New York, safe in the corporate headquarters of Burford Department Stores, Inc. Then he remembered what it was like to be constantly kissing Ransom Burford's ass along with all the other vice-president bum-boys, and he turned back to the matter at hand.

"The Ritual" was underway. The man nodded to his female assistant. She handed him a wicked-looking instrument. He took it, leaned over Charmain, poised. Laddy flinched and he felt Leda grab his arm. On the table, Charmain shifted slightly, but it was only to open her legs a bit wider. She was perfectly calm and in control. The man seemed to make a decision. He brought the instrument down and…

"Charmain!"

It was a whisper, but it cut through the low music like a knife. Everyone in the room was startled.

Charmain sat up sharply, fury etched on her face, screaming. "Marta, what the HELL are you doing? I told you NO interruptions…"

Charmain was facing the bedroom door and Laddy could see that it was open just a crack. Marta Kane, Charmain's trusted personal assistant, had opened it slightly so she could be heard. She wasn't looking inside.

"Oh, Charmain, I'm so sorry, but it's Vidal Delaney. He says it's an absolute MUST that he speak to you right this minute."

There was a respectful silence. Even Charmain calmed down visibly. Vidal Delaney was on that very short list of Hollywood heavy-hitters, like Spielberg and Ovitz, whose calls you always take.

Charmain cursed and strode stark naked from the room.

"This had better be fucking good!"

CHAPTER 6

CITRUS CORNERS, FLORIDA
1985

MEN started looking at Charmain Burns when she was just a little girl.

That phenomenon did not escape the notice of two sharp-eyed—some would say busybody—old maids who spent a good part of every day shopping, then stopping for lunch at the diner on sleepy Main Street in Charmain's hometown, Citrus Corners, Florida. These biddies would see Charmain, at age eight or nine, skipping along in short baby-doll dresses her mother should have had her out of ages ago, for heaven's sake! They would cluck in dismay at the sight of grown men glancing furtively at Charmain's long, shapely legs. "That girl's too pretty for her own good, you mark my words," they'd sniff. By "pretty," they actually meant "sexy," although neither would dream of using such language.

These withered crones were fond of engaging Charmain's mother in supposedly friendly conversation, telling Selena Burns, for instance, that her little girl was "so mature" and had "that Shirley Temple look." Selena, who was nothing if not shallow, would preen. She'd prod Charmain, who was rarely shy about performing, to do one of her dances, sing a song, or recite a poem. The old bats would roll their eyes, and throw each other meaningful glances as Selena prattled on about how Charmain loved to sing and act out scenes for her Daddy—unaware that the comparison to Shirley Temple referred to the twinkly little star's innocent, but nonetheless powerful, sexual aura, which had been written about by film critics in her era. One of those writers had, in fact, been sued for publishing remarks that implied the nymphet's appeal was based as much on seductiveness as childish charm.

When Selena and Charmain would leave, the old maids would gossip on and on, the conversation always the same with minor variations. The older one would say, "My Uncle Billie, who was only five years older than me, and no better than he had to be, put his hand right up my dress once when I was barely nine years old and whispered, 'You look just like Shirley Temple.'"

And the other biddy would reply, "Why, Shirley had a figure just like a little woman. And those short dresses. I remember Momma whacking Daddy real hard on the arm when we were sitting in the Rialto movie theater that used to be right where the hay and feed store is right now, watching a Shirley Temple movie. And when Daddy moved and looked at Momma all startled, I looked down in his lap and saw just why she was so upset. The man was positively bulging. I didn't know what I was seeing at that age, of course."

Like Shirley Temple as a child, Charmain had the look of a tiny, perfectly formed woman. Her smooth baby fat sculpted a voluptuous curve to her buttocks and subtly hinted at the promise of budding breasts. And, like America's little movie sweetheart, young Charmain had a presence and poise that commanded attention. Total strangers would turn and stare at her as she passed, nudging their friends and saying, "Isn't that the prettiest little girl ever?!"

Charmain rarely wore rompers or jeans, always insisting on short, frilly, feminine dresses. Even fine, upstanding men who'd slaughter a pedophile as quick, or quicker, than they'd stomp a rattlesnake, caught themselves looking twice at eight-year-old Charmain skipping down Main Street in a brief, flouncy dress. Their eyes would wander unbidden up her long, smooth legs and somewhat heavy thighs.

Who knows what passes through a man's mind? Did those who caught themselves staring too long at Charmain sublimate any stray synapse of unbidden desire the way their fathers had when faced with Shirley Temple's twinkling gams, suppressing unbidden thoughts and quickly saying to the nearest person, "Isn't that the prettiest little girl ever?"

Charmain's mother, Selena Burns, had never wanted a child. Incredibly, she'd never mentioned this until after her marriage to husband Lawton, a passive, mild-mannered man who made an adequate living selling insurance to Florida citrus growers, farmers, and cattle ranchers. Lawton had been so horrified and angered by his new bride's unexpected refusal to bear him a child that she finally acquiesced and was careful never to show anything but happiness about motherhood ever again.

Most men would have probed and questioned why a wife would suddenly admit an aversion to bearing offspring. But Lawton never asked. He seemed content that the problem had resolved itself. Selena and Lawton never spoke of it again, and, after Charmain's birth, he never suggested that they have another child.

And neither did Selena.

Truth be told, Selena had married Lawton in desperation, to get away from her oppressive father. She was the daughter of a fundamentalist preacher, the Reverend Galen Holcomb, who had broken away from the Baptist church to form and rule over what he called his "ministry." It was actually an obscure cult numbering, at most, forty members. The cult was based on sexual self-denial. Members were allowed to have sex only for procreation and had to participate in a bizarre ritual. Each couple would come to Reverend Holcomb and ask his permission to join sexually in what was called a "sanctifying." The date and time of the sanctifying would be announced to the congregation. It would be on an evening picked by the Reverend after he interviewed the woman exhaustively about her menstrual cycles and likely fertile periods.

On the appointed day and hour, the congregation would gather at their tiny church in the woods outside the village of Timson, Georgia, just across the north Florida line. The couple would enter, strip naked in an anteroom, and don white robes. Reverend Holcomb would lead them to a curtained area to one side of the altar. Once out of sight, the couple would disrobe and commence fornication as the congregation softly sang hymns. Reverend Holcomb would begin to pray aloud for a successful implantation of the seed. He'd exhort the couple to cry out in a strong voice and let God hear the ecstasy he wanted them to feel on this special occasion. When thumps and cries signaled impending orgasm, the Reverend Holcomb would raise his hands to the heavens and shout, "Burst forth for Jesus, husband. And ye, woman, open thy womb for thy master's holy seed."

He'd signal the congregation to sing louder, faster. Sweat would begin popping out on faces contorted in beatific empathy. And, as the sanctified couple achieved the noisy, blessed sacrament of climax, who knows how many of the faithful quietly achieved solitary satisfaction in their pews?

After the sanctifying, the couple had to wait a minimum of two months to see if pregnancy occurred. If it did not, they were allowed to try again. And so on. Strangely enough, unlike many a preacher man who wielded absolute power over the sex lives of his flock, Reverend Holcomb actually practiced what he preached. He faithfully and scrupulously abided by the strict church laws he'd laid down and never had sex with his wife, Selena's mother, a shy, beautiful country girl named Rena. Nor did he ever possess or know another woman carnally.

One awful consequence of this lunatic self-abnegation was that Rena began to sexually abuse their only daughter, Selena. It happened the first time after a sanctifying at the church. The couple joining in most holy union that evening had been wildly passionate. The woman's screams in achieving her ecstasy had been the most uninhibited the congregation had ever heard. Rena was more aroused than usual. And sadly, fervent prayers to be delivered from her body's salacious treachery didn't quench the fires licking at her womb.

That night, after putting seven-year-old Selena to bed, Rena and the Reverend Holcomb retired to their separate rooms, sleeping apart as usual. But sleep would not come to Rena. She dozed fitfully. Several times she jerked awake to find her hands near her sex. This was a sin she hadn't committed since her grandmother caught her doing it at age nine and whipped her mercilessly.

Had Rena known her husband masturbated wildly every night before dropping off to deep, blessed sleep, she might have allowed herself similar relief. But Rena knew only what her reverend husband told her. And he told her nothing.

As Rena tried to sleep, a violent lightning storm sprang up. Strangely, the rumbling and thunder and splash of rain calmed her. And just as she fell asleep, she became dimly aware that little Selena had slipped into the bed, whimpering that she was afraid. Hours later, or it might have been moments later, Rena hovered on the knife-edge of dreams and half-awareness as her body writhed and contracted in waves of sexual desire. In a moment of comprehension and fleeting horror, Rena thought her hands had betrayed her. But no...she felt something outside of herself rubbing insistently against her throbbing sex...and she experienced a heated rush of ecstasy that triggered a glorious release.

Two years later, Selena was delivered from the sexual abuse that began that night. Her mother died suddenly, struck down by a flu that turned into pneumonia. Selena became a virtual handmaiden for her father and gratefully escaped his house when Lawton Burns came by one day to sell the Reverend some church insurance, and was smitten by the Reverend Holcomb's comely daughter.

Selena's revulsion for motherhood didn't change after the birth of her own daughter. But she carefully hid from Lawton her resentment and subconscious fear of her own child. She didn't understand her dark feelings toward Charmain, so she supressed them. She had a only vague recollection of the abuse she had suffered at the hands of her mother, having pushed these memories into the deepest corners of her mind.

Selena was at once fascinated and repelled by her daughter, but had no idea why. Nor did she dwell upon these strangely ambivalent feelings. Outwardly, Selena was a good mother. She cared for Charmain meticulously, but with little passion. She often ignored her for hours at a stretch, yet always made sure the child was clean and well-fed.

One night, when Charmain was six years old, a thunder storm crackled across the sky. Selena awoke and, without realizing what she was doing or thinking about it, rose like a sleepwalker, went to Charmain's room and took the child back to her bed. That night, the pattern of abuse begun so long ago renewed itself with a new, unwilling partner. Just as her mother Rena had done, Selena would rub her little girl's body against her own. And after the intense release was reached, she would begin to scold the child, spank her, and call her naughty.

At first, Charmain was confused and frightened by her mother's swift and terrifying mood changes—from seductive to violent. But she was smarter and tougher than her mother had ever been. Even as a little girl, after many nights spent crying herself to sleep, Charmain instinctively came to understand that her mother was sick, that something was wrong, that she was not at fault for what was happening.

As time went on, that knowledge made Charmain feel powerful, superior to her mother. Gradually, she exercised her power. And learned things from her mother that most little girls never learn. Charmain discovered the power of seduction. She flirted outrageously with boys, even grown men, testing her powers. And gradually, she began to experiment with physical sex. Never with older boys, but with girlfriends or boys her own age or younger.

Charmain became acutely perceptive in sexual matters. She learned early on that her mother rarely surrendered to sex with her father. Charmain would hear them arguing behind their bedroom door. The pattern was always the same. Lawton Burns would plead and beg. Selena would refuse him. Finally, he'd explode with rage and bellow that she was his wife and, by God, he had conjugal rights. He'd beat Selena and rape her savagely. Then, for long weeks and months, Lawton Burns would revert to the role of meek, even submissive, husband, in atonement for his wickedness.

Months would pass. Inevitably, Lawton Burns would plead again for consensual sex. Selena would spurn him. And he'd beat and rape her again.

Charmain suddenly got it into her head that she should tell Daddy what was happening to her. He'd always been benignly distant to her, showing affection mainly by way of little gifts and souvenirs he'd bring her after long sojourns on the road. But Charmain gradually began to see her father as a fellow victim. She went to him when she was nine and tried haltingly to explain what Selena did to her on those hellish nights. He looked at her, then said something like, "There, there now...it's just nightmares you're having." He reached in his pocket and pulled out a dollar. "Here," he said, "some ice cream money."

Then he picked up his newspaper, held it in front of his face decisively, and shook it like a witch doctor chasing an evil spirit with a rattle. It was at this moment that Charmain was overcome by the aching realization that she was totally alone in this world.

By the time she was twelve, she had performed an amazing variety of sex acts with younger boys and girls. She'd done everything short of actual penetration, although during one session with a little boy four years her junior, a lad she had turned into her favorite sex slave until he'd moved away with his parents, Charmain had inserted his tiny penis into herself. As far as she was concerned, it hadn't really counted. She sensed a barrier that hadn't been breached. She knew instinctively that the time for full penetration by an older boy, or even a grown man, would come soon enough.

Charmain and her mother spent a lot of time alone in their modest, isolated home—located on ten acres at the outskirts of rural Citrus Corners. Lawton Burns was constantly on the road, selling insurance to ranchers and farmers.

It was during one of these periods that Charmain, about a month shy of her eleventh birthday, decisively ended the sexual abuse. One night, her mother came to lead Charmain to her bedroom. When they got into bed, Charmain suddenly became the aggressor, licking and biting her mother's breasts, running her hands between her legs, trying everything she could to excite Selena. It was as if she had finally acquiesced in her abuse and had become a willing, even eager, partner to it: victim turned agressor.

The effect on Selena was electric, immediate. Instead of responding, she recoiled from her daughter's caresses and pushed her away, saying, almost piteously, "No, no, stop it. No, don't, please. No, don't. Go away. Go away. Go back to bed. Go away." Charmain said, "No, Mommy, no. I won't go away. I want to do it with you. Let's do it, Mommy." Her hand darted between Selena's legs.

Selena sat upright in the bed and hit Charmain with every ounce of force she could muster, knocking her off the bed. Charmain sat on the floor, rubbing her face and taking her hands away in surprise after seeing blood on her fingers—blood that had trickled from her nose. Charmain stood up and smiled at her mother as she wiped away the blood.

"Goodnight, Mommy," she said. Then she turned and left the room.

Selena never attempted to abuse Charmain again. Her daughter had become Selena's equal. A new relationship evolved that was built on a mutual hatred that had not existed before, even at the height of Selena's abuse. Mother and daughter had always been silent around each other. Now that silence was fraught with tension.

And a hint of impending violence.

CHAPTER 7

11:31 A.M.
WILSHIRE BLVD.
BEVERLY HILLS

NO smog. California sunshine. Light traffic. Vidal Delaney whipped through the bright Beverly Hills morning in his new Jaguar convertible, reveling in the breezy feel of riding in a ragtop. It had been an impulse, buying one of these new Jags the car mags were raving about. But what the hell? He could afford it and it felt…like, bitchin' dude!

He laughed, recalling the surfing jargon of his youth in Redondo Beach. Goddamn, he thought, this baby makes me feel like a kid again. Last ragtop I owned was a Volkswagen, but with a surfboard strapped to it. He glanced approvingly at the Jag's leather interior, the richly polished walnut dash with its kick-ass stereo. And the custom-installed phone/fax system complete with state-of-the-art scrambler and encryption coding to guarantee secure communications.

Security.

It was Vidal Delaney's watchword. He'd made millions in Hollywood by convincing stars and power brokers that fame and fortune exacted a terrible price: vulnerability.

"Information is power," he used to say back in the early days when he personally pitched every potential client.

"If you can't keep information secure, power is a pipe dream. You're vulnerable. Someone can take it all away. Think about it. If you're ignoring your security, a total stranger has the potential to harm you monetarily, psychologically, even physically. You've worked hard to get to where no one can touch you. But can you tell me today that you're truly as safe and secure as you want to be?"

Paranoia. It's a fucking growth industry, as Vidal was fond of saying—but only to himself. If he had any superstition, it was keeping his mouth shut about what he half-jokingly thought of as his "secret formula," a fantastic idea that had hit him one day in 1985 as he'd paddled out to catch a wave off Malibu. A light had exploded in his brain. A message started flashing insistently, like a neon sign on an all-night diner:

PARANOIA = CA$H…PARANOIA = CA$H!…

Just like that! BAM! His secret formula for success. And it had made him a power in this town.

One day he was a strapping blonde wanna-be actor making the odd buck working nights as a bouncer at rock clubs along Sunset. A year later he'd formed Delaney Protection Partners, Ltd., and had six clients—including a TV star with a hit series and an exec-VP of development at MGM. Vidal (real name, Joe) Delaney was on his way.

Vidal slowed and stopped for a red light at Canon. A horn beeped behind him. He looked in the rearview, then grinned and waved back at Sharon Stone. She blew him a kiss and the light changed. Oh, sweet Sharon. What a piece of ass. He'd pitched her a couple of weeks ago as a prospective client. Vidal sighed. Signing Sharon Stone would almost be a shame. She'd flirted outrageously with him during the pitch at her manager's office. "So, a good-looking guy who's not married and not gay," she'd purred. "I'd fix you up with a girlfriend, but I'm afraid I'd get jealous even though I'm married now."

He'd let her take the lead, responding with boyish grins, keeping it professional. He'd invited her to lunch at The Ivy, and she'd accepted. She was married, but...he felt like something could happen between them. Hadn't pushed it. Business came first. And if he did sign her as a client, that ended it.

Vidal *never* fucked a client. Not in the carnal sense.

He looked in the rearview. Sharon was gone, lost in the traffic behind him. His gray eyes lingered in the mirror. Hey, check out that new mustache. Looks good, he thought. Gave him a maturity, softened his blonde, aging-surfer-boy good looks. People told him he looked like that *Dukes of Hazzard* guy, the pretty boy, John What's-his-name.

Sharon had liked the mustache.

"Where I grew up, people used to call them 'cookie-dusters,'" she'd said. Flirting.

Amazing. Ten years ago, who'd have dreamed that someday he'd have A-list stars like Sharon Stone or Charmain Burns coming to him? He'd been lucky, but it was more than that. Vidal knew show biz. He was tuned into the La-La Land psyche. And he'd been the first to exploit Hollywood's fear of the emerging power of tabloids like *The National Enquirer, The Revealer, The Star*. Every time paparazzi jumped out of the bushes and went "Boo!," Vidal's stock headed north.

Any star worth his or her twinkle had been stung by the tabs. Problem was, the rags had become too damn accurate. And the truth, as they say, hurts. Even worse, from the standpoint of the Hollywood publicity mill, was how the public's perception of tabloids had changed in the past decade. People had come to realize that not all supermarket papers were purveyors of looney-tune sleaze à la "Three-Headed Appalachian Babies Spawned By UFO Invaders!"

The Enquirer had proven that decisively when they turned up those damning photos of O.J. Simpson wearing his supposedly non-existent "ugly-ass" Bruno Magli shoes. And when their tip to the LAPD turned up the murder weapon that put the murderer of Bill Cosby's son, Ennis, behind bars.

The uncomfortable fact was that today's tabs were ferreting out stories the so-called "mainstream" press would kill for.

Vidal promised protection. His technique was simple and often devastating: he spied on the spies. He'd managed to buy off a few tabloid insiders, low-level freelance stringers mostly, who'd tip him off when a star client had been targeted for scrutiny. Vidal and associates would devise countermeasures to block reporters and photographers from weddings, private parties, yacht excursions, discreet orgies, etc.

He shook his head, grinning. One thing he'd never understood was why celebrities got paranoid about weddings. In the Hollywood of old, stars had loved seeing photos of their nuptials splashed across the front pages. Today, Whoopi Goldberg painted FUCK YOU on her roof for photogs in choppers.

Give the clients what they want. And Vidal gave value for money. He provided bodyguards, souped-up escape limos chauffeured by ex-race car drivers, helicopters, private jets, safe houses, so-called "clean" credit cards that didn't leave a paper trail, makeup artists expert in disguise techniques—even celebrity "look-alikes" to lead the paparazzi on wild goose chases.

Vidal was good. The big tabloids laughed at the *Keystone Kop* antics of most Hollywood security firms, but Vidal had earned their grudging respect by batting about .350.

Then a nightmare worse than tabloids woke Hollywood up screaming.

Stalkers!

Lunatic "fans" who became obsessed with stars and made their lives hell. Like real-life clones of the relentless zombies from *Night Of The Living Dead*, stalkers had always plagued The Biz. But in the late 80s and into the 90s, stalking had become a scourge. Vidal, ever ready to exploit a new branch of star paranoia, had a brand-new pitch for terrified potential clients:

"Yes, Mr. and Ms. Show Biz, you still have to worry about those annoying tabloids. But now it's time to think about warped wackos who want to rape, torture, and kill you! Don't worry, though. Delaney Protective Partners, Ltd. has a new anti-stalker plan that's...well, it's a lifesaver. Sign here on the dotted line, please. How much does it cost? Ask instead, how much is your life worth? Ah, I knew you'd see it my way...Here, use my Mont Blanc pen..."

PARANOIA = CA$H!

Oh yeah! He'd signed five new clients after a wacko lesbian with a rifle invaded Sharon Gless' house. Business soared when an ex-con tried to abduct Donna Mills; David Hinckley gunned down President Reagan for love of Jodie Foster; Rebecca Schaeffer was murdered by a sicko; and a madman climbed Madonna's walls screaming that he wanted to cut her throat.

One truly bizarre stalker death plot had terrified the rock world. A raving maniac mailed a booby trap primed with sulfuric acid from Florida to the London home of Bjork, the nymphet singer from Iceland—and videotaped himself blowing his brains out while listening to her song, "I Miss You." Luckily, Scotland Yard had intercepted the death package.

And then there was the highly-publicized case of the vicious ex-con who'd targeted Steven Spielberg for rape.

Vidal steered right onto Beverly, pulled a sharp U-turn, and braked in front of his favorite newsstand. A smiley Latino with a limp moved quickly to the car.

"Hey, Mr. Delaney! Here's the trades and the new *Vanity Fair*. You got all the tabloids yesterday, right?"

Vidal nodded, handing him a ten and waving off the change.

"Yeah, thanks, Ramon. Mañana, hombre."

He gunned the Jag and hung a right, marveling at the car's power as he darted into a gap in the Wilshire flow. Wow, this baby kicks ass!

Yeah, business was great. Paranoia sent stars flocking to his door. He wasn't their first stop, though. Usually they went crying to the cops after a serious death threat came by mail or phone. Then they got their first big shock. They learned that the law can't help much when some creep threatens you. You're expected to sit around helplessly and wait until the stalker actually rapes, shoots, stabs, or beats you. Or sends you a bomb. Then, and only then, can your police force swing into action. Hopefully, you're still alive to cheer them on.

Vidal had lots of pals in the LAPD. Cops kept an eye out for big security firms that might hire them when they took their twenty-year pension. More often than not, gold badges tipped Vidal off when stars secretly contacted them about stalkers. They recommended Delaney Protective Partners, Ltd. with a clear conscience because the firm did good work. It screened client mail and incoming calls, so threats could be analyzed by an army of experts in psychiatry, psychology, forensics, handwriting, and voice analysis.

Vidal stopped for a red light. He glanced at his Vacheron-Constantine watch. In just three hours, he'd sit down to hear reports and recommendations on two troubling new stalkers. One was a female sending up to ten letters a day to Tinkerbell, the hot new rock star who dressed like a fairy....literally. The letters were bizarre, always three pages long and handwritten—with each word penned in a different color. One word red, the next green, the next blue, and so on. Scary. Females rarely got violent, however. A more serious matter was a weirdo Vidal's experts had pegged as a truly dangerous stalker, a male who'd gotten close enough to kill Charmain Burns. Vidal sensed that this guy was real trouble. Violent, building to some sort of climax that wasn't far off...

He turned up the radio volume. KFWB news had just mentioned *The Revealer.*

"…Early reports say the editor's name was Steve Bellini and he was a guest at the Camino Rio Hotel. Police are not ruling out foul play in the death. And in a bizarre twist to the story: when the tabloid newsman fell from his 14th-floor suite, he landed on a seventh-floor balcony at the feet of *Die Faster* producer Noel Gold and Broadway star Meryl Olivier, who were reportedly having a business meeting.

"As they'd say at Bellini's own paper, *how's that for an item?…*"

"Shit!" Vidal shook his head in disbelief. Weird. Steve Bellini, of all people, goes skydiving without a chute. "Fuck!" he said more quietly. An impatient horn beeped behind him. He hit the gas, then punched the memory button keyed to Charmain's unlisted home number.

"Hello," said the speakerphone.

"It's Vidal. Get Charmain!"

Marta, Charmain's assistant, talked to big Hollywood names every day. She didn't intimidate easily. But Vidal scared her so bad her bladder reacted.

"Uh…Vidal, she says she can't be disturbed becau—"

"GET HER NOW!"

Marta hit the Hold button. There was a long pause. Vidal felt unease gnawing at his gut. Coincidences were rare in this business. Steve Bellini, the tabloid editor Charmain hated more than anyone in the world, suddenly falls to his death? Just two weeks ago, Charmain had threatened to file a $300 million lawsuit against Bellini for a shocking story he'd published about her in *The Revealer.* When her lawyers advised she had almost no chance of winning, Charmain had raged, "I'll KILL that cocksucker!"

The speakerphone clicked and her voice snapped, "What the fuck is so goddamn important?"

Vidal took a deep breath. NEVER lose your temper with a client. "Charmain, the news just broke that Steve Bellini is dead. He took a dive from the 14th floor of the Camino Rio Hotel. The cops don't know if it was suicide or foul play."

The phone went silent. Vidal thought he'd lost the line.

Then she said slowly, "No…How could that be? I didn't want that. I just don't understand how—"

Vidal cut her off sharply. "Charmain! You're in shock. Hang up. Stay at the house and speak to no one about any of this until I get there. Who's with you…Marta?"

"And some friends," she answered. "I'm having a little…party. Followed by a light lunch."

Good, Vidal thought. Plenty of witnesses. "Get rid of them fast. I'll swing by the office first and see you in an hour."

"Goddamnit, Vidal. You can't give me orders like I'm—"

He broke in fast.

"Charmain, you hired me to make you secure. I'm doing that. Hang up NOW!" Vidal hit the "Flash" button before she could protest, got the dial tone back and punched the memory that dialed Charmain's personal manager, Mike Kelso. The Jag made a screeching U-turn just before La Cienaga and he headed back up Wilshire to his office.

Charmain put down the phone. For a wild moment, she felt an uncontrollable urge to burst out laughing. She steadied herself, gauging the emotion that washed over her. Goddamnit, she thought, it's not fear. It's like…I'm excited…

"HAH!" The explosive yell burst out of her, bleeding off the hellfire boiling inside. She punched a fist in the air, then walked back into the room where her friends and the white-coated man and woman awaited. The man, sensing the crackle of tension, asked:

"Are you upset? Should we postpone, or…?"

Charmain shook her head sharply. Turning to face her mesmerized clique, she hiked herself up onto the table, laid down, and opened her legs.

"I feel perfect for this right now," she said. "Do it."

The man frowned and pointed at her shaved vagina. The lips were moist, burgeoning.

"I can't do you like that," he said. "We either postpone until you've calmed down, or…"

Charmain smiled and arched her back. "The only way to deal with a volcano is to let it erupt, Doc. I'm so hot with all these eyes on me, it won't take long."

Everyone in the room had stopped breathing. In the heavy silence, Charmain's hands slid down to her swollen, aching flesh…

CHAPTER 8

11:02 A.M.
***NATIONAL REVEALER* NEWSROOM**
LOS ANGELES

EXACTLY fourteen minutes after Steve Bellini's body crashed Noel Gold's pitch meeting, the phone rang at Cameron Tull's desk in *The National Revealer's* Los Angeles office.

"Gossip Desk. Mr. Tull's line!" chirped Eva Martin.

She listened for a moment, then said: "Stop. He'll want to speak to you himself, immediately."

After fifteen years with America's best-known gossip columnist, Eva always knew what Tull needed to hear fast. She patched the call through to his Malibu ranch. Tull picked up the phone in his study. He hit the "mute" button on his VCR remote control, killing the sound but keeping his eyes locked on an amusing video tape.

It had arrived anonymously in the morning mail, and contained scenes of a famous married actress energetically fucking an Italianate-looking young stud of the type so adored by Cher. Tabloid TV would happily pay in the half-a-mil range for this little ratings-getter, Tull guess-timated. But he would never sell it. After he viewed it, the tape would be hidden away, with his sizable secret collection of similar show-and-tell tapes, films, and photos. They often proved effective at calming down a star who threatened a lawsuit over a story.

"What is it, Eva?...When? Christ!...Okay, put my source through to me. Then tell Mary to clear the fucking decks. I'll talk to her in exactly two minutes."

Eva patched the call through to Tull, then punched her direct line to *The National Revealer's* editor, Mary Campbell, a tabloid legend fabled and feared from Fleet Street to Tokyo. She was popularly known as "Mary, Queen of Scots."

"Mary here," she responded. It was a quiet, almost kindly voice, but it never lulled those who knew her into being any less wary.

"It's Eva, Mary. I'm quoting Cameron, who said to clear the effing decks, he'll call you in exactly two minutes."

"Can you tell me what he wants, Eva?" Mary asked in her gentlest Scottish burr.

"I don't know, Mary," she lied.

"Of course you do, dear," Mary sighed and hung up.

At that moment, staring blankly out his study window at the Malibu Hills rising above him, Cameron Tull was on the phone, listening to his secret source at the Camino Rio Hotel relate how Steve Bellini had met his death. He interrupted the breathless narrative, barking into the phone:

"Alright! You've told me enough for now. It's dangerous for you to keep talking to me on a hotel phone."

"Don't worry—it's a pay phone," said Clark Tremain, not-his-real-name, a handsome young desk clerk who hoped very much to be the next Tom Cruise. Clark desperately needed the tip money Tull paid him. Drama coaches were expensive.

"Listen to me wanna-be actor boy," Tull snapped. "Don't you think somebody might wonder why an assistant manager with access to hotel-phones would suddenly choose to use a lobby pay phone just minutes after a notorious tabloid editor wrote his last 30 on Noel Gold's patio? Hang up and find out everything you can. Exactly forty-five minutes from now, take a coffee break, leave the hotel and call me again."

Tull was gone before Clark Tremain could ask what the phrase "wrote his last 30" meant. It sounded so cool. Hey, Cameron Cool. Maybe I'll call him that some time, Clark thought, knowing he'd never dare.

Tull punched the direct line from his study to Mary Campbell's desk. Mary picked up and said, "Good morning Cameron, you're almost a minute late." She listened intently, pursing her lips when she heard Tull's news. Then she asked:

"Accident? Murder?"

"Murder, Mary," said Tull. "It's ninety-nine percent certain. My source at the Camino Rio was first on the scene with Phil Monte, the hotel detective. Phil's a pal of mine, so I'll talk to him later. When they got upstairs, Steve's door was wide open, a bouquet of flowers was lying in the corridor outside the door, and inside the suite there was a trail of food and utensils that had fallen off a room service table, one of those things on wheels. The table had smashed into the balcony railing. One of Steve's shoes was lying there, apparently jarred off by the impact."

"Sweet Jesus, the poor lad," breathed Mary. One week earlier, in a moment of professional disagreement, she had referred to the deceased as "a fucking prima donna."

"The way Phil Monte puts it together is like this," Tull continued. "Someone, probably posing as a delivery guy, hit Steve with a fist or blunt instrument, put him on the trolley and shoved. They'll know more when they examine the body."

"Who DID this, Cameron?" Mary's voice had risen to the high-pitched sing-song that signaled her staff it was time to deliver. "Who killed our Steve?"

"Hollywood, Mary. Hollywood killed him—and Hollywood is going to pay."

"Please be less fucking dramatic and a bit more specific," Mary snapped.

"You'll know who when I know who," said Tull.

He hung up, took a deep breath. His early years in the Orient had taught him the value of meditation at moments of great stress.

My mind is racing at 800 miles an hour, he told himself. Slow down. Suppress the emotions. Start sorting out possible motives, possible culprits. Stop thinking about the fact that your friend is dead. Do the job. The job always comes first. Personal feelings cloud judgment and have to be set aside. Tull had never forgotten the first time he'd learned this lesson. He was a young reporter, working for a wire service in Japan, and had been sent to the city of Nagoya to cover a devastating tidal wave. The tsunami had smashed in from the city's busy harbor and raced across the countryside, leaving thousands dead and nearly a million homeless.

It was the first really big story of Tull's career, and he'd gotten lucky. The tsunami had smashed or sunk every boat in the harbor. But one night, because he happened to sit at a tiny sidewalk noodle stand, he met the executive editor of the top Nagoya newspaper, who took a liking to Tull because he spoke decent Japanese. The editor allowed Tull to accompany a Japanese reporter and photographer team into the flooded area in a sixteen-foot motorboat the paper had flown in from Toyko.

On the morning Tull and the Japanese team arrived where the flooded areas began, he had been appalled at the sight of water-logged corpses piled to a height of about thirty feet. As a young reporter, Tull had seen plenty of dead bodies, victims of bullets, blades, baseball bats. But those had been fresh bodies, not these rancid corpses decomposing under the rising sun.

The real horror for Tull had been the doll-like bodies of little children. Grief had torn at him with angry claws. But his genuine conviction that he had been born to observe and to report, dispassionately and accurately, steeled him against emotion. He did his job. Still, for many years, the image of that grotesque death scene would flash across Tull's mind. Most vividly, for some curious reason, whenever he took a shower. Water triggered memory, filling his nostrils with that smell, that paralyzing stench.

Mind control, Tull told himself. Meditation. He had to put the story first. Keep emotion at bay, under control. As the reality of Steve's death hit him, the anger was building. He'd liked Steve a lot. Young guy. Terrific reporter, turning into a great editor. Dead. Probably because someone wanted him shut up. Tull felt the fury wash through him, trying to take him over. He wouldn't let it. He'd fought these emotions before. Reporters often went into stories raging over some injustice or tragedy caused by human villainy or stupidity. Or by God's random, moving finger. But if you were any good, you learned to suppress your feelings and get the fucking story. Just as he would now.

But underneath the anger, another emotion struggled to surface. Harder to define, but just as disturbing. It had to do with the subtext of every story about death: the survivors. The loved ones, who suddenly learn that death is one jarring affirmation of how painful it is to be alive. The most disturbing thought for Tull right now was that he had to be the one to tell Jessica Bellini, Steve's sister.

Jessica. The woman he never stopped thinking about. He'd met her a year ago. Hadn't seen her since.

But that was another story.

What was important now was finding Jessica Bellini, fast. It was unthinkable to let her hear the horrifying news on radio or TV. Tull glanced at his watch. The news can't break on the air for at least five more minutes, he told himself. I have less time than that. Think, he willed himself. Think. Think. Think…

CHAPTER 9

11:38 A.M.
***NATIONAL REVEALER* NEWSROOM**
LOS ANGELES

THE staff hit the phones and the streets immediately after Mary Campbell finished an emergency meeting with the top editors.

It had been brief. Mary had wrapped it up by invoking the name of Dalton Lupo, the paper's owner, a reclusive billionaire who'd come late to the tabloid game. But in the early 80s he'd launched *The National Revealer,* a tabloid that now rivaled—and often beat the pants off—the mighty *Enquirer.*

"Mr. Lupo called personally," Mary told the grim-faced newsmen. "He knows you will not rest until we find out who murdered our colleague. He is offering a $1 million reward to anyone outside this organization who helps us find the killer, or killers."

Mary paused, then added:

"He will pay double that amount to anyone INSIDE this organization who does the same. And he wants everyone in Hollywood to know it."

Mary didn't elaborate on her conversation with Lupo. He'd been brief and blunt as usual:

"Nobody kills one of my people. And Bellini wasn't killed by some random hotel thief or lunatic. Only a handful of our staff knew he was 'in the can' at the Camino Rio. My gut tells me this was a payback. I know you're getting together a possible list of suspects. Turn up the heat, Mary."

Moments later, Lupo phoned Tull. The publisher and his columnist weren't friends, but they'd done a lot of business together since meeting in the Orient many years before. Lupo had been CIA then. Tull, like many U.S. journalists working overseas, had cooperated with The Agency on a few low-level research jobs. Tull had never met anyone more single-minded and ruthless than Lupo. But the man gave his staff what he demanded most—loyalty. And he paid generously for it.

"I can't say this officially, Tull, even to Mary, but I want you to spread the word in that town—discreetly but forcefully—that somebody had better cough up our killer. OR we'll start printing things we usually ignore."

Lupo paused. Tull pictured his tall, powerfully-built boss, in his mid-60s but 40-ish looking, with a full head of lightly graying hair and piercing black eyes. He would be standing at the floor-to-ceiling glass wall of his study, looking out over the virgin valley far below his Colorado mountaintop hideaway.

"Actually, Tull, I might have to ask you to come up with a few devastating items from that film and photo archive you've built up over the years."

Lupo clicked off. Tull put the phone down slowly, anger mounting. It's impossible, he told himself. He must be bluffing. How could Lupo know about my secret files?

Meditate. Control. The story comes first. Tull took deep breaths, then he picked up the phone and dialed the most powerful man in Hollywood on a private number known to only six people.

The number rang and was picked up instantly. "Yes?"

"It's Cameron Tull."

A pause.

"Are you waiting for me to ask how you got this number? I won't. How can I help you?"

"Well, I've suddenly come up with an idea for an original screenplay. It's high concept. I'd like your reaction."

"Very well."

"Okay, here goes. Everybody in this town knows there are stories the tabloids are aware of, but never print. Stories about stars, directors, producers, studio executives that are incredibly sordid. Stories that are true, but maybe only eighty percent provable. Now, stories like these don't get published for various reasons. One is that no tabloid wants an open-ended legal battle they may lose just because jurors don't like finding against a movie star.

"You know the stories I'm talking about. Like that male star a certain studio keeps covering up for when he goes into steroid rages and beats up women. Or how about an in-depth look at the two macho male superstars—not including the one already apprehended—whose passions for transsexual prostitutes have not yet been revealed.

"Now here's the hook to my, um...screenplay: what if a tabloid got really angry because, just for example, some Hollywood player wanting revenge for negative publicity murdered one of the paper's editors? That tabloid might decide on a little payback of its own. It might pass the word to Hollywood that you'd better help us find the killer, or we'll hurt you—bad."

A pause.

"I'm infatuated," said Hollywood's most powerful man. "Can you make me fall in love?"

"Think of it as a surefire screenplay that writes itself," said Tull. "Remember, you know you've got a great story when you can reduce it to a headline—one sentence on a sheet of paper. And here it is:

"What if a tabloid was pushed to the wall and decided to print EVERYTHING it knows—and told Hollywood: sue and be damned?!"

Another pause. Tull waited. Then, "I'm ready to go to the prom. But will this play in Peoria?"

Tull chuckled mirthlessly. "You know every player in Peoria, pal. Ask them."

There was nothing more to be said.

Except, maybe, *fuck you.*

"Thank you for bringing me this project," said Hollywood's most powerful man. "I'll get back to you."

"Yeah. Ciao."

CHAPTER 10

2:00 P.M.
CITRUS CORNERS
1989

ONE hot Florida summer day, when Charmain was twelve, she and Selena were alone at home. A hot wind was blowing through the pines. It masked the sound of a pick-up truck, driven by a pair of no-account drifters who'd mistakenly turned down the dirt road leading to the Burns' house.

The road ended in a cul-de-sac, ringed by orange groves that surrounded the house. As the two hard-eyed crackers turned their pick-up truck around, they spotted Selena, who was still a very good looking woman, out in the backyard hanging up clothes.

The wind was ripping her dress almost to her waist. She made no attempt to pull it down, not realizing she was being observed. When she went back into the house, the two men watched for awhile. They saw Charmain come outside and help her mother, then go back inside. They realized the women were probably alone.

Minutes later, they burst into the house, demanding money and valuables. Charmain and Selena screamed and were slapped into silence. One of the drifters held a gun on Selena, stepped in close to her and ran his hand up between her thighs.

"You ever been fucked by a real man?" he said, grinning through tobacco-stained teeth. "Maybe I might just take it into my mind to give you a good fuck. I saw your legs out there when you were hanging clothes."

The drifter looked over at his friend, hoping for some encouragement. The other one paid no attention, checking for valuables, pulling open drawers, emptying Selena's purse on the kitchen table and taking cash from it.

He said, "Let's get out of here. Come on."

The other one shrugged, gave Selena an evil grin and cupped one of her breasts.

"Get off her and let's go, goddamnit."

The drifter released Selena and started to turn away.

She said very softly, "Well, I thought you were some kind of man. I thought you were going to show me what a good fuck was. What's wrong with you? Haven't you ever seen a real woman before?"

The drifter stopped, looked back at her, and shook his head. He turned to his buddy and gave him a look that said he wasn't taking any more shit about this. He gestured at Charmain.

"Get that little girl out of here."

His friend shrugged, grabbed Charmain by the neck as she struggled and kicked, and shoved her into a closet, slamming the door. Then he walked over to the stove, poured himself a cup of coffee and watched in mild disgust as his sidekick curled dirty fingers into the neckline of Selena's thin summer dress and ripped it clean off.

"Let's see them big titties!"

He yanked her white cotton bra up to her neck. Selena's large, firm breasts fell out of the bra and bounced down on her ribcage.

"WhooeEE! Looka them babies jump around. Man! I'm gonna get me some now. Pull your panties down, girl. Show me a little of that striptease."

Selena hesitated. The drifter's hand shot out and gripped one of her nipples. He squeezed. Hard. Selena shrieked.

"Aaahhh, STOP! Alright…alright…"

She slipped her fingers into the waistband of her panties, pulled them down to her knees and slowly stepped out of them. She was all but naked now, save for the tattered dress and the bra swinging uselessly up around her neck. The drifter reached for it, pulled it over her head, and dropped it on the floor. Then he stepped in close to her. Selena, breathing hard, flinched as he put his hands around under her ass, lifted her up, and walked her backward over to the the sturdy oak kitchen table. He put her down on it, then shrugged out of the dirty overalls he was wearing. He stood there in his shirt, no underwear, and pushed her legs apart.

"Now you're gonna get some real country fuckin', girl."

Selena pulled him close, put her mouth next to his ear and whispered, "I'm gonna do some real screamin' and hollerin' so my little girl can hear it. And you've gotta hit me some and then wreck the house a little. Understand?"

The drifter didn't move for a moment. Then he grinned and hit her once, twice, three times, grunting as he put some power behind it.

Selena screamed, "No…don't hit me…please!"

Then gave him a crooked smile as blood trickled from her mouth.

The drifter tilted her ass back on the kitchen table and pushed into her. Selena sobbed and yelled, making it sound good. Then the yells were moans…

And then it was over.

The drifter caught his breath, turned to his sidekick.

"You want any? It's prime."

The other one shook his head impatiently.

"Let's go."

Selena looked over at him tauntingly.

"Wouldn't you like a little?"

The guy looked at her quickly, then away. He shook his head.

"Shy, huh?" Selena said.

She lowered her voice.

"Maybe you'd like some young stuff. Tell you what. Why don't you fuck my girl? She's just ready for fucking. Did you see those new, tight titties on her? She's ripe. She's ready. Why don't you give it to her?"

Her voice rose. The two men looked at her, still on the kitchen table, legs apart, ranting like a wild woman, the juices of her assailant running down her thighs. Now even he was looking at her with disgust.

"Woman, you are just plain crazy and sick," he said.

He turned to his companion. "Let's go."

He reached over to the phone hanging next to the door and ripped it out of the wall. They left without looking back. A moment later, Selena heard the truck engine roar into life, the sound of tires ripping through gravel.

She ran to the open door.

"Goddamnit," she yelled after them. "I told you to wreck the house a little. This has got to look good. Shit!"

Selena tore back into the house and began knocking over chairs, breaking dishes, trying to make it look like the scene of the violent rape she was about to report to the sheriff. Then she went to the closet, removed the chair her captor had stuck under the doorknob. Charmain stepped out of the closet and stared at her mother, dry-eyed.

"This is terrible," Selena said. "I've been raped. I have to go and call the sheriff. The phone Daddy uses for business in the den should be working." She walked into the den, picked up the phone from the end table next to her husband's La-Z-Boy, and started to dial.

Charmain, who had heard everything that transpired through the closet door, reached back into the closet and picked up a baseball bat that belonged to her father. She walked into the den, gripping the bat with both hands, stepped up behind her mother and smashed it down on her skull.

Selena grunted heavily, dropped the phone, and fell to her knees, hanging on to the end table. Charmain hit her again with the bat. And again. And again. And again. Blood spattered all over Daddy's favorite chair. Selena slowly sank into a pool of her own blood on the hardwood floor and Charmain thought fleetingly of how she used to feel sorry for the hogs when Daddy knocked them in the head before butchering.

She didn't feel sorry for Selena.

Charmain waited until the raspy death rattles subsided. She stood there a moment and shivered once, violently. Then she smiled, walked into the dining room and selected a silver candlestick holder from the sideboard. She brought it into the kitchen, sat on the table where Selena had experienced her final illicit passion, and pulled down her panties. She inserted the ornately ridged holder into her vagina. Slowly at first, then more violently, moving it around, gasping against the pain.

She looked down and saw the blood trickling down her thighs. She hobbled quickly across to the kitchen sink, turned on the hot water and washed the candlestick thoroughly. She ripped a paper towel off the holder, wadded it up and stuffed it between her legs. Pulling her panties up to hold the makeshift tampon in place, she walked back to the dining room and replaced the candlestick holder on the sideboard.

Charmain looked carefully to make sure she hadn't left any blood spots from kitchen to dining room. She walked back into the den and picked up the telephone, still greasy with Selena's slowly caking blood. She dialed emergency, waited calmly until she heard the dispatcher's voice, then screamed at him:

"Mama's dead and the bad men did bad things to me. The bad men did bad things to me. Mama's dead."

The dispatcher alerted the nearest patrol cars.

"We've got a hysterical little girl who says her mommy is dead...and I think from the sound of it that she's maybe been raped."

It took less than 24 hours for sheriff's deputies to round up the two drifters. They put them in a line-up and Charmain identified them. At the trial, she gave testimony that made the entire courtroom weep. Telling how these men had broken into her house, raped her mother, raped her, and then killed her mother. Both drifters were sentenced to life imprisonment without parole.

They protested their innocence.

After the trial, Lawton Burns and his daughter went home to the little house near the orange groves in Citrus Corners. Lawton, like so many married men who find themselves suddenly alone, was at a loss to understand what turn his life would take now that he was rid of a woman he had hated for years. He sat at the kitchen table, his head in his hands.

Charmain walked into the dining room, to the sideboard where the silver candlestick holder reposed in polished glory, and opened one of the cabinet doors. She retrieved the bottle of whisky traditionally there for those rare moments when her father had a drink.

She poured him one and took it to him at the kitchen table, sat down next to him. When he turned to face her, she took his face in her hands and kissed him sweetly.

"Don't worry, Daddy. I'm going to take care of you now. We're going to be very happy," she said.

CHAPTER 11

CITRUS CORNERS
1989...

FOR the next few years, Charmain and her father lived quietly.

At first, there was talk of putting her into foster care because of her age and Lawton Burns' long absences from home on business. But Lawton pledged to spend less time on the road, and he hired the old maid aunt of Frank Clanton, the mayor of Citrus Corners, to live in as a housekeeper.

By the time Charmain was fifteen, she'd run the addled old lady out of the house. Nobody said much about foster care any more, even though Lawton had shown no inclination toward re-marrying. Everyone in town knew Charmain could take care of herself.

In high school, she joined no cliques and courted no one. She would have been wildly popular if she hadn't been so feared. Girls and boys alike were intimidated by her heart-stopping beauty and fearless, arrogant air. She never went out of her way to be mean or aggressive, she just didn't care. No one fucked with Charmain. Everyone, including the teachers, gossiped about her endlessly. Her childhood rape was a popular subject. And her sex life, because she didn't seem to have one. Charmain's promiscuous sexual experimentation had all but ended with the death of her mother. She didn't date any of the local boys, although she did show up for school dances and boogied with both sexes because she obviously loved to dance and showed tremendous talent at it. But when the other kids paired off for make-out sessions, Charmain caught a ride home alone or called Lawton to be picked up.

In a small town like Citrus Corners, if you don't have a sex life, people will make one up for you. Especially if you're beautiful and sexy.

It was safe to say that not just schoolboys, but every male in Citrus Corners—with the exception of Mr. Carson, the high school art teacher—had thought at least once about gettin' naked with Charmain. And more than a few females had drifted off into Sapphic daydreams about her.

So rumors abounded. Some said she skinny-dipped in the irrigation pond near the orange groves surrounding the Burns' acreage, and met the gym teacher there for sex. Others said she was a lesbian and often strapped on a dildo with her one good friend, Millie Johnson. A year older than Charmain, Millie had dropped out of high school in the ninth grade after reporting a pregnancy that turned out to be a false alarm.

Still others hinted darkly that Lawton Burns was in no hurry to get married because his daughter, as one of the boys down at the volunteer fire department pinochle sessions put it, was "taking care of him just as good as any wife could...know what I mean?" And just why did the mayor's old maid aunt suddenly get fired from her housekeeping job?

None of it was true, of course, except that Charmain did occassionally swim naked in the irrigation pond, and had been spotted by a lucky orange grove foreman out checking his crop. She had indulged in girlish pajama party diddling with Millie Johnson once or twice, but nothing serious. And certainly not involving dildoes.

But one rumor that did have more than a grain of truth sprang up when Charmain was in her senior year. The rumor that Buddy Billings, the captain of the football team, had fucked her. And he'd made her suck his dick and come in her mouth. Truth was that Charmain had asked Buddy and his girlfriend, Ruth-Ann Mayes, for a ride home after a school dance.

Ruth-Ann was loaded after too many nips of a tepid rum-and-coke mixture one of Buddy's pals had been passing around at the dance, plus a few hits on joints lit up furtively out in the parking lot. Her home was on Route 4, on the way out to the Burns' place, so Buddy had solicitously suggested dropping her off first. On a sharper night, Ruth-Ann wouldn't have gone for it, but she was too fucked up to care.

When Buddy turned his Ford pickup off the road into the Burns' driveway, he cut his headlights and stopped far short of the house, still hidden behind Australian pines and orange trees.

"What are you doing?" asked Charmain.

She knew damn well what he was doing, of course, and made the instant decision that she'd have a little fun because she was feeling damn horny lately and couldn't face another night of touching herself and fantasizing about finally filling her aching void with a big, fat cock. Buddy was perfect, Charmain figured, because he wouldn't talk. Ruth-Ann would kill him. Charmain was safe. So...just a *little* fun.

"Hey, listen, Charmain, you know, I always thought you were beautiful and I...uh—"

"Shut up, Buddy," she said. "You say one goddamn word from here on in and I'm gettin' out of this truck and goin' in. You hear?"

Buddy nodded dumbly. Charmain pulled her pink cotton sweater over her head, unsnapped her bra and turned to him.

"Scoot over here," she commanded.

He slid over on the bench seat, eyes wide as he looked at her fantastic tits, which looked even bigger than when she had clothes on.

She reached over and undid his belt buckle.

"Unzip and pull your pants way down...no, down to your ankles. That's good...now, don't move...ah..."

She lifted her skirt up to her waist and swung halfway around to face him, straddling his knee. She reached down to the crotch of her panties and pulled them aside so that her bare pudenda made contact with the bony part of his knee. His cock was erect. She looked at him and laughed. He was nearly as rigid as his dick.

She slid her fingers around his cock and started stroking, leaned forward and put her breasts into his face.

"Help yourself, Buddy…and don't say a word. Now or ever."

She humped his knee and jerked him slowly, not wanting him to come before she did. But it was over fast. She really was horny and his flesh on hers felt so damn good. Her clit found a bony ridge, stayed on it and…

"Ah…ah, Jesus…Charmain…I'm coming…"

He ejeculated all over her tits and the warm spray made her feel good. Complete.

She came. And that was it. Perfect.

Except that Buddy opened his big mouth. The excitement of having had what amounted to a heavy petting scene with Charmain wiped out his normal fear of saying anything for fear Ruth-Ann would hear about it.

Buddy confided in three of his best friends, and told them he'd not only fucked Charmain long and slow and hard…but actually made her get down on her knees and swallow his come. Buddy's buddies swore they'd never tell anyone. But they did, of course, and the hot gossip boiled and bubbled all over high school and Citrus Corners.

Then Charmain heard it. From Millie Johnson.

The next day she walked into the high school corridor and made straight for Buddy's locker, where he was hanging out with his usual gang of football studs, groupies and the adoring Ruth-Ann, possibly the only person in town who still hadn't heard the rumor.

Charmain stopped in front of Buddy, her arms cradling her schoolbooks to her breast. She smiled sweetly and said softly, "Hi, Buddy."

Buddy searched her face warily. It had penetrated his jock brain just the day before that Charmain might actually hear that he'd been talking about her. But when he looked in her eyes, he imagined he saw love. So did everyone standing there, including Ruth-Ann, who felt jealousy rising in her craw. And in years to come, when Charmain was a famous actress, they'd all marvel at the acting job she'd done that day.

"Buddy…?"

Charmain said it softly, plaintively. Instinctively, he stepped closer to her. Charmain looked up into his eyes and said again…

"Buddy…?"

"What…?"

Charmain's knee shot up and smashed into his balls. Buddy's scream escalated into a note so high-pitched that dogs started barking in the next county.

It sounded like "AAAAAAHHHHHEEEeeeeeeehhh-h-h-h-h—!"

Charmain and the dumbstruck kids watched Buddy writhe on the floor for a moment, then she said to Ruth-Ann, "You haven't heard yet, but your boyfriend's telling people he fucked me and made me give him a blowjob. It's a lie. He made a move on me the other night, but I just laughed at him."

She looked down at Buddy and suddenly shrieked, "I'll make you a deal, you piece of shit. If you can make that pathetic pecker of yours work again by sundown, I'll let you stick it anywhere you want. But I'm guessin' that Ruth-Ann is in for a long dry spell. Have a good football practice, Buddy-boy."

And she walked calmly off to her first class. Just after the first period bell, an ambulance came to cart Buddy off to the emergency room.

CHAPTER 12

3:25 P.M.
CITRUS CORNERS
1994...

IN the late spring of Charmain's senior year, the president of a marketing cooperative called the North Florida Dairy Farmers Association dropped by the Burns' place to sign some renewal papers on an insurance policy Lawton Burns had sold them. It was a hot day and Lawton offered his client, a fifty-ish man named Bill Vries, a glass of ice-cold, homemade lemonade.

They sat sipping and chatting on the back porch when Charmain emerged from the orange groves. She'd been swimming in the irrigation pond and was wearing a bikini bottom and a white T-shirt. It was still damp, and as she walked across the backyard toward the house, her nipples faintly showed through, two spots of dusty rose that bounced lightly as she moved. Under the burning sun, her water-slicked hair shimmered, a golden-red helmet that emphasized her startling green eyes and high cheekbones.

She skipped up the steps to the porch and smiled incandescently when her father introduced her to Bill Vries. She went inside and Vries said:

"Lawton, that is a fine-looking young woman and if you have no objection, I think I've ended my search for the North Florida Dairy Farmers' next 'Miss Milk Maid.' You know, we do our little beauty contest every year over in Tallahassee and the winner does personal appearances for us, wins some nice prizes and a fair amount of cash, about $5,000. What do you say?"

"Well, that's fine, but what if she doesn't win?"

Bill Vries laughed heartily. "Now you just trust me, Lawton. She'll win. Hell, I'm the head judge."

Now they both laughed heartily.

Charmain graduated in early June. She asked no one to sign her yearbook, although quite a few asked her to sign theirs. Mostly boys, but some girls. The big surprise was Ruth-Ann Mayes, who was still going with Buddy Billings. Ruth-Ann wrote: "I think you are an honest person. I always wanted to be your friend."

Charmain didn't attend the senior prom. No boy dared ask her, and she sent signals to none of them. A week after graduation, Lawton drove her to Tallahassee for her first beauty contest. For the talent section, she dressed in a skimpy sailor suit, did her hair in pigtails, walked onstage and announced she would present her interpretation of Shirley Temple singing "On The Good Ship Lollipop"—if Shirley had been seventeen instead of seven years old when she'd first performed it.

Her hip-swinging, high-kicking song and dance was a spirited, vampy eye-popper that brought the house down. When the emcee ran onstage after Charmain took her bows, he cracked, "Whew! Turn up that air conditioning."

An hour later, Charmain was crowned "Miss Milk Maid." After her victory promenade, she posed for the local press, smiling seductively into every flashing camera.

Bill Vries said to Lawton, "Hell, she would have won even if I hadn't had the fix in. She's like a goddamn movie star, Lawton."

Then he pushed through the crowd of photographers, reporters, and well-wishers and posed with Charmain for a victory picture. He put his arm around her waist; she put her arm around his. As the cameras went off, Vries casually slid his hand down to her ass and squeezed gently. She'd been expecting it. And didn't mind. She actually thought he was kind of cute. She had a secret passion for older men and imagined she'd surrender her cherry to one someday soon. But not to one this old. She let her hand drop as casually as his had and gave his ass a squeeze back.

She looked up at him and said, "Thank you, Mr. Vries." Then she stood on tiptoes and kissed him on the cheek. Everybody cheered and Bill Vries pretended to be embarrassed. He said in her ear, "How about we get together for a quiet dinner later?"

She looked him in the eye, smiled sweetly, and shook her head in a gesture of utter finality.

He shrugged. Grinned.

"You'll be our best 'Miss Milk Maid' ever, honey."

Charmain loved being a beauty queen. She felt like she was born to pose and perform, just the way she'd been doing it secretly for years in front of her bedroom mirror. Only now she had crowds of adoring people watching and applauding. They loved her. Really loved her. She felt their emotion wash through her, lift her up and make her stronger. As she traveled around North Florida making personal appearances for the Dairy Farmers, she felt for the first time that she had friends. Just the way she liked them. Always there for her when she wanted them. Crowded around her at arm's length.

But no closer.

Charmain started to learn about the beauty contest circuit when promoters approached her and invited her to join other competitions. Like most people, Miss America and Miss Universe were all that came to mind when she thought of beauty contests. But there were loads of contests on local and state levels. And if you were good enough, you could earn decent money, free clothes, cars, giant TV sets and other prizes, even college scholarships.

The next contest Charmain entered was a new one organized to promote a just-opened theme park outside of Jacksonville, Florida, called "AdventureLand." The winner picked up a cool $15,000 in cash and prizes. When Charmain arrived and sized up the other contestants, she knew she'd stepped up to a more competitive class. Some of the girls were absolute knockouts. This was no "Miss Milk Maid" for local yokels. And there was no Bill Vries to give her that friendly edge among the judges.

The way this contest was set up, every girl of the fifteen who made the semi-finals was interviewed one-on-one by each of the seven judges, six men and one woman. Charmain decided she needed an edge. So she brazenly promised every male judge she'd have sex with him if she won. She knew she was taking a big chance, that maybe one of the men might get all righteous and blow the whistle on her. But every instinct she had about men told her they made decisions with their dicks and wouldn't say a word when offered her jewel supreme.

Except maybe, "You swear?"

She was right.

That night, the emcee opened the final envelope and bellowed: "Our new Miss AdventureLand...Charmain Burns!"

The audience erupted and she took her victory promenade.

Two hours later, she was back in her hotel suite, waiting, when the first knock came on the door. She'd told each judge, including the woman, to join her at 11 p.m. sharp. Charmain walked over to the door, opened it.

It was a male judge.

"Hi, you're right on time," she said, waving at a room service table piled with liquor bottles and mixers. "Come on in and make yourself a drink."

The judge, a prosperous-looking Jacksonville businessman with a tan that revealed a white circle on his ring finger where his wedding band had been until a few minutes before, came in wearing a nervous smile. "Well, a drink would be nice," he said. "You should be drinking champagne."

Another knock on the door. Charmain opened it to welcome another male judge. The first male judge looked a bit confused at this new arrival. What the hell, wasn't this a private party, goddamnit...?

Charmain waved the two over to the drinks table. And before any uncomfortable conversation could start, there was another knock.

This time it was two judges who'd met in the hallway after getting off separate elevators. When they spotted the other judges, they looked like they'd been shot. One made an involuntary motion as if to back out of the room, but Charmain swept him inside and shut the door. Chattering brightly, she took drink orders and handed them out, acting so perfectly natural that she carried them all along in the fantasy that maybe they'd misunderstood and that each would get their illicit moments alone with Charmain...tomorrow night, perhaps?

The next knock on the door was the female judge, a Miami advertising executive, and the only one who actually believed they were all just there for a celebratory drink.

Within five minutes, the other two males judges arrived, got that stunned look on their faces, and made the best of things by joining the party. And by the time everyone was working on their second drink, it started to feel almost comfortable in the room.

The judges figured they'd either misheard the day and time for their payoff—or Charmain was simply welshing on the deal.

After ten minutes of this, Charmain tapped on her glass and said:

"Could I have your attention, please? First of all, I am so thrilled that you voted me the winner. And I know that I made promises to each and every one of you, except for the lady with us..."

The men got a strangled look and the lady executive looked mystified.

"Promises?" she said.

"Yes," said Charmain. "I promised each and every male judge here that I would have sex with them if they voted me the winner. Now I'm ready to pay off, so who's first?"

She smiled impishly at the lady executive.

"I know I didn't promise you anything, ma'am, but I'm so grateful. You're welcome to stay and have me if that's your thing. Or you can just watch."

There was a thick, dead silence. The men were frozen. No one could, or would, speak first. Then, a loud snort. An explosive, suppressed giggle that broke into a braying laugh as the lady executive could control herself no longer. Slowly, the men swiveled to look at her, then back to Charmain.

Wounded looks. Little boy looks. Charmain burst out laughing.

"Oh, come on, y'all...you didn't really believe I was going to put out, didya? Hell, I'm still jailbait until next month. Y'all should know better, I swear."

Some of the men opened their mouths as if to speak, but no sounds came out. Now Charmain and the lady executive were almost pissing their pants, laughing hysterically as tears ran down their faces. Slowly, the men shuffled out of the room, not looking back.

Charmain ran over to the door and slammed it.

"Ohmygawd, did you see their faces?"

It took a moment for the lady executive to catch her breath. She looked at Charmain seriously for a moment and said, "I really should blow the whistle on you, but...it's too goddamn PRICELESS!"

She exploded again, giggling helplessly.

After a few minutes, the two of them calmed down a bit. Lady exec took a breath and said, "Well..."

Charmain said, "Let me freshen your drink."

She poured another white wine, handed it to her. They smiled and clinked glasses, sipped for a moment. The lady exec looked into Charmain's green eyes and said, "You know, actually..."

Charmain leaned forward and kissed her gently on the lips.

The lady exec said, "Oh...oh!"

Charmain took her glass, set it down on the table, then kissed her again. Hard.

CHAPTER 13

6:54 P.M.
TWO WEEKS EARLIER...
LOS ANGELES

THE Presence slipped the Sig-Sauer 40mm automatic out of the holster hidden in the small of his back as he approached his apartment door. He punched the Swedish-made combination lock with the index finger of his left hand, pushed the door open, and paused in the doorway.

His eyes flicked to what looked like a smoke detector on the ceiling. A tiny red light in its center blinked on and off. Good. It would be glowing steadily if anyone had entered in his absence. The "detector" was a barometric trigger. It measured the slightest changes in air pressure. Opening a door or window even a crack triggered a response.

The Presence holstered the Sig as he stepped into the modest one-bedroom apartment. He had lived here since leaving The Job. It was comfortable, nothing more. All he needed now. He sensed that the time of extraction was drawing near. His heart leaped every time he thought of it. He'd seen the signs, felt them. A nascent resonance in the earth. The faint, intermittent shimmer of a nimbus girdling the North star. Soon. It would be soon. He felt exalted, yet anxious. He had to be ready. It was time to move swiftly. But carefully. No mistakes.

He walked straight into the tiny den, put the latest copy of *The Revealer* and a micro-tape cassette on the blond wood desk, and fired up his Apple PowerBook G3. As he waited for it to load, he stepped back and ran his fingers through thick dark hair styled neatly in a modified crewcut. He stripped off his sport jacket, polo shirt, slacks, Bass loafers, socks, briefs. He was the kind of man who looked well-built and athletic with clothes on. Naked, his body was awe-inspiring. Muscles cut like sculpted marble, brutal shoulders, cord-like abs, long legs topped by rippling swimmer's thighs. A wall mirror caught a reflection of his chest. He smiled grimly, wondering what his ex-comrades-in-arms would make of its...accoutrements. He never took his shirt off in public anymore. Not that he had much occasion to. He worked alone now.

He dropped to the floor and executed twenty one-armed pushups, ten on each arm. He did them slowly, not pausing to rest at the upper or lower extension. As he finished, the phone rang. He ignored it as he typed in his password and the file name "Queen" on the PowerBook. The screen flashed up a color photo of Charmain Burns in a gold mesh bikini, her first-ever publicity photo. It had run in Cameron Tull's column shortly after she'd arrived in Hollywood three years before.

The Presence reached out and touched the computer screen, lightly running his fingers over Charmain's image. He hit a key, then another, and another. Headlines popped as he rifled through news clips that chronicled a Hollywood career in hyper-drive…

- Newcomer Charmain Burns Scores As a Sizzling Teen Sex Bomb in Her First Movie!
- Charmain Burns Signs as Sexy Troublemaker on TV's Red-Hot *BevHills High* Series
- BURNS ON FIRE!! Picks Up First-Season Emmy
- Charmain KO's Director with Karate Kick After He 'Called Me a Filthy Name Women Hate!'

That headline was the one that had first attracted the attention of The Presence.

- *BevHills High* Producer Larry Buckley Refuses Charmain's Huge Salary Demand: '$100,000 a Week—Or I Walk,' She Says!
- Movie Offers Pour in as Charmain Tells *BevHills High* Producers: 'I'm Too Sick to Work!'
- Buckley Caves In: Charmain Gets Her Hundred Thou!
- Woman Motorist Claims Charmain Pulled Gun on Her During Traffic Argument!
- Charmain Gun Charges Dropped as 'Victim' Refuses to Testify! *BevHills High* Producer Mum on Settlement Rumors…
- Charmain Suspended After Slapping Co-Star Linda Kole!

He nodded, remembering how proud he'd felt. This was an imperious woman who brooked no challenge to her authority.

- It's Char-mania! Star Drops Top at Party After Winning Second Emmy!
- Love at First Sight as Hollywood's Hottest Sex Symbols 'Meet Cute...' Charmain Pulls Gun on Bad Boy Connor O'Toole, Ends Up 'Lip-Locked' Moments Later!
- Burns Burning Up in Sizzling Romance with Hunky Connor!
- Charmain & Connor Shock Diners as They Make Whoopee Under a Table!
- Cops Break Up Wild Club Brawl, Arrest Charmain Burns and Connor O'Toole!
- Secret Service Eject Charmain and Connor as She Drops Top and He 'Waves' Indecently at White House Ball: Witnesses Say President and First Lady 'Looked Amused!'
- Wild Child Charmain Front-Runner for Coveted Lead Role in Movie Version of Runaway Best-Seller Novel *Medusa*!

•Connor O'Toole 'Suicidal,' Pals Say, After Charmain Dumps Him Amid Rumors of Lesbian Affair!

As the news stories and photos he'd scanned into the PowerBook flashed by, The Presence picked up the latest *National Revealer*. A powerful photo dominated the front page. It showed Charmain Burns, her lips drawn back over perfect white teeth in a mask of rage, slashing a wild-eyed, terrified horse across the face with a riding crop. The headline screamed:

"NEW CHARMAIN HORROR: She Brutally Lashes Innocent Horse! Exclusive Photos!"

And the subhead below read:

"Animal Rights Groups Unite to Boycott Network Unless She's Fired From *BevHills High*!"

What fools, thought The Presence. Did they not understand? Charmain lived her life by a simple code: "I must bend you to my will...right or wrong, you must obey me." The media sold papers by painting Charmain as a spoiled, petulant, demanding bitch. And the stupid masses bought it. Why couldn't they see what was so self-evident? Charmain is a queen. A strong woman born to rule. Totally courageous, utterly ruthless. A noble woman. The type of queen his planet needed so desperately.

Using a tiny razor-tipped cutter, he clipped the latest *National Revealer* article and photos of Charmain. He switched on the high-resolution flatbed scanner next to the PowerBook. Moments later, the new adventures of Charmain were entered permanently into the "Queen" file. Now it was time to focus totally on his mission. Much still had to be decided. He was almost certain that Charmain was The Chosen. But he needed a sign, some indelible indication of unique nobility.

A sense of urgency nagged him nearly every moment now. He had begun routine surveillance of Charmain nearly three months earlier, but now it was time to launch an around-the-clock effort. The Presence picked up the micro-cassette tape he'd laid on the desk and snapped it into a tape machine. He'd retrieved the tape the night before from a recorder buried at the base of the phone pole he'd climbed weeks before to tap Charmain's phone line. He punched "Play," turned the volume up to "Max," and walked into the bedroom.

The tape reeled off messages to Charmain's answering machine and her phone conversations over a three-day period. As he listened, he dressed swiftly in black trousers, navy turtleneck, a belt with no reflective metal on the buckle, and lightweight black running shoes. He listened intently to a call made just an hour before, then walked back into the office-den and played it back.

"Hello?"

"Charmain, hi...It's Dina. What's up?"

Dina Buckley, daughter of the *BevHills High* producer. The Presence turned the volume down a bit.

"Not much. Just hanging out at the pool."

"Me too…I am so totally bored. Let's go out later."

"Where? BuzzBuzz?"

"Unless you want to do The Viper Room? That new group 'Shitface' is opening."

"The perfect group for that shithole. The fucking Viper Room sucks. I'll see you at BuzzBuzz around ten."

"Okay…"

Charmain left her Beverly Hills home at 9:34 p.m. She whipped out of the driveway in her red custom Callaway Mercedes and headed for Sunset Boulevard. The Presence followed her to BuzzBuzz, where she turned into an alley behind the club and parked next to an empty office building. He cruised slowly into the alley behind her, lights out. He saw Charmain enter the club through a door marked "Staff Only." He drove through the alley and parked out on Sunset. Then he slipped back down the alley on foot, unnoticed by the security guards and bouncers standing out front.

The Presence settled into a dark spot between a dumpster and a phone pole that commanded a view of the dimly-lit rear staff entrance. Charmain would exit from there. He had followed her here more than once. It might be hours. He settled himself into the lotus position and passed into a meditative trance. Images of the mother planet swirled through his mind…

It was a quiet night for BuzzBuzz. By 10:15 Charmain was bored. The place, just over a year old, was trying desperately to become the hangout for movers and shakers. It featured chic California nouvelle dining at velvet-covered banquettes, bands that looked punk but played disco, a medium-sized dance floor—and astronomical prices to discourage tourists and wannabe's. BuzzBuzz worked well when it was jammed with celebs jostling to ogle each other. Tonight it wasn't working at all.

A sneer settled on Charmain's face as she sized up the room. It was crawling with non-creative types—the demi-monde of film, TV, and music bureaucrats who kept the town running—managers, business managers, agents, mid-level studio execs, publicists, hack writers for *Variety* and *Hollywood Reporter*. No tabloid types tonight. They rarely showed up. They didn't have to; half the fucking staff was probably on their payroll.

A semi-interesting person finally walked in. Greg Bellson, a writer-producer who'd just scored his second hit series on TV. Charmain and he had never met, but at this point they were the two most famous people in the room, so Greg stopped by Charmain's table for a ritual "quickie schmooze."

HE: (*Reaching across table to take her hand*) Well, hh-h-i-i-i there. Congratulations!

SHE: (*Stays seated, but purses her lips in a long-distance "air kiss"*) Thanks…I love your work.

HE: No, really…Two Emmys in two years. I'd die to work with you.

SHE: Me too!

HE: (*Big smile and wink*) If Buckley doesn't treat you right, you call me!

SHE: (*Arching her breasts and offering a fresh perspective of her sequined tank top*) Oh, I will…I will.

HE: No, he's great. I love Larry. Wonderful vision. (*Suddenly peers across the room and sets up his exit line*) Whoops, is that my agent? Maybe I can get him to pick up the check. Ha, ha…Well…

SHE: So great seeing you.

HE: Let's talk soon, really.

SHE: Love to…Bye…

HE: Bye.

A waiter stopped by. "Will you be eating or…?"

"I'm waiting for someone. Bring me another drink."

"Another Cuervo? Of course…"

Goddamnit, where was that fucking Dina? Charmain fished her cell phone out of her Judith Leiber bag and punched Dina's memory button. The line connected. Shrieking punk rock blared into Charmain's ear.

"Hello?"

"You fucking cunt! If you love that fucking Viper Room so much, just stay there. How dare you keep me waiting here?!"

"Charmain, I'm on my way. I just stopped by to hear the band, and the lead singer started talking to me. He's such a fan of yours and I thought, like…you know…he could…Uh, like…come there with me and—"

"Fuck you, you're high, you little junkie bitch. What are you on, Angel Dust? Why don't you go under the stage and shoot up like River Phoenix, then suck all the Shitheads' dicks and DIE OUT ON THE SIDEWALK?!"

Heads were turning at BuzzBuzz. A young actor Charmain detested, Dennis Hawes, had just walked in with three nobody starlets. As he passed Charmain's table, he said in a stage whisper, "Hope she takes her own advice." The starlets giggled and shook their asses.

Dina was pleading on the phone, "So please don't be mad…Charmain?…I'll leave right now. I'll be right over…Wait for me…Okay?…Okay, Charmain?…"

Charmain's eyes had never left Dennis Hawes' back. She stared icily as he and his pussy posse were seated, then spoke into the phone.

"Don't come, don't call…And Dina, don't talk to me on the set anymore!"

Dina was crying. "Charmain, I'm sorry…You're my best friend, don't hang up, plea—"

Charmain clicked off. The waiter arrived and deposited her Cuervo. Charmain knocked it back neat, stood up and said, "I'm leaving. Put it on my tab and give yourself ten bucks."

As the room's most famous person, every eye was on her—and pretending not to be—as she sauntered over to Dennis Hawes' table. He didn't look up, suddenly engrossed in the menu. The bimbettes tried staring Charmain down, but blinked as they realized they were face-to-face with the craziest bitch to hit Hollywood since Roseanne. And the most violent since Shannen fucking Doherty.

Charmain folded her arms and said loudly, "Well, well, it's Hawes and his 'ho's...Phheeww! If you girls can't afford a decent feminine hygiene spray, the chef will loan you a bottle of vinegar. And there's a hose out in the alley."

Dennis Hawes looked up, red-faced.

"Now listen, Charmain..." he started to bluster.

"ASSHOLE!" Charmain screamed, slamming her fist on the table. Everyone in the vicinity, including three waiters who'd sidled up to hear the action, nearly jumped out of their skin. One of the bims pissed her pants and started crying.

"You'll never work on my series again because you can't memorize ten lousy lines without holding up production. You have a brain the size of your dick, your hair's starting to go, and you have bad skin. Your own agent told me the word's out on you. He can't get you a job. It's porno or driving a cab for you, Hawes! And next time you see a star, drop your fucking eyes, you piece of shit. Any problem with that? Or do I need to pound your fucking face in?"

Dennis tried looking defiant, but failed. One of the bims, finding some courage, said, "Don't argue with her, Dennis. She's probably carrying that fucking gun of hers!"

Just what Dennis had been thinking. His guts contracted. Charmain, ever perceptive, saw people at nearby tables suddenly shift uncomfortably. Fuck, she thought. They think I might whip out my piece. Better leave before I start a panic.

She suddenly laughed and said, "Oh, I wouldn't shoot Dennis. He's on the Endangered Species List—the 'Zit-Crusted Asswipe.' Good night, ladies. Don't forget to look at his HIV card."

Charmain headed for the rear exit. She grinned and felt better as she heard, behind her, the buzz rising in BuzzBuzz.

She strutted through the kitchen, out the staff entrance, and into the alley. It was dark, littered with empty boxes and garbage cans. As she headed down the alley toward the office building where she'd parked her car, Charmain stiffened when she heard a metallic click. She saw the glow of a cigarette lighter. Three men were standing along the cement block wall that ran down the alley. She caught an acrid whiff of...Shit, they were smoking crack! That's all I need, crackheads. Run back to the club? Ah, fuck 'em, she decided. She kept walking. They turned to watch her pass. Young. Creeps. One of them, Tom Petty's zombie twin, fingered his long, dirty blonde hair and leered.

"Hey man, look…prime-time TV pussy."

His pals snickered in the time-honored tradition of street scum. Dirty Hair held out his crack pipe.

"Suck my dick and I'll let you suck on this, baby…"

Charmain probably could have gotten by them if she'd been willing to ignore a few loathsome sexual insults. But, as was her custom, she refused to take shit. Her right hand was out of their sight. She reached into the bag hanging from her shoulder and…Fuck! No gun. She'd left the 9mm Kahr in her nightstand. Shit! Okay, she was almost past them now. They made no moves, just kept up their litany of filthy anatomical references and depraved sexual rape fantasies.

She glared. Assholes. But so what? She'd heard worse. No sweat. Just ignore them. Oh, how she wanted her gun. Guys freak out when a chick pulls a piece…Good, she was past them now. Just keep walking to the car. Don't look back. They'll think you're scared…

She was almost home free when Dirty Hair called her the one word she never tolerated.

"Fuck you, stuck-up cunt!"

Charmain whirled and screamed, "I'd rather lick dogshit than fuck you, you smelly hairball! The only cunt you've ever played with is spelled F - I -S - T."

Right away, she knew she'd pushed it too far. They swarmed, knocking her to the ground. Dirty Hair yelled: "Let's show this fucking cunt what it's like to get fucked by three cocks at once."

He grabbed a fistful of hair and yanked her head up. He twisted her to face one of his slobbering buddies and snarled: "He'll fuck you in the ass!" He shoved her face at the other one: "He'll fuck you in the cunt. And I'm gonna shove my cock all the way down your friggin' throat."

"I'll bite it off, I swear," Charmain hissed. Dirty Hair slapped her. They manhandled her into a kneeling position. Skirt and panties were yanked down her thighs. Dirty Hair had her arm twisted behind her. Now she knew she was going to get hurt. Hurt bad. For a bizarre moment, the whole tableau congealed into slow motion as the two behind her, fried on crack, had a tough time unzipping their pants. She struggled furiously. Dirty Hair hit her.

"Come on, start fucking her," he yelled. "When you get going, hold her good and I'll put my dick in her mouth. Right, bitch? And you even try to bite me, I'll knock your fucking teeth out and cut your throat."

Charmain recoiled in horror as she felt a penis stabbing at her thighs and buttocks as one of the creeps probed for whatever orifice he intended to penetrate. She started to scream. Dirty Hair cursed. A knife was at her throat. The point broke skin. A hot trickle of blood ran down her neck. Violence exploded around her. Thuds and blows and cries. The hand gripping her hair jerked away. She was thrown to the ground. Cringing, curled in a fetal ball, she waited…for the knife…blows…the rape…pain…But nothing touched her. Nothing. She heard violence, but it was like a soundtrack.

She opened her eyes. Images suddenly matched sounds. A black man, arms pumping in short piston strokes, was systematically beating up her assailants. It was beautiful, brutal. He hit with blinding speed, yet seemed to be taking his time. He slammed a fist straight into Dirty Hair's mouth. Blood splattered on Charmain. Something hit her face and stuck. She put a hand to her cheek, brushed it off. A tooth.

She laughed, yelled, "Kill the fuckers." Dirty Hair was down. Two to go. They kept trying to skitter past the black man, run down the alley. Hopeless. He was a panther. They shuffled, he moved. Wherever they went, he was there first. Stabbing with jabs that traveled inches. Toying with them. Inflicting pain because he could. Now they begged for mercy. Charmain thrilled to their fear, to the black man's power. He's a boxer, she realized. Only a pro moves like that.

The black man tired of the game. He unleashed a savage uppercut. A punk went down. One to go. This one slobbered, cried, covered his face. The black man grabbed his shirt front in his left hand and said, "You ain't been hit good until you've been busted by Buster Brown." He drove a piledriver right straight at the nose. Blood sprayed. The guy hit the ground and never twitched, lay there like a pile of dirty clothes.

Charmain said, "Yay!!" and pulled up her panties. The black man walked toward her. He never sensed The Presence, poised on the wall above him, ready to spring. Charmain sat up and said, "Where's my skirt?" The black man spotted it, picked it up, and handed it to her. He held out a hand to help her up. "You okay?"

On the wall, The Presence relaxed. Charmain was safe. His mission still intact. He had observed everything and was impressed, once again, with Charmain's courage, her refusal to compromise. She carried herself like…a queen. Physical dominance by three men was no shame. She had defied them, fought them, never begged. He had been ready to rescue her until the boxer came up the alley like a black whirlwind. For a split second, The Presence had considered joining in. He'd been looking forward to the joy of a light workout. Then he'd recognized the black man and knew he could handle it. A difference in style, of course. The three would heal, revive, and continue their pathetic lives. They would not have survived an encounter with The Presence.

Charmain was on her feet now, brushing herself off. "How are you feeling?" said Eddie "Buster" Brown.

"Fine, outside of the fact that they nearly ripped my fucking hair out by the roots." Charmain looked at her savior and said, "Who are you, anyway? You've got to be a boxer with those moves."

"That's right," he said. "Eddie 'Buster' Brown. Career record of 33, 6 and 2."

"I don't know shit about boxing," said Charmain. "I've never heard of you. But anyway, thanks for fighting off those punks, Buster. You're an okay guy."

Suddenly Buster said, "Now I know who you are. You're on TV. You play that bitchy girl on that high school show."

"That's right, Buster. I'm Charmain Burns."

She held out her hand.

"Yeah, I don't watch TV much, but I remember seeing you in that swimming pool scene where you almost drowned that girl who was messin' with your man. You were wearing that little tiny bikini. You sure are one fine-looking woman."

Buster's eyes flickered. Charmain knew that look in men's eyes. She sensed he was suddenly remembering how she must have looked moments ago, naked from the waist down, panties around her ankles.

She looked at Buster more carefully. He had a rugged handsomeness. And she noticed that he had broken a light sweat in his tussle with the punks. Charmain stepped closer and caught a slight scent of his musk. It stirred her, and for a moment she remembered her days as a girl in the South, giggling with other sweet young things about that most taboo of subjects: sex with black men. Charmain had idly fantasized about it, but it wasn't on her Top 10 list. Now, she felt aroused. The fear, the adrenaline, the proximity of a male who had proven his maleness beyond all doubt caught up with her.

"Buster," she said, "I think I owe you a drink."

"Well," said Buster, "I was goin' to see my friend here. He works in the kitchen. He says he'll introduce me to the manager so maybe I can get work as a bouncer. But, yeah, I'd like for you to buy me a drink."

"No, I didn't mean in the club," said Charmain. "There are some people in there I don't want to see. Let's go up to my place and I can get out of these clothes. I want to burn them. Just the thought of those punks' hands on my things makes me sick. I need a shower."

She turned and started walking away, totally confident that Buster would follow. And he did. Before Charmain and Buster reached her car, The Presence was already sprinting like a big cat up Sunset. He was in his car with the engine ticking over when Buster and Charmain passed him in her Mercedes. The Presence slid out after them.

Buster Brown had lived his entire life in Los Angeles but he'd only driven through Beverly Hills two or three times. Word was that the cops there didn't take to strange black men driving through their elegant, palm-lined streets after sundown.

Like any average American, Buster had wondered, dreamed about what a Beverly Hills home would look like inside. Now he felt like movie scenes were flashing before his eyes. After arriving at the house, he'd barely gotten a glimpse of the lavish art deco interior before Charmain poured them both a stiff drink and dragged him out to the patio area. It was a beautiful moonlit night. Charmain immediately stripped naked and dove into the pool. She broke the surface, shaking herself like a sleek young seal.

She told Buster, "Take off your clothes and get in here. It's great."

Shyly, he turned away and took off his clothes. He dove in quickly. Charmain giggled. They splashed around in the cool water for awhile, Buster warily keeping his distance. Then Charmain climbed out. She stretched, throwing her arms over her head and shaking the water from her hair. Buster was awed by her incredible body. Her pale white skin picked up the glow of moonlight. She reached for her drink, raised her glass at Buster in a mock toast, and slugged back a warming mouthful of eighteen-year-old Macallan single malt Scotch whisky. Then she picked up Buster's drink and beckoned him out of the pool.

"Toss me a towel," he said.

"Uh-uh."

"Come on."

"You come on."

Buster shrugged, came out of the pool, and accepted the whisky Charmain held out. She stepped in close. Buster saw that her nipples were rock hard. The moonlight appeared to give them a slightly purple tinge. It seemed to Buster that he never had seen anything as white as Charmain's skin at that moment.

He gasped as he felt her hand reach down and encircle his manhood.

"Wow!" breathed Charmain. "You know what we call these in the South, don't you, Buster? We call them blacksnakes. I've never played with a blacksnake before. Does it bite?" she teased.

Charmain's hand gripped, released, caressed. She reached up with her free hand, put it around Buster's neck, and pulled his face down to hers. She kissed him, then whispered in his ear, "Let's go upstairs and see if we can find a rubber that'll fit this big boy."

Charmain turned and sprinted through the house. Buster followed her through the carpeted living room and up a broad hardwood staircase to the second floor master bedroom. As he trotted into the room after Charmain, Buster blinked. At first, it seemed to be totally dark. But there was very dim lighting that bounced off the smoky mirrored paneling on the walls and ceiling. A huge bed dominated the room. Charmain was sitting on it cross-legged, a large glass bowl between her legs. At first Buster thought it was full of brightly colored candy. He chuckled when he got closer and saw the bowl contained various brands of condoms.

"Here's a Japanese one that'll work just great, I think," said Charmain. "I know the Japanese are supposed to have teeny dicks, but they make a special brand for export that seems to work best for some of my...bigger boys."

Buster reached out his hand as if to take the condom. Charmain snatched it away, pulling him down on the bed, forcing him to lie full-length.

She looked over his equipment judiciously and said, "You know, I think we Southern girls believe all these stories about how big you black guys are. But I read somewhere that that's not really true. That black dicks look bigger when they're not stiff and white dicks look small until they do get stiff. But once you've got a hard on, they're all about the same size. What do you think, Buster?"

He jerked instinctively as she carefully placed the condom on top of his shaft and then rolled it carefully down its length. Charmain felt suddenly light-headed. Excited. Adrenaline pumped through her system as her body reacted to the night's events. The near rape. The fight. The sight of Buster's naked, well-muscled body as he'd climbed out of the pool and stood beside her. Charmain needed release and she went for it. Straddling Buster's body, she lifted up her hips, still holding his cock.

"Don't move," she told him. Slowly, deliberately she lowered herself onto him, then stopped, teasing herself, building up the already unbearable tension. With a little cry, she plunged down onto him and felt him deep inside her. Then she collapsed onto his chest.

"Fuck me, Buster Brown," she breathed.

Excitement shot through Buster like he was on an electric wire. He turned her over on her back, dominating her, pounding into her. Charmain gasped. She dug her heels into his rock hard buttocks. A frenzy overtook her and she thrust back up at him with a fierce energy that surprised him. He thrust back at her even harder, dominating her. Images swirled through Charmain's mind. The leering punks standing over her, stiff penises bouncing against her body, about to penetrate...then the blinding flash of Buster's muscles as he pounded their faces, their guts, smashing them, blood spurting everywhere.

Charmain felt the muscles in her belly begin to twitch and jump and jerk. Wildly exultant, she tensed as her body prepared to release. She opened her eyes, knowing the sight of Buster's black muscles would trigger her orgasm.

She looked up at the mirrored ceiling...and screamed in horror.

A figure, a man, was standing near the foot of the bed. She jerked her head away from Buster's insistent kisses. The man came closer, his eyes staring intensely into hers.

She screamed again.

"Come, baby," said Buster as he thrust into her even harder. "Come, baby. I know you're coming. Come, baby."

Charmain shrieked and beat her fists against Buster's back. She wanted to run, to escape this freakish nightmare. All the emotions of the night caught up with her. Fear; lust; now the sheer horror of a stranger staring straight into her eyes as her body bucked uncontrollably.

She slid over the edge into a wrenching orgasm. A moment later, Buster cried out and spent himself inside her. In that first split second release, Charmain's eyes closed as her head snapped back in a reflexive spasm. When she opened them again, the man was standing closer. She watched in fascinated horror as he reached out and curled his fingers around the back of Buster's neck. He squeezed hard. Buster slumped unconscious on top of her, a dead weight.

With a casual shove that told her how strong he was, the man pushed Buster's dead weight off her, exposing her body. The man's eyes darted downward. She knew her thighs were slick and wet. She felt violated. For the first time in her life, she was terrified beyond control.

She opened her mouth to scream but the man swiftly held his hand up and said, "Have no fear. I will not hurt you." His voice was deep, resonant, full of authority. Charmain fought to control her fear.

"Who the fuck are you? How did you get in here?"

He held up his hand. "It is not necessary for you to speak. Only to listen. I am Randak 2000. What I am, who I am are matters that do not require your understanding now. I go where I wish, when I wish. I have observed you for some time now.

"The question before us is this: are you worthy?"

Charmain felt the panic rising to her throat again. This was obviously some nut, here to kill her. Her mind raced desperately for a way out. She thought of the gun in her nightstand, but he was standing too near. She wouldn't have a chance. But thinking of resisting helped to control her fear. He's just a man, she told herself. Con him! She sat up, covering her breasts with her hands. No, too submissive! She dropped her hands. Let him look. She glared at the weirdo. "Okay, you said you're not going to hurt me. So, what the fuck do you want? An autographed eight by ten-glossy? A pair of my panties? Fine. What would you prefer, freshly-washed or slightly-used?"

Charmain, like any good actress, was a student of human nature. She watched the man's face intently for any hint of a smile. A sense of humor would be good. But there wasn't a flicker of it on his face.

Shit, she thought, a real fucking psychopath. The man spoke as if he was simply continuing his statement. As if she had not made any interruption.

"You have spirit. That is why I have been observing you. But I must have a greater sense of your power. Your daring and ruthlessness. You are perhaps destined to be a great leader. You must give me a sign. I'll be watching."

The man paused. Responding to the look of total bewilderment that crossed Charmain's face, he said, "Do not try to understand. I am Randak 2000. I am your observer. There is great trouble in the universe I inhabit. Perhaps you are the key to the survival of my race. I will contact you."

At that moment, Buster Brown began to stir in the bed beside Charmain. Randak 2000's right hand moved like a snake. He hit Buster at the base of the skull. Buster stopped moving.

Randak 2000 looked at Charmain. "When he awakens, tell him you were surprised by a jealous ex-lover, who struck him. He will believe you."

In one swift motion, Randak turned and bounded toward the open French doors of the second-floor balcony and leaped straight out into the night air.

Charmain gasped. JESUS CHRIST!

For a moment, all was silent in the darkened bedroom. Buster breathed heavily. For a moment, Charmain shook in reaction to the wild emotional roller coaster ride she'd had that night.

Buster was regaining consciousness. "What the hell...What's up? What happened?" he said weakly, rubbing his head. "What the fuck happened? What's going on?"

Charmain looked at Buster for a moment, then shrugged and fed him the story the weirdo had suggested.

"Look, I'm really sorry, okay? My ex-boyfriend still has a key. He got in here, and came up behind you and hit you in the neck. Are you okay? How do you feel?" Buster was sitting up by now, rubbing the back of his neck.

"Shit," he said. "I've been hit harder than that by sparring partners. Yeah, I'm okay, I think. Where is the fucker?"

"I got ahold of my gun in the nightstand and scared him off," she said. "Look Buster, you've got to get out of here. Let me think for a minute."

She suddenly decided that the first call she'd make would be to Vidal Delaney. But she didn't want Vidal to know she'd had Buster in her bed. She started to suggest calling a cab, but thought better of it. A cabbie might remember Buster's face. Picking up a black man at the home of a famous white female TV star was something a cabbie would remember. Worse, he might tip *The Enquirer* or *Revealer.* And walking was out of the question. A black man walking through Beverly Hills would be picked up and questioned by the town's overzealous cops.

"Buster, here's what I want you to do," she said. "Take my keys and take my car. Drive it to the BuzzBuzz parking lot and leave it there. Put the keys under the front seat. I've got an extra set of keys and I'll pick it up tomorrow. Don't tell anybody you've been here. I don't want any more trouble."

Buster suddenly realized the night was ending. He hadn't told Charmain about his big dream, and she could help him. "Listen, baby," he said. "I want you to help me out. I need some help."

Charmain patted his cheek. "Sure, I'll give you some money, Buster. I'm so grateful to you. What do you want? Like, I'll give you a couple grand, or even more. What do you need?"

"That's not what I need," said Buster. "I don't need no runnin' around money. I want to be an actor. I could be the next black action star like Shaft. Or like Action Jackson, you know, Carl Weathers. You remember him in *Rocky?* I could be just like him. I'm tougher than him and I'm better lookin' too."

Oh God, Charmain thought. Hollywood. Even the boxers want to be actors. Why can't I just give him a couple grand and get him out of here? But she sensed that Buster was too proud to fall for that, and he wasn't really looking for a hand-out. Just wanted to be an actor. Just like her.

So she said, "Look, Buster, here's my phone number. See, it's right there on the bed stand. Copy that down and now you have my private line. Call me in a couple of days and we'll talk about your career. I'll do everything I can, okay? I'm really grateful to you for helping me get away from those creeps. But right now, I've got a lot of things on my mind."

Buster was impressed. "Wow, that's your private line, huh?"

"That's right, Buster," she said, thinking, hey, I change telephone numbers more often than most women change pantyhose.

Buster took her hand and kissed it gently. "You're a very nice lady. You really are."

"Okay, Buster, look, I promise, I'll try to help. Okay? But you've got to call me in a couple of days. Now take my keys and get out of here. And don't tell anyone you've been here, okay?"

"Okay. Okay. I won't call you for you a couple of days, but you think about it, alright?"

"I promise, Buster," she said.

Moments later, she heard the front door close. She picked up the phone and dialed Vidal Delaney. She heard her Mercedes going down the driveway. Buster was gone. Vidal answered.

"Vidal, listen, it's Charmain. My god, some creep, some weirdo, just got into my bedroom. I woke up and the son of a bitch was staring down at me. I was terrified. I don't know what to do."

"Hold one second. I'm gonna get somebody up there. Just hold on. Stay on the line." Vidal clicked his second line and called his chief of security, Boris Szabo.

"Boris, Charmain just had a problem up at the house. Somebody broke in. She's alone now. Call your contact in the Beverly Hills P.D. and have them send a car out there right away. Then you get up there with a couple of our guys and make sure they're posted around the perimeter. I'll be there within twenty minutes."

Vidal clicked back. "Charmain, there'll be a Beverly Hills police car outside within a minute. Boris Szabo and a team are headed over. I'll be there within twenty minutes. Who was this creep? Are you okay?"

"Yeah, I'm okay, Vidal. I don't know. I'll give you the details when you get here. All I know is he called himself something like Randak, Randak 2000, I think."

There was silence on the line.

"Are you sure?" said Vidal.

"Well, I don't know. Yeah, yeah, Randak 2000. Yeah, I'm sure."

"Holy Christ," he breathed.

"What's the matter?" Charmain yelled.

"I'll tell you when I get there."

"No, tell me now, Vidal, goddamnit."

But he'd clicked off the line. Vidal was in his car heading for Charmain's house within a minute. He dialed a number on his car phone.

"Dr. Crane," a voice answered.

"Dr. Crane, sorry to wake you so late. It's Vidal Delaney. An emergency."

"Yes, Vidal, what can I do for you?"

"Dr. Crane, remember a couple of months ago I brought you some fan mail for Charmain Burns and showed you in particular one from some wacko who called himself Randak 2000? Do you recall that?"

After a moment's pause, Dr. Crane said, "Yes, I do recall that Vidal."

"Didn't you say that this guy was one of the dangerous ones?"

"Yes, I did Vidal. He is potentially very dangerous. Why do you ask? Have you had more mail?"

"It's worse than that, doc. Apparently, this guy, or someone calling himself Randak 2000, was just in Charmain's bedroom."

"My god, is she alright?"

"Apparently she's okay," said Vidal. "The guy has left. Doc, can I come by and see you first thing in the morning?"

"You certainly can Vidal. How about 8:30?"

"That'll be fine doc, thanks a lot."

Vidal clicked off and gunned it. It was time to learn more about Randak 2000.

CHAPTER 14

Citrus Corners 1995

SHORTLY after her eighteenth birthday, Charmain took her next step up the beauty circuit ladder and entered the "Miss Hula Girl" contest, a big-time event sponsored by a tanning products and beachwear company.

Elimination contests were staged in sexy resorts worldwide and culminated in a splashy finale on the Hawaiian island of Oahu. Charmain entered the contest held in Orlando, Florida. First prize was $25,000 in cash and $50,000 in prizes, with the chance to compete in Oahu for a jackpot worth $250,000.

Charmain spent two months at home in Citrus Corners, swimming nude in the irrigation pond and running for miles through the orange groves toning her body. She also spent hours firing at targets with the compact Kahr 9mm pistol she'd bought and carried with her everywhere since she'd been attacked by three men as she drove home from the "Miss AdventureLand" contest.

She'd pulled in at a Florida Turnpike rest stop at night and was exiting the ladies room when they swarmed out of the shadows, dragging her toward their car as she kicked and screamed. What truly terrified her was that they called her by name, knew she'd just won the beauty contest. Obviously, they'd been stalking her.

She was a heartbeat away from rape and God-knows-what when an 18-wheeler truck pulled into the rest stop, headlights punching through the dark to reveal the brutal struggle.

The driver hit his air horns loud and long. The men fled, but the Florida Highway Patrol, alerted by a CB radio call from the trucker, caught them before they reached the nearest turnpike exit.

The next day, Charmain drove to Luther's Rod & Gun in Citrus Corners and bought the Kahr, a state-of-the-art combination of light weight and heavy firepower. She paid Luther an extra $100 to meet her on Sunday morning out at the orange groves and teach her how to shoot. She was a fast study. Before Luther left that day, she could put five out of five shots into the "heart" of a human silhouette. Luther taught her the difference between plinking at targets and actual combat shooting. He taught her draw, point and shoot techniques and how to fire two quick shots in succession rather than squeeze off one at a time—the professional "double tap."

After a few weeks of practice, she could pick three widely-spaced oranges on a tree, draw, double-tap three times and blow each one up in a spray of fruit juice.

Just before Charmain left Citrus Corners for the "Miss Hula Girl" contest, Lawton Burns—who'd had little control over her since her mother's death—suddenly suggested that he quit the insurance business and become her manager.

"After all," he said, "you're starting to make money and I don't want to see anyone take advantage of you."

Charmain looked at him squarely.

"You're going to protect me? You never lifted a finger when Momma took advantage of me, did you, Daddy? You didn't protect me then, when I begged you to. I have never trusted you from that day. And I never will."

It was a memory Lawton Burns had suppressed since that awful moment when he'd looked into his little girl's imploring eyes, then turned his back on her like the lousy coward he knew himself to be, deep down in his soul.

"I…I didn't know what to do, Charmain…I just—"

"You let her hurt me. Let her do all those terrible things."

Tears were running down her father's face.

"Charmain, I know you must hate me, but—"

"I don't hate you, Daddy. I just know you're a weak man. That's why I've always had to be strong. No, I don't need you to manage me. I've always had to take care of things myself, and I'm doing just fine now. So it's about time I left this place, isn't it? Because there's no reason to be here anymore."

Two days later, Charmain took off for Orlando. Knowing it might be a long time before she saw Citrus Corners again, she asked Millie Johnson to come and spend the week in Orlando with her.

It turned out to be the happiest time Charmain had ever had in her life. It was fun having a girlfriend along to share the excitement of parties and photo shoots in the days leading up to the beauty pageant. The girls stayed in a luxury hotel suite, ate out at great restaurants, played at Disney World and sampled Orlando's raucous night life.

And then, it was time to compete. Charmain finally felt like a pro. Didn't feel like she needed an edge this time out. She'd looked over the competition. She knew—just knew—that she was going to win.

And she did.

It was fantastic. Her first truly big win. In the hierarchy of pageants, "Miss Hula Girl" was just a rung below the big time—Miss Amerca and Miss Universe. Hula Girl founder Frank Emmet, a Georgia country boy who'd made millions after mixing the first batch of tanning lotion in his momma's galvanized washtub, personally escorted Charmain to a gala celebration at the Orlando Hilton that followed her crowning and victory promenade. At 11 p.m., he turned up the volume on the giant TV screen and hollered:

"I think we're on the news, folks."

And sure enough, there was Charmain on NBC News, the camera tight on her face at the exact moment the emcee had announced:

"And here's our winner…the new Miss Hula Girl…Charmain Burns!"

She was on national TV. Millie grabbed her and screamed in excitement. Charmain felt the room spin as she saw herself—for the first time ever—on a screen.

O GOD! She really *was* beautiful.

After years of hearing others say it, of taking it for granted, she suddenly saw what others felt when they looked at her. There she was—not just a pretty TV picture, but a latent force projecting beauty, sexuality, and charisma that lit the screen as the camera fell madly in love with her.

Frank Emmet pumped his fist in the air, shouted "My Hula Girl!" and hugged her hard. He aimed the remote control at the TV screen and began channel surfing.

Now the whole party crowd screamed.

There was Charmain again…and...again…on CBS, CNN, ABC, and two local channels. It was her first magical night as a star.

She swore right then it wouldn't be her last.

Hours later, after fighting off several rich, persistent, and not unappealing men, Charmain and Millie made it back to their suite. Exhausted, they stripped off their clothes and flung them in every direction, then collapsed into their beds. Still revving on champagne and adrenalin, neither could relax.

Millie said, "Sugar, what we need is a joint."

"God, do you have one?"

"Sure do."

Millie unscrewed the handle of a plastic hairbrush. It was hollow. She fished out two thin, tightly-rolled joints.

"One each, hon. I don't feel like sharin'."

Charmain toked. "Oh, YEAH!"

Millie said, "Can I tell you something, Charmain?"

"What?"

"I know you're going to be a big star and stuff, and I'll probably never see you again. But I want you to know that this has been the most exciting night of my whole life, and I love you for bringing me here with you. I'll always love you, hon."

"Oh, Millie…"

Charmain jumped out of bed and onto Millie, and hugged her.

"It wouldn't have been so wonderful if you hadn't been here to see it with me, Millie. And don't say you'll never see me again. You will. No matter what happens. And listen, I have a great idea."

"What?"

"Well, tomorrow I pick up my winner's check. I'll be loaded. So let's take off and hit the big time. Go down to South Beach in Miami. Hang out with Madonna and all those hunky male models and Cuban beach boys."

"Oh, God, Charmain, that would be so damn neat. You mean it?"

"Yeah. Let's go and let our hair down, girl. Maybe it's time I lost my cherry."

Millie squealed. "I've been trying to get you to do that for years."

"Yeah? Well, maybe you can show me how. If you can remember. How old were you? Ten?"

"Bitch! I was thirteen!"

"You were twelve, Millie. Stop your lyin'."

CHAPTER 15

11:20 A.M.
SOUTH BEACH, FL

TWO lithe Cuban boys leaned against the sea wall, muscles shiny-hot in the South Beach sun. Watching all the girls go by. Looking like they'd spritzed with coconut oil. Smelling like it, too. They lounged arrogantly, hips cranked out to display neon Speedos that bulged like Wonder Bras.

As they strolled past, close enough to reach out and squeeze those packages, Charmain and Millie took a heady whiff, trying not to roll their asses.

Charmain hummed under her breath, "Tall and tan and…and *hung* and horny…The boys from Ipanema are hunky…"

Millie giggled and whispered, "Oh God, Charmain, this bikini. They can see every inch of my butt."

Charmain grinned. "So what?"

"It's too BIG!"

"Millie, it's not. Men like something they can get their hands on. They hate skinny butts."

Still walking, she turned back, flashed a flirty smile at the leering duo, and smacked Millie's ass hard enough to raise red.

"Ow…CHARMAIN!?!"

The boys were making that lip-squeaking sound so *en vogue* among Latin males in heat.

"God, what is that?" said Charmain.

"Sounds like they're…callin' a pussy," said Millie, deadpan.

Both girls shrieked.

It was their second day on South Beach. And it was a blast. They'd checked into the drop-dead Delano Hotel on a discount deal set up by Frank Emmet, the Hula Girl owner, who knew everyone in the world.

After unpacking, they hit one of the sidewalk cafes for an early lunch, and Millie immediately started feeling insecure.

"Charmain, look at these girls. They're gorgeous. Jesus, hon, they all look like models. Oh, man, I don't know about walking around here in my bikini."

"You aren't gonna be."

"What do you mean?"

"We're going shopping. For thongs."

"Thongs? Are you crazy?"

"Millie, stop bitchin'. First of all, you know you've got a body built for sin. That's why you had Florida State college boys driving all the way over to Citrus Corners to get some. Guys have been trying to get their hands on those big boobs of yours since I was flatter than an ironing board."

"Charmain..."

"Now stop it. And we could both do with a makeover. So right after we buy thongs, we'll go to that hairdresser the concierge recommended."

"Who?"

"It's a place called 'Fluff.'"

"No, I mean who is the 'cone-see-urge,' or whatever?"

Charmain laughed. "That's the guy who stands at that little desk in the lobby and answers questions for the guests."

"Oh, the queer guy?"

"Millie, nobody says 'queer' anymore. It's 'gay.'"

Millie held up her hand.

"Okay, okay, let me try this."

She pursed her lips and mouthed, "Good *day*...I'm the *gay* cone-see-urge."

Later, looking fine in new hair and thongs, they prowled the beach until the sun was low over the cobalt water, then headed back to the hotel. After a shower, they stood naked in front of a mirror, checking their tans.

"See, that's why thongs are great. You get tan all over."

"Yeah, because you're showing ever' damn thing God gave you. But you're right, Charmain. That's the good thing about thongs. In fact, let's thing a thong about thongs."

"Thay *what*?"

They laughed, then slathered aloe vera gel over each other. Millie said, "Hey, don't you think you've done my boobs enough?"

"Yeah. I just like the way they feel."

Millie slapped her hand away. "We're both too horny for our own good."

"You've got *that* right. Come on, let's get dressed to kill and then hit that place, Liquid, that Madonna's girlfriend owns. Frank Emmet's got us all fixed up to get in VIP."

"Yeah, and remember what he told us. Miami is a weird place and we should watch ourselves."

"Millie, are you about to have your period? I swear, I never have heard one girl bitch so much in one day."

That night they boogied down in Liquid with the South Beach hotties. Charmain got eyes the minute she walked in, sexy in a figure-hugging black spandex mini-dress with spaghetti straps, bare legs, stiletto sandals, 1-carat diamond earrings she'd won in the beauty contest twinkling in her lobes, hair short and gel-slicked à la Sharon Stone. Millie was poured into a white knit skirt and circulation-stopping tube top. Charmain asked a waitress if Ingrid Casares, Madonna's girlfriend and owner of Liquid, was in the club.

"No, she won't be in tonight," the waitress said. "Say, aren't you the girl who won the Hula Girl contest?"

"She sure is," said Millie proudly.

It was the first time Charmain had ever been recognized in public. About a dozen people came out of the packed, jamming crowd to say they'd seen her win "Miss Hula Girl" on TV. It was sensational, a huge thrill.

One guy, a thirty-ish businessman Charmain vaguely remembered from the victory party in Orlando, introduced himself as Ronnie Berman, a good friend of Frank Emmet, and started hanging around them. He was with a group of wealthy-looking men and women, and they all ended up sitting together in the VIP corner.

Then, a flurry of excitement. The crowd parted. Five men, all very macho-looking young Latinos, dressed in expensive suits and dripping with gold chains, rings, and Rolexes, strutted into the VIP section as the velvet rope was quickly lifted.

"Hola!" said one of them to the obsequious flunky holding the rope. "Dónde está Ingrid?"

"Nueva York, señor."

"Ah!"

One of the other men laughed. "Maybe she's getting down with Madonna, man."

Ronnie Berman and his crowd were suddenly all over the newcomers, flinging around Latin names and exchanging macho bear hugs.

"Ramon...Paco...Gordito...Miguel..."

And the Latinos were crooning, "Ronnie...Cynthia...Bill...Vicky..."

Hug hug. Kiss kiss.

A club manager hustled over with an ice bucket and two bottles of chilled Cristal champagne at $250 each. On the house. As he popped the first bottle, Latin-tinged disco music suddenly blared. The manager signified that this was in honor of the newcomers.

"Who the hell are these guys?" Charmain said to Millie.

"I don't know, but I'm ready to conga with that one they're callin' Ramon. Eeeww, he's cute. That boy can stuff my taco anytime."

Charmain laughed. God, she was having a good time. She felt a weight lifting off her, and was suddenly hit by a truth that went off like a flashgun in her head—the realization that for years, maybe most of her life, she'd been struggling up out of a deep, black pit.

A moment later, Ronnie pulled her over to meet the Latino boys, who made a huge fuss over her beauty queen status. For the next hour, Charmain and Millie were danced ragged and loved every minute of it. Except when the one called Paco dragged them onto the floor. He was crude and lewd, groping and grinding in slow dance tempo even when the music was flat-out boogie.

He reeked of a pungent, vile cologne. Actually bragged about it.

"I get it sent from Europe," he told Charmain. "You can't get it here. It's called 'Congrève.' Great, huh?"

"It beats armpits, I guess."

He looked at her sharply. Then laughed.

"Ah, you are a funny *chica*, eh? You American girls are always making jokes. Not like Latina women, who respect their men."

"Go find a fucking Latina, then. They're all over Miami."

He laughed unpleasantly. "No, I like you. You are *muy caliente*. That means 'very hot.'"

Paco kept his eyes on her all evening. He sat out most dances, swilling Cristal, hitting the john a lot. Cocaine was firing his cylinders. Not that he was unique. In the ladies room, Charmain and Millie marveled at the cacophony of snorts and sniffles emanating from the stalls.

"No wonder they call it the powder room," Charmain cracked after they'd peed.

Dancing with Ramon, Millie asked, "What do you guys do?"

"Oh, international shipping, importing. You know."

"So what do you import?"

He laughed. "Whatever people want, baby."

The night was packing heat. The crowd boogied down on the thudding beat, sweating, jammed tight, undulating like one great beast.

Ronnie Berman swooped by and yelled in their ears, "We're moving on. You're invited. Coolest private party ever. You'll meet Don Diego. You won't believe his place. Fabulous."

"Who's Don Diego?"

"Billionaire. The Man. In this town, the top half of the top ten."

CHAPTER 16

12:42 A.M.
DON DIEGO'S PENTHOUSE
SOUTH BEACH

A limo ride later, they stepped out of a private elevator thirty stories above Miami onto the marble floor of a room so spacious and stunning Charmain thought fleetingly of an art museum. It was a penthouse apartment surpassing even Hollywood's wildest wet dream of how the rich and famous live, stretching eighty feet to a panoramic expanse of floor-to-ceiling glass doors that opened onto a huge terrace.

Even the walls were marble, intercut with slabs of exotic hardwood. The room was dotted with free-standing sculptures and paintings lit by spotlights beaming from a domed ceiling, which featured a trompe l'oeil mural of a sky at sunset.

Furniture was modern, minimal, until the floor dipped gradually into a wide, carpeted conversation pit lined with leather sofas and centered by a Steinway concert grand piano manned by a striking blonde woman in a tuxedo. Very Dietrich.

She was playing Cole Porter, brilliantly.

There were perhaps forty people milling around, some sitting at a large wet bar that overlooked the pit. The room didn't feel crowded. Waiters discreetly took orders for drinks, hors d'oeuvres, hot snacks. A Japanese sushi chef served by the bar. In a knot of people at the far end of the pit, Charmain caught sight of the man who seemed to be their host. Older, silver-haired, distinguished. He made no move to come over, so Charmain ignored him.

Millie was clutching her arm. "Oh God, Charmain, this is like the most fucking outrageous place. Come on, let's go out on the terrace."

They walked out under the stars. A night breeze rustled the potted palms and foliage, wafting exotic tropical scents up from the Gulf Stream. Millie, Ramon in tow, had quietly melted into the darkness. Charmain walked to the railing and looked out, breathing deeply. God, this was so romantic. If she only had a man. Miami's glittering streets stretched out below her to an inky-black ocean pinpricked by the lights of ships sailing out toward the night horizon. Her eyes drank in Biscayne Bay, South Beach. And Star Island, where all the celebrities lived.

Moments later, Millie and Ramon appeared. "Charmain, Ramon says this is a two-story penthouse. Can you believe it?"

Ramon nodded. "It's probably the most expensive real estate in Miami. Don Diego's living quarters are on the floor below this. And down there, on that dock, is his yacht. It's 170 feet long, even has a swimming pool."

"You and your friends all work for him?"

"Sí. We are in shipping, importing. A bit of finance."

Millie looked up at him adoringly. Ramon kissed her, his hands caressing her ass. Charmain sighed and walked back inside. She asked for a cranberry spritzer and sat on a sofa, watching couples dance as the blonde pianist sang a smoky version of "I Get a Kick Out of You." The waiter brought her drink and put it down on a small table. She sipped, put it down, then stiffened as her nostrils picked up a familiar, pungent smell.

She turned to face Paco.

"Hola, chiquita mía," he said with his trademark leer, dropping his sweaty hand to her thigh. "What do you say we get out of here, eh?"

"Oh," she said, removing the hand. "You mean leave this boring scene and go someplace really interesting?"

He looked at her, puzzled. "No…I mean…"

"Yeah, I know what you mean."

Paco got his leer back. "No, I mean, you must be getting tired…I can tell you are getting cranky, no?"

"Gee, I wonder why that would be? DUH!" Charmain said loudly.

People sitting nearby were noticing this exchange.

Paco, fueled by a tankful of Cristal topped with primo coke, winked at them, then said to Charmain:

"What you need to wake you up is a big *chorizo.* You know what is a *chorizo*?"

"Nothin' I want, I'm sure."

"No, it is a very special Spanish dish…A sausage. And I want to give it to you."

She turned away from him, then whirled in a fury as his hand scrabbled onto her thigh again.

"Here's the only Spanish I know, Paco…FUCK OFF, AMIGO!"

The people around her laughed. Paco glared, angry. Got up and lurched off. The people applauded lightly. She smiled, glanced around.

And then she saw him. Standing next to Don Diego. Tall, dark hair, a light stubble of beard, white linen suit, luminescent blue eyes that had locked on hers. Hard.

Her stomach flip-flopped. Breath stopped. She felt powerless, suddenly shy as his eyes pierced her, drank her in. She wanted to look away. Just for a second. Compose herself.

But she was…caught. He had her. She knew it. He knew it, too. He smiled slowly and she melted. God! Oh thank you God! This was him. This was her man. The man she'd seen in the shadows of her dreams. The man who'd come for her someday. Now he was here. And she couldn't stop looking at him. She was frozen. Her numbed brain attempted to send messages. One finally got through. It said:

Smile at him, you stupid bitch. You're starin' like a deer caught in headlights. Smile, goddamnit. She felt her lips part dryly. Stuck to her teeth. Shit, she must look like a moron.

"Madame, another drink?"

Mercifully, a waiter stepped in and interrupted the laser beam locking their eyes. It gave her the moment she needed.

She took a quick sip from the dregs of her spritzer, handing the waiter the glass. "Yes, please."

Now. She straightened up, arranged her legs, let her mini-dress ride up another inch, thrust her breasts out subtly, cocked her head and adjusted her smile. As the waiter moved out of their line of sight, she caught her breath. Would he still be there, still looking at her…?

He was, but…His mouth formed words and she thought he was speaking to her. But he was too far away to be heard. For a moment, she was confused.

Then, he arched an eyebrow at her, shrugged and turned his head slightly. And she realized he was talking to Don Diego. Another man joined them and they became engrossed in conversation.

But every minute or so he'd look over, catch her eye and re-establish their wordless communication. God, she thought, please let him come over here. Now.

But he didn't. Someone asked her to dance. She brushed him off. Ronnie Berman stopped by and sat a moment, said he and his friends were leaving. Did she need a ride? No? Okay, see ya. He gave her his card and said, "Call any time." She started to ask if he knew the tall man with Don Diego, but didn't. For all she knew, he'd go tell the guy she had the hots. But so what? She did have the hots for him, so why not? Oh DAMN, why doesn't he just come over here?

She checked her watch. Nearly 3 a.m. Millie reappeared and sat down.

"Listen, hon, are you gonna be mad if I don't go back with you tonight? Ramon has asked me to…uh, join him for a little quality siesta time. We're both getting sorta smashed and we can stay right here. There are spare bedrooms and Don Diego said it was okay. In fact, you can stay here too, if you want." Millie giggled. "Not in our bedroom, of course."

Charmain shrugged. "Sure, you stay. Millie, where's Ramon?"

"He's getting me a drink. Why? Something wrong?"

"Yeah. I can't get that guy over there to talk to me. He looks like he's interested, but won't make a move."

Millie followed Charmain's eyes and said, "WHOA! Stud muffin! And real elegant. Y'all want to play with the grownups, eh, hon?"

"Oh come on, he's maybe thirty-three?"

"Try thirty-six. That's double eighteen, but hell, you're legal at least. Anyway, here's Ramon. Baby, who is that handsome man over there talkin' to Don Diego?"

Ramon handed her a flute of Cristal and grinned.

"Hey, I leave you alone for two minutes and you're checking out guys."

"Charmain wants to know, hombre."

"Ah. Well, that's Patrick Taulere. A heavy guy."

Charmain said, "What do you mean?"

"Well, he's a man of respect."

"Ramon, you are not being real helpful here. Who *is* he?"

"He's a real rich guy from an old family in Savannah. He's not married. Real ladies' man. Comes down here on business a lot."

"What business?"

Ramon hesitated. "Well, like us. You know, shipping, import-export."

Millie said, "So you can introduce him to Charmain?"

Ramon shook his head. "Too weird. I don't really know the guy. Anyway, I think you've missed your chance. Looks like he's gone."

Charmain's heart skipped a beat. Her eyes searched for him. But he wasn't there. Shit.

Millie said, "I'm sorry, Charmain. Hey, maybe he just went to the john."

Charmain, suddenly wanting to be alone, said, "Yeah. Maybe. Look, you go on and don't worry about me. See you sometime tomorrow. And you be good."

Millie winked. "Oh, hon, am I ever going to be good. Mucho bueno, if you get my drift?"

Ramon pulled her up, said goodnight, and they drifted off toward the elevator.

Charmain sat there, checked the room again. Still no sign of…Patrick. She said the name aloud softly. Oh God, why had he left? Please let him be in the john. Then she realized something. Don Diego wasn't in the room, either. Or the man they'd been talking to, so maybe they were off somewhere talking privately.

A few minutes later, the piano player sang softly, "When your lover has gone…" and tears stung Charmain's eyes. Shit.

Then she smelled it again. That *awful* cologne. Paco!

He sat, put his drink down next to hers, and said, "Hey, don't get mad, okay? Look, you must be tired, so why don't we do like your girlfriend and Ramon and catch a little nap in one of the bedrooms? Come on, *chica,* you know you're tired."

He was slurring his words. Higher than a fucking kite.

"The only thing I'm tired of, Paco, is you. So screw off."

She turned away from him and was about to get up when a woman who'd sat down near her asked if she was really Miss Hula Girl. Charmain forced a smile and started chatting, hoping Paco would get lost if she ignored him. At one point, she reached for her drink on the low table in front of her and started to put it to her lips.

"DON'T DRINK THAT!"

It was almost a shout. She and everyone in the room looked up, startled.

It was Patrick Taulere, striding toward her from the direction of the elevator. Oh God, he was here! But what…?

He reached down and took the glass from her.

He extended his other hand and helped her up. Now she was looking right into those beautiful, powerful blue eyes.

He said, "We haven't had a chance to meet. I am Patrick Taulere."

No man had ever made Charmain feel faint. Now she felt like her knees might buckle. She wanted desperately to clear her throat, afraid her voice would be a croak.

"Charmain…Charmain Burns."

She sounded just fine. He smiled warmly.

"May I ask you to join me?"

"Yes, but…" She looked at her drink, still in his left hand.

"Ah, your drink. Well, I do not think it's a healthy drink. Let's find you a new one, shall we?"

People were muttering, exchanging knowing glances. Some looked over fleetingly at Paco, who sat glowering at Patrick Taulere.

"Hey, *maricon*…who the fuck you think you are? Give her back her drink."

He got to his feet and lurched forward. "What the fuck you saying? You saying something about me? Motherfucker!"

And suddenly Charmain got it. She looked up at Patrick and said, "He spiked my drink?"

Paco bellowed, "What did you say, you fucking bitch? *Puta*! You better watch your mouth—"

"PACO!"

Don Diego's voice froze the action. Paco, looking like a child suddenly slapped, put out his hands.

"*Jefe…*"

Don Diego's eyes were black holes.

"Take the drink from our friend, Paco."

Patrick held out the drink. Paco took it, looked at Don Diego.

"Drink it, Paco!"

"*Jefe, por favor…*"

"NOW!"

The room was hushed. Every eye on Paco as he lifted the glass, trembling, to his lips. He drank, slowly. Stopped. Looked at Don Diego. Begging.

"All of it, Paco," Don Diego said softy. "Drink it all."

Paco drained the glass. Don Diego smiled.

"*Bueno*. Now come over here to me, my son."

Paco swayed, then moved forward, his legs turning to rubber. He lurched, almost fell. Recovered. Took three more steps, tripped and crashed to the floor almost at Don Diego's feet.

Don Diego gestured curtly to three hard-looking men, who quickly scooped Paco up and removed him from the room.

He stood up, waved at the piano player, who started tinkling a cheery chorus of "Let's Face the Music and Dance."

"My friends," he said loudly. "Join me on the terrace for dessert—a very special flaming cherries jubilee."

He walked over to Patrick and Charmain and said quietly, "My deepest apologies. And congratulations to you, my old friend, for having such sharp eyes. In every way," he added, eyeing Charmain approvingly. He leaned over and touched his lips lightly to her hand.

"This is Charmain Burns, Don Diego," said Patrick.

"You are charming," Don Diego said to her. "*Mi casa es su casa.*"

"Thank you," said Charmain.

"Don Diego, with your permission, we will not join you for dessert. The young lady is fatigued and..."

"Of course, of course," said Don Diego. Roguishly, he added, "Just don't tell me she needs her beauty sleep."

Patrick smiled and shook hands with Don Diego, who pulled him into a macho bear hug, bowed again to Charmain and headed for the terrace, the hard-eyed men following behind.

Patrick, taking both of Charmain's hands in his, looked down at her and said, "Do I presume too much, Charmain?"

She smiled. "That would be impossible, Patrick."

CHAPTER 17

11:51 A.M.
PACIFIC COAST HIGHWAY
LOS ANGELES

CAMERON Tull pushed the Aston-Martin hard as he headed north on the Pacific Coast Highway. Thank God for small miracles, he thought. Jessica wasn't far away. He looked at his watch and made the calculation. Yeah, with luck he'd get to her in time. He nudged the accelerator to eight-five.

In those frantic moments after the tip about Steve Bellini's death, Tull's first thoughts had been about Steve's sister, Jessica. Phil Monte, the Camino Rio hotel detective, had asked in that first phone call: "Who's the next of kin? Was he married?"

"No. His parents live in Europe most of the year. I don't know how to contact them. He has a sister. I know her."

"You'd better get to her fast, Tull. She's gonna get a nasty shock if she hears about her brother's death on the news. And it won't be long before she does."

"I hear you."

After the conversation with Phil Monte, Tull had taken a moment to work it out. He didn't know Jessica's whereabouts. He smiled wryly. No surprise there. She had made quite a point of not keeping in touch with him. More precisely, she had stopped answering his calls. Which raised the question he'd avoided asking himself: should he be the one to give her this heartbreaking news? A moment's reflection yielded a more relevant question: who else? Jessica, by choice, had never met anyone on *The Revealer* staff. Indeed, his own meeting with her had been by the merest chance. Her parents lived in Europe. And by the time police managed to find and inform her, she'd have heard it on the news. Tull shrugged. Why was he hesitating?

He dialed Jessica's Los Angeles home number. It rang, then the answering machine came on. Her voice said, "Please leave a message..."

His nerve ends twitched noticeably. Jesus! Even now, she still got to him. After the beep he said, "Jessica, it's Cameron Tull. It is extremely important and urgent that you call me immediately." He left his private number, which would forward to his cellular phone, then clicked off and tried her office. A female voice answered.

"Miss Bell's not in. Would you care to leave a message?"

He asked for Madeline Huber, Jessica's business manager.

"She's not in. Would you care to leave a message?"

Tull sighed. A fucking receptionist zombie. Probably gorgeous. Probably stupid. Experience told him that playing it straight with Brenda Bimbo would be a waste of time. She'd have orders to tell nuthin' to nobody. And she wouldn't have the brains or balls to ignore those orders if Mars invaded Earth. Worse, she'd blab to her co-bimbos the second she hung up the phone. And in an office like Jessica's, a fashion house, somebody would be wired into a tabloid.

He put an edge into his voice:

"Miss, I'm Detective-Lieutenant Frank Kramer of The Los Angeles Police Department Intelligence Division. This is a police emergency and I need to get in touch with your boss immediately. I've tried her home. Where is she?"

"Well, I really can't give you that infor—"

"Miss, we can do this the hard way or the easy way. I'm in my cruiser and less than five minutes from your office. If I have to go there to get this very simple and reasonable information out of you, I will charge you with impeding an official police investigation. What is your name?"

"Ohh, no…I…uh, okay…she's supervising a photo session…uh, you know, models, like, on location, for the new ad campaign—"

"WHERE, GODDAMNIT? What is this, a fucking state secret? I'm warning you, if you don't tell me right now, I'll…"

"I'm sorry, I'm trying to…"

Tull heard the first choke of tears. He felt like a prick, but suppressed it. Time for a gear change. Easy does it…

"Look, Miss," he said quietly. "I appreciate your caution in giving out your boss's whereabouts. I can't impress upon you how urgent it is that we find her immediately. She's not in trouble with the police, but she might be in great danger. Now you're probably asking yourself, 'How do I know this man is from the LAPD?' Okay, I don't have much time, but write this number down—213-555-1800. Now put me on hold and call the ID—the Intelligence Division. They'll confirm that I'm Lt. Kramer, Badge No. 5048. But make it quick, please!"

"No, it's…okay. I believe you. She's up at Sandy Point, above Malibu Beach. She's leaving there in about an hour to come back here."

"Good. Now, as soon as I hang up, set your mind at rest and call that number to verify I am who I say I am. I must caution you, however, not to contact your boss. That could put her in great danger. I'm calling you on a scrambled line, but your phone may be tapped. If you contact her or anyone else, we'll formally charge you with obstruction of a police investigation. It's a serious charge."

"I won't tell anyone. I swear…Is…is she going to be alright?"

"We think so. Thanks. And again, you're welcome to call that number.

You've been very helpful."

Tull clicked off, grinning. Ah, the joy of conning reluctant sources. He rarely used the policeman ploy. It worked better with women, especially ordinary working girls. He'd take hundred-to-one odds that Jessica's receptionist wouldn't call the "police" number he'd given her. If she did, a special line would ring at his *Revealer* office and his assistant would answer crisply, "LAPD Intelligence Division" and verify the existence of Lt. Frank Kramer. After that, the line would never be used again. The number would be changed and, in the unlikely event the real cops ever followed up, they'd learn that 213-555-1800 was an out-of-service pay phone number—all courtesy of Tull's contact in the phone company. Most tabloid editors had phone experts who could get any celebrity's private, unlisted number. Tull's guy could do a lot more, including—in very special cases—foolproof phone taps. All very naughty stuff, and strictly against *Revealer* policy, which was never, ever to use illegal means in news-gathering. Tull agreed with the spirit of this policy. But gathering information was the name of the game in the cutthroat business of news, and everybody bit the bullet and took their favorite shortcut—everybody! From the *New York Times* to the *Washington Post,* from the wire services to the TV networks. Official policy was one thing; getting the news was sacred.

Tull had his own policy: never publish information gathered through questionable methods. Use it only to point you in the direction of reliable—and legal—sources.

He rang his assistant. "Eva, I've got two more brief calls to make and then I'll be in the car. Tell the Queen of Scots I've located Jessica and I'm on the way to break the news to her. I'm off the scope for a couple of hours. Hold my messages unless it's a Category 5. Oh, did you get a call on the special number?"

"No. Will I?"

He grinned. "I doubt it. I think my performance was Oscar material. A nomination, at least."

"Yeah, you should be in pictures," said Eva.

Ten minutes later, the postcard-perfect scenery of the Pacific Coast Highway above Malibu was unrolling in front of the Aston-Martin. Tull scanned the radio for news broadcasts of Bellini's death. He heard the KFWB newsbreak at the same moment Vidal Delaney picked it up on Wilshire Boulevard. Goddamn, I hope Jessica's not hearing this, he thought. Chances were she wasn't. The atmosphere on a professional film or video shoot was always intense and business-like. Serious money was spent with every tick of the clock. Nobody stood around listening to a radio.

The trip to Sandy Point took fifteen minutes. Tull pulled off and parked on a shoulder overlooking the beach. He stepped out of the car, blinking at the shimmer of sunlight on the sweep of sand below. The beach was deserted except for a camera crew, a covey of models—and Jessica. He stood for a moment, watching as they filmed an odd scene: two female models in bathing suits striding seductively past three well-muscled men who were, incongruously, lifting weights while standing knee-deep in the boiling surf.

"CUT!"

The scene ended. Jessica conferred with a tall, slim man who was obviously the director. Tull squinted. It looked like Peter Melton-Tilford, a pretentious Brit who made lousy movies but superb TV commercials. Jessica had hired the best. And why not? Her name was getting hotter by the minute. God, even at a distance she looked classy and sexy, dressed in a cool-looking white suit with short skirt and sandals, jet black hair pulled back and tied with a silk tangerine-colored scarf. He shook his head sharply. Remember why you're here, damnit. He walked down to the beach.

Jessica looked up, saw him. Seconds later, she realized she'd stopped breathing. She tried to concentrate on what Peter was saying...

"...light and sun and air all around the models, Jessica, that's what I'm going for...I don't want tight close-ups...Space, don't you see, dahling? I'm carving out a very special piece of space..."

"Peter, please don't forget I'm selling clothes. I want them to be seen."

"Clothes? Jessica, my love, consuming America can see *clothes* hanging on racks at K-Mart. First, give them fantasy. Project them into the fantasy and they'll be panting for your adorable workout outfits and slinky swimwear, dahling. I know it's your first national TV ad campaign, but you must trust Peter, eh?"

Jessica knew she was smiling just a bit too widely as Tull walked across the sand. She tried to frown. Her lips trembled, but the smile stayed. Ridiculous! How many times had she seen him? Twice? Three times? He looked so handsome. What was he, forty-ish? To her thirty-ish? Navy linen jacket over a black t-shirt and chalk slacks, graying hair, receding in a very attractive way. Deep chest. Shoulders to die for, and—Jessica wasn't overly susceptible to handsome men who wore clothes well. They were no novelty in the fashion business. So? Was it his charm? He was cocky, but fun. Intelligent, wryly witty. Great skin. Beautiful hands, masculine yet expressive. And lips that...

Now she frowned. God! Get a grip, girl! Next you'll be running across the sand in slow motion like some panting virgin in a French art film. Forget that he's the perfect man...Just think, he's all wrong for you!

Her eyes focused. She took a deep breath and said, a little too brightly:

"Hello. What a surprise. Just passing by, or...?"

Now he was close enough to look into his eyes. Suddenly she felt cold. Sensed pain. She felt an urge to run. Peter, still beside her, started to speak. She waved him away.

"Tell everyone to take a break, Peter…Please!" The director looked at her, puzzled, then nodded brusquely at Tull and moved off.

The wind freshened, blowing Jessica's hair. She reached up to brush it back. Her mind felt frozen, numb. Her eyes searched his face and Tull sensed she felt some foreboding of his hellish news. No time to search for eloquent, comforting words. Just tell her. Swift and straight.

"Jessica, I didn't want you to hear this on the news…Steve has been in a terrible accident…He was killed instantly…I'm so sorry…"

For a moment, she couldn't take it in. "No, it can't be…I just spoke to him last night…Are you sure it was Steve?…No, no, it's probably a mistake…"

She looked at him desperately, pleading for some small sign of hope. This wasn't happening. Time *could* be turned back. Tull watched her struggle through the first shock of denial. He reached out as if to steady her. Jessica threw up her hands, stepped back. Her breath started to come in short gasps, the panic rising up to overwhelm her.

"You said…You said it was an accident? When? What happened?"

"It happened this morning, Jessica. Steve fell from the balcony of his hotel suite."

"He *fell*? How could he fall?"

Her voice rose sharply.

"In broad daylight he *fell?*"

She stared at him, frantic. Tull pursed his lips. He hadn't planned to tell her everything. Now he had to.

"Jessica, we don't know anything yet…But the police aren't ruling out foul play. Neither are we. Our entire staff is on this case and we won't rest until—"

Her hands flew to her mouth. "Oh, God, no, no…Not Steve…My baby brother…He's not even thirty years old…"

Her body suddenly hunched and shook violently. She straightened up, tears pouring down her cheeks. "Steve…Steve," she sobbed. "God, how could this happen?…Why? This will kill my mother…How can I tell my parents?…How?"

She blinked suddenly, clenching her fists. Fury crossed her eyes as she looked at Tull and snapped, "You said he might have been murdered? Who would do that? Did it happen while he was on assignment for your paper? Why would—"

Tull cut in. "Jessica, please listen. I only said that the police can't rule out foul play. We don't know why he fell. Nothing is clear yet, but we're investigating and so are the police, and I promise you that—"

"Nooo…NOOOOOO…"

The keening wail burst out as the pain finally hit her. She hunched forward and swayed. Tull stepped in quickly and caught her in his arms. She collapsed against him. He held her, saying nothing. Slowly, the spasms that shook her subsided.

After a long moment, she said quietly, without looking at him, "Could you bring me my bag, please? It's over there near that umbrella."

He released her carefully. "Are you sure…?"

She stepped away and straightened up, taking a deep breath. "I'll be okay," she said.

Tull walked across the sand to the umbrella about twenty paces away.

The crew and models down the beach stopped to watch him until Peter Melton-Tilford clapped his hands and said loudly, "Are we working here, people? Places, everybody, please!"

Tull picked up the bag, walked back and handed it to Jessica. She took it wordlessly and rummaged for tissues, a compact, and lipstick. Tull turned away, staring out at the rows of sunlit whitecaps stretching endlessly to the Pacific Rim.

"Cameron?"

A tiny shock danced on his skin like St. Elmo's fire. How many times had he heard her say his name? His reaction amazed him. He turned and walked over to her as she stuffed her repair kit back into the bag. She straightened up and faced him.

"I want to thank you," she said, "for being kind enough to come here. I know this wasn't easy for you and…"

"Jessica…"

She held up a hand to silence him. "I know you're a decent man, Cameron. My brother respected you and he was the most wonderful—"

She paused a moment, fighting back the tears that threatened her again. "Anyway, thank you. Now I have to think about what to do, I guess…"

Tull said, "Jessica, let me help you through this until your parents arrive. Can you reach them by phone?"

"Yes. I…God, it seems so weird to stand here on a beach and call them on a cellular. But I guess…?"

She looked at him, wanting his help. It made him feel like a white knight rescuing the damsel. Silly. But he liked the feeling.

"Let me suggest this. My house is only fifteen minutes away in Malibu. You can phone your parents there in complete privacy, then call whoever else you need to. You should not be alone. Then I'll drive you back to L.A. if you want. I'm at your disposal, Jessica. Please let me help."

She nodded bleakly. "Do you think it's wrong not to call them right this minute, or…?"

"Jessica, stop being hard on yourself. You are in shock. You need time to compose yourself for this. A few moments…"

He caught himself before saying the words "won't matter." It sounded harsh. But it was true. Steve was beyond earthly comfort. The pain of his survivors had to be managed now.

Jessica nodded. "The shoot is almost finished, except for one key shot. I should be there, I think." Her lips trembled and tears sprang into her eyes. "Daddy used to tell Steve and me, 'Be a professional, always.' I'm going to finish the shoot." She looked at him. He nodded.

Jessica handed him her bag. "Would you hold this please?" she said. Lifting her chin and squaring her shoulders, she walked resolutely down the beach toward the waiting models and crew.

Tull, watching her, thought, I'm standing here holding her bag—and liking it. A flash of guilt shot through him. How can I feel that way in the face of her pain? He shrugged. He'd learned, over the years, to trust his judgment, his emotions. Was it repugnant, on this woeful day, to experience spontaneous joy? Am I a heartless sonofabitch? He grinned thinly. He knew exactly what that felt like.

And he didn't feel like that at all…

CHAPTER 18

1:45 P.M.
PACIFIC COAST HIGHWAY
MALIBU

JESSICA withdrew into herself on the ride back down the coast to Malibu. No tears, no talk. Until she asked, "Don't I have to make arrangements…? I've never done this, so I don't know…"

Tull looked over at her. "Jessica, everything is being taken care of until you're ready to cope. Steve's in good hands. What's important now is your family. You need to be with them. That's all you need to think about."

She nodded, staring at the road ahead. Not seeing it. The car phone rang once. He reached over, punched it off. Yeah. Time to shut off. He slipped into the meditative state he'd learned to find so easily all those years ago in Japan. Tune out thought. Tune in tires humming on hot asphalt. Just drive.

Jessica blinked. It seemed like only a moment had passed, but Tull was saying, "We're here." He got out and walked around to her door, opening it. She stepped out onto the driveway of crushed river-rock gravel and stood still, trying to focus. Tull took her elbow gently. "Are you okay?"

"Yes. I just…lost track for a minute."

She knew vaguely that they were in the canyons above Malibu. The air smelled fresh and the beating sun had been cooled by a canopy of oaks towering over the driveway. Trees everywhere. The effect was like a forest grove, vaguely Oriental, dotted with stands of bamboo. Jessica looked up the slope of the driveway and saw a rustic house. It sat on stilts, tucked against a rock face softened by vines and hanging plants. The house was dominated on its second level by a huge redwood deck.

Tull guided Jessica up the drive and past a three-car garage that looked like an old carriage house. They entered a path that wandered through a thicket of bamboo and past an exquisitely raked Zen garden. Even in Jessica's numbed state, the scene evoked a sense of tranquility, a feeling of having arrived at a haven. The path opened onto a terrace of smooth stones set in a carpet of grass. It led to three deep flagstone steps and a massive wooden double door, which opened at their approach.

"Hello, Mrs. Gordon," said Tull to the motherly-looking older woman who stood aside as they entered the house. "I'm glad you're here. This is my friend Jessica."

"It's nice to meet you, dear," said Mrs. Gordon, who sounded like she'd grown up next door to Robin Leach. "It's the day to change the linens, Mr. Tull, so I came a bit early. I was just about to put on some tea. Would you like some, Miss? Won't take a moment."

Jessica shook her head. "Thank you, no. But is there some mineral water? And then..."

Tull broke in smoothly. "What she needs is a place to catch her breath and make some calls, Mrs. Gordon. I'll take her into the study. There's some mineral water there. Then I'll have tea out here at the bar."

Mrs. Gordon, exhibiting that finely-honed feeling for social undercurrent peculiar to Brits, Japanese, and other island-dwellers, sensed the mood and left the room. "I'll be in the kitchen if needed," she said.

Tull guided Jessica into his study. A massive, 14-foot-long French antique pine farmhouse table commanded the room. Behind it, a dark oak credenza bristled with computers, tape recorders, and other high-tech gear. The floor was Spanish tile topped by a forest green Oriental rug. Across the room, next to French doors that opened onto a small balcony, was a nook formed by two saddle-leather sofas. They sat at right angles around a rough pine coffee table edged with hammered iron. The sofas faced a big-screen TV/entertainment center housed in an armoire that matched the coffee table. At the intersection of the sofas was a small table. It held a lamp and a telephone.

"Think you'll be comfortable here...?"

Tull waved a hand at the sofa nook. Jessica sat down. He walked over to the credenza and opened a door that hid a small refrigerator. He extracted a bottle and held it up.

"Pellegrino okay?"

Jessica nodded. He selected a crystal tumbler from a silver tray on the credenza, walked over to the coffee table, poured the tumbler half-full, and handed it to her. He set the pale green bottle on the table as she sipped the mineral water.

Tull stood, looking down at her. Indirect sunlight filtering in from the French windows gave her skin the glow of ivory and painted bluish highlights on her thick black hair. Like a painting by Botticelli, he thought. An all-American girl by birth, but she looked so Old World at this moment.

"Jessica," he said. "I don't know how to help you with this."

She took a deep breath and looked at him. "I have to do this alone."

He nodded. "You'll have privacy in here. Once I close that door, it's practically soundproof. If you need me, just hit the intercom button on the phone."

She gave him a wan smile and nodded. He wanted to reach out and touch her, make some gesture...

He turned and left the room, carefully closing the thick oak door behind him. He walked across the hardwood floor of the great room to a granite-topped bar. He stepped behind it, opened one of the dark oak cabinets above and took out a snifter. He set it on the bar, reached underneath and came up with a bottle of Remy XO. Pouring himself a generous shot, he took a sip, then walked across the room and opened a set of French doors that led to his favorite spot, the massive redwood deck that jutted out over the wooded area he and Jessica had just walked through. A friend had once dubbed it the "Zen forest."

Standing at the rail and savoring the cognac, Tull had a sudden troubling thought. It was tragic that Jessica had to break this awful news to her parents by long-distance phone—but it would be devastating if she wasn't able to reach them immediately at their home in Italy. Tull knew Bellini Sr. was retired and loved to travel around Europe with Jessica's mother. They owned an apartment in Paris, a St. Tropez villa, a ski chalet in Chamonix, and God knows what else.

He shook his head, remembering…

Learning about Steve's family had been a shock. Who'd have guessed that the all-American boy and Yale grad was a scion of the famed European jewelers, Bellini Frères? The centuries-old firm had opened its first U.S. store on Fifth Avenue back in the 1950s with the proud boast: "Patronized by Benjamin Franklin and other distinguished Americans."

His mind drifted back to the day he'd learned about the Bellini family tree. The day he'd met Jessica. A year ago. He'd been invited to a Palm Beach wedding…

It was a typical sun-drenched South Florida afternoon. Palm Beach society had turned out to witness the young bride and groom joined in holy matrimony. Not to mention what was—for that old-money crowd—the equally important ecclesiastical validation of the prenuptial agreement.

The ceremony was held at the island's exquisite church, Bethesda-By-The-Sea. When it ended, guests were shuttled up South County Road to the Breakers Hotel for a reception. Tull loved the magnificent old Breakers. He'd taken a small ocean-view suite there, thinking he might stay a few days. But standing among this group of chattering strangers and sipping Cristal champagne, he had second thoughts.

He'd forgotten how Palm Beach bored him. Old money and pompous old farts. Fertile ground for society columnists, perhaps, but not for Tull. Who even cared about so-called society anymore? Outside of the William Kennedy Smith trial, Palm Beach's last sexy moment had been the Roxanne Pulitzer scandal. Ah, yes. Trumpets and lesbians. And, speak of the devil, there was Roxanne now. Working the room, greeting people like a society matron. In Palm Beach, Roxanne was still an outsider—but she was *their* outsider. And still with a hardbody women half her age would die for. Moments later, she rushed up and kissed him heartily.

"Cameron, you stud. Thanks for the mention of my novel in your column. Did you get my card?"

Tull grinned. In a Maurice Chevalier accent, he crooned, "Ah, yes…I remember it well." And he did. The card had featured semi-pornographic French art, with a thank-you note inside. He liked Roxanne. She hadn't let the town harpies kill her.

"When are you leaving?" she said.

"I'm not sure. Maybe tomorrow."

"Stay. Let's have dinner and raise some hell. Are you staying here at The Breakers?"

"Yes."

"I'll call you in the morning and talk you into staying. I'd offer you my body, but I'm sure that's no incentive. Bye."

Tull heard a voice at his side say, "Man, she still looks great. Is she into younger guys?"

Tull turned and blinked in genuine surprise. It was Steve Bellini. "What are you doing here? Don't tell me we're covering this?"

"I'm a friend of the groom, Roger Sarstead. And my sister went to school with the bride. What are you doing here?"

"I'm a friend of the groom's father. He was Vice-Consul at the U.S. Embassy in Tokyo when I was over there working for the *Asahi Evening News*. We've kept in touch."

Steve grinned. "Uh-huh. And since Phillip Sarstead is the President's oldest friend and unofficial advisor, I'll bet you keep in touch. What a great source."

Tull smiled and said nothing. People assumed that anyone he knew or talked to was a source. In the executive suites of Hollywood studios and TV networks, where the ongoing game was trying to figure out who was leaking gossip to the tabloid press, a person could be fingered as Tull's snitch just by being seen with him. That had screwed up what could have been some beautiful friendships. No matter. Life was a tradeoff. Tull believed he had the best job in the world.

Steve said, "I want you to meet my sister." He raised his voice over the din of chatter and a six-piece society combo.

"Jessica!"

Halfway across the room, a woman in a group clustered around the bride turned toward them. Tull caught his breath. She was dark, elegant, and beautiful. Steve waved and beckoned at her.

"Wow!" said Tull quietly. "That's some sister."

And then he recognized her. "My God…Jessica Bell? The fashion designer?"

Steve grinned. "That's right. My big sister is getting to be quite a name. And speaking of names, the reason she changed 'Bellini' to 'Bell' isn't because she's ashamed of being a *paisan*…She just didn't want to trade on the family name. We're pretty famous. And the business is closely related to fashion."

He looked slyly at Tull. "Figured it out yet, Cameron?"

"Bellini...?"

And then Tull got it.

"Your family is 'Bellini Frères.' The European jewelers."

He tapped the watch on his wrist. "I bought this Vacheron-Constantin at the Fifth Avenue store ten years ago. Amazing. I had no idea. Does anyone at the paper know about your, ah...glittering antecedents?"

Steve shrugged. "My family never asked me to keep it quiet. But a son in the tabloid business might scare off the carriage trade, so...Ah, here she is."

Jessica Bell, poised and unsmiling, stood before them. "Sis, I want you to meet a man who thought he knew everything about the rich and famous until just about a minute ago..."

Jessica did not hold out her hand. Uh-oh, thought Tull.

"Your fame precedes you, Mr. Tull," she said. "I'm one of the many millions who have seen you on TV. You are ubiquitous."

Tull smiled and bowed slightly. "I apologize for being hard to avoid."

"Not at all. One always has one's remote control."

She softened the zinger with a smile that broke like sunlight through a storm. Okay, lady, I'm your slave, thought Tull. Aloud, he said:

"Why do I suddenly feel like Quasimodo?"

Steve was enjoying the exchange hugely. "I should have warned you, Cameron. The snooty Signorina Bell does not approve of sleazy tabloid types like her brother."

"A true statement, as far as it goes, Mr. Tull," said Jessica. "Let me hasten to add that the snooty Signorina Bellini loves her brother dearly, even though he is, occasionally, a total asshole. And for that, I do not blame your tabloid at all."

"How relieved they will be to know it," he grinned. "Listen, I can barely wait to continue this Noel Coward repartee, but I wonder if you'd let me bring you a drink. The Cristal is wonderful, and I know they have a decent Chardonnay..."

"You're very kind, Mr. Tull."

"Not really, I just need to get away for a bit and think up some really clever things to say."

"Then you won't be long, I'm sure," she purred. "Chardonnay, please."

Tull walked off. "Somehow, sis, you're not convincing me that you find him to be a totally disgusting tabloid scumbag," said Steve sarcastically.

"You never did understand subtlety," Jessica rejoined.

"You're being about as subtle as a cheerleader in the boy's locker room."

"Mr. Tull is more...interesting than I would have expected. And you wouldn't want me to be rude to a colleague!"

Steve rolled his eyes. "Jessica, I haven't seen you like this since high school."

"Let's have dinner later at Taboo," she said quietly as Tull approached with her drink. "I'll bring that overly-endowed little blonde thing you like, and you invite Mr. Tull."

An hour later, the foursome piled into Jessica's limo and were chauffeured to Worth Avenue, the most chi-chi shopping strip in America east of Rodeo Drive. Dinner at Taboo was fun, with Tull and Jessica fencing with each other about the arrogance of the media in general—and what she called "the totally useless function of tattle-tale tabloid reporting." Steve, totally absorbed in the Wonder-Bra'd delights so unselfishly displayed by his giggly companion, showed no interest in philosophical discussion.

Miss Wonder Bra's only contribution was:

"I just LOVE the tabloids. I buy them all every week, and after mummy reads them we give them to the maids."

Two hours later, Steve and his amorous companion took off for parts unknown. Jessica offered to drop Tull at The Breakers on her way to the Bellini beachside mansion. He accepted, then asked her to drop into the bar for a nightcap. She agreed. Moments later they drifted outside, drinks in hand, to the darkened balcony that ran along the beach. It was a travel-folder Florida night, lit by a full moon that illuminated the whitecaps of endless waves surfing gently onto the white sand beach.

"So," said Tull, as they stood watching the midnight scene, "you hate what your brother—and I—do for a living."

"You've summed it up neatly, Cameron," she said.

"Yet—and let me see if my logic is flowing here—you manage to actually love your brother. So don't you think, then, you might manage some small affection for me in the future? Hypothetically, of course."

She turned and smiled up at him. "The flaw in your logic is that blood is thicker than tabloid ink. But charm can overcome many flaws."

"Does that mean you find me charming?"

"Oh yes," she breathed. And they kissed in the moonlight…

A muffled scream from the study snapped Tull back into real time. He raced inside and threw open the door. Jessica sat hunched over on the sofa, sobbing hysterically.

"Jessica, what is it? What happened?" Tull crouched in front of her. Hot tears salted his hands as he reached out to hold her. Head down, her body shuddered as she continued to sob helplessly. He waited a moment, hugging her lightly and stroking her shoulders as he spoke soothingly.

"Jessica, I know this is terrible for you—but let me help. Did you reach your parents?" She nodded, trying to regain control.

"I heard you scream," he said patiently. "Did something happen when you talked to them? Are they…okay?"

Goddamn, he thought. What happened? Is this just natural hysteria? Did her mother threaten to kill herself, or…?

"Please, Jessica. You've got to tell me what's wrong. You're scaring me. Is it your parents? Are they okay?"

She struggled to get herself under control. She started to speak, sobbed reflexively, then looked at him, tears streaking her face.

"It's…It's not what you think. I spoke to my father. He took it badly at first, but he's a very strong man. My mother…" Her shoulders jerked in a spasm of agony and she covered her eyes with her hands. Then she shook her head and looked up again.

"My mother was out shopping. My father will find her and tell her. They'll fly here immediately, but…"

Tull held her arms tightly and looked into her eyes intently.

"Jessica, you've got to tell me! Why did you scream?"

She tried to speak, then pointed at the telephone. Tull sensed the hysteria rising again and spoke sharply to cut it off.

"Jessica, tell me exactly what happened! Tell me now!"

She took a deep breath, struggled for control.

"I called my apartment to see if anyone had called. And…and there was a horrible message…it was a woman, mocking me…asking about Steve—"

Tull stood abruptly, lifted the phone, and punched the redial button. As he waited for the answering machine to pick up, he asked Jessica:

"What's your code for retrieving messages?"

"Zero, zero, zero," she answered.

Tull shook his head. Amazing. It seemed like nobody ever programmed a secret code retrieval number into answering machines. They just left it on the factory setting so that anyone could pick up their messages. A daily modus operandi among tabloid reporters was running through their list of private phone numbers of stars and moguls too dumb or too lazy to encrypt their answering machines. It was a constant source of information, sometimes trivial, occasionally newsworthy. But always interesting. The phone messages of busy people were a road map of their lives.

The answering machine picked up.

"Hello, you've reached 555-1619. Please leave a message."

It beeped and Tull punched in three zeros. Bingo! He heard a woman's voice. It said in a sneering drawl:

"*Hi, Jessica…How did Steve like the flowers?*"

A pause…a derisive laugh…and the click of a hang-up.

"What's your code for 'repeat?'" Tull snapped.

"Two," Jessica answered.

Tull hit "2" and listened again, intently.

The female voice was low-pitched, almost sultry. Not menacing, but venomous. The message itself, delivered in an unhurried drawl, was exactly what Jessica had called it—mocking.

Tull's held back from blurting what leaped to mind the moment he'd heard the woman's voice.

Charmain Burns!

Goddamnit, he wasn't one-hundred percent sure. But, after hearing the replay, he was at ninety-five and climbing. That slight Southern lilt in the voice. Shit! This was unbelievable, but…

Jessica, still on the edge of shock and hysteria, came up off the sofa and cried out, "Oh GOD! It was a woman…a woman murdered my BROTHER! Why? Oh God, WHY?"

She was pacing, frantic, hugging herself as if trying to hold back the pain. Tull went to her, gathered her in his arms, and again tried to calm her.

He started off with a lie.

"Jessica, listen, we don't know that. It could have been some vicious kook who heard the news on the radio and thought she'd play a prank."

She struggled against him, trying to pull away. "No, no, no! Don't tell me that. I can feel it in her voice. She knew him. She murdered him…"

Tull was relieved. Jessica hadn't caught his lie. She was in shock and had never asked the exact time of death. If she had, she'd have realized—after hearing the machine's robot voice announce the time of the message as 10:07 a.m.—that the call had been placed almost an hour before Steve died. But his relief was short-lived. Jessica stepped back and said steadily:

"What did she mean? About the flowers?"

He hesitated. "Well, I'm not sure…"

"Don't!" she said sharply, holding her hand up as if to ward off untruth. "Don't lie to spare my feelings. You know something. Tell me, Cameron. I can handle it. Please!"

He sighed through tightened lips. "Alright, I'll tell you what we know, which isn't much. It looks like someone delivered flowers to Steve and there was an attack of some kind. He was hit, punched. He fell backward onto a room service trolley. It rolled out onto the balcony and he was pitched over the railing. It could have been a murder attempt, or…"

She cut him off impatiently. "How could it not have been murder? You heard the phone call. Obviously someone meant him harm."

Tull nodded. "Harm, yes. It looks like someone was sent to beat him up. But they might not have meant to kill him."

Jessica stared back at him intently. He could see her struggling to take it all in, to comprehend. Then her eyes lost their focus. She turned away and walked to the window.

"I just can't seem to concentrate. I'm so tired, so tired…"

She swayed and almost lost her balance as he rushed over and caught her. "Sit down," he said, leading her back to the sofa. "Jessica, will you please listen to me?"

"Yes," she said wearily. "I'll listen. Just tell me what to do. I can't think anymore."

He lifted her feet up onto the sofa and took off her shoes. He massaged her feet and said, "I'm going to get that tray of tea from Mrs. Gordon. And I'm going to insist you take a bracing sip of Remy Martin. You're exhausted and you need a pick-me-up. Then we'll talk about what to do. Now just sit here a moment and don't move. I'll be right back."

He stood and arranged a cushion behind her. Jessica lay back and covered her eyes with her arm. Tull walked quietly out of the room and shut the door behind him.

"Mrs. Gordon?" he called.

She came out of the kitchen. "Yes, sir? You want the tea now? It's ready."

"Yes, please. We'll have it in the study. Mrs. Gordon, I wonder if I could ask a favor. My friend has suffered a terrible loss, a death in the family. Her brother, actually. It just happened and she's finally starting to calm down. I think she should rest here a few hours before coping with all the arrangements. Could you stay with her while I run down to L.A.? Perhaps three hours, tops?"

Mrs. Gordon clucked sympathetically, "The poor dear. Of course I can stay. Let me go and get that tea. That's what she needs." She bustled off into the kitchen.

An hour and a half later, Tull was on his way to Jessica's place in L.A., with the key she'd given him. She'd protested at first, wanting to come with him. But he'd convinced her that was a bad idea.

"You might be in danger from whoever left that message," he told her. "Right now, no one knows exactly where you are. Let's keep it that way. The important thing is to get your answering machine while that message is still recorded on the computer chip. We can have it transferred to tape, then turn the machine over to the cops, I guess. It could be valuable evidence."

"It's not a computer chip," she said. "I've had the same machine for years. It uses those little micro-cassette tapes."

"Whatever," said Tull. "The important thing is to make sure we grab it."

"Okay," said Jessica. "I'll take a little nap, I think. I'm just useless right now."

"Fine," said Tull. "I won't be long."

CHAPTER 19

2:53 P.M.
PACIFIC COAST HIGHWAY
MALIBU

TULL sped down the PCH in his Aston-Martin. He felt hot, tight, excited. Story fever. Fire in the belly. He still got it, even after all these years. Just like that first night on the lobster shift at the *Boston Record-American.* After months of obits and rewrite, Sid White had looked out over the sleepy newroom and barked: "Tull. Mob rubout in Southie. Two bodies. Here's the address." As he eagerly grabbed the slip of paper, Sid had looked at him hard, appraisingly. "You're all I've got, boyo. But I think you'll do." Goddamn. He'd felt so fucking proud. And he'd nailed the story, whipping the *Boston Globe* with an exclusive on a witness at a nearby gin mill who'd seen a white Ford laying rubber after shots were fired.

Yeah. Story fever. Kept you cranked better than speed. Every good reporter had it. Great reporters had something else. Control. Knew how to move fast, but not too fast. The trick to cracking a story is sifting and sorting the known facts constantly. Keep them running in your brain like a video loop, over and over. Don't get trapped by tunnel vision. Step back. Look for the pattern, the big picture. And history. History's everything. Who are the players? What's their m.o.? Their background? What drives them? How about sudden changes in lifestyle? New problems. Drugs. Booze. An illicit affair. Business gone sour. Legal problems…

"YEAH!" He yelled into the onrushing wind. That was it!

Just days earlier, Charmain Burns' lawyer had warned *The Revealer* of a lawsuit he was about to file over the paper's publication of shocking photographs showing Charmain brutally whipping a horse across the face. Just another moronic lawsuit that would be dropped or settled for *bupkes.* No one at the paper was worried about it. Charmain's lawyers claimed that the photos were misleading and maligned her; that she was simply training a horse using time-honored techniques. But the pictures spoke for themselves. In a brief chat Tull had with the Queen of Scots, she'd mentioned that, in her opinion, Charmain's lawyer's heart wasn't in the suit.

This was just another case of a star with money to burn forcing an attorney to take action—even after being advised she couldn't win. Why do stars insist on suing fruitlessly? Because stars are often big, silly babies. And they love being in the news. Hearing some hair-sprayed TV newsanchor tease breathlessly:

"MAJOR STAR SUES *THE REVEALER!*...DETAILS ON NEWS AT SIX!"

Yeah, this was starting to fit. Tull's gut felt right. He stacked up the story points:

One: the voice on Jessica's answering machine had sounded like Charmain.

Two: the story about the horse-whipping had been under Steve Bellini's byline, so chances were it had whipped Charmain into a fury for revenge.

Three: the star's penchant for gun-toting violence was a matter of...well, history.

Tull punched out the number of the Camino Rio Hotel on his carphone. "Camino Rio Hotel. Good day..."

"Phil Monte, please."

"Monte!"

"Phil, Cameron Tull...You said our perp was probably posing as a delivery guy. Were there flowers at the scene?"

"Yeah, on the floor. The cops are trying to trace where they came from. And for DNA. How'd you know?"

"Just a guess, Phil. I'll share later."

"Hey—"

Tull clicked off. Goddamn. He pounded the wheel. That fucking bitch Charmain! He took a deep breath. Control. You know nothing yet. Don't pre-suppose. Don't let impulsive thoughts block the truth. He laughed. His swordmaster in Tokyo used to tell him, in his fractured English, "Don't be hot like sun. Be cool like moon. Never stare into enemy's eye. You are like moonlight. You look at nothing, see everything. Nothing surprise you, okay?"

He glanced at his watch. Nearly three. He'd be at Jessica's apartment in twenty minutes. Get some answers. He kicked the Aston in the ass, scoping the rearview for cops. He thought of Jessica. Should he call back, see how she was? He suddenly wanted to hear her voice.

And then it hit him. He'd be seeing where she lived for the first time. Walking into air inhabited by her, redolent of her essence. He'd see the furniture she sat on, slept in. Touch her books and knickknacks. Her clothes...He shook his head, laughed sharply. Christ, I sound like some pervert about to rifle through her underwear drawer. But oh, man...

Seeing her again had brought it all back. Like it had just happened. His mind took him there once more—as it had every day for a year—to that heart-stopping moment. That kiss in the moonlight in Palm Beach. It had electrified him...and her.

"Oh," she'd said, moving as if to step back out of his arms. She'd swayed and he'd steadied her.

"Well," she'd said. "Well..."

Her bosom rose and fell visibly as she caught her breath.

"That was quite unexpected," said Jessica.

She blushed.

"Not the...not what you did. But the...ah, the..."

She laughed and looked at him helplessly.

"I know exactly what you're trying to say," he said.

"You do? Well, you're a writer. You tell me."

He drew her in to him. "You're saying that it was quite unexpected you'd feel like...this..."

He kissed her again. And it was the same, only hotter. Like melting together. Her blood/his blood. Her bones/his bones. Fusing. Bonding. Consilience. Forged by heat he'd never felt with any woman. Spiritual. Sexual. Dizzying.

Finally, he released her. She opened her eyes as he gazed down into them. She blinked, then met his gaze steadily.

He said, "I have never wanted so badly to say the perfect thing. To phrase the perfect phrase. Without fear of sounding corny."

"Just say it," she said.

He cupped her face in his hands. "I want to live inside you."

She closed her eyes and breathed softly.

He said, "A moment ago, I felt like I was inside you. No...I felt like we'd melded. Like we were one person. I mean this, every word. I'm not just..."

She opened her eyes and smiled.

"Trying to seduce me, Mr. Tull?"

He looked so wounded, so hurt, that she had laughed. "I'm sorry. I was teasing. I know you mean it."

She stretched up and kissed his mouth.

Then she said quietly, "I felt it too."

"You did?"

"So strange. Like our hearts were beating together."

They kissed again and again. Now, at last, it was carnal. He grew against her and she retreated slightly, then surrendered against his hardness. He sensed it immediately. She'd given him control. He took his lips away. She moaned. He tilted her chin up at him and laughed softly.

"What's so funny, mister?"

"Now," he said.

"Now...what?"

"Now I'm trying to seduce you."

"Really?"

"And I'm telling you because I want everything to be honest between us. My intentions are strictly honorable. Outside of the seduction part, that is. If I'm making myself clear."

She squirmed in his arms. "Nothing's clear to me right now. And I like it."

"You are so beautiful," he said. He covered her face with gentle, slow kisses. "I have never felt like this…Never…I—"

"We've got to stop, Cameron."

He stopped. Startled by her almost brusque tone.

"What…?"

"You've heard of that old adage: 'If they're wet, they can't think.' I need to think."

Tull was speechless.

Jessica giggled. "Oh God, I can't believe I said that! You've got me acting like an idiot."

Tull laughed. "Then I must be doing something right."

"You've been doing everything right. Now there's just one last thing. Let me go."

"Never," said Tull. "No. That I will never do."

"I mean, let me go home now."

"Why now?"

"I want to go home and dream about this."

"Look," he said. "I don't want this night to end. And I'm not saying it has to end in my bedroom. I'll sit on the beach with you and watch the sun come up, I'll…"

She reached up to kiss him. Then she said seriously, "I wouldn't mind ending up in your bedroom, the way I feel right now. Look, Cameron, I'm not a girl and you're not a boy. So let's not fence around. You have a powerful physical effect on me, okay? If I fall into bed with you right now, I'm sure it will be astounding. But it might add up to a one-night stand, which I don't do. If I get away from you for awhile and still feel this ga-ga, then I'll know it's something very special."

Tull stroked her hair. "Look, how can I put this? I'll do anything for you. I'll wait a year…a decade…"

"Let's not go mad," she said. "I was thinking more like…tomorrow night?"

"Really?"

He grinned like a naughty schoolboy.

"Let's meet for an early breakfast," she said. "I like that watching-the-sun-come-up thing. Later we'll have lunch, then dinner. You'll have the whole day to seduce me. And guess what?"

"What?"

She kissed him softly.

"I'm betting you do just that."

Next morning, the sun had barely lit the Gulf Stream when Tull joined Jessica on the patio of the Bellini beachside cabana. They breakfasted, then changed into bathing suits, swam, walked the beach and talked in the fresh morning air. After a tour of the family mansion, one of the oldest in Palm Beach, they changed and drove over to Worth Avenue. And Jessica discovered that Tull loved shopping. Not buying. Shopping. She tried on clothes at Saks and Lili Pulitzer. And giggled when he tried to steer her into Indiscreet, the lingerie boutique that was Palm Beach's answer to Victoria's Secret.

Later, over lunch al fresco down one of the shady alleys off Worth, they held hands under the table. And exchanged their pasts, dreams, desires. Under Jessica's gentle questioning, Tull found himself speaking of things few knew. His teenage years. The father who walked out on his mother one day and was never seen again. The horror of two policemen meeting him at high school to say his mother had been killed by a city bus that ran up onto a sidewalk.

A small settlement kept him going through high school. Alone and ready to quit, he finished because he knew it's what his mother would have wanted. He went on to college in Boston, then quit in his second year and started working at his chosen craft—writing. He did freelance articles for the *Boston Phoenix* and other magazines and tried to break into daily newspapers. He fast-talked his way into a copy boy job at the *Record-American.* And finally worked his way up to reporter. Ended up in the Far East as a foreign correspondent, working the Pacific Rim from Tokyo to Vietnam.

"You never married?" she asked.

"No. Came close once. It's not a life choice. It just never happened. You?"

"You just summed me up. Once, almost. I guess I'd love to, and I think about it more lately. The old biological clock giving me a wake-up call. But things are just getting so busy now. I worked hard to build my business. Suddenly it's exploding. And I love what I do."

"Yeah. As do I."

They were silent for a long while. The lunch crowd had departed for the Palm Beach siesta. They were alone in the cool passage, swimming in each other's eyes. Then Jessica reached over and took his hand, placing it on her heart. And she began to speak in Italian, the language of her girlhood, a language Tull had no fluency in. Long melodic phrases poured out of her as she spoke to him from a heart he felt pounding beneath his fingers.

He listened, understanding nothing. And everything. His eyes stung as tears responded to her voice.

When she finished, he leaned across the table and kissed her softly. They left, got in the car, and drove aimlessly for a while. Jessica picked up her cell phone and punched in a call. "Graciella…is my brother there? Ah, si. Okay." She said something in Italian, then hung up. Tull looked at her questioningly.

"That was our maid at the house. Stefano…Steve…just left for the airport. He and the little blonde slept late and she took a cab. Steve left you a message. It was 'Good Luck.'"

"What a strange message," said Tull, grinning.

"You're looking awfully smug about something, Mr. Tull."

"Who…me? By the way, what did you tell the maid in Italian?"

"I gave her the rest of the day off."

"Oh."

"Suddenly you're monosyllabic?"

"Uh-huh."

He looked at her, gave her the schoolboy grin again.

Jessica shook her head.

"This is ridiculous," she said. "Take a right here."

"Where are we going?"

"To my house, as if you didn't know."

She slid across the seat and snuggled up to him.

"God," she said, "I didn't even hold out until dinnertime."

For three days, they never left each other's sight. Alone, on the plane back to L.A., he felt whatever had connected them pulling him back to her. He phoned her from somewhere over Texas.

"This is no poetic metaphor I'm describing, Jessica," he told her. "I feel like my fucking heart is going to tear out of my chest. And I can't believe I'm talking like this."

"I can't believe I haven't stopped crying since you left," she said. "Cameron, it won't be long. We'll be together in just one month. In New York."

But New York never happened.

Never.

Tull found Jessica's house on a leafy street in Pacific Palisades and drove up to the closed gates. The place was expensive-looking, but not pretentious. Wood and glass, with lush landscaping. Tull hit the gate beeper Jessica had given him, drove up the circular drive, parked and let himself in with her key. The burglar alarm chirped as he punched in the code.

He went right to the answering machine, paused reflectively, then hit PLAY to check the tape. Nothing. He punched it again. Shit. He flipped up the cover.

Empty! No goddamn tape. Impossible. He'd just heard it, what…? An hour ago? It had to be here. Was there another machine? Jessica hadn't mentioned one, but…He searched desperately. There were two other phones, one an extension, the other a separate line. But no other machine.

What the *fuck?*

He sat down at the desk in the tiny den she obviously used as a study. His mind raced. Came up with one sobering conclusion: someone had taken the tape. Seemed impossible. But had to be.

Who even knew the tape existed? *Answer*: the person who left the message. Why did they take it? *Answer*: it's potentially incriminating evidence in a murder case.

Who could break in and bypass a first-class alarm system? *Answer:* only a pro!

It all added up: Charmain had left the message, realized she'd been stupid, and turned for help to the best in the business—her very own security guy, Vidal Delaney. Charmain wouldn't know how to find a top-flight burglar on short notice. But Delaney would. Sonofabitch! Tull slammed his fist down on the desk and yelled in frustration.

"Goddamn you, Vidal. You want to play rough? I'll use your fucking eye sockets for ashtrays, you sonofabitch!"

The curse rang loud in the empty room.

And was duly recorded.

CHAPTER 20

3:01 A.M.
"CREOLE TIME"

THE limo rolled slowly through the Miami streets, Patrick's driver waiting for him to name a destination. Charmain snuggled back in the leather seat and sighed happily.

"Well, I took you away from dessert," Patrick said with a wry smile. "And it's not breakfast time."

"Not yet," she said, smiling back.

"I know a place that might be amusing. But perhaps you have a suggestion."

She said, "You know what I'd like? I never did try any of that terrific champagne...what's it called?"

"Cristal?"

"Yes. Cristal. Everybody was drinking it. I never tried it. And I know I'm never going to drink a cranberry spritzer again. What do you think that sonofabitch put in my drink?"

"Almost certainly it was rohypnol. Very nasty."

"You mean that stuff they call 'roofies?' The date-rape drug?"

"That's the one."

"Jesus. That filthy, scummy bastard. You saw him do it?"

"Yes. I'd just walked back in the room. Another couple of seconds and...well, it's over and done with now."

"God, he could have raped me. Patrick, I can never thank you enough."

He touched her shoulder lightly and grinned. Her heart turned over.

He said, "You were saying...? You'd like to try some Cristal?"

"Oh, yeah. You know what I'd love? Is there a quiet place that overlooks the water? I love the water."

"Do you like boats?"

"Oh, yes. Is there a place like that on a boat?"

"Yes. The place I was going to suggest."

His eye caught the driver's in the rearview. The driver winked and hit the gas.

Five minutes later, they drove out onto a dock and stopped next to a sleek motor yacht.

"Oh, it's gorgeous," said Charmain. "But I don't think they're open. I don't see any lights inside."

"Well, let's go aboard and light some."

"Wait a minute, this isn't a restaurant. There'd be a sign."

A moment later, as Patrick led her up the gangway, Charmain got it.

"It's yours, right?"

"Right."

"Wow!"

"Like it?"

"What part of 'Wow!' is confusing you?"

He smacked her lightly on the bottom.

"Don't be naughty."

It took her a second to catch her breath.

"I won't...if you promise to do that again."

He threw back his head and laughed, white teeth gleaming as they walked along the darkened deck.

"Here we are," he said, sliding open a door and stepping in ahead of her. He threw a light switch and she followed him into the main salon. Its decor had overtones of an elegant Victorian parlor. Brocade, plush sofas and loveseats, tables topped with crotcheted cloths, and lamps of etched glass and antique brass. An ornate bar that looked like it had come out of an English gentlemen's club dominated one side of the salon. Patrick walked behind it and rummaged while Charmain looked around.

"So you live on the boat?"

"Well, I do when I'm in Miami, or wherever. When I'm at home in Savannah, I might spend a night or two aboard each week. Going out fishing, that sort of thing. Here we are."

He stepped out from behind the bar carrying an ice bucket containing a bottle of Cristal and two flutes. He led her out on the afterdeck, sat her at a table, popped the cork on the Cristal, and poured.

Patrick raised a glass. "To you," he said.

"No."

She stood, raised her glass and said, "To you...my hero."

They sipped. Looked at each other in the moonlight. The stubble on his face stood out darkly against his skin. She wondered how it would feel scraping across her cheeks, her thighs...

"How do you like it?"

Startled, she thought for a split second he was reading her mind.

"Oh! You mean the Cristal?"

"What else? You said you hadn't tried it."

"It's like drinking gold fairy dust."

Ohgod. She couldn't believe she'd said that. She sounded like a child.

He looked at her intently.

"Perfectly put. You're somebody very special, Charmain Burns."

She got that faint feeling again. Did he really mean that, or was it just part of his seduction routine? Who cared? She was crazy about this man. She'd figure it all out later.

"Patrick?"

"Yes?"

"Please kiss me now."

He took her in his arms. Unhurried. "Yes. You're very, very special…" he breathed.

She kept her eyes open until his lips found hers. Gently. Sweetly. God, he was delicious. She was very aware of her breasts mashing against his chest. The kiss got hotter. She felt his stubble tickle her skin.

"Mmmmm…"

The moan was wrenched out of her. Inside her head, everything started pulsing in technicolor. Almost frightened by the whirl of emotions overtaking her, she opened her eyes. Saw the moon, silvery and calm. She closed her eyes again. Let him sweep her away. And he did. Literally. She lost contact with his lips and suddenly felt herself lifted up in his arms. She opened her eyes. Saw his burning into her.

Patrick said, "Can I ask you to do one thing?"

"I'll do anything for you, Patrick," she said.

"Just snag that ice bucket and our Cristal. It will be nicely chilled later."

She smiled shyly up at him.

"For breakfast?"

"For breakfast."

He carried her back through the salon, opened a door and went down a short staircase into the master bedroom. Low-key lights were already lit, bathing the king-size bed in a pale glow. He put her down, set the ice bucket on a bedside table. And looked at her.

"My God, you're so exquisite," he said. "Breathtaking."

She stood there, hands at her sides, not posing. Just totally without defenses.

"Tell me what to do, Patrick. Do you want me to take off my clothes? Or do you want to do that?"

What's wrong with me? she thought. Now I'm sounding like a slut. But I can't help it. I'm just saying stuff. Oh, please let him like me.

He smiled. It was the warmest smile she'd ever felt.

"*Tu…tres adorable. Jeune. Trop sexuelle.*"

"I…I don't…is that French?"

"My family is French Creole. I'm sorry, but it really is the language of love."

"Oh. Oh, Patrick."

She reached down swiftly, grasped the hem of her dress and stripped it over her head. She was bra-less. She stepped out of her panties. Stood there for his inspection in her little black fuck-me sandals.

"*Mon Dieu!*" He breathed it like a prayer. "*Tu es formidable.*"

And then she was in his arms, head whirling as he covered her with kisses. Lips. Face. Breasts. Shivering as stubble raked her nipples. Down on the bed. Cool, silky sheets like she'd never felt. Hands reaching for him hungrily. Finding him. Grasping the heat of him. Ohgod, he's huge. A soundless, giddy giggle…She thought, wait till he finds out I'm a virgin. Would it hurt? Didn't care. Ohgod, these expensive sheets. Would she bleed? Didn't care. Oh, he felt so good. She wanted to eat him. Did. He groaned. Oh, he likes that. She did it again, tonguing exactly the same way. Another strangled groan. He thrashed on the sheets. Was between her legs.

Rough beard on her thighs. Her core melting now. On fire. Wetness like she'd never felt. Time fell away. Drowning. Then he was on top of her. Charmain looked into his eyes. Pale blue fires.

"Patrick," she whispered.

"Yes?"

"It's…okay if you speak French."

"*Ah, ma petite chérie. Tu es encroyable.*"

A moment later, he slid inside her. Gently. Hurt like hell, but she was braced. Ready for it. Didn't wince. Didn't care. Didn't want her cherry holding him back. Needed the full force of him.

"Oh, darling Patrick."

The pain drove her to say it louder than she'd meant.

"It's so good. FUCK ME HARDER, BABY. FUCK ME!"

Magic words. Made pain go away. Thrilling ecstasy. Driving her toward the moment of her life.

Her back arched as the wave hit her. She cried out.

"Patrick…"

CHAPTER 21

12:25 P.M.
"CREOLE TIME"
THE COAST OF FLORIDA

"MILLIE?"

"Hi, hon. Where are you?"

"On a beautiful yacht."

"Ohmigod. Mr. Sexy owns a fucking *yacht*? Ramon and I heard you hooked up with him after that asshole Paco tried to dope you. Can you believe that? And then…what's his name…?"

"Patrick." Charmain still tingled every time she said it.

"Yeah. Patrick. He comes charging up like Mr. White Knight and saves your pretty white ass. My GOD, girl, didn't you just cream your jeans??"

"Ooohh, yeah!"

Millie lowered her voice, got closer to the phone.

"Is he wonderful? I mean, you did…right?"

Charmain giggled. "The last time was about twenty minutes ago."

"God! Listen, are you coming up for air, or stayin' there? I mean, don't worry about me, but—"

"No, I'm coming back. If I can still walk."

"Eeeww, that's right. Girlfriend's cherry got popped. Sore City, huh? Look, I want to hear everything! So get your ass back here."

"What time is it?"

"About 12:30."

"Okay, in an hour. Not even."

"Okay."

Charmain hung up, walked out of the yacht's main salon and onto the afterdeck, where Patrick was reading the *New York Times.* She was fully dressed for the first time in hours.

"I'm ready," she said.

"Why, darling, I almost didn't recognize you with your clothes on."

He stood, kissed her and went to call the car. She evaluated the kiss. Decided he'd done it like he meant it. So far, so good. No sign of a morning-after brushoff yet. Everything had been perfect from the moment he'd awakened her just after dawn for more lovemaking. Slower this time. Even more satifying. Then he'd let her doze for an hour, brought her a glass of orange juice in bed, grinned and announced:

"Breakfast is served on the fantail, madame. I've given the help the day off, so madame can dine nude if she wishes."

She came up on deck wearing his silk robe embroidered with the yacht's name, "Creole Time." Sunlight danced on the water as they dined under a canopy. And she knew he truly liked her when he served French toast with a flourish and said, "Am I right in assuming that you like anything French?"

They lingered over the meal, laughing and talking animatedly. She couldn't believe how they went from one subject to the next. That she found it so easy to converse with him. Charmain's bullshit meter, cranked to supersensitive, told her he was actually interested in what she was saying. Despite the fact that he was twice her age.

And she drew him out. He told her about Savannah, a town he loved.

"Wait till you see it," he said. "You'll understand why it's called 'The Jewel of the South.'"

Hearing about it hours later in person, Millie gasped.

"You mean, just like that? He invited you to go back with him to Savannah?"

"Not just *go* back, you silly child. *Sail* back. On his *yacht*!"

They both screamed.

"Oh God, Millie. I am so in love. And I am so scared. What if his fancy friends in Savannah don't like me? What if he dumps me?"

Millie looked at her solemnly.

"Don't worry about it. Be tough, like you always are. And just enjoy the ride. Hell, girl, no matter what happens... You just lost your cherry. On a yacht. To a *French guy.*"

They screamed again.

"Oh shit," Millie gasped. "Now look at you. Laughin' so hard you're cryin'...Charmain?...Hon?...Migod, you *are* cryin'! What's wrong, sweetie?"

Charmain, sobbing uncontrollably, collapsed into Millie's arms. When she could finally speak, she said, "But I didn't lose my cherry to him. I lost it way back when...you know...when those men..."

Millie hugged her hard. "Now you stop that talk, Charmain. You were a little girl and you were attacked. And that just doesn't count. What the hell is virginity, anyway? It's just in your mind. Hell, by the time they actually get dicked, most girls have had everything in the world up there. Vibrators, dildoes, cucumbers. Their own fingers. And God knows who else's."

Charmain laughed a bit. Millie dried her tears as she wailed, "But he'll find out. Someone will tell him. Millie, I love him. I've got to be honest with him. And what will he think?"

"Whoa, slow down, girl. You've got plenty of time. Let's see if he's honest with you before you start worrying about this. Right now, he has no right to know anything. It's not his damn business yet. I know you're crazy in love, Charmain, but go slow here. It was just one bad thing in your past, that's all."

Charmain looked at her and shook her head.

Millie said, "What?"

"There's more. Even worse."

And she told her. About her mother. Everything.

An hour later, exhausted from sobbing, they both took a nap and slept until nightfall.

Patrick came by and took them to dinner. Charmain told her to invite Ramon along. Millie shrugged and said, "He's 'not available' until later. Bet you anything the sonofabitch is married or has a girlfriend. But he's a fun lay. And *I'm* not in love."

As Patrick's limo swooped up to the hotel entrance, Millie patted Charmain's cheek and said, "Remember…nothin' but smiles, girl."

Patrick took them to the legendary Joe's Stone Crabs. Over dinner, he told Charmain that he'd changed his plans slightly so they could leave for Savannah in two days.

"I'd planned to stay here until next week," he said. "But I can hardly wait to show you my city. I do have business in the Caribbean. Antigua. So I'm chartering a plane to fly me down there in the morning. I'd take you, Charmain, but it's going to be a lot of meetings and you'd be on your own a lot. I suggest you stay here and shop some more with Millie. What do you think?"

Charmain said, "Fine."

Millie laughed. "I think she's not going to sleep a wink until you get back."

Patrick grinned. "Millie, I have an idea. Why don't you sail up the coast of Florida with us, say as far as Jacksonville. That lands you pretty close to home, right?"

Millie's mouth dropped open. She looked quickly at Charmain. Then said, "Well, I don't want to be third spoke in the wheel…"

Charmain beamed at Patrick. "What a great idea! Patrick, you are the best." He likes my friend, she thought. Another good sign.

Millie protested. "But I don't want to be in the way…"

Patrick winked. "You won't be. There's a lock on my stateroom door."

They all laughed and attacked the stone crabs.

For the next two days, the girls hit the beach in the mornings, shopped in the afternoon, and in the evenings Millie slipped out to meet Ramon. Charmain stayed in the room. If she couldn't spend her nights with Patrick, she wanted to spend them thinking about him. In one or two moments of insecurity, she wondered if he'd actually come back for her. Once she even had a cab take her by the dock to see if his yacht was still there.

It was.

She realized what was going on inside her. For the first time in her life, she'd found someone she thought she could trust. Who was strong enough to protect her. It was her dream. She wanted desperately for it to be true.

On the morning Patrick was due back, Millie and Charmain had breakfast at a South Beach café. Millie had news of the evil-smelling Paco.

"Ramon says he's in deep shit. Don Diego's bodyguards beat the crap out of him after the party and put him into the hospital. He's out now, but Ramon says he's finished in this town. He says Don Diego put him out of the big-time. Whatever that means. I guess he fired him."

Charmain said, "It sounds worse than that."

"Ramon says he's a mean little bastard. Said let him know right away if he shows his face. He doesn't think he's any danger to you now, but keep your eyes open."

Charmain curled her lip. "That piece of shit's the one who'd better hope I don't see him. Nobody's raping me again. I'll kill him where he stands."

Charmain's hand flashed into her purse and she drew the 9mm Kahr under the table. It was a fast move. Millie, who'd grown up around gun-toting Florida crackers, was impressed.

"Damn! Where'd you get that?"

Charmain grinned. "You see the apple in that fruit bowl over there?"

"Yeah."

"I could drill it twice before you could spit."

"Wow! If you weren't a girl, I'd marry you."

"Ha, ha, very funny" said Charmain, sliding the pistol into her purse. "Patrick will be back in an hour. Let's finish packing."

CHAPTER 22

"Creole Time"
Sailing Toward Savannah

THE sun never stopped shining on "Creole Time" as it sailed inland of the Florida shore up the Intracoastal Waterway. Day after day of perfect weather. Nights anchored in some quiet cove bathed in moonlight.

Patrick had a skipper, a mate, and a chef aboard. The men had their own quarters and were rarely seen, except when the mate assisted the chef at mealtimes. Breakfast was always served on the fantail with the boat at anchor in the morning sun, after the girls had a swim off the stern. Lunch was catch-as-catch-can. Sandwiches and a drink on a tray wherever you wanted it. Dinner was served in the main salon. Patrick insisted that they change and dress formally for the evening meal, which started with Belvedere vodka martinis mixed by the master himself, followed by Cristal champagne and fine wines.

Patrick was the perfect host, charming and attentive. Charmain and Millie had never sailed on anything larger than a bass fishing boat before, and he turned the trip into an adventure, filling their heads with seafaring lore and fish tales, pointing out the sights passing by on port and starboard. Patrick was always up before the girls, at dawn. He'd drink café au lait, make phone calls, then go below to the radio room and bring up the *New York Times* and *Wall St. Journal* on the yacht's computer.

When the girls rose, he'd join them for breakfast and hand them printouts of news stories he thought might interest them. He was so attentive, so kind, that Millie admitted to Charmain:

"Hon, I hope you appreciate I'm holdin' back here not to fall for your man. He is not just the handsomest thing on two feet, he treats us like ladies, not wet-behind-the-ears girls just north of jailbait."

Charmain gave Millie a look of mock warning. "You'd better not even think of it, girl."

Millie snorted. "Ha, not that I'd have a chance. At first, I figured he was just another guy going crazy for you, like they all do. But he's got me convinced he's in love with you. The way he *looks* at you? WHOA! And I know you're gettin' more than your share of sugar time. That man does love his siestas, doesn't he? Or should I call them *matinées*?"

Millie ducked as Charmain swatted a towel at her. It was true. Every afternoon, the skipper would find a quiet stretch of water, slow the boat to a crawl, just above idling speed. Patrick would dive in and swim alongside for thirty minutes. Then he'd climb aboard via the stern ladder and go below for a shower and a nap. And every afternoon at that precise time, Charmain would stretch casually and tell Millie, "See ya later." Millie would roll her eyes.

Charmain would go to the master stateroom, slide between the silken sheets, and get her brains fucked out. And then, there were the nights. Glorious, passionate couplings as moonlight filtered through portholes.

Three days rolled by. Then, Jacksonville. Late morning. The skipper slipped the yacht neatly alongside a marina dock. Patrick had arranged for a car to meet the boat and take Millie to a hotel where she'd spend the night and catch a bus to Citrus Corners the next morning. As they stood at the bottom of the gangplank hugging each other, Charmain and Millie burst into tears.

"Millie, you take care of yourself, hear?"

"I will. Oh god, good luck with Patrick. Call me."

"I will. I will. Oh, Millie, I miss you already."

And then she was gone.

Patrick and the chef made a quick foray into the city to stock up on fresh vegetables and fish. Patrick came back loaded down with newspapers and magazines, including all her favorites.

"Here's *The Enquirer, The Revealer, People,* and every fashion rag I could lay my hands on. Oh, I'm sorry, *chérie*, I forgot *Good Housekeeping.* Shall I go back for it?"

Charmain laughed. "Very funny."

He said seriously, "You sure you don't want to spend a day on dry land? Do some shopping? See a movie?"

"I want to spend the day flat on my back on those sexy sheets, monsieur. *Tu comprends*?"

He'd been teaching her French.

"Ah, bon français. Oui, je comprende. Onivir!"

"Creole Time" knifed through the waterway, up the Georgia coastline. Past the Cumberland Island National Seashore, Jekyll Island, Sapelo Island, Ossabaw. Patrick started telling her about Savannah, the city he loved so dearly.

"Now, darling, you already know a bit about the state of Georgia, because it's right next to you down there in North Florida. A lot of Georgia is like that. Rural. Real down-home. Folks proud to be backwoods cracker Baptists. It's the Bible Belt. Now, Savannah, it's a completely different ambience. More…hell, I don't know, more passionate, more decadent, more go-to-hell. It's nothing like Atlanta, for instance. It's more like New Orleans or Key West. Did you see the movie, *Midnight In The Garden of Good and Evil*?"

"No. I heard the book was real good, though."

"The book is brilliant. You've got to read it. Anyway, there's a line in the movie where this writer from up North tries to explain Savannah to his New York agent. He calls it, '*Gone With the Wind* on mescalin.' And that's about right. People here are quirky, eccentric, offbeat. Savannah is a truly original city and a state of mind. In Atlanta, the first question people ask you is, 'What business you in?' In Macon, they ask, 'Where do you go to church?'

"In Savannah, the first question is, 'What would you like to drink?'"

Charmain's heart was banging in her chest as "Creole Time" nosed into Savannah's natural deep-sea port, which had originally attracted British settlers—and later, pirates—to its shores. They sailed up the Savannah River, docked and were met by Patrick's chauffeur-driven Bentley. Bags loaded, they drove along the bustling riverfront dotted with boutiques, artists' studios, galleries, pubs, and restaurants.

They turned away from the river. Charmain got her first look at a Savannah trademark, live oaks draped with hanging Spanish moss. The architecture was breathtaking, like stepping back in time, gingerbread-trim houses with deep verandas, painted in pinks and reds and blues and greens.

Patrick explained that the city was built around neighborhood squares. As they moved south on Bull Street, Patrick pointed out two of the most beautiful, Johnson Square and Wright Square.

"Now we're coming up on Chippewa Square, which you might recognize, because right over there is the bench Forrest Gump sat on and told the story of his life."

They drove past Savannah's focal point, Forsyth Park, where crowds strolled and sat around its picturesque cast-iron fountain. They swung around the park and headed north on Abercorn Street. Patrick lived two blocks from Calhoun Square. When the car pulled up, Charmain gasped.

"Oh, Patrick, it's just beautiful...like a fairytale castle."

"It's almost a perfect copy of a villa in Monaco from the late 1800s, built by a cotton merchant for his young mistress, who later murdered him in the drawing room. But don't get any ideas. They caught her and hanged her. Legend, or a smart real estate promoter, has it that both their ghosts still walk the halls. But I've never seen them."

A maid opened the front door. She said, "Welcome home, sir. Welcome, ma'am. My name is Marie. What would you like to drink?"

They walked inside. It was exquisitely furnished. "Sort of ante-bellum Southern-fried French decor," said Patrick. "But I like it."

"How long have you lived here?"

"Nearly ten years. We're an old New Orleans family, but I fell in love with this place."

"So your parents live in New Orleans?"

Patrick's face darkened. "No, they died some years ago. Just one sister now, some cousins, aunts, uncles. You know. Come, let me show you your room."

Charmain pouted as they walked up a winding staircase to the second floor. "I thought I'd be sleeping with you."

Patrick laughed. "Come on, Charmain. Start learning to live like the upper crust, darling. It's the only way. Man and wife always have separate bedrooms. One does one's toilette, changes clothes, or sleeps in one's own bedroom. Fucking is done—by appointment only, mind you—in the master's bedroom. The master, however, can visit milady's sleeping chamber and ravish her anytime he pleases."

Charmain rolled her eyes. "Sounds good, the way you explain it. Ohgod, what a gorgeous room. It's all so pink and girly. This is where you bed all your women?"

Patrick walked over to a dressing table, picked up a large engraved business card and handed it to Charmain. She looked at it and tears stung her eyes. It read: ROLF TALIAFERRO, INTERIOR DESIGN.

On it, a handwritten note: "Patrick...Not bad for a week's notice, eh? Hope she loves it...Rolf."

She said, "You did this for me?"

"Like it?"

"Tu es l'homme parfait," she said, still crying. She wiped her eyes. "Did I say that right? I tried to say you're a perfect man. But it sounds like I called you an ice cream."

"I don't mind being called an ice cream."

She laughed and threw herself at him. "You're an ice cream cone...let me lick you!"

"Have you made an appointment, madame?"

For the next few weeks, Charmain walked in a dream. Patrick and Savannah wove her in a spell so powerful she felt reborn. A new person. Patrick seemed truly in love. He proudly introduced her to his circle of friends. Upper-crust to downright weird, they all were exciting, fun, smart. She and Patrick had breakfast most mornings at Clary's Cafe, a hangout for colorful Savannah insiders, where Patrick introduced her to John Berendt, author of *Midnight In The Garden of Good an Evil.* And to Lady Chablis, the notorious black drag queen made famous by "The Book." That's how it was known in Savannah, as "The Book." And it had affected, in some way great or small, the life of every Savannahian. After it hit as a runaway best-seller, tourism in the city increased by a whopping forty-six percent. Real estate prices soared. Many local folks were making money selling souvenirs, conducting walking tours. Lady Chablis had not one, but two Internet websites. And everybody talked about "The Book." The old guard aristocrats hated it, or so they said. The gay community loved it. And everyone was fascinated by it.

Patrick bought Charmain a copy and she shyly offered it to John

Berendt for his author's signature one morning at Clary's Cafe. Charmain started reading it avidly, and the very first night she said to Patrick: "Darling, I just love the writing. Listen to this..."

And she read him a passage. After a while, she stopped, but he motioned her to continue. The next day, he tossed another book at her, *Dialogues & Monologues for Actors*. From a play called *Dark Moontide*, he chose a soliloquy by a character named Sloane and said, "Would you read this to me, darling? The character is talking about meeting the first man she ever loved."

Charmain smiled. "That should be easy for me to read," she said.

She began. The words caught her. She was swept up into the soul of an Irish girl, not much older than she, facing a lonely death in the emergency ward of a foreign hospital and recalling the sorrow of a love lost, but never regretted. Wrenched by a growing passion that shook her soul, Charmain spoke Sloane's final words:

"A part of me is him until death takes me. And even then...and even then..."

Charmain suddenly became aware that her words were still ringing in the room. Not like an echo. But hanging in the air somehow. Patrick stared at her. Then, slowly, he began to applaud. Clapping his hands, and not softly. Still applauding, he got up and walked across the room and stood before her. He stopped finally, and said, "That was a brilliant reading."

She said, "Sorry. I got a bit carried away."

Patrick looked at her thoughtfully.

"Could I ask you a favor, darling?"

"Anything, Patrick."

"Well, it's been years since I read 'The Book.' Most of us in Savannah read it the day it came out, practically. I often think of reading it again. Would you mind reading it to me? From the beginning."

"Oh Patrick, I'd love to."

"You don't mind reading aloud?"

"No. Actually, it's kind of fun. In fact, would you do something for me? Would you stop me if I mispronounce words, or drop my g's like a Florida redneck? And tell me what words mean if I don't understand them?"

"It's a deal. Let's begin tonight."

CHAPTER 23

**PATRICK TAULERE'S MANSION
SAVANNAH**

IN May 1981, a rich antiques dealer in his fifties, Jim Williams, stood behind the desk of the study in his magnificent redbrick mansion on Savannah's Monterey Square and faced his blonde, twenty-one year-old male lover, Danny Hansford, a street hustler described as "a walking streak of sex."

According to testimony in his four murder trials, Jim Williams claimed that Danny, known for a violent temper and intemperate use of drugs and alcohol, was brandishing a pistol and threatening his life. Danny fired, missed. Jim whipped an antique German Luger automatic out of a desk drawer and shot Danny to death.

Self-defense, as Jim Williams claimed? Or murder? The case, with its succulent overlay of steamy, illicit sex and hanky-panky in high society, mesmerized Savannah through years of trials that ended in Jim Williams' acquittal. And it fascinated the nation when John Berendt, a New York writer and producer who'd moved to Savannah after falling in love with the city, wrote the story and made it a best-seller.

Now "The Book" had worked its voodoo on Charmain. Night after night, she read it to Patrick. Then they'd talk endlessly about the story and rich characters, some of whom—like Lady Chablis and Berendt—Charmain had already met. Patrick had even known Jim Williams, who'd died in 1990, even though the crime had taken place years before he'd left New Orleans for Savannah. One evening, Patrick asked Charmain if she'd mind if he invited an old friend over to hear her read.

"Oh, Patrick, no one wants to hear me read except you. And you only listen because you love me."

"That's not true..."

She threw him a pout. "It's not true that you love me?"

"It's not true that I only listen to you because I love you. I do love you. But I think you read brilliantly. In fact, I think you show great talent as an actress, and I'd like to..."

"So it is true you love me?"

Patrick grinned. "Darling, stay focused, please. Look, there's a brilliant old man named Merce Buckingham who was quite a successful producer on Broadway back in the 1940s. And when he was a young actor, he worked in England's Royal Shakespeare Company. He's a smart, crotchety old bastard and I've asked him to listen to you and see what he thinks. Maybe give you some tips."

"Oh Patrick, I don't know. Me, an actress?"

"What are you going to be in life? A beauty queen? It's a career with built-in obsolescence, *chérie*."

Charmain smiled slyly. "I thought I might become a cute little housewife with an apron. Take cooking classes in Creole cuisine, *mon amour*."

"And after sampling all those rich sauces in your kitchen, your ass will acquire great volume and spread out until you have great difficulty negotiating the kitchen door, *petite chou*. I'd rather come home at night to fuck a slinky actress who has to watch her million-dollar derriere."

"French pig. *Cochon!*"

"Oink-oink. So, what do you say, babe? Tomorrow night. You'll love Merce. He's a character."

She smiled and snuggled up to him. "Okay. But only for the sake of my ass."

"Speaking of your ass, darling, shall we retire to the boudoir?"

"Love to, monsieur."

Merce Buckingham was a riot. Over dinner at Patrick's mansion, he told hilarious anecdotes about show business in its most glamorous days. Even when the stories were about people Charmain had never heard of—Noel Coward, Talullah Bankhead, Ethel Merman—she found them fascinating. When she told him that, meaning it as a compliment, color mottled the parchment-white skin of the still-handsome old man. He jabbed a finger at her and roared:

"Why *don't* you know these people? Why? And don't tell me it's because you're too young to have known them, goddamnit! Have you no sense of history? Don't you know that those who ignore history are doomed to repeat its mistakes? Or am I going too fast for you, little cracker girl? It may surprise you to learn that Julius Caesar wasn't a school chum of mine, but I still know WHO THE FUCK HE WAS!"

Charmain sat very still, arched an eyebrow, and gave him a level stare.

"Julius who?" she said sweetly.

A moment of stunned silence. Merce Buckingham fixed her with his most intimidating glare...then burst into laughter.

He told Patrick, "You were right. She's an actress. She's got the instincts of a diva—which is quite different from just being a bitch, you know, although it's part of it. And her comic timing when she delivered that line. AH! Delicious. Devastating. Now, let's go hear you read."

After one chapter of "The Book," Merce held up his hand.

"You must forgive me, beautiful young creature, but the days when I happily stayed up till dawn, drunk on wine and heady words from the mouths of actors, have long since passed.

"Now, let me sum up as I see it. Your diction is slovenly, but not hopeless. Not bad, actually, considering your background. And don't be offended by that. One way or another, we are all hicks, y'all! Diction can be easily fixed. Work on it!

"Your instinct for dramatic tension is promising. You go for the throat. And I have already mentioned that your timing is flawless. Charmain, I have saved the best for last. What's extraordinary is that your energy is almost frightening. Wolf-like. Devouring. You have awesome resources for a career on the stage. Including the two MOST important."

"What are those…er, they?" she asked.

"Terrific tits and a great ass, of course. Congratulations, my dear, and good luck to you."

Merce struggled to rise from the comfortable wing chair as Patrick leaped to assist him.

"Congratulations to you, too, my boy," he said with a broad wink.

"Thank you so much for coming," Patrick said.

"It was a wonderful meal. I'd like to steal your chef. Look, there's only one way for her to develop her talent. And that's to work. And to work, she needs to go to New York, or London, or even that hellhole Los Angeles. She's got something. It's what she does with it."

As Charmain drifted into sleep that night, the colorful world Merce Buckingham had described filled her dreams…

A musical fanfare blared. Curtains rose. She was on a stage. Alone. Lights blinded her, but she lifted her chin and walked forward, seeking the audience. She sensed them out there, ravening, waiting to devour. A pack of wolves. But no! She was the wolf. She would devour, not they. Flinging out her arms, smiling, she cried, "Do I make you believe? Am I an actor?" Shouts. A roar of applause. Her soul caught fire. She felt pure joy, like a newborn. House lights up. She peered from the stage into the crowd and—Dear God! There…in the first row, cheering and clapping wildly.

Her mother.

Sitting between the two drifters, who grinned and winked slyly at Charmain, shouting…

"Bravo!…BRAVO!"

Charmain screamed, jerked awake sobbing, drenched in sweat, thrashing as Patrick reached for her.

"What's wrong, *chérie*? Sshh…You were having a nightmare."

He held her, rocked her. She drifted back to sleep.

CHAPTER 24

PATRICK TAULERE'S MANSION
SAVANNAH

LIFE settled into a pleasant routine in the mansion off Calhoun Square. Patrick had hired a diction coach for Charmain, a Mrs. Lily DuChamps, an ancient English lady who had toured the provinces of Great Britain in minor roles with the Royal Shakespeare company after the war, then married the visiting heir to an old Savannah fortune.

Mr. DuChamps, sadly, had expired after drinking and gambling away most of his inheritance. His still-elegant widow supplemented the nest egg she'd prudently socked away by giving acting and diction lessons. She came to the house every morning after breakfast. Never a great actress, she was a brilliant teacher.

She told Charmain: "Remember, the purpose of all these interminable exercises in stretching your facial and glottal muscles is not to teach you to speak in some affected, quasi-British fashion. It is to allow you to have the vocal tools necessary to shape your natural voice and inflections any way you choose. A comely bustline and trim ankles are powerful weapons in a lady's aresenal, but a pleasing first impression can be quickly ruined by a shrill, squeaky voice and careless diction."

After each lesson, Charmain would walk out into the garden and practice everything she'd learned. She'd walk up and down under the moss-covered oaks hanging over riotous flowerbeds, and made strange sounds:

"EE-WAH-WAH-EE-WOW-WOW-WOOOOOOO...DWA-DWA-DAY-WEEEWWW..."

And on and on.

After the vocal exercises, she'd choose a monologue from the actor's audition manual Patrick had given her and attack it aloud, first turning on a tiny portable tape recorder. She'd listen to the tapes every few days, and was secretly elated when she heard her voice turn richer, deeper, more precise. And she now had the ability to control her accent, modulating its natural Southern undertones, from a whiny redneck twang to a sexy drawl redolent of magnolia and mint julep. Damn, I sound so cool, she thought. I can play my voice like an instrument, just like Mrs. DuChamps said. Folks in Citrus City wouldn't believe it was me talkin'.

Patrick spent most mornings locked up in his study, doing business. Charmain still wasn't clear exactly what his business was and had never been introduced to any of his business associates, only social friends. The few times she'd inquired casually about his affairs, Patrick had shrugged off the subject. He left the impression that he came from old money and conducted business mainly to keep himself occupied, enjoying it as a sort of game one played to maintain mental alertness.

Not that Charmain had confided much about herself. She'd told Patrick the bare bones: that her mother had been murdered in a horrible home break-in; that her father was still living in Citrus Corners. If Patrick had pressed her, she probably would have told him everything. She knew she was incapable of lying to him if he really wanted to know.

For the first time in her life, she truly wanted to share her soul. But Patrick didn't pry, exercising what she figured was a gentlemanly reserve. And that set the pattern. They talked endlessly about everything under the sun. But never about the past. Charmain wasn't troubled about it. Life was too perfect. Why talk about what could never be changed when the future looked so exciting, so hopeful? Looking forward to every new day was a new feeling for Charmain.

Most days, Patrick would seek her out in the garden just after noon. They'd take a swim in the pool, then eat a light lunch served by the staff. They'd sit, chatting and laughing, and plan the rest of their day and evening. Sometimes Patrick would hustle Charmain into the shade of a thick arbor of honeysuckle and hibiscus, where they were invisible from the house or the street, and take her standing up. Then they'd go inside and change. Once or twice a week, they'd go out deep-sea fishing on "Creole Time" and spend a night aboard.

Other days, Charmain would take off on afternoon shopping expeditions. Patrick rarely accompanied her, but always handed her a wad of cash, telling her to send the chauffeur home for more if she needed it. It bothered her at first to take his money, but when she objected, he thrilled her by saying, "It gives me great pleasure to make you happy, *chérie*. Now, why do you want to make me sad?"

Patrick enjoyed fine restaurants. Three or four nights a week, they dined haute cuisine at Elizabeth on 37th, The Pirate's House, or Charmain's favorite, the ritzy 45 South, where Patrick introduced her to the exquisite grilled venison with sweet potato au gratin. Once a week, on Friday night, Patrick hosted a dinner party for no more than ten guests at the mansion. Charmain took to playing hostess easily. She treated these soirees as a vehicle for testing her diction and role-playing ability. She'd catch Patrick looking at her proudly and thrilled when he told her, "You are the belle of the ball, *ma belle*."

For Charmain, nights were the rich topping of every delicious day. She adored the custom of separate bedrooms. Each evening, she'd go upstairs alone, draw a bath and soak luxuriously, then apply light eye makeup and select a sexy nightgown, silk pajamas, or camisole. At this point, she'd call down to Patrick on the intercom, suggesting he come up to bed. Next she'd select a pair of mules with high platforms. She'd bought about a dozen pairs after Patrick told her he loved her to come to him shod in anything high-heeled. After checking herself in a full-length mirror, she'd walk to Patrick's bedroom and knock softly on the door.

"Entre, belle du jour," he'd always say.

She'd sashay in, strike a pose and say innocently, *"Monsieur...desirez-vous quelque chose?"*

And the games would begin.

Once, just once, Patrick had broken her tidy routine. She had barely settled into the tepid water of her bath when the door opened and he strode in, naked under his silk dressing gown, in obvious arousal. She said, "Patrick, what the hell...?" and was yanked out of the tub and up into his arms. He stood her in front of the wide marble counter. Before she could speak, he turned her around roughly to face the waist-high counter. He put his hand on her back and forced her down. Belly and breasts shivered as they mashed into cold marble. Charmain looked into the scene reflected in mirrors running the full perimeter of the bathroom. An erotic montage of angles never seen, only dreamed about.

She gasped as he thrust into her. Her eyes closed. She felt his fingers twist in her hair. He pulled, forcing her head up.

"Open your eyes and see how gorgeous you look when I'm fucking you, little girl," he said.

He pulled back slowly, barely inside her now, teasing. Suddenly snapped his hips and drove into her. Yanking back on her hair again just as her eyes involuntarily started to shut. She faced the mirror and looked deep into her own soul. Watched her eyes widen and roll as she moaned in helpless pleasure.

Patrick was relentless, working her like a machine, never letting her close her eyes. For the first time ever, Charmain witnessed her own wrenching orgasm. And his.

After she caught her breath, she looked at the mirror and focused on Patrick's eyes. Still inside her, caressing her breasts, he said, "Sorry to break your nightly tradition, sweet girl. But I needed you immediately. And in this house, I am the master."

He winked and slapped her ass.

She shifted weight, cocked her hip. Ground it into him.

"Did you hear a complaint...master?"

Often, they'd talk in the dark after making love. One night, he said to her, "You know, I've been thinking a lot lately about how lucky I am. I've tried to look ahead at my life and see where I'm going. Make a new plan. It sounds corny, like one of those self-help magazine articles. But setting goals really works. You just kind of imagine yourself in a place doing something, and suddenly one day you're there. It really is damn near magical. It could work for you."

Charmain got attentive. "Like how?"

"Well, let me tell you. First, I got this idea years ago when I was just a kid starting out. Like any young guy, I wanted to do something big, exciting, important. Most of all, I wanted to get rich. I mean, I had some money, of course. But I wanted to build a real fortune. I started reading a lot about success and making money. I wanted to crack the secret of how to make things happen. One day, I read this amazing story about the president of Matsushita, a giant Japanese electronics company. This man had written out a one-hundred year plan for his company. Imagine that, Charmain!! A detailed plan that laid out exactly where the company would be in one century—long after this man was in his grave.

"Now this wasn't the usual blah-blah crap about working hard, keeping one's eye on the ball, using good business sense, et cetera. No, this man spelled out, step-by-step, exactly how the company would achieve its goals. It was a mind-blower. I started thinking. And realized that I'd never really looked ahead more than a few days, weeks maybe, into my own life. I mean, in a serious way.

"And then it dawned on me! Most people were just like I was, just moving along in life, day by day, with no specific idea of what they really wanted and how they'd get it. And most people, like me, hadn't made a big success of their lives. Sure, everybody wants success. Money, fame, respect, security. But the majority never get it. Successful people are a minority. And that's the minority I wanted to join. So I started studying successful people. Tried to figure out their secret.

"Well, to make this long story short, I discovered that they share certain attributes. You know, willingness to work hard, early to bed, early to rise—all that *merde*. But when I boiled it down to its essence, the secret ingredient common to every success story—outside of lucky stuff like winning the lottery—is planning. Setting the goal, formulating a detailed plan and a rigid timetable. So I sat down and did it. Actually wrote it out. And, boy, did it ever work for me."

He squeezed her in the dark. "Have I put you to sleep yet?"

She hugged him back. "No. Don't stop. I love this! What happened?"

"Well, I knew something about the shipping business, but it wasn't until I set my plan in motion that I started to achieve success. And most of my goals became reality even quicker than I'd expected. And I've had so much success that, in just the past few months, I've achieved every goal in my plan. I now have all the money I'll ever need in life. So—it's time for a new plan. Time to do something other than just make money. I want to help people. Maybe set up a foundation to help kids. I'm writing the plan now. That's why I've been so busy lately."

"Wow!" she said. "You sound like one of those motivational guys on TV!"

Patrick laughed. "What a great business they've got! Selling the product called success. Everybody wants to buy. How about you, my darling? You have a really exciting destiny as an actress. I've been thinking about bankrolling you myself, maybe going to Hollywood and becoming a producer. I believe everybody should seek their own destiny. You want to try my secret for success? Make your own plan for life?"

"It sounds so exciting, Patrick. But how do I start?"

"With the hardest part of all. Deciding what you want from life. Not just, 'I want to be rich,' but precisely *how* rich. Then you spell out exactly how you plan to become rich. And exactly when! Then you live life according to the plan. It's that simple, darling. Want to try it?"

"Okay," she said. "My biggest goal is to—"

His fingers pressed lightly on her lips. "Not now, my sweet. Bedtime is for dreaming. Start tomorrow. On your own. Get a yellow legal pad or something and start writing everything down. It will take you a while. It's not as easy as it sounds. But it'll be one of the most exciting things you'll ever do. I promise you."

"Oh, Patrick, I love you." She snuggled up to him. "You're sexy, you're handsome and smart. You *must* be smart. You're so goddamn rich!"

Next morning he awoke early, as usual, and she was gone. A note was pinned to her pillow:

"Darling—Won't be having breakfast with you. Working on 'The Plan.' Canceled Mrs. DuChamps. See you at lunch. Love you! Charmain."

Just after noon, he was sitting in the garden and heard a taxi pull up out in the narrow service alley that ran alongside the house. A moment later, Charmain sailed through the side gate, wearing shorts, a skimpy halter, sunglasses, and a big floppy hat.

"There's my wonderful lover man. *L'homme formidable.*"

She jumped on his lap and kissed him.

"Sweetheart, I've missed you so much," she said. "But I felt like I was with you. Every minute I could hear your voice, telling me how to write"— she dropped her voice comically, mimicking him—"The Plan!!"

He laughed. "So that's what you've been up to. I wondered what could get you out of bed ahead of me. But where were you?"

"Down at the docks, sitting on the afterdeck of 'Creole Time.' The chef brought me cappucino and croissants. I had absolute peace and quiet. And look!"

She fished a yellow legal pad out of her purse and waved it triumphantly.

"I've done pages and pages of my plan, but I have lots more to go. You're so right, Patrick, the hardest part is what I thought would be the easiest—just trying to figure out exactly what I want in life. But I think I made a great start. Listen to this—"

He held up a hand. "Whoa! Don't discuss your plan until it's finished."

Charmain pouted. "But, darling, I want you to hear it. Please? I'll just read a little bit."

"Well, okay, but…Whoops! Look what's happened," he said, deftly untying the top string on her halter top.

"Oh, bastard," she squealed, squirming out of his lap as she pulled the top back up over her breasts. "Marie might see us. Stop trying to distract me."

He grinned broadly, white teeth flashing against his tan. God, she thought, he's so handsome. She suddenly got hot, wanting him.

"Okay," he said, "here's the deal. I've been working on my new plan, too, as I told you. New goals, new directions, the works. And I'm damn near finished. So, tonight we'll have dinner here at home, just the two of us. And we'll both unveil our plans. I have high hopes that mine will interest you very much."

Her heart leapt. Something in the way he'd said it…

She felt suddenly shy. "Does it have me anywhere in it?"

He shrugged his shoulders and threw out his hands. Teasing. Looking very Gallic. Oh God, she thought, her heart racing. Something's goin' on here.

He said, "Dinner at 8 o'clock, then?"

Charmain, fighting to appear calm, smiled seductively. "Okay. But I need to see you before then. Say, at siesta time?"

"On a strictly non-verbal basis, I presume?"

"Presume your muscle-bound ass off, Frenchie. I swear my lips will be sealed, if y'all catch my meanin'?"

He raised his eyebrows. "My 'muscle-bound ass'? What the hell have you been smoking, girl?"

She burst out laughing. Marie came out of the house bearing a tray. Lunch was served. Later, over iced tea, she looked at her watch, then gathered up her purse and kissed him.

"Patrick, I really do have two or three things to pick up at the shops. But I will be back in time for a siesta. I got up so early this morning."

He patted her behind. "I'll 'get up' the minute you get back—if y'all catch *my* meanin'?" he said, winking.

She giggled, kissed him again. "Okay if I take your car?"

"Everything I have is yours, as the song says, *ma chérie*. Hurry back."

"Bye, Patrick!"

"*A bientôt, belle fille…*"

At the gate, she looked back. He waved.

CHAPTER 25

3:05 P.M.
PATRICK TAULERE'S MANSION
SAVANNAH

CHARMAIN arrived back at the mansion just after three o'clock. As Patrick's chauffeur opened the door and helped her out, a distant rumble of thunder drifted through the hot, still air. Clouds rolled in from the bay and spread softly across Savannah.

"Looks like we're about to get it," said the chauffeur. "Would you like some help with those packages, Miss Charmain?"

"No, Claude, I'm just fine. The garden could use the rain, though. It's been dry this month."

Perfect siesta weather, she thought. Nothing more romantic than afternoon rainfall. She tingled, looking forward to the sex. Why does missing sleep always makes me horny? Well, nothin's nicer than a nap after a good fuck.

Claude's sing-song voice cut through her daydream.

"...and so if you and Mr. Patrick don't need the car, Miss Charmain, I'll take it on down to get it gassed up. Don't think I'll get it washed, though. Wait to see what this rain's goin' do, first. Uh-huh..."

She spoke over her shoulder as she unlocked the black iron gate.

"No, that's fine. We don't need the car right now."

"Yes, ma'am. I'll be back in a few minutes, anyhow. Marie's probably wantin' me to get some things at the market. Says y'all are dinin' in tonight."

She heard the car drive off as she walked up to the front door. She half-expected Marie to open it and stand there, smiling, greet her. She often did when she heard the car pull up. But not this time.

Charmain fumbled for her key, found it, and opened the door. She walked in, kicking it shut behind her, and put her bags down on the hall table. As the sound of crinkling paper subsided, it struck her that the house was strangely still. She paused. Looked down the hallway to her left toward the closed kitchen door. Where was Marie? Ordinarily, she'd be bustling through it by now if—

Charmain cocked her head. Something strange...her senses struggled to identify it. Was it in the air?

"Marie?...Patrick?..."

Her voice echoed emptily.

Again, she sensed…what? What *was* that? She breathed in sharply. Now the appropriate sense kicked in. Smell. Some faint smell in the air. An odor alien to this locale, this house. But what…?

Olfactory glands fired her memory. Identified the scent.

No!

Her mind denied it.

Ohgod, no…no…NO…

Couldn't be!

But it was.

Unmistakable.

In a split second, her ears filled with a shrieking, keening wail. Like a siren. A wild animal dying. *Her* voice. Screaming. Standing there paralyzed by sheer terror. Knowing now this house she loved had been invaded…violated…knowing it as her lungs filled with that never-forgotten sickly-sweet smell.

Nausea lurched her gut…

That filthy, vomitous scent.

Cologne…!

"NoooOOOOOOOOOHHHHH!…NOOOOOOO!…PATRICK!"

Sudden fury ripped through her panic. Adrenalin pumped, releasing her paralyzed limbs. She snatched at her purse, yanked out her 9mm and ran down the long hallway that stretched straight ahead. Toward the closed double doors of the great room, where Patrick often sat in front of the fireplace, reading, sipping a drink. She prayed she'd find him there now.

"PATRICK?…ANSWER ME!…PATRICK!"

She slammed through the doors. Saw the back of his chair. For one split second, her heart almost leaped out of her chest.

Yes, he was there. There's his arm…

All wrong, She knew it. His right arm hung limp. Something shiny encircled the wrist. Oh Jesus.

Handcuffs.

She swung the gun around the room.

He could still be here.

Finger hot on the trigger, she shrieked his name.

"PACO!!"

"MOTHERFUCKER!…I'LL KILL YOU!"

Nothing. She ran to Patrick. Faced the chair. And everything…everything…just drained out of her. Her gun dropped to the floor. Instinct made her hold out her hands. To comfort, to heal.

But the blood…too much blood…in his lap…and…dripping from—She saw the spike then. Her body spasmed, chilled by the cold steel glinting under the lamp that had lit Patrick's final agonies. It pointed straight up out of his right eye, like some obscene signpost marking death's final path.

Charmain fell to her knees. Looked into his poor, dead face. Dry-eyed, she spoke softly to him, hugging her arms and rocking back and forth. Long, shuddering sobs wracked her. Then wild, howling screams as her soul struggled to burst out of her and find him again.

No one heard.

After a time, her hand clawed out, searching the floor.

Found the gun. Held it mindlessly. Screaming. Screaming.

A voice said, "Oh, sweet Jesus."

She felt an arm go around her.

The voice spoke, quiet and calm in her ear.

"No, Miss Charmain, no more death in this house today. Mr. Patrick would not want that, Miss Charmain. You know he wouldn't, now. You know I'm tellin' you the truth."

She shuddered. The screaming stopped. Still she stared rigidly at Patrick. Oh, God! My sweet Patrick…

Claude slipped the gun out of her hand. Put it in his pocket. He knelt beside her, holding her around the shoulder, rocking her gently.

"Police and ambulance here in a minute, Miss Charmain. You just hold on now. You just hold on!"

She thought she heard screams again.

But it was sirens.

CHAPTER 26

11:40 A.M.
WILSHIRE BLVD.
BEVERLY HILLS

AFTER his carphone conversation with Charmain, Vidal Delaney U-turned back up Wilshire and gunned it. He speed-dialed his office on the carphone.

"Szabo."

"I'm two minutes away. I need you for a fast briefing. Have three of our best agents on standby. Full alert."

"Got it."

Vidal clicked off, dialed a number he knew well.

"Kelso Management, good morning."

"Vidal Delaney for Mike Kelso."

"Just a moment..."

"Vidal? What's up?"

"This is important, Mike. I need you at Firefly's in forty-five minutes."

Vidal had code names for clients. Firefly was Charmain.

"What's the—"

"I'm on a carphone. Just be there, Mike."

He clicked off as he rolled through the gates of the five-story Delaney Building. Boris Szabo, the cold-eyed ex-CIA agent who'd taken early retirement to become Vidal's No. 2, was waiting for him in the soundproof executive conference room. Vidal briefed him quickly on Bellini's death and his conversation with Charmain, including her unsettling remark: "I didn't want that."

Vidal said, "That's when I told her to speak to no one and hung up on her."

Szabo whistled softly. "You think she's involved?"

"I'm hoping she's not, but let's prepare for the worst. Make sure you've got specialists in every area standing by, including our three in-house guys. I'm heading over to Charmain's house. I don't want her seen coming here or doing anything out of the ordinary. You stand by here. I'll communicate on a portable scrambler phone. Okay, that's it. Have somebody from technical meet me downstairs with that scrambler unit, chop-chop."

As Vidal rolled through the gates of Charmain's mansion twenty minutes later, her entourage was leaving, most of them total strangers to

Vidal. That bothered him. He recognized Bonnie Farr and Laddy Burford. He got out of the car and said hello to Laddy.

"You must be the reason she's throwing us out," said Laddy. "She'd promised us lunch."

"Sorry," Vidal said.

"Oh, she's sending us over to the Beverly Hills Hotel pool for cabana munchies. Her treat."

"Great."

An unmarked van pulled through the gates. A man in a pale blue jumpsuit got out. Vidal pointed him to a gate leading to the pool and strode into the house.

Charmain was just coming down the staircase in a robe, looking pouty.

"Have your buddies been here all morning?" he asked.

"Yes," she said.

Good, he thought. An alibi.

Charmain's manager, Mike Kelso, fifty-ish and mild-mannered, arrived moments later. Charmain started to talk, but Vidal motioned for silence and led both of them them out onto the pool-patio area.

He said quietly, "No talking until the technician I've brought with me does his job."

They watched as the man in the coveralls swept the area with a wand attached to a black box, then went inside the house for several minutes. Finally, he emerged and gave a thumbs-up to Vidal.

"All clear," he said.

Vidal nodded and told him, "Walk the perimeter. Make sure our meeting stays private. Keep a particular watch for photographers."

Kelso, annoyed now, said, "Vidal, will you tell me what the hell's going on?"

"That was a sweep for bugs and now I've posted security, Mike. Come inside. We need to talk."

He looked at Charmain. "How about the den?"

She shrugged and led them inside. They sat and Vidal said:

"First, everything said in this room is off the record forever. Right?"

Charmain and Kelso nodded.

Vidal said, "Okay. Mike, have you heard on the news about the death of Steve Bellini, the *Revealer* editor?"

"No. Isn't that the guy who did the horse story we're suing over?"

"That's him. He went out a window at the Camino Rio Hotel and crashed on a patio seven floors below. Bizarre. He practically fell into Noel Gold's lap while he was pitching a project to Meryl Olivier. Neither of them was hurt and had nothing to do with this, apparently."

Kelso looked at Charmain, then said, "I'm still mystified. Why are we all sitting here?"

Vidal shrugged and said matter-of-factly, "Because Charmain gave me an indication, during a brief phone call after the event, that she was involved somehow. We're here because our job is to protect Charmain."

Vidal looked at her. She stared back. He pursed his lips and waited.

Kelso spoke, like he couldn't quite catch his breath. "Charmain, is it true? Did you have something to do with this? You've got to tell us."

Charmain snapped, "I don't have to tell you *shit.* You work for *me,* motherfucker!"

Kelso held out his hands appeasingly, but said nothing. He'd been here before.

Vidal said quietly, "I believe I just said that we are here to protect you, Charmain. We know we work for you. But how can we help you if—"

Charmain said impatiently, "Goddamnit, I want a joint."

She jumped up, walked to the doorway and yelled, "MARTA! BRING ME A JOINT."

She turned and smiled in mock sweetness at the men. "Join me?"

They shook their heads. A moment later, Marta came clattering down from upstairs. She handed Charmain a perfectly rolled joint and a Bic.

"Anyone want anything?" Marta asked.

Vidal said, "Nothing for me. Mike? No?...Marta, why don't you go and have lunch now. Come back in an hour."

"But I usually eat my lunch here...and..."

She slowed down like a wind-up toy under Vidal's steady stare.

She said, "Jesus...okay, I'll...just go and..."

Vidal said, "One hour. Not before."

Marta left. Charmain fired up the joint, inhaling deeply. She held it, exhaled slowly. Smiled like she'd been jump-started.

"Sooo, okay...What happened was, I wanted to scare Bellini. That's all. Kick his ass. Make him back off. Like, I couldn't believe it when you said he was dead. I mean, I don't even know why he's dead. I sent this guy to his hotel. This guy I just met. He's a boxer. A pro. The real thing. He was just supposed to go to Bellini's room like he was delivering something, then pop him once. I even told him, don't beat the shit out of the guy. Just one good shot, y'all...BAM! So what happened? How did Bellini end up dead? If Buster threw him out a window, that's on *his* head. It's not my fault, right?"

Vidal started to speak, then chilled.

Charmain paced, long legs flashing out of the robe. Took another hit, held it, exhaled.

"So, you want to ask me why I did it, right?"

She was right on the edge. Both Vidal and Mike Kelso had seen her in this mood. Anything could touch her off. Vidal thought, Thank God she's toking. It should calm her. Jesus, what a nasty mess this is.

Charmain faced them. "Okay, look. This bastard prints those pictures of me whipping that horse. And we're going to sue his ass, right? But I'm thinking, hey, why not just pop him? Scare his ass. And then offer not to file the lawsuit, which the lawyers say we probably can't win anyway."

Vidal shook his head. "I don't get why you had to scare him. Why not just drop the lawsuit?"

Charmain took another hit, exhaled. "Uh-uh. Kick his ass first, let him know I'm serious. Then drop the lawsuit to sweeten the deal."

"What deal?"

"*The Revealer* agrees to kill the story on my childhood that they're working on. Back in Florida. That's the last fucking thing I need right now, Vidal. I have to stop that story. Every time *The Revealer* does one of those 'Childhood Of The Stars' things, they always dig up dirt. They go back to your hometown and talk to every asshole who ever claimed to know you. And they'd never kill the story if we sued them. They'd go all out to dig up dirt on me. Stuff to use against me in the trial."

Vidal and Mike Kelso exchanged glances.

"Charmain, what trial?" Kelso said quietly. "Civil suits like this rarely go to trial. They're settled out of court. Am I right, Vidal?"

"Yeah. Charmain, what dirt? Those stories are just about kid stuff. Is there something...?"

"Vidal, what the green-eyed hell are you running your mouth about? Aren't you the one who talked me into paying you a whole lot of money to protect me against the tabloids? And maybe I'm losing my goddamn mind, but aren't you the one who told me, 'They can always dig up something on anybody'? Or am I just a dumb ol' Florida cracker?"

Vidal looked at her steadily.

"Both of you better start thinkin' about my career," she said. "First of all, it doesn't take a genius to figure out that if we file the lawsuit it's just going to keep that shit story about the horse in everybody's minds. Better if people forget about it. Especially Clive Tinsdale. Because it turns out that Mr. Red-Hot Director is one of those English gentleman types who loves horses more than pussy. He's some kind of mucky-muck in that horse organization that Princess Anne and Bo Derek and a bunch of Hollywood horse nuts run.

"So y'all listen, goddamnit, and listen good. Clive Tinsdale is one director I don't want to piss off. And you know why, Mike? Because I want the female lead in his next movie more than I've ever wanted anything in my life. I will star in 'Medusa' or die trying. Shit! If this had gone the way I laid it out, the horse thing would have faded away and Tinsdale wouldn't see me as some kind of horse-beating monster. Especially after I announce that I'm making a big fucking donation to their next horse charity show. Neat, huh?"

Charmain flopped down in a leather chair, took another hit, and said, "Look, that's the way I saw it. So Bellini's dead. Now what?"

Kelso was staring at the floor. Vidal cleared his throat, then said carefully,

"I'm not up to speed on this Medusa thing. Mike?"

Kelso looked like a man just back from a weekend in hell. He cleared his throat. Twice.

"Tinsdale is the hottest director in town right now, Vidal. His new film will be based on the legend of Medusa. You know, the harpy with snakes for hair, whose glance can turn men to stone. It's a modern version, about an actress who'd do anything, even commit murder, to become a leading lady. Every actress in town wants it." Charmain took another hit.

"I'd kill to get that part," she sighed.

A beat of silence. Both men glanced at her, anticipating an acknowledgement of the irony. Nothing.

Kelso went on. "Charmain is perfect for the role. And I think she has a chance. I've been talking to the studio, but it's really up to Tinsdale."

Charmain said, "The only good news is that Tinsdale's been in London for the past few weeks, so hopefully he didn't see that vicious item Cameron Tull wrote in his column. It said, 'A betting man would put Charmain Burns dead last in the *Medusa* horse race.' That sarcastic prick."

Vidal walked to the window, stared outside for a long moment. He turned to Charmain.

"My job is to protect you. What has happened can't be changed. But I must insist that in the future you keep me informed of any plans you make that could lead to legal difficulties like those we are facing now."

Charmain was on her feet, screaming at him.

"Don't you preach at me, goddamnit! I didn't get where I am in this town without bustin' a few balls. And NOBODY tells me what to do, you understand?"

"Perfectly," said Vidal, holding up a hand to cut off her tirade. "Now let's start figuring this out. First, I don't quite understand why you're so worried about this childhood profile that *The Revealer* plans on doing."

"You don't understand, Vidal. Those stories always make you look bad."

"Not unless you have something bad in your past. What are you worried about?"

"I'm not worried about anything in particular, goddamnit, and I'm not going to say it again. I just don't want them doing shit about my childhood...period!" she snapped. "My guy Buster was just supposed to warn him to stay out of Florida."

Vidal looked over at Kelso, who was glassy-eyed. Vidal thought, Jesus, how many different ways did she want to incriminate herself?

"Okay," he said. "Tell me about this boxer. Buster?"

"His name's Buster Brown. He's a professional boxer I met a couple of weeks ago. Some creepazoids outside BuzzBuzz hassled me and he beat the hell out of them. He's a real nice guy, very cool."

Annoyed, Vidal said, "Yeah, he's very cool...but he ended up killing Bellini. And that makes you an accessory to murder."

Charmain, genuinely puzzled, said, "Now who's talkin' crazy? It's not my fault this guy hit him too hard, or whatever."

Before Vidal could speak, Kelso broke in. "Charmain. Charmain, listen to what you're saying. Don't you understand that this boxer, this Buster, was in Bellini's room because you sent him? And if Steve Bellini died as a result of that, the law says you are complicit in the murder, or the accident, or whatever it is.

"And, do you think this Buster fellow is going to keep silent about your part in this when the police pick him up? I can assure you he will not. He will point the finger at you. Oh, my God, this is a nightmare. A nightmare. Weren't you thinking? About your career? After all our hard work—"

"SHUT UP! SHUT UP! YOU FUCKING OLD LADY! YOU PUSSY...YOU..."

Vidal moved swiftly, grabbing Charmain just as she leaped at Kelso and started clawing at him. He dragged her over to the sofa, tossed her down on it.

"Stop, Charmain...Right now, stop! We can't do this. Be cool. We're here to help you. You've got to help us."

He pinned her into a pile of throw pillows. She stopped struggling.

Kelso stood up and walked over to retrieve the still-lit joint that had flown out of her hand and burned a pinprick hole in the carpet.

"Here, Charmain, take a hit," he said, holding it out. "It will make you feel better. And stop being angry at us. That's not what this is about."

Charmain looked up at Vidal.

"May I have one arm free, please?" she purred. "Pretty please? So I can suck on that gorgeous joint? If I can say that in mixed company?"

Vidal laughed in exasperation. He let her up. Charmain reached out, as if to take the joint, and patted Kelso sharply on the cheek.

"I'm sorry, Mike-y," she crooned. "You do love me, don't you?"

Kelso laughed shakily. "You know I...we all do, Charmain."

She took the joint from his hand, slowly, caressing his fingers. She took a long drag, then reached down to rearrange the robe over her legs, which had been exposed in the struggle.

"Thank heavens this is one of those rare occasions when I'm actually wearing panties," she said, glancing up seductively. "There is something so reassuring about sensible white cotton panties, don't you think? Now, let's figure out what we're going to do, boys."

Charmain looked at Vidal questioningly.

"Obviously," he said, "what we're going to do is lay this whole thing on the boxer. We've just got to figure out the right spin. And it would be better if we get to him before the cops. Even if we do, we have no idea what he'll tell the police once they start grilling him. Even if we pay him off, there are no guarantees once someone realizes he's facing years behind bars."

That hit Charmain hard. Fuck! No guarantees? Years behind bars? Vidal's right, she thought. I can't trust Buster. And how about Vidal?

He started firing questions at her. Have you seen or heard from Buster Brown since Bellini's death?

No.

Did you pay Buster any money?

Yes.

Do you know where he hangs out?

At some gym.

What gym?

Don't know.

Will he contact you again for more money?

Not money. Help in becoming an actor.

When will he contact you?

Don't know.

Anything else about him I should know?

No.

She giggled inwardly. She wanted to answer:

Yes, I fucked him.

Just to catch the look on his face.

Vidal said, "The first thing to consider is that he can blackmail you."

"I don't think so," Charmain said.

"Why not?"

"Because he's ga-ga over me, for one. And he can't stop talking about becoming the next black action hero in the movies, for another. Look, I know the acting bug when I see it, honey, and this guy's bit bad."

Vidal said, "Okay. I guess we sit tight until we know more. I've got my people checking their police sources. Charmain, are you sure there's nothing more I should know? Anything that could connect you to this?"

Charmain paused. "Well, it's no big deal, but…I left a message on his sister's answering machine."

Vidal turned to stone.

"What do you mean?"

"Well, you know, I kinda wanted to rub it in, so I called that bitch, Jessica Bell. You know, the designer, who changed her fucking name from Bellini, that stuck-up cunt. I hate her because of that time she dissed me when I was—"

Vidal roared, "Goddamnit, Charmain, what did you say to her?"

"It wasn't much," she pouted. "I said something like, 'Hi, hope Steve liked the flowers'…and that was it, I swear…"

Kelso held his head. Migraine time.

"Oh, God, Charmain. What were you thinking?"

"Shit, she won't know it's my voice."

"But there are ways to ID a voice electronically."

"Oh, fuck, more paranoid old lady bullshit. Who's gonna do *that*?"

Vidal, who'd gotten very still, said absently, "She will, once she finds out her brother's dead. Do you know where she lives?"

"Not exactly. Somewhere in Pacific Palisades, I think. Vidal…?"

He ignored her, walked swiftly out of the den and outside to his car. He clicked on the portable scrambled phone and punched in Szabo's direct line. They talked for three minutes. Vidal briefed him on what he'd learned from Charmain.

Szabo, fast on the uptake, said, "You want me to send someone to retrieve that tape, right?"

"Yes. If she hasn't heard it already. And if she's there when our agent arrives, break off. I don't want any heavy stuff. This is bad enough already."

"Understood. And I suggest that our man leave a bug in her residence. Then we can learn if she did hear the message."

"And other useful things, perhaps. Good idea. Now, what do we know about the Bellini investigation? You talked to our cop shop sources?"

Szabo filled him in. Vidal hung up, went back inside.

"The news isn't all bad," he told them. "The cops have no suspect and no good leads. What they've pieced together is that someone posing as a flower delivery man slugged Bellini. The blow knocked him back onto a room service cart, which then shot out onto the balcony and pitched Bellini overboard."

"That's *it!*" Charmain exclaimed.

"That's what?"

"That's why Buster hasn't called me. He doesn't know Bellini's dead. He probably popped him and turned right around to scoot out of there. I'll bet he never saw Bellini fall back on the cart and go out the window. And believe me, Buster's not the kind of guy who listens to radio or TV news. And it won't hit the papers until tomorrow. He probably hasn't heard anything yet."

Vidal mulled it over. "You could be right. That makes it even more important to get hold of him right away. Before he does hear anything. If the cops get to him first and tell him, he'll be so freaked about the possibility of a murder charge that he'll finger you. You're sure you have no idea how to find him?"

"Look, you're the goddamn investigator, Vidal. Why don't you investigate?"

Vidal nodded. "Fair enough. Let's find him and get this behind us."

Kelso said, "Don't you think we should call in Charmain's lawyer? What if the police find Buster and suddenly show up here?"

"There'll be time enough to call your lawyer, before you say anything to the police."

"I don't know."

Vidal paused, then told them seriously, "Look,. I am here to protect

Charmain and will do everything legally possible. And maybe a few things that aren't so legal. We agreed this conversation never took place. It's off the record forever. But let me make one thing clear, without trying to scare anybody. I cannot allow myself to become an accessory to a murder. That can't happen. Understood?"

Charmain smiled. "Well, fuck you, too, buddy."

Kelso said quickly, "I think we're all getting a bit carried away here. In the worst case scenario, it would be a plea bargain to manslaughter. Charmain would probably never do jail time."

"Jesus. Thanks for the 'probably,'" she said.

Vidal said, "I'm no lawyer, but I agree with your assessment, Mike."

Kelso nodded. "It's still potentially messy. Even if she gets off with probation, her fans might get turned off because she hired a pro boxer whose hands are registered weapons—"

Vidal whistled. "Whew! The media will have a field day with that!"

"But," Kelso went on, "with some careful spin-doctoring and long-range planning, her career might revive after two years, so it's not a total disaster even if...JESUS!"

He ducked as the massive Lalique crystal vase barely missed his skull and smashed though the den window. Charmain, her voice strangled with rage, shrieked:

"SHUT THE FUCK UP, YOU LOUSY BASTARDS!!"

Vidal moved toward her, then backed off as she snatched up a silver candlestick.

"Charmain!"

"How DARE you fucking stand in front of me like I'm not there and talk about me going to jail, or losing my fans. You PRICKS! How much do I pay you, you fucking leeches? You want to lose my weekly checks, you bloodsucking BASTARDS? DO YOU!?"

"No...Charmain, we were just—"

"I'll NEVER go to jail. You understand? NEVER! NEVER! YOU GOT THAT?!"

"Yes...Yes, Charmain..."

"YOU do your fucking job, Vidal! And you, you old pussy, YOU get me that fucking lead in *Medusa*. Now, do you both understand your fucking jobs? DO YOU? AM I GETTING THROUGH TO THOSE FUCKING PEA BRAINS?"

Vidal threw her a mock salute and split. Like he'd just recalled an urgent appointment for a blowjob.

Kelso did what he always did after Charmain's eruptions.

Grinned weakly.

And got hard.

CHAPTER 27

1:05 P.M.
CHARMAIN'S MANSION
BEVERLY HILLS

SILENCE. Mike Kelso knew not to move or utter a word.

Charmain sank into the sofa pillows, threw her head back, closed her eyes. Went still. Kelso had seen this before. It was a meditation she did, a retreat inside herself. It lasted for minutes or hours. If you spoke, she would not answer. If you persisted, God help you.

The assistant before Marta had made that mistake. Charmain had thrown her through a French door. An expensive deal. Medical bills. Payoff money.

He thought, Why do I do it? Invest blood, sweat, and money into beautiful young girls. Like Charmain. They come to Hollywood, get off the Greyhound like a bubbly Mary Tyler Moore, and think, "I'm gonna make it...after all." Yaaay-y-y!

Fresh-faced babies just out of high school, with maybe six months at Hooters for seasoning. And they think, hey, Marilyn Monroe did it...why can't I? Well, you can, baby. Just like Marilyn did it. Blowjobs or handjobs to the photographers and hack newspaper guys in exchange for publicity photos and stories. Sleep with a casting director or two. Then start fucking the brains out of an important agent who's old enough to be your grandfather. And if you make it, enjoy it while you can.

Marilyn did.

Before her clock got punched at age 36.

Kelso sighed. Ruthless expolitation of female flesh was a time-honored tradition in this town. Practiced mostly by schmucks who couldn't get laid any other way; who thrilled to the exquisite sweetness of power that forced beautiful women to grovel.

Mike had seen it all.

And hated it.

He'd come to town as a young man out of a Midwestern college with a literature degree, wanting to be a writer. Hadn't made it. So he drifted into studio publicity, first at MGM, then Warner's. And he made friends with an older agent at ICM who thought he had a good way with people and a head for business. Then Mike got his break. A gang of young turk agents led by wunderkind Mike Ovitz broke away from ICM and William

Morris to form the renegade agency CAA. ICM and William Morris freaked. Kelso was hired in a moment of desperation by his ICM agent pal, who'd moved up a notch and needed new blood in the agency.

Mike had done well, learned a lot as an agent. But three years into it, he quit. It was too bloodthirsty, too impersonal for him. He liked finding and developing talent. But he quickly discovered that the top agents, the real killers, didn't give a damn about developing anybody's career. They fought to sign established names, then sat back and took orders for their clients' services.

So he'd gone into personal management. And specialized in those fresh-faced girls who got off the Greyhounds. He'd find them waitressing, maybe even stripping out by the airport, or just hanging out on Melrose or at the discos.

Occasionally, he found them hooking.

Oh yes, there were other "personal managers" in town who specialized in apple-cheeked young stuff. Pimps. A special breed who recruited for well-heeled producers, directors, studio execs, and actors who made no bones about a preference for hookers. Not tired, beat-up whores. Lovely young things. The kind that girlie pimp Heidi Fleiss used to line up for Charlie Sheen's wild, violent orgies. The kind that the late action-movie king, Don Simpson, hired so he could make them kneel and piss on their heads.

Whores, for Hollywood's rich and powerful, were a convenience.

Instant gratification.

Chinese take-out.

And if you were hungry two hours later, no problem-o! Just dial again. 24-hour service.

One of Kelso's first hot finds had been a young runaway from the Northwest. He'd seen her walking down Sunset one Saturday morning. When she ducked into the legendary Duke's Coffee Shop, he'd pulled over impulsively and parked.

He strolled in, ordered coffee, and watched her order a huge breakfast of four sunnyside eggs, bacon and sausage, home fries and pancakes, large orange juice and whole wheat toast. Coffee. She was dressed in dirty, ragged clothes. Her nails, though neatly clipped, weren't done professionally. Her hair was freshly washed and she projected a youthful radiance that was breathtaking. But she hid it. Never looked up. Never flirted with the table of wannabe rocker boys who kept leering in her direction. Ate like she was starving. Looked fourteen but was probably more like seventeen.

Runaway, thought Kelso. Written all over her. Just in from out of town. Finally ran out of money. And probably just pulled a trick and was eating her first square meal in days.

He watched her closely, pretending to read *Variety*. She had a quality, a vulnerability. An intelligence. Then he saw her smile, almost too fast to catch, when the waitress came and offered her a free refill on the coffee.

The girl looked up, flashed an eyeballs-and-teeth grin that made you want to hug her. The waitress, a hard-boiled type, caught the enchantment, too. She smiled back, patted the girl on the shoulder.

Mike Kelso made up his mind. He'd approach her. Always tricky. At age fifty-three, he didn't look ancient. Just blah. Gray hair, glasses, sober suit, no charisma. Your typical dirty old man, if you were a teenage girl and saw him approaching.

He dropped a business card on her table. She looked at it, then up at him.

"I'm a legitimate personal manager of show business talent, Miss. I have clients on several top TV shows, like Nila Shane on *The Love Sisters,* which is number one in its time slot, and Carla Barlow, who's on TV's hottest series, *BevHills High*. You don't have to talk to me now. But I wish you'd call my office. I think you have a look that could work on camera. That is, if an acting career interests you."

She looked at him solemnly. "My name is Rebecca Schilman. I'll talk to you now."

He took her back to the office, held all his calls, and talked to her for hours, sending out for lunch. He realized after a while that she was in a sort of shock. She was only seventeen. Her mother, a widow and closet alcoholic, had thrown her out, calling her a whore when she caught her jerking off a persistent boyfriend on the front porch, the only place where she'd been allowed to consort with the opposite sex.

Rebecca had bought a bus ticket to Hollywood. And quickly ran afoul of Jenna Stanley, a thirty-ish ex-hairdresser who'd taken over the Heidi Fleiss trade.

"This woman would come downtown near that overpass at 1st and Central where a lot of the kid runaways hang out," Jenna told Kelso. "I'd ended up there after my money ran out and I couldn't get a job. She'd just cruise around and ask the girls if they wanted to make some easy money giving sex to rich Hollywood guys. She recruited some of the boys too. I turned her down two or three times, and she stopped asking me.

"Then one night she came down and, man, she made a beeline for me. She told me she had a special job that paid a lot and I was perfect because I was so young-looking.

"Anyway, she took me to this producer's house in Beverly Hills. It was, like, a mansion. And there were posters of all these famous movies he'd produced. But years ago. I knew some of them, though.

"He'd paid this woman to get my clothes and hair styled so I looked like a twelve-year-old schoolgirl. I mean, she actually told me that that's how old I was supposed to be. It was truly weird. Like, he'd set up a room with a blackboard and a teacher's desk and a small student's desk for me. It was creepy. He even had an American flag, like a classroom. He'd stand at the teacher's desk and give me lectures. He'd even give me little written tests.

"Then he'd stand over my desk and sort of look down my blouse. Or he'd drop his pencil on the floor and look up the plaid mini-skirt I always had to wear. He'd brush up against me, and touch me. Then he'd send me home. The woman put me in a hotel and she'd pick me up every day for 'school.'

"Finally, after three days, he started the sex stuff. First he claimed I'd sassed him, and he got a pointer and made me pull up my skirt and he whipped me with it. Then later that day, he put me on his lap and pulled down my panties and spanked me with his hand. And on and on. And finally, on the fifth day, he raped me."

Kelso was mesmerized. He knew the producer well. Hadn't had a monster hit in years. Not a player. But still in action. Hung out with some big names. A good-looking man who could certainly get sex on his own. But sex wasn't the deal. It rarely was. Power! The guy just needed the illusion that he was still powerful. And illusions are always for sale in Hollywood. Just pick up a phone and order. Something exotic. Convenient.

Chinese take-out.

Kelso sent Rebecca Schilman out to shop for new clothes with his secretary. When they returned, he told the girl, "Your new name, your star name, is 'Danae Winslow.' Like it?"

Danae smiled. "I love it."

That night, he took her to dinner. And it finally occurred to him to ask where she was staying.

"Wherever," she'd answered. "I'll find a place when I have money. Otherwise, it's behind a dumpster."

"Do you have money now?"

"A little. Not much. Enough for two or three days."

"Okay, I'm going to find you a nice hotel."

She shrugged. "Can I stay at your place? You said you're not married."

"Okay," he said. "Sure, why not? Just until we find you something."

He knew she expected him to slip into her guest room bed that night. God knows she was sexy, but this was business. He was excited by this girl. Danae Winslow could be hot.

And she was. He got her a small role on *Night Nurses,* playing a high school candy-striper. It quickly grew into a recurring role. Then a regular spot. In the second season, she was a featured player, getting more scenes and incurring the hatred of the other two star actresses on the show.

By year two, Danae Winslow was the star. And one of Mike Kelso's greatest successes.

At the end of year two, she had her lawyer phone Mike Kelso to inform him that he was fired as her personal manager. He tried to reach her by phone, but the former Rebecca Schilman—aka Danae Winslow—never took his calls again.

Welcome to Hollywood.

Kelso took it like a man. In this town, you picked your ass up and danced every time they hit you. This wasn't the first time a girl he'd built up from nothing had dumped him. Kelso was far from a stupid man. He knew it wasn't coincidence that all his star clients were teenage girls. And that he got too emotionally involved with them. He even realized that part of the strange pattern was the fact that he never, ever hit on the girls. That's because, his conscious mind told him, it's business. But way down deep, he yearned for one of these girls, these fresh-faced young women, to fall in love with him. To turn to him and say, "I want you. I want to be with you."

It had never happened—until Charmain.

And, as it always was with Charmain—and with life, for that matter—it hadn't happened quite the way he'd dreamed it. It was....

"Kelso!"

Charmain snapped him out of his reverie. Her eyes were wide open again. She patted the sofa beside her.

"Come here, Mike-y."

He walked over and sat. Again, she patted his cheek. And purred, "I'm not mad at you anymore. It's been a very rough day for me, Mike-y. Look, I know you're my tiger and you work real hard for me. And I know you'll get me *Medusa*."

"I'm going to do it, Charmain..."

"I know you are. And you know what that means. I reward people who come through for me."

She leaned forward and patted his cheek again.

"Now, I've been thinking. And I know what to do. We're going to get Buster Brown out of the country."

"We can't do that. It's too risky. Besides, you don't even know how to find him."

"Oh yes, I do."

"Jesus! Why didn't you tell Vidal?"

"Because I can only trust Vidal so far. He's the kind who always thinks of coverin' his own ass first. You heard him. If this thing gets too hairy, he'll sell me out in a heartbeat."

"Charmain, I don't think that's fair. Vidal's cautious and tries to operate within the law. He's already put his neck on the line, if you think about it. I'm surprised he didn't advise you to turn yourself in to the police before things get worse. I think that's what your lawyer might advise you to do, but—"

"That's why we're not contacting my lawyer, Mister. Like Vidal said, we're keeping this between us and off the damn record. Right now, I trust only two people all the way—me and you. Vidal knows only what I want him to know. Okay?"

"Okay."

"Swear, Mike-y."

He held up his right hand in mock solemnity.

"I swear, Charmain."

"Good. Now let's talk to Buster."

She crossed over to the desk, dialed 411.

"Shit, it's so fucking hot today...Yeah, in Los Angeles...ABC Poolroom...or ABC Pool maybe?...What? Yeah, that's it...Hey, what's the address?"

She jotted it down, waited for the number, hung up. Dialed. Glanced at Kelso.

"I remember Buster telling me, 'It's as easy to remember as ABC.'" She held up her hand.

"Yeah, hello. ABC Poolroom? Is Buster Brown there?...Just tell him it's the blacksnake lady...Yeah, he'll know. Just be a good boy, blood, and go get his ass."

Charmain looked at Kelso, grinned. Put a finger to her lips.

"Hello? Buster? You know who this is, right? But don't say my name, okay?"

Inside the ABC Poolroom, a dingy emporium in the derelict hell of downtown L.A., Buster Brown grinned and pumped a fist silently in the air.

"Okay," he said.

"Now listen, Buster. I've been thinking about what we talked about, and I can help you with your dream. But you can't tell anyone you're talking to me, right?"

"Right."

"So what happened today? You just, uh, popped him and...it went okay?"

"Yeah. It was nuthin'."

"So...what, you just went like, 'bang'...and that was it?"

Buster chuckled. "Yeah, one right hand. You've seen my right. He went flyin'! Then I flew, too. Right on out of there, you know?"

Charmain covered the phone, gleeful.

"He doesn't know, Mike-y. He says he hit Bellini and left. He doesn't know he killed him. Hasn't heard the news."

Charmain turned back to the phone.

"Buster, listen, I've got a great plan for you. I'm sending my, uh, my producer down there to pick you up and and drive you down to a hotel in Mexico. I'm going to join you there tonight and we'll spend a few days in the sun relaxing and going over script ideas.

"What? No, don't go home and pack anything. I'll buy you clothes down there. Anyway, you aren't going to need a lot of clothes on the beach...or in our suite, loverman. But you gotta swear you won't tell anybody you've hooked up with me or where you're going. The first thing you have to learn about being a star is never talk about what we say to each other. Now, can you be standing outside there in, say...thirty minutes?"

Buster looked across the poolroom. His buddies waved him back to the table.

It was his shot.

He took it.

"I'll be there," he said.

Charmain hung up, hissed, "Yess!"

She wrote rapidly on a notepad, ripped off the sheet and handed it to Kelso.

"First, I've written the address of the poolroom I got from 411. Also, the name of the hotel in Baja Mexico where you're going to take Buster. The Casa Del Sol. God, I've got to get, what? Ten grand or so out of the bank in cash."

She walked to the door, screamed upstairs. "MARTA!"

"She's not back yet. Vidal sent her out, remember? Charmain, for God's sake, slow down. This is going too fast. We've got to think. And why am I driving Buster? I can't just up and leave my business on short notice."

"What are you talking about? You'll be back tonight. You're not staying. Look, you're driving Buster so he doesn't get out of our sight. And we don't want him seen crossing the border with me, right? I'll drive down alone later tonight."

"And then what?"

"I'll stay with him a day or so, give him some bullshit about how I've talked to some studio about his career and they're interested. And then I give him ten grand to stay out of the country. You can live forever on ten grand in Mexico. I'll send him books on acting, and some of those tape cassette courses. Tell him he's got to study for at least six months, a year."

"You think he'll buy that?"

"Why not? You remember how I was when you first found me? I would have done any damn thing to get a chance. This guy's a boxer who's going nowhere. And he's smart enough to know it."

Charmain sunk back into the sofa.

"You know what? My bet is he'll shack up with some cute señorita down there and stay forever. And even if we keep him there for a year, this thing will be all blown over."

Kelso took off his glasses, polished them nervously on the back of his tie.

"We should let Vidal handle this, Charmain. What if this fella blows all your money and starts blackmailing you? Even if he doesn't know he killed Bellini, he knows he could hurt your career by saying you sent him to beat someone up."

"You do what you're told," she snapped. "This is my fucking career. And I'm the one whose ass is on the line. You just don't have any balls."

She gave him a lazy, calculating look.

"Am I still your goddess?"

He shrugged. Nodded.

"Answer me, slave."

"Yes," he said. "You are my goddess."

Charmain arched an eyebrow.

"How long has it been since I allowed you to…worship?"

"A long time."

She shrugged open her robe, smiled coldly.

"Hurry!"

He got up, knelt by the sofa, thrilled as he put his mouth to a protuberant nipple. Charmain often allowed him to see her naked body. But her breasts were the only part she allowed him to "worship." Touching was rarely allowed.

"What do you call them, Mike…my nipples? I never can remember."

He balanced her rubbery hardness on his lower lip, reluctant to break contact even briefly. He said:

"Light bulb nipples."

She laughed.

"Oh, right, because they sort of puff out like the rounded ends of light bulbs. And they're rare, right? Who did you say had the best ever? That ex-porn actress…uh, Traci Lords? God, the things that turn men on. You're like baby animals."

Minutes later, she pushed him away. "You've got to get going. But today you get a special reward, slave. You can come. On the hem of my robe."

Kelso considered himself a dignified man. No matter how many times he endured the humiliation, he asked himself, "Why?" And always swore it would be the last time. Knowing it was a lie. He grasped the hem of her robe, unzipped, extracted his engorged member, stroked it across silken texture. Eyes on her breasts, imagining their heft.Their softness.

She sighed. Contempt shaded her voice.

"Hurry up. I need you to get on the road."

His eyes pleaded.

"Alright, slave. You can squeeze one of my girls. Either one."

He groaned. Touched.

"Now come!" she snarled.

"Then get out."

Her voice was a whiplash, triggering the explosive starburst of guilt.

He came.

Gasping that which always had to be uttered:

"Goddess!"

CHAPTER 28

1:38 P.M.
LOS ANGELES

KELSO drove, cold dread soaking through his soul. Jesus Christ! What lunatic destiny propelled him down these dirty, hostile streets? How, why was he suddenly meeting at the ABC Poolroom with a thug named Buster Brown?

Jesus.

Buster Brown...Buster Fucking Brown...

The cartoonish name struck him like an insane joke. He giggled, suddenly hysterical, out of control. He felt his left cheekbone still burning from the furious slap Charmain had delivered just minutes ago. Even *that* seemed funny now. He fought to stop the wild, aching laughter. Recalled her last words:

"Kelso, don't *ever* tell Vidal about this. He'll look for Buster, but Buster will be nowhere to be found. And that will be the end of it.

"Now whatever you do, don't let Buster listen to the radio. Or watch TV. Not that it will matter, once you get into Mexico. They're not going to run a story about an American newspaper guy on Mexican TV.

"This is working great, Mike. Buster doesn't even know he killed a man. It's so cool."

She'd fixed him with that crazy stare she got sometimes. It always made him drop his eyes.

"I'm going to tell you again, Mike. Your only job is to get me the part of Medusa. Every bitch in town wants it. But I'm going to get it. It's the greatest movie role for a woman in years. And it's going to be my first feature film.

"Nothing's going to fuck that up. Not *The Revealer* and its stupid pictures of me disciplining a horse. Or Steve Bellini going out a window.

"You get that role for me, Mike, and you're the hottest personal manager in town. You fuck this up...you're dogmeat."

"Charmain, I've got to tell you one more time that I think this is all wrong, that—"

She smashed him across the face so hard he went blind. He shook his head, felt for his glasses. Gone. Jesus. Staggered, caught the wall. Held on. His vision cleared. He felt her hands fumbling on his face.

"Here, for Chrissake, here...Your glasses. Shit. They almost went out that broken fucking window."

She was laughing. God help him. It actually made him feel good. Like she cared. She took him in her arms and hugged him close for a long moment. He felt tears form in his eyes.

She whispered, "Here's a thought to speed you on your way, old buddy. You get me that part, Mike, and I'll play with your cock while you worship."

As he negotiated downtown L.A. streets he rarely traveled, Kelso knew he was slowly going mad for this woman. Every instinct he trusted screamed at him to get out of this degenerating situation, insist that she turn herself in to the police. Right fucking now.

But all he could think about was, How do I get her that part? How do I make Charmain Burns "Medusa?"

He recalled a conversation he'd had with Charmain's agent, Jay Lonstein. Jay had put the *Medusa* deal into focus.

"Trouble is, Mike, she's too young. Not in the age sense. She's just too TV. Not seasoned enough. No real movie experience. No proven marquee value. There's only one question studio heads ask today: can she put asses in seats? That's it! Bottom line. The days of using unbankable stars is over, unless you're looking for an art movie award at Sundance. Oh sure, Charmain's a terrific actress. Two Emmys. She's got charisma, fire. But every name actress in town wants *Medusa*. Streep and Streisand. Who'll never get it. Pfeiffer, who's a good actress, but too light. Bridget Fonda, too weird. Sandra Bullock, too cute. Julia Roberts, strictly comedy, a flop in drama. Kate Winslett? Too tubby. Kim Basinger? Her Oscar was for *L.A. Confidential*, which only did so-so at the box office. Sharon Stone? Long in the tooth, but she's got a shot. Gwyneth Paltrow? Maybe. It's probably Winona Ryder's if she wants it. That girl can play anything. AND sell tickets.

"My choice? Drew Barrymore. Anyone leaning toward Charmain would split the difference at Drew. She's got a track record in features and some hits, like *Wedding Singer*."

Jay Lonstein had it analyzed cold. As far as it went.

But Lonstein was a fucking agent. A meat salesman. You don't want filet mignon? He'll sell you a T-bone. Prime rib too rich? He's got a special on the New York strip. Ah, you can only afford rump roast? Sure, whatever you want. All nice for the price.

Agents! Kelso despised them. They had no passion for the talent. Like waiters, they pushed what they wanted to sell. Everything's delicious, they tell you. But if you don't like the specials, look at the main menu. We've got something for every taste. And if you don't see what you want, let the chef whip up something special. We don't give a fuck what you eat, we just want you to eat *something*. How about some Stallone bolognese? No? Schwarzenegger schnitzel? Ragout of DiCaprio? Paltrow paté? A Cruise-burger, maybe?

Agents were K-mart.

Personal managers, like Kelso, were Tiffany's.

Agents had a list of clients as long as your arm. They'd sell you anyone on it. And if no one bought the talent over a period of time, the talent was dumped. Personal managers had a few select clients. They nurtured them, protected them, advised them with an eye to their long-term career. Even loved them.

He had to get Charmain that role. Had to. But she needed an edge. Something to break her out of the pack. Like a hot news story to get her name in the headlines. Not like the photos of her whipping the horse. The worst part of that story wasn't that it made Charmain look bad. Even a negative story can help a star's career. But it had to be juicy. Something you could keep on talking about, speculating about. Gossip with legs. News to make you whisper. The horse-whipping coverage had upset Charmain, but nobody cared. Bottom line? A fucking one-day wonder. A yawn.

Charmain needed big headlines. Front page, not the *People* columns. A romance with a bigger star, like Leonardo DiCaprio, maybe. She needed to jolt the public. Become a household name. Get right in the face of American ticket buyers.

Who'd ever heard of Hugh Grant before he did a few laps with Divine? Or Anne Heche before she turned gay for Ellen DeGeneres? Outrageous news could make you a star; make the studio honchos believe your name on a marquee would sell millions of $7.50 tickets.

He grinned wryly. What fucking irony. Here he was, sitting on the perfect news story. Sensational enough to make Charmain an international star. A murder, no less. Committed by a murderous actress. It fit glove-perfect with the movie role of Medusa that Charmain wanted so desperately—the gory tale of an actress who'd literally kill for a part.

Man! It was *so* bizarre…a perfect scandal story, the kind that sells papers and racks up huge TV ratings. The press would go rabid!

For a wild moment Kelso wondered…could it work? Yeah, maybe! Hell, just be audacious. Phone Clive Tinsdale and say, "You want a man-killer? You want a real-life Medusa? Look no further, my friend!"

Get Charmain to turn herself in. Hire the best attorneys. Spin the story that she hadn't meant to hurt Steve. Just told Buster jokingly that she wished he'd knock Steve's block off. Buster, a fan, had taken her too seriously. Now this tragic death. Charmain breaks down in tears on national TV. America loves a confession. Walters or Sawyer, maybe. Lots of weeping. Lots of spin. Charmain gets off with probation. Signs for *Medusa*, and the movie opens at No. 1 and grosses $200 mil. Farfetched? Crazy? Kelso shook his head. The weird thing was, in today's Hollywood, it might just work.

He thought, I'm the one who's crazy. What am I doing here? Why the hell don't I just bail out of this now? Call the cops, turn her in. Taking

Buster out of the country was dangerous. It made him an accessory. He wanted to turn around, drive back, tell her to go to hell. But he knew he wouldn't. Why? That's easy, he told himself. You're in love with the bitch. Obsessed. You're a sucker for star power, and she's a pure, fucking original. A glamourous 24-carat diva headed straight for stardom, even legend.

If somebody doesn't kill her first.

Charmain Burns had made enemies. She'd come roaring into town ready to kick Hollywood ass, not kiss it. The L.A. male power elite—the executive boys club—didn't scare her for shit! She was one of the new breed. Hollywood 90s women like Roseanne, Shannen Doherty, Sharon Stone, Madonna, Courtney Love, Drew Barrymore. Strong, fearless babes who understood pussy power. Who never let men patronize them. Who refused to be "good little girls" or "ladies." Oh no.

That shit was over.

A journalist once asked Charmain, "Do you call it feminism?"

"I call it…about fuckin' time!" she snapped.

The guy persisted.

"So how do you handle a dispute with a producer? Or a casting couch pass, for that matter?"

"With a swift kick in the *cojones*!"

Johnny Journalist came back fast and catty:

"Well…speaking of balls, Charmain, where *did* you get yours?"

CHAPTER 29

3:51 P.M.
PATRICK TAULERE'S MANSION
SAVANNAH

"*WHAT* a fuckin' mess!"

"You got that right, lieutenant," said Detective-Sgt. Charlie Slade. Never hurt to agree with the boss. And on this ratfuck, Slade agreed wholeheartedly.

Lieutenant Joe Fell, head of the Homicide Squad, surveyed the murder scene.

"You were the first dick to arrive, Charlie? You and your partner?"

"Yeah, Sam and I were right behind the black-and-whites, damn near. Just so happened we were a couple of blocks away over on Whitefield Square when we heard the call."

Joe Fell nodded. "Okay, run me down chop-chop, Charlie. I just found out that Langston Burdine himself is on his way over."

"Jesus. The Chief of Detectives? At a crime scene?"

The lieutenant shrugged. "Patrick Taulere was a big fish. Maybe Langston just wants to make sure he's dead."

Charlie Slade grinned, flipped open his notebook. "Oh, he's dead, all right. Okay…the body was discovered by Charmain Burns, the victim's girlfriend, who has resided on premises for several weeks. Police were actually called by one Claude Valjean, the victim's chauffeur. Says he dropped Miss Burns outside, went to Abercorn Street to gas the car, came back a few minutes later.

"He entered the house through the kitchen. Found a Miss Marie Pritchard, the maid, or housekeeper, whatever, dead. She got it in the back of the head. Blunt weapon. The chauffeur says he heard Miss Burns screaming, came in here and found her kneeling in front of the body, hysterical. No sight of a perp. Says he touched nothing, found the victim just as you see him."

"Physical evidence?"

"Well, just what you see. That spike in his eye, or whatever it is, actually killed him. Although he would have bled to death quick enough from the other stuff. The M.E. says he hasn't spotted any hair or fibers, but he's not finished yet. Fingerprint guy says the perp was wearing gloves."

Lieutenant Joe Fell looked at his watch. "Where's the M.E.?"

Slade pointed toward the kitchen. "He's taking a look at the maid."

Fell lit a cigarette, blew out smoke. Said, "You haven't mentioned Miss Burns, Charlie."

"The twist? Sorry, sir. She looks pretty clean. Chauffeur says he spent the afternoon with her."

"Anything going on with her and the chauffeur?"

Slade grinned. "No, sir. Doubt that. He's a pretty old guy. Not the type, ya know? And there's packages on the hall table that check out she was shopping. We're calling all the stores, of course."

Fell shook his head. "I'm sure she's clean. I don't think a woman did this."

A flurry in the hallway. A rich baritone voice acknowledging respectful greetings from the gaggle of cops that filled the house. Chief of Detectives Langston Burdine, a tall, barrel-chested man wearing a Panama hat, swept into the room. Medical Examiner Francis K. Fuhrman, one the world's great ass-kissers, although a solid forensics guy, eddied in Burdine's backwash.

"Gentlemen."

Burdine, who was in his mid-fifties, nodded at one and all and fired up a cigar. Everyone in the room knew it was a Cuban. Lucky bastard, thought Charlie Slade.

Burdine puffed, made sure he had an even glow going, and said, "It is hot out there and getting hotter. I, for one, wish that damn cloudburst that's been threatening all afternoon would piss us all some relief."

He walked closer to the corpse. Took a long look.

"Well now. This saves us all a lot of trouble."

Burdine turned, beckoned to the M.E., who stepped in close, eager to please.

"Now Francis, what I see here is a grown man in good health handcuffed from every limb to the rungs and arms of this very fine antique chair. Looks like a Louis 13th, or a fine copy. Our perpetrator then, it appears, removed our victim's balls while he was still alive.

"Now, Francis, I'm just eyeballin' here, so tell me if I'm right. Our perpetrator then takes the victim's severed balls and skewers them like shish-ke-bab on this long, thin spike. In fact, this thing could be one of those shish-ke-bab skewers like Mrs. Burdine has at home for when we barbecue. Which is almost never. I'm no fan of greasy, burned meat."

Francis K., respectfully refraining from interrupting the Chief of Detectives' narrative flow, nodded furiously, signifying his absolute agreement that, yes, it was probably a shish-ke-bab skewer. No one in the room was certain whether he was agreeing on the barbecue question.

"Next up, it seems to me, was that the perpetrator taunted the victim. Showin' him his balls on a skewer, that kind of thing. And then, stick with me here, Francis, because this is just a guess on my part, he actually tried to make the victim eat his own balls. And again, that's just a guess based on these tiny little holes, some of them bloody, around the victim's mouth.

These indentations here would be poke marks from what I'm presuming is the sharp end of this skewer. Which the perpetrator then plunged into the victim's brain pan, via his right eye. Am I right on everything so far, Francis? If so, I'm ready to ask my $64 question…"

Francis K., practically on the verge of whiplash, nodded even more enthusiastically.

"…and that question is: how do you get a big, tough gent like Patrick Taulere into a chair to put handcuffs on him? This is a man who knows the score. Even if you're holding a gun on him, he figures he's a dead man once he's cuffed down. So, Francis, tell me if I am right in guessing we're going to find a big bump on the back of his head where the perpetrator clubbed him, that he snuck up as the victim sat reading that newspaper lying there on the floor? *New York Times*, isn't it? Never one of my favorites."

Francis K., apparently overwhelmed by the spectacle of Langston Burdine in deducing mode, spoke, his voice croaking a bit.

"Right as rain, Chief," he said.

The big man puffed on his Punch #3 and winked at Lieutenant Fell.

"Well, it's like ridin' a bicycle, isn't it, Joe? Once a detective, always a detective."

"Yessir," said Lieutenant Fell.

"I do miss being in harness. Well now, Mr. Patrick Taulere was one of those French Creole gentlemen from New Orleans, and you know what the French always say in a case like this, don't you, Joe?"

"Er…no, sir. I'm not much on French stuff."

Francis K. Fuhrman piped up. "I believe they say, '*Cherchez la femme*,' don't they, Chief?"

Langston Burdine nodded, smiled. "That's exactly right, Francis. '*Cherchez la femme*.' Find the woman."

Joe Fell shot the M.E. a look that said, Watch it, asshole!

He said to Burdine, "Charlie Slade here can fill you in on the scene as he found it, sir. Charlie?"

Slade flipped his notebook open again and went through his routine for Langston Burdine.

"Slade, did you talk to Miss Burns?"

"Yessir. Very cooperative. And her alibi seems to check out, as I said. I asked if she had any idea who might have done it. She just looked at me funny and said..." Slade checked his notebook carefully. "…Uh, she said, 'Do you smell anything strange?' I said I didn't. Asked her what she meant? And she just shrugged and went back to cryin'."

"Joe, it's your investigation, but I'd like to talk to her."

"Yessir, of course. She's back there in the dining room. Policewoman's with her."

Langston Burdine followed Joe Fell into the dining room. Charmain was sitting in a chair by the window, looking out at the garden.

"Excuse me, Miss Burns," said Burdine. "I'd like to talk to you for a moment if you're up to it."

Without waiting for a reply, he sat down at the dining room table and removed his hat. Charmain turned and looked at him. Burdine returned her gaze impassively. He'd heard on the Savannah grapevine about Patrick Taulere's new toy. A beauty queen, alright! Country, but not trash.

Her eyes met his, and he smiled inwardly. Tough. Not hard yet, but on the way.

"My name is Langston Burdine. I'm Chief of Detectives for the Savannah Police Department. Now, Miss Burns, I have just a couple of questions. Can you help me out?"

"I'll talk to you."

He nodded. "That's good, ma'am. Because you and I share a common goal. We want justice for Mr. Taulere."

He paused. "By the way, does this cigar bother you?"

Charmain shook her head.

"Thank you. I've been convinced for years that cigars aid my deductive reasoning powers. Probably no truth to it. Just one of those excuses people make for smoking. Well, first off, let me put my cards on the table. It seems you are under no suspicion in this murder. My detectives are still checking your alibi, and I can't officially rule you out as a suspect yet, but I'd bet my pension fund that you had nothing to do with this terrible crime."

Charmain snapped, "Are you gettin' real close to making your point here?"

Oh yeah. Tough. Not just cocky. A real core to her. He sensed the fury. He'd seen that cold, implacable stare before. In the eyes of hillbillies and swamp rats consumed by blood feuds. Hellbent for revenge.

Langston Burdine gave her an easy smile. "Excuse me, ma'am. I'll cut right to it. I think you know who did this. Or have a pretty good idea. I want you to tell me all about that, right now, please."

Charmain stared at him.

Langston Burdine sighed. "You said to one of my detectives, 'Do you smell anything strange?' What did you mean by that?"

"I don't know. I don't remember saying that."

"It might be helpful if you recalled anything like that. Some smell that didn't seem right to you. That could be a valuable clue. Could you try to remember just what you smelled?"

Charmain looked away, then back at him. "Look, I was in shock. I still am, goddamnit. I don't know why I said that, if I did. I don't know who did this, okay?

"Look, I loved Patrick Taulere. I want his murderer. You're asking me if I know who might have done this. No, I don't. I *don't* fucking know, okay, sheriff? Or chief, whatever the hell you are! Patrick lived in this town, so maybe you have an idea who killed him. Do you?"

Langston Burdine puffed on his Punch #3, regarding her calmly. He was right. He felt it. Sure as hell, she knew something. And she'd never tell him. Tough little cookie. Stubborn. In the old days, he might have taken her into the basement downtown and worked her gut over with a phone book. Not anymore. Changing times. Changing tactics.

"Miss Burns, you had known the deceased for a matter of weeks. Met down in Miami, am I correct?"

"Yes."

"And are you aware of what business Mr. Taulere was in?"

"Yes. The shipping business."

"Uh-huh. Yes, ma'am, that he was. But did he ever tell you any more exact details of his business? Introduce you to business associates? Or any family members?"

Charmain shook her head. "No. I didn't care about his business. We were in love. That's what we talked about. Us. I never met his family. I know they're an old New Orleans family, that's all."

Langston Burdine shook his head almost sadly.

"Ma'am, Patrick Taulere came to live in our fine city some years ago. He was a socially pleasing young man, as you know, and seemed like a law-abiding pillar of society. Said he was in the shipping business, with offices in New York, Miami, London. And we heard him speak vaguely of a fine old family in New Orleans.

"Now about two years ago, I got a visit from a bigshot out of Washington, D.C. This gentleman is a coordinator for the DEA, the federal Drug Enforcement Agency. He'd come to talk about your Mr. Taulere. And when he'd finished, I was surprised as a 'coon dog with no fleas to scratch.

"Your Patrick Taulere was in shipping, all right, in a mighty big way."

He paused, savoring his cigar. Looked at her. Hit her with it.

"What he shipped was drugs."

Charmain recoiled. "No, it's not true," she said. "Not Patrick! It couldn't be, he—"

Burdine nodded. "I know, ma'am, I know. I reacted the same way you are right now, and I'm a policeman.

"You know, when we think of drug pushers, we conjure up images of sleazy lowlifes, scum. Not classy gentlemen like the deceased. We don't think about the higher-ups, who work behind the scenes and finance the deals. The ones even we regular cops never meet. And that's what Patrick Taulere was. A kingpin. Never got near the dirty stuff. He leased cargo liners and financed shiploads of cocaine, marijuana, and heroin from South America. And those ships never even docked in this country.

"They'd sit up to fifty miles offshore, waiting for high-speed boats to pull up for off-loading at night. The speedboats would run into shore on overcast nights, too damn small to be picked up by radar. And if a boat got intercepted by the Coast Guard or Border Patrol, so what? Mr. Taulere's big ships were safely out of reach in international waters, off Florida, Georgia, Louisiana, Texas, California, Canada."

Charmain said, "If it's true, why wasn't he arrested?"

"Not enough evidence. He stayed clean away from the dirty end. He met no one, signed no papers. All he needed was a phone and Swiss bank accounts for payoffs. It's hard to nail a big player. Which is why the DEA wanted me to help put together evidence against Mr. Taulere.

"Well, I told them I wouldn't be much help, probably. Even though Mr. Taulere lived here, my guess was he'd never so much as spit on the sidewalk in Savannah. He truly loved our city. Considered it his home. He always stayed squeaky clean here. No big ships of his ever anchored off-shore of Savannah.

"That's how I know about Patrick Taulere, ma'am. Courtesy of the DEA. I've seen their evidence and it's compelling. Not enough for a court of law, maybe. But it's clear enough to me that he was a bigtime criminal."

Charmain took a deep breath. "He told me he came from old money, that his family had been in shipping, and—"

The Chief of Detectives chuckled. "His family are career crooks going back two or three generations, so I guess you might call them old money. Or old dirty money. And shipping was their trade. They smuggled contraband of all kinds, including drugs. In the old days, they hijacked cargo ships and robbed docks up and down the Mississippi. Strictly small-timers.

"They were probably the reason he wanted to leave New Orleans. Make a fresh start. He was a smart fella, way above the river rats his kin were. Probably could have made money in anything legitimate, if he'd had a mind to."

Tears welled up in Charmain's eyes. "That's what he'd been talking about. Changing his life. Doing good things. I didn't understand what he meant exactly. Now I do. Oh God! Patrick!"

Langston Burdines stood, picked up his hat. "Ma'am, I will not press you now, as I know you are truly grieving. I assume you will be staying here in Savannah until the funeral?"

"Yes."

"Well, Miss Burns, I hope that after you have recovered somewhat from this painful ordeal, you will tell me your ideas on who might have done this."

Charmain stood, swayed slightly, then composed herself.

Looking him right in the eye, she said, "I don't know who did this. That is my final word, believe me."

Langston Burdine bowed slightly, put on his Panama hat and left in a trail of aromatic smoke.

CHAPTER 30

PATRICK TAULERE'S MANSION
SAVANNAH

FOR the rest of that day and into next morning, Charmain didn't eat, sleep, make phone calls or accept any. It took hours for the cops to clean up the crime scene and she spent most of the time sitting in Patrick's study. Earlier, after she'd left the dining room, she'd walked in on Lieutenant Fell rummaging through Patrick's desk.

"What the fuck do you think you're doing?" she screamed.

"Miss Burns, this is a police investigation and—"

"Don't shit me, you sonofabitch. You're investigating a murder, period! Do you have a fucking search warrant?"

"No, but—"

"GET OUT! GET OUT!"

Patrick's Savannah lawyer, Weldon Phillips, a white-haired old gent, showed up and offered to help with funeral arrangements.

"His kin in New Orleans should be informed," he said. "Do you know them?"

"No," she said.

"Then allow me to do that for you. As for the police poking around in Patrick's effects, I'll have a word with them. It won't happen again. Now, were you aware that Patrick has a lawyer in New York who handles all his business afairs?"

"No, I thought you did."

"All I handled for Patrick was local business, household affairs, his will, that sort of thing. I'll call the other lawyer. Please don't concern yourself."

The skipper and chef from "Creole Time" arrived. The skipper took charge of dealing with phone calls. The chef tried coaxing Charmain with food, which she refused. Outside, the chauffeur fended off reporters and TV crews, who finally left after getting shots of the body being wheeled out to the meat wagon.

Charmain had begged to accompany Patrick to the morgue. Weldon Phillips told her it was impossible. No contact was allowed until the Medical Examiner officially released the body. She watched from behind a curtained window as they carried Patrick down the front steps.

For the first time in her life, she fainted.

That night, she went up to her bedroom, bathed, put on light eye makeup, dressed in a satin nightgown and matching pegnoir Patrick had adored her in, slipped on high-heeled mules, and went to his bedroom door. She knocked softly and said,

"*C'est moi, mon amour. Votre belle du jour…*"

She opened the door and for one split second, he was there, reading, glancing up at her with his roguish twinkle.

She went to the bed, lay down next to his pillow. No tears, she told herself. Time to cry later. Think of the good times.

She woke just after midnight. Patrick had come to her, telling her, "Go to the the hidey-hole."

She arose, went downstairs and through the darkened house, to a small den that looked out on the garden through leaded bay windows. Patrick loved to sit there on rainy days and watch the water drip off the Spanish moss on the oak trees. In front of his favorite chair was a low, rough pine table, an antique from Europe, on which he loved to rest his feet. It was round, with four small drawers.

Charmain opened the drawer facing the windows, pulled it out of the table and laid it down. She reached into the hole it came out of, found a knob, and pulled. Out slid another drawer, cleverly concealed under the table in the middle of the other four.

"I call it my hidey-hole, chérie," he'd told her. "Mostly I keep cash in it. Mad money. I rarely keep anything much in my wall safe in the study. That's for business stuff. This is for personal things and money I can grab and spend. If you ever come home and I'm not here, help yourself to whatever you need. If you take it all, just let me know so I can refill."

Charmain looked into the drawer. There was a fat wad of cash. She picked it up and counted it.

Jesus Christ! At least thirty thousand dollars.

There was a small notebook in the drawer. She picked it up, opened it, recognized his handwriting.

On the first page, in large block letters, were the words: "New Plan." She sat there for an hour, reading his future. And hers.

And finally, written in his own hand, were the words he'd pledged to share with her over dinner. Tears fell on the page as she read:

"<u>Goal</u>: Persuade Charmain to marry me.

"<u>Target date</u>: ASAP!

"<u>Method</u>: Prove I love her. Buy ring."

She looked in the drawer. Picked up a small leather box. Opened it. And there it was. Glittering and immense. Four carats? She felt a flash of self-loathing at thinking about the size. Then she started laughing, knowing how Patrick would have teased her about it.

She slipped the ring on her finger. It was so beautiful. She kissed it softly.

Oh, Patrick! I love you. I love you. I will always love you…

In a daze, she put the money back in the drawer, and went back upstairs to Patrick's bed.

Next morning, the chef awoke her gently. He'd prepared a breakfast tray. She ate ravenously and fell asleep again.

About an hour later she woke up, showered, and dressed in the darkest thing she had, a simple navy dress. She brushed her hair slowly, trying to think, still numb. The only person she even thought of calling was Millie. But she couldn't face anyone now. There was a knock on the door, the skipper's quiet voice: "Miss Burns, I'm sorry to bother you, but there's someone here who, ah…says she has to see you."

"Who?"

"Says she's Mr. Taulere's sister. I've asked her to wait in the dining room."

"Tell her I'll be right there, skipper."

My God, she got here quick enough, Charmain thought. She looked in the mirror, smoothed her hair and dress and went downstairs.

The moment she walked into the dining room, Charmain knew she was dealing with trash.

The hard-looking woman sitting at the head of the long table had the bottle-blonde look down cold. Forty-ish and hefty. Blood-red pointy fingernails. Her only resemblance to Patrick was fair skin and piercing blue eyes.

Charmain stopped short of approaching her. Didn't hold out her hand. "I'm Charmain Burns."

The woman stubbed out her cigarette in a crystal ashtray.

"I know goddamn well who you are. You're my brother's fancy tramp. Well, I'm Solange Taulere, his sister and next of kin. And you, little missy, have exactly one hour to pack your crap and haul your ass out of my house. Start now or I'll kick the shit out of you, and maybe cut up that cutie-pie face of yours with my razor."

Solange Taulere patted her handbag.

"You understand, bitch?"

The woman eyed her. Charmain forced herself to say, "Yes, ma'am. I surely do. I…I'll just get my purse and go pack."

Her handbag still sat on the dining room sideboard where she'd left it the night before. She walked over, picked it up, then looked at the sneering face of this woman who, unbelievably, had come from the same womb as the man she loved.

"Ma'am…May I call you Solange? What a pretty name. It's French, *n'est-ce pas*? I'd like to ask you a favor. Would you show me your razor, please?"

Solange tensed. Smelled the danger.

"Would I…what?"

The 9mm pistol snaked out of Charmain's purse.

"SHOW ME YOUR FUCKING RAZOR, WHORE!"

Solange froze. Three quick steps and Charmain had the muzzle pressed into her cheek.

"MOVE AND I'LL BLOW THAT PIG SNOUT OFF YOUR UGLY FACE!"

Charmain grabbed Solange's bag. Tipped the contents out on the dining toom table. Poked through the mess and came up with a pearl-handled razor. She flicked the blade open.

"Ooohh, look at this," she said, brandishing it under Solange's nose. "So shiny. And scary-sharp. Where I come from, only black pimps use razors. Is your boyfriend a black pimp, you fat peroxide slut?"

Solange shifted in the chair, opened her mouth to speak. Charmain jammed the gun harder.

"Don't talk, bitch. Don't even move. So…this is the razor you were going to cut my face with, huh? Why, I'm shocked. We were almost sisters-in-law. Yeah, that's right. Don't believe me?"

She lifted her hand and gave Solange a closeup of the ring.

"Where do you think that came from, a crackerjack box? We were just about to announce our engagement. But that ain't gonna happen now. And just for your information, there's nothing more I want from Patrick. I got what I wanted—his love. DO YOU UNDERSTAND LOVE, YOU FILTHY, SCUMMY CUNT? DO YOU?"

Charmain put the razor on the table. Her free hand curled into the neckline of Solange's black silk blouse and ripped it open. She snatched the razor and cut one bra strap. A big white breast flopped out, exposed.

"Don't ever forget me, you pig," Charmain breathed in her ear. "Think of me every time you look at my mark."

She sliced quickly, precisely, bold as a surgeon. Blood bubbled up in a delicate line, barely breaking the milky skin.

Solange whimpered.

Charmain laughed. "Music to my ears, honey. Now here's how it's gonna be. You get out of my house, 'cause it's mine until after the funeral. I'll see you there, along with any other of your no-good kinfolk. You will be polite. If you so much as eye me, I'll kill you where you stand. After the funeral, I'm gone. If I ever see you again, I'll kill you."

She stepped back, pointing the 9mm right at those blue eyes.

"Do *you* understand, bitch?"

Solange nodded.

"Good," said Charmain. "Now get the fuck out of here before you bleed on my floor."

CHAPTER 31

6:03 A.M.
PATRICK TAULERE'S MANSION
SAVANNAH

THE day of Patrick's funeral, Charmain awoke at dawn. She walked through every room of the quiet house, remembering the first day she'd seen it all, hand in hand with Patrick.

She stepped out into the garden, still and beautiful under the golden wash of a sunny Savannah morning. She walked slowly, touching favorite trees and flowers. Sat on a stone bench under the ancient oak trees he'd loved so much. For the rest of my life, she thought, I will look at Spanish moss and think of him.

She spoke aloud.

"Patrick, honey, this is where I'm going to say goodbye to you. Not at the funeral. I know you're here right now. I can feel you real strong. After today, you'll always be in my heart. But I don't think you're ever gonna actually *be* here the way you are right now...you know what I'm sayin'?

"Now, you do understand why I didn't tell the police anything? Like they're going to believe me that I know who killed you just because I smelled his cologne? Even if they did, that motherfucker probably has an alibi all worked out. No, let him think he got away with it. That's what I want him to think. Now, don't you worry about me, Patrick. I know what I'm doin'. I've been doin' for myself since I was a little girl. I never told you about it all, but I was dying to. And I would have. Now you know, I guess. You were my hope, Patrick. A man I could lean on."

She sat there an hour, sometimes silent, then speaking aloud to him. She explained that she'd wear the engagement ring to the funeral, then take it off forever and put it away for her first granddaughter, if she ever had one.

"I wanted your child, baby. A girl first. I wanted her so bad. And I would have been the best mother, Patrick. I swear. I'm so sad because I keep thinking I'll never have children. I know you'd tell me I'll go on and meet someone and have kids. I just don't think so, Patrick. And it will never be like it was gonna be with us."

She cried. For the last time.

The sun rose higher.

"Miss Charmain?"

The chef found her sitting there, insisted she move to the garden table and eat a light breakfast. She managed some juice and his delicious cappucino, but couldn't eat. She went upstairs and changed into the black suit and hat she'd bought for the funeral. She threw the last of her things into a small bag. She'd packed her luggage the night before and had Claude take everything over to Habersham House, an old inn near the waterfront. She'd check in for a day or two right after the funeral.

She walked downstairs. The skipper, chef, and Claude were waiting, looking stiff in their black suits. She kissed them all and said, "Thank you for being so kind to me. I will miss you and this place so much."

They walked outside and got into two cars. Claude drove her in Patrick's limo. They arrived at the church after everyone had gone inside, but the press was still at the curb, waiting for her. She was a notorious person in Savannah now, not just because she was a beauty queen who'd landed one of the town's most eligible bachelors.

Yesterday's paper had featured a front page article headlined: "DEA Investigated Taulere as Drug Kingpin, Police Admit!"

And a subhead over *her* picture: "Did Beauty Queen Know?"

Charmain stepped out of the car. Flashguns flared. Video cameras blocked her path. A female reporter shoved a microphone at her.

"Charmain, did you know Patrick Taulere was a drug bigshot?"

"No. And neither do you!" she snapped, pushing past as Claude stiff-armed through the pack.

A moment later, they were inside. Heads turned as she entered. A seat had been reserved for her in a front pew, but she sat at the back.

An hour later, at the cemetery, she left the car and stood to one side as words were said over the coffin. She looked at Solange, sitting with two younger men who looked like they might be kin. Solange glanced over once, then quickly turned away. One of the men actually winked at Charmain. She didn't look at them again.

As Patrick was lowered into the ground, she walked to the graveside and dropped a single white rose on the coffin lid. She turned to leave. Several of Patrick's friends came forward and offered condolences. Charmain was polite, but kept moving toward the car. And finally, she was speeding away.

It was over.

Almost.

Claude dropped her at Habersham House. Charlie Slade, across the street and down half a block, keyed his car radio.

"Dispatch. What you need, Charlie?"

"Patch me to the lieutenant."

A moment later, the speaker crackled.

"Fell. What's up, Charlie?"

"Subject's back at her hotel."

"Okay. Keep on her tail. Burdine has a hunch she might lead us right to the killer. And he's the boss. Don't lose her. Your partner there?"

"Yeah. He's just grabbin' a nap."

"Just make sure you both don't fall asleep."

Charlie shoved his middle finger at the speaker.

"No sir, lieutenant."

"Report right to me on anything unusual."

"Sir?"

"Yeah?"

"What if she starts drivin' out of state?"

"That's Langston Burdine's call. You just let me know before she does."

"Yessir."

"Over and out."

About an hour later, Charmain came out of the hotel, dressed in jeans and a slouchy shirt, her long auburn hair tucked up sloppily under a ball cap. She was wearing sunglasses. She started walking along the riverfront. Charlie Slade got out and followed on foot while his partner drove. He stayed well back, watching as she walked in and out of boutiques, a video rental place, a department store, a book store. Bought a few things, rented a video. Nothing unusual. Just a woman shopping. Late in the afternoon, she stopped at a riverfront cafe and ate a light meal outside. She sat there for a long time, then left and went back to the hotel.

His partner said, "You gonna report in to the loot?"

"Naw. Nothin' to report. I need to catch some sleep."

"I got it covered."

The next day, Charmain stayed in the hotel most of the day. She came out once, in late afternoon, dressed about the same as the day before. Again, she seemed to be shopping casually. She stopped to look in windows, wandered into a few shops, bought little. Only once did Charlie Slade spot anything unusual. She stopped in at an optometrist's.

Motioning to his partner in the car to take over the tail, Slade darted into the store, interrupted the only salesman, who was talking to a customer and protested until he saw the badge.

"Did that last customer, that young woman in the sunglasses, buy anything?"

"No, she didn't."

"What was she looking for?"

"Nothing, really. Said she was just browsing. Looked at some glasses.

Asked about contact lenses."

"Okay. Thanks."

Slade hit the sidewalk at a jog. His partner was parked half a block up. He pointed to a bookstore, signaling Charmain was inside. Slade slowed down and caught his breath. Ten minutes later, Charmain came out, hailed a cab, and went back to her hotel.

She never came out again that night.

In the morning, at about 11:30, Slade got nervous. He went to the hotel's front desk, flashed his badge and asked if a Charmain Burns was registered. She was.

"Any idea when she's leavin'?"

The clerk checked the registration card.

"We've got her down for two or three days. Don't know exactly, of course."

"Okay. Thanks."

Slade went back to the unmarked car, opened the door, and slid in.

"She's still there," he told his partner.

"Why don't you just have the front desk call us if she checks out, Charlie?"

"Because Langston Burdine wants this to be unofficial. We make too much of a fuss and one of those clerks will tip off the newspapers and TV for a quick fifty bucks."

"I'm gonna go get some doughnuts. You want coffee, or what?"

"Coffee."

He was back in twenty minutes. Ten minutes into a sugar high, they glanced up as a stylish brunette with short-cropped hair walked out of the hotel and crossed the street. She carried no luggage, just a handbag. She got into a car parked at a meter and drove off.

Later that afternoon, nervous that Charmain still hadn't emerged, Slade checked the front desk again.

Gone.

By the time they figured out she was the brunette and the car was a rental, she was long gone. They'd lost her clean.

Joe Fell told a very unhappy Langston Burdine, "She had the rental people deliver the car to the street. A bellman put her bags in the car before she came out. She cut her hair and dyed it. Slade says she looked five tears older, not like a kid. She could have gone in any direction, sir. Do we put out an all-points bulletin?"

The Chief of Detectives smiled. Not pleasantly.

"There's one direction we know she didn't go in, Joe, and that's east. Because east is the goddamn Atlantic Ocean, and I'm surprised a detective of your caliber hadn't figured that out. No, we're not putting out a goddamn APB. I'd look like a fool calling this woman a suspect on the run when I just had her in my jurisdiction, now wouldn't I? Forget it. I had a hunch, that's all. Now she's gone. That's it."

Joe Fell, wilting under the heat, said, "She did disguise herself."

Langston Burdine reached in his desk humidor, extracted a Punch #3 Havana and clipped it deliberately.

"Tell you what, lieutenant. You go ahead and put out that APB. And when the press comes roaring in here to find out why, you can just explain to them that we're hunting down a woman because she decided to change her goddamn hair color. That'll play real good on the evening news."

As Lieutenant Fell and Chief Burdine concluded this conversation, Charmain rolled across the Florida state line. She glanced at Patrick's watch. A Patek Phillipe. Warm and heavy on her wrist. It was five-fifteen. She was making good time. She rubbed the watch, feeling him. It was the only personal item she'd taken from the house.

The engagement ring, which she'd taken off right after the funeral, was back in its box, in her handbag on the front seat.

Along with the fat wad she'd taken from the hidey-hole.

It had counted out to $34,860.

CHAPTER 32

12:08 A.M.
MIAMI

IT took a week to find Paco.

She checked into a cheap motel in downtown Miami. Bought a cheesy bouffant blonde wig and a thrift shop dress she wore in the daytime. Stayed away from South Beach until nightfall. When the sun dropped into the ocean, she transformed herself, like some disco vampire.

Sitting naked at the rust-spotted mirror in the room, she'd apply dead-white makeup, heavy eyeliner, a beauty spot on her right cheek, red-black lipstick. Her cropped black hair was slicked with gel. Light brown contact lenses were popped in. Then a black Wonder Bra, metallic silver micro-mini dress, and cork platforms with silver straps. Or her alternate outfit of black spandex pedal-pushers, gold Carmen Miranda high heels, and gold see-through shirt hanging loose and nearly unbuttoned. And always, the dark Gautier glasses.

Around ten, she'd drive over Biscayne Bay bridge and hit the clubs. Night after night.

She didn't spot him.

The first three nights didn't discourage her. She wasn't ready for him yet, just wanted to locate him. There were things she had to get, most not that hard to come by. She'd fretted about one item, worried it might not be available.

Then she ran into the right guy, who giggled and told her, "*Hola*...no problemo, *chica!* This is Miami, man. You got the money, honey? We got the vice!"

Mira!

On the fourth night, she was ready. Burning up. Hot to find him. Hit every club, boogied with guys to make it look good, kept her eyes open. Nothing.

On the fifth night, desperate, she cruised a few late-night snack joints like Versailles.

Tasted her first *media noche*, the delicious Cuban sandwich kissed by God himself.

Still nothing.

Where are you Paco? Motherfucker!

I want you…

On the sixth night, on the dance floor at a club called "Rippoff," her heart jumped when she suddenly looked into the eyes of Paco's buddy.

Ramon.

Millie's three-night stand. Maybe Millie was still fucking him, for all she knew. Shit! Suddenly Charmain lost all confidence in her disguise. Ramon was so close she could touch him. Dancing with a zaftig blonde. Checking *her* out.

She cringed, waiting for the look of recognition. He stared right at her. Then looked down, digging her tits bouncing under the see-through. He stayed on them a few seconds, caught her eye again. And winked.

Relief flooded her. Fucking fabulous! He didn't know her. She was cool.

It must have been an omen. The next night she hit "Tumbao," a new club down the end of South Beach catering to Latins. The crowd was still thin just after midnight. Sitting alone at the bar, she looked up into the mirror…and froze.

Paco!

Alone.

He'd just walked in. Stood near the door, adjusting gold chains and bracelets. *Macho peacock fuck!* Wearing that arrogant sneer. A jolt of adrenalin fired her nerves. Staring at him in the mirror, she felt her lips curl over her teeth. Caught her own image. A she-beast looked back.

Must be cool, she told herself. Very cool.

She'd visualized this moment. The first laying on of eyes. Seeing the killer who'd taken her man. Knowing she'd experience the fury. Knowing she'd have to chill, be in control.

Cool.

Very cool.

Now. It was the moment. He came walking along the bar, checking out the talent. Two cute Latinas without escorts were standing together, laughing self-consciously as they sensed his approach, arching their backs to accentuate that most devastating Latin male magnet: the big, shapely ass.

Paco leered, but passed them by. He wanted to check out a blonde sitting by herself a few stools down from Charmain. She turned slightly away, so he had to pass her, then look back. Charmain grinned. Knew it would be no sale.

It wasn't.

The woman was a well-preserved divorcée or widow, a Miami Beach type. Or maybe Boca Raton. Lean, tanned, still amazing for mid-fifties. Rich enough to support a plastic surgeon. Cruising for a Latin toyboy.

The woman looked at Paco, smiled. He rolled his eyes. Kept moving.

Now. Her turn.

Cool…very cool…

Look him in the eye…don't flinch, goddamnit!

He stopped, facing Charmain. Jesus! Her stomach churned. That smell. The cologne. Triggering images that she shut down instantly. She forced herself to swing around. Looked at him, seductively, over the rim of her Gautiers. Then slowly turned away in classic feigned indifference that was test, not turndown.

She tensed. Had he recognized her? What'll he do if...

"Hola, chica. Hablas Español?"

She wheeled around on the stool. Time to test the accent.

"You tawkin' to me?"

Ohgod. That sucked.

Paco grinned. "Hey, you from New York?"

Relief.

She tilted her chin, gave him a cocky, tough once-over.

"Yeeah? So?"

"Come on, baby, give me a break. *I love Nueva York.* I go there a lot. Hey, I bet you come from the Bronx."

"The Brawnx? Fuhgeddaboudit!"

"Okay, okay. Hey, I bet Brooklyn."

"Whaddaya know! Chico here is a regular Albert Einstein."

"It's Paco. Hey, I buy you a drink, okay?"

"Well," she said slowly.

"BARTENDER! Hey, *hombre,* the lady is thirsty!"

Now she was cool.

Very cool.

The accent sounded stupid, but good enough to fool his Latin ear. In Savannah, she'd rented a videotape of a comedy she'd seen once. *My Cousin Vinnie.* She'd studied it over and over in the hotel. Never laughed once. Just studied the star, Marisa Tomei, her New York attitude and accent. She'd tried the "Noo Yawk" thing out on a few people since Savannah. No one laughed in her face. And it did cover her Southern accent.

Goddamn.

It was working.

Her first acting gig.

CHAPTER 33

1:45 A.M.
PACO'S APARTMENT
MIAMI

IT had been too fucking easy.

She let him buy her a couple of drinks. The silver micro-mini floored him. His eyes raked her thighs and pushed-up tits in the black Wonder Bra. He kept asking her to dance, but she put him off.

"I like to tawk. So, you're Cuban, right?"

He puffed up, indignant.

"No! I am Colombian."

She batted her eyes. "Oooooh, you don't say? Isn't Colombia where they grow that great coffee? And other stimulants?"

She giggled to cover the shock of his hand on her thigh. Her skin crawling. Knew she had to let him touch her. Get used to it, she warned herself.

He said seriously, "Colombian people are toughest of all Latins."

"You know, I heard that," she said. She lowered her voice. "My old boyfriend up in Brooklyn? He was a wiseguy, ya know?"

"Ah. Mafia? *Sí.*"

"Yeah. And Vinnie always said, 'Never fuck wit' no Colombian.' "

"That's right."

"Vinnie, he was real tough. Did some real bad things to people. Like, broke their bones, ya know?"

"Broken bones? It's nothing."

She said mockingly, "Oh, yeah? So what do you do, big man? Mr. Badass Colombian? Huh? What?"

He leaned over, put a hand on the side of her breast, spoke in her ear.

"One guy, he fucked with me, I cut his balls off."

He paused, added, "Down in Colombia, you know?"

She shrugged. "Big deal. I heard Vinnie cut a guy's balls off once."

He gripped her breast and squeezed.

"Yeah. Well, I put this guy's balls on a sharp whatchoocallit and showed them to him. Told him he'd have to eat them. But the *maricon* died on me!"

It was all she could do not to vomit in his face.

Deep breaths, she told herself. Deep breaths.

He took her sighs for passion. Squeezed the other breast. Breathed in her ear. Called her by the name she'd given him.

"So, Tina, you like guys *machos hombres*, eh?"

"Oh, yeah. Let's dance," she said.

She led him out on the floor, then stopped, fanned her face, and said, "Gawd, it's so hot. I don't want to sweat all over you. Wait here. I'm just gonna get a hankie."

She walked back to the bar, rummaged in her purse, fished out a handkerchief. And the hard-to-find item.

Which hadn't been so hard to find.

She vamped back onto the dance floor. She swung her hips, shook her ass, hiked the mini to the redline and bent over, showing dangerous cleavage. Let him take it all in. After a few minutes, she moved in, started slow dancing up against him. He ground against her, reaching around, grabbing her ass.

After two records, Paco was in heat. Bumping his erection against her.

She said in his ear, "Are we gonna stay here all night?"

He dragged her off the floor, signaled the bartender for the check.

"Hey, calm down," she whined. "I'm not goin' anywhere until I cool off in this air-conditioning. Let's drink these and have one more. A nightcap."

The bartender moved off, came back with another round.

Now Paco was all over her, hands swarming, sweaty. He tried to kiss her. She shoved him hard. The tough Brooklyn chick.

"Not here," she said. "I don't like heavy making-out in public. It's low class. Let's talk for a minute, for Chrissake!"

She got him talking. He liked soccer. She told him she didn't know shit about it, asked him to explain the game. He babbled non-stop. Downed his drink, started on the next.

Ten minutes later, he shook his head, yawned. Looked at his watch.

"Man, I'm getting sleepy," he said. "I started work early today."

"Let's go," she said. "Let's get cozy at your place. Then you can tell me more about soccer. You have a car?"

He rubbed his hands over his face. "Car? No, no car. Parking is bad on the beach."

They went outside, hailed a cab. He gave the address, dozed off. She woke him when they arrived at his place, a small house near the beach. More like a big, one-room cottage, really. Run-down bachelor pad. He got the door open, walked inside, and flopped down on the couch.

"Hey…uh…get us a drink…I sleep *un poco*…"

He slept more than *un poco*.

She slapped his face. Once…Twice…A third time, harder.

He woke up then, tried to speak. But all that came out was a garbled mumble as he tried to talk around the rubber ball filling his mouth and the duct tape sealing his lips.

Disoriented, eyes streaked with terror. Charmain standing over him.

What the fuck? He was on the bed…?

"Uuummmm…UUUMMMHHHH!"

He struggled to rise. Metal bit into his wrists, ankles.

Madre de Dios!

Handcuffs.

His mind fought to concentrate. Cloudy. He shook his head. Looked at her. She looked…different.

"Remember me, Paco?"

Charmain walked closer, leaned over him, pulled her hair back from her face. She'd scrubbed it clean of makeup, taken out the contact lenses after she'd dragged him over to the bed and immobilized him.

"Think of me with lighter hair, reddish-blonde. You were hot for my body. Remember? About two months ago? The beauty queen? At Don Diego's?"

A flicker in his eyes.

"Ah, so you do remember? You filthy fucking pig. I never forgot you and that stinking, cheap fucking cologne. Do you ever get laid, Paco? Can any woman get past that smell without heaving? Or is that why you have to rape girls? Like you tried to rape me."

Charmain stepped back, studied him.

"Look at you. All helpless. Just like I would have been if I'd swallowed my drink that night. You were going to use rohypnol on me! Knock me out with the 'date rape drug.' Then, fuck me. Right, Paco?

"Bet you were gonna slip your dick in my mouth, too. Eh, Paco? And, oh, I know, after that, you were gonna turn me over and fuck my ass. Right, Paco? Sure! That's a power trip for a macho man like you. I'd just be lying there helpless. Like you are now, motherfucker."

She smiled. He glared back. Defiant.

"Oh, you eyein' me, boy? Got attitude?"

She leaned close to him. Whispered.

"Let's pretend it's the night you tried to rape me. And you've got me here, all helpless. Only I'll be you and you be me. Role reversal. Okay?

"Now, let's see, the first thing you would have done was…? I know! Rip off my top and look at my tits. Am I right? Like…*this!*"

She yanked hard. Buttons popped, exposing his chest.

"Oh, you don't have tits. So what do I do? Play with your hairy chest? You sure got a lot of hair. I bet you rub that cheap shit cologne in your chest hair every night before you go out and rape girls."

She sat down on the bed, reached to the night table, picked up an ornate blue and gold bottle.

"Here's your cologne. Let me put some on for you."

She took out the stopper, drenched his chest.

"WHEW! What a stink! This shit throws out some fumes. Worse'n gasoline. Don't you ever worry it might explode?"

Charmain reached out again, picked up a cigarette lighter.

"Aren't you scared some girl you're lookin' to rape might light a cigarette too close to your chest, and..."

She flicked the lighter.

FFFWWOOOOOOMMMM!

Blue fire. He screamed through the gag, lunged upward, shaking wildly.

Flames licked the hair, burned off and died. His chest smoked like a woodlot after a forest fire.

His muffled screams segued into whimpers. Charmain leaned over and whispered:

"You're on your deathbed, Paco. Scared yet?"

She looked at his eyes.

Glazed.

"This role-playin' is fun, huh, Paco? Now I know why you love rohypnol. You can get people all helpless and play any way you want. That's why I went out and bought some myself."

She saw the flicker of comprehension.

"That's right, asshole! I slipped rohypnol in *your* drink. What a hoot, huh? That's how I got you tied down here like a hog for slaughter."

She whispered in his ear again. "I'm a country girl, Paco. I've helped my daddy slaughter pigs."

She stood, winked at him.

"You've got a ways to go yet, bubba. A ways to go."

Tears ran down his cheeks.

"Aw, don't cry, macho man. You're Colombian, right? The toughest of all Latins, didn't you say? And you've had a wonderful life, raping girls, and traveling, seeing the world. You're quite a tourist, aren't you? Been to Savannah lately?"

Paco shook his head violently.

"NNNNNUUUUHHHH!"

"You tryin' to say 'no'? Don't lie, Paco. Not now. You even told me what you did to my man, back at the bar."

She walked across the room to a low table in front of the couch. Picked up her handbag, walked back. Put it on the bed and sat down next to him. She rummaged in the bag and removed some items. Paco strained to see. She ignored him.

"You know, some people would say I should have told the police in Savannah that I smelled your scummy cologne, and that you murdered my Patrick because he saved me from gettin' raped by you. But I thought, shit, the courts couldn't convict O.J. Even with all that blood, and bloody footprints and hairs...all that evidence. How were they gonna convict you on one lousy smell?

"So I thought, 'Charmain, you've got to do for yourself, girl, because nobody's going to help you. Patrick was my man. I loved him. He was going to protect me forever. Then you came along, Paco, and you...you—"

She felt the tears feathering at the edge of her self-control. Can't let that happen. Got a job here.

Cool…very cool…

"Don't know if it's right, but it feels right to me, Paco. And if I don't do it, who will? You'll be walkin' around free. No. I don't think so."

She looked at him.

"Oh, I almost forgot our game. Remember? I'm you and you're me. So what would you have done to me next, Paco? Oh, right, you'd pull down my panties and look at my pussy, touch it a little before you fucked me. Okay…"

She got up, yanked his pants down to his ankles, then his underpants.

"Okay, I'm lookin' at it. It ain't much. But it'll do. The real fun is in having someone all helpless, right, Paco?"

She sat on the bed again. Held up her hands and showed them to him, back and front. She was wearing rubber surgical gloves. She'd put them on after Paco passed out. Before she'd touched anything in the room.

"Neat, huh? Let's play doctor, Paco."

She selected the last item from her bag of tricks. and held it up so he could see it

The straight razor.

She flicked it open.

Wiggled the blade in the lamplight, watching his terror-stricken eyes reflect the bright flash of razor-sharp steel.

"Know where I got the idea for a razor, Paco? It's an old family secret. Not my family. Patrick Taulere's!"

He whimpered again, shaking his head violently, eyes pleading.

Charmain smiled, stood up.

"Look on the bright side, Paco. You finally get to see me naked. But not helplesss, of course, so I guess you won't get turned on."

She unzipped the silver mini, pulled it over her head. Stripped off the Wonder Bra, panties, garter belt.

Posed.

"What do you think, Paco?"

She looked at his cock.

"No reaction? That's a shame. It would have made this…neater?

"Oh, and in case you're wondering why I got naked, don't think I'm kinky or anything…it's for the blood. Can't leave here in messy clothes."

He started thrashing back and forth, screaming…screaming…

She swiftly bent at the waist, gripped the knob of his penis in her rubber-gloved hands and pulled up, stretching it taut. Laid the sharp edge of the blade at its base.

And sliced.

"Motherfucker! MURDERER!"

She held up her trophy.

Threw it in his face.

"UUUUMMMMMHHHHHH…UUUMMMMHHHH!"

He bucked and heaved. She bent over him again, found his scrotum, stretched it.

The razor flashed.

Ohgod, so much blood. But this part she knew. Done it on the pigs with Daddy back home. Working fast now. Her gloved fingers found one testicle. Sliced. Found the other. Sliced.

"UUUUUMMMMMHHHHHH…"

His face turned to bright, mottled red as he screamed through the duct tape. She stood up, held out a rubber-encased palm. Showed him his balls.

And dropped them on his burnt chest.

She stood. Stripped off the gloves. Observed him for a moment. He was howling, thrashing, but getting weaker. She leaned down, shrieked in his ear, over the noise of his death throes.

"Patrick Taulere says hello, Paco. He's watching you go to hell with no cock and balls!"

Charmain tossed the gloves and razor on the bed. Went into the bathroom, showered for three minutes, came out and dressed.

She looked around. Good. Nothing to tie me to this but hair and fibers. They always find those. Not that it'll do them any damn good. Not without a suspect. And nobody suspected her.

Just in case, though…

She walked over to the bed. Looked at him. Still alive. Not for long, probably. But better safe than sorry.

She picked up the nearly full cologne bottle. Started sprinkling it over him, the bed, and the newspapers she'd spread on the floor to soak up his blood.

"Paco," she said, "I hope you can hear me. But even if you can't, I know you can still feel pain. And that makes me real happy. Because there's nothin' worse than burning to death…just like you're gonna burn in hell."

She hefted her bag onto her shoulder, walked to the door and flicked the lighter. She bent, lit the newspaper, watched the flames race toward the bed.

"Said you had a ways to go yet, Bubba. Goodbye, you piece of shit!"

And she was gone.

CHAPTER 34

9:28 A.M.
I-95 NORTH
FLORIDA/GEORGIA BORDER

CHARMAIN goosed the rented Mustang GT convertible north up I-95 toward the Florida-Georgia border. She felt strange, tingly and numb all at once. Sad, yet weirdly jazzed. Patrick was gone. A ghost. But the blood debt was paid. It was as right as it could be.

Her skin twitched the first few times she spotted a state trooper, but she got over it fast. Fuck it. They caught her, fine. She really didn't care. It was all fate, anyway. A life lesson: bad shit can happen to beautiful people. Okay. Got it. No one ever fucks me over again.

No one.

Just before she hit Jacksonville, a huge DOT sign posted destinations. First listing for North was "Savannah." Charmain's chest heaved. She swung the wheel toward the setting sun, shot across the interchange marked West—"I-10." And cried until there was nothing left.

She drove all night across the Florida Panhandle, stopping once for coffee and pancakes at a Waffle House and again at a deserted rest stop to do some cocaine she'd bought in Miami. Keep her awake, she figured. Halfway between Tallahassee and Pensacola, she had a strong urge to leave the I-10, turn north toward Citrus Corners and fall into Millie's arms. No, she thought, past is past. Over. Done. Head for the sun. Hollywood, here I come. Ha, ha.

Just before dawn, Charmain pulled into a Red Roof Inn outside Mobile, Alabama, and crashed until late afternoon. She awoke ravenous. Drove into Mobile, ate a huge steak, then pushed the Mustang through the night to New Orleans. The Big Easy. Patrick's hometown.

She checked into the Royal Sonesta Hotel on Bourbon Street, but didn't sleep. She showered, called room service, ordered coffee and *beignets*, a local confection of delicate fried bread and powdered sugar. Patrick had told her about *beignets*, said they'd share them at their first New Orleans breakfast together. Two words: dee-lish.

She left the hotel, walked through the French Quarter until she reached the Mississippi. She wandered along the bank, watching barges and paddlewheel boats drift up and down the river; imagined Patrick as a boy playing around the docks, diving into the river on hot summer days, fishing from the banks. Suddenly, she stopped, shook her head. What had she expected? That he'd magically reappear, speak to her again? That she'd feel his spirit as strongly as she had that day in Savannah, in the garden? Stupid.

"Goodbye, baby," she said.

She turned away from the mighty river, walked back through the French Quarter, checked out of the hotel without sleeping. And left him behind forever.

HOORAY FOR HOLLYWOOD!

CHAPTER 35

12:22 P.M.
THE POLO LOUNGE
BEVERLY HILLS

"CHARMAIN hit this town like a goddam cyclone," said Mike Kelso.

"That she did," agreed Cameron Tull.

It was mid-afternoon, mid-week. This was the hour when the Polo Lounge at the Beverly Hills Hotel, poised between lunch and cocktails, was quiet, almost deserted, a perfect place to conduct an interview. Tull scheduled them here often. It was his first ever with Mike Kelso, a mid-level talent manager who'd been kicking around for years. Not a bad guy, but a lightweight. Smart enough, but no killer instinct. Mike specialized in managing the careers of nubile young hotties. Never got romantically involved with them, apparently, but obviously had some kind of murky letch for young stuff.

Mike Kelso worked hard; supported his chickies until they got jobs. Yet invariably, every time he got a girl's career to where she was getting some buzz, she'd dump the poor putz for a big-name manager or agent. Uncle Mikey just couldn't con any broad past voting age. So sad.

Welcome to Hollywood.

Rumors abounded about how Mike Kelso landed roles for his girls. Some were true, and Tull knew it, but who cared? Time was, he wouldn't have wasted ink on Kelso and his stable of struggling nymphets. But suddenly, this over-the-hill schlepp had heat. The Show Biz Fairy Godmother, that fickle bitch, had tapped his limp dick with her magic wand and led him to discover TV's hottest new star. Now Kelso and his happening client, Charmain Burns, were first-classing it on the Hollywood Express. And Charmain looked like she just might be more than flavor-of-the-month.

Even the stodgy *L.A. Times* had written: "Her acting's raw around the edges, but Charmain Burns has star quality to, well...burn. If you've ever wondered what Hollywood means by 'It,' this stunning 'BevHills High' newcomer might be, well...*It*."

Charmain had just completed her first season on TV in a blaze of front page headlines. Most of them scandalous. Many generated by Cameron Tull's *National Revealer* gossip column.

Sipping his perfectly-foamed Polo Lounge cappucino, Tull considered again why he was here, interviewing Mike Kelso, rather than Charmain herself. It was just a hunch, but he figured that probing Kelso for unique insights into his client might be invaluable preparation for the main event. More importantly, he was thinking of doing a book on her. He'd interview Charmain in good time. Right now, he wanted to bond with Kelso and hear his take on how a barely-legal Florida cracker gal had triumphed so swiftly in a town that endlessly conspires to murder talent at birth.

Tull had become the acknowledged journalistic expert on Charmain. He had several sources close to her; one in particular who was, in a word, fantastic, knew damn near everything about her. So when the inquiring minds of Larry, Maury, Sally, Geraldo, Barbara, Diane, or Katy needed to know, Tull was the *primo* "talking head" in their Rolodexes. He earned hefty fees yammering on TV about Charmain and why she was so deliciously bad. Then just days ago, he'd had a call from Random House publishing wunderkind Liza Wyman, who'd urged him to make Charmain the subject of his next book. Tull had written two celeb books, both bestsellers.

"This could be a blockbuster," Liza enthused. "There are at least two proposals at major houses right now. The writers are nobodies, so I'm not vomiting blood or anything. But someone will do this book and you're the right guy. Cameron Tull does Charmain Burns? Wow! I'm *itching* to write you a fat advance check. So say the word. But say it fast. Or I'll probably go ahead without you."

Tull laughed. "You're *itching*?"

"Scratch me, baby," she cooed.

"I'm fascinated. We'll talk."

Charmain Burns truly did fascinate Tull. She was that rare animal, a bona fide overnight success. Came out of nowhere, hit the bigtime in one swift leap. And she'd done it without grinding her way through the "starlet mill"—sucking up to agents and producers; taking acting lessons; strutting the meat at auditions; cruising film premieres to pose desperately for the papparazzi; showing tits and ass in low budget straight-to-video flicks.

And, Tull was fairly certain, she hadn't gone the time-honored route of fucking her producer. Tull knew Larry Buckley, the staggeringly successful creator of *BevHills High*. He didn't play couch games. Not with the talent, anyway. For Buckley, "fuck" was a business verb.

No, Charmain hadn't needed a sugar-daddy, or heavy hype. She'd hit town Hollywood-ready. She had The Power; that special inner fire that pulsed almost visibly through the skin; glowed in the eyes. All the greats had it: Garbo, Gable, Garland, Rooney, Monroe, Dean, Brando, Taylor, Sinatra, Connery, Cruise, Madonna, Jackson, De Niro, and Roseanne, who typified the new breed of star women.

But danger accompanied this gift of heavenly flame. It could rage quickly out of control, consume a career, burn out the core of talent in a firestorm of booze, drugs, and fear; shrivel a giant to a hollow husk. Like Rooney, Garland, Monroe, Brando, Michael Jackson. Roseanne had come close to immolation...and yes, even Taylor.

Tull grinned inwardly, listenening as Kelso chattered on about his client. The guy's adrenalin was pumping hard. This was an exciting career first for him, being interviewed by an important columnist.

"You know, Cameron, getting a break in this town can be murder, even if you've got talent," he said, with the air of a man revealing a great, hitherto unknown, truth. "Then, every once in a while, somebody comes along who makes it to the top just like *that*!" He snapped his fingers. "But even then, they need expert guidance and management. When a talent make a really bad move, something that could kill their career before it starts...well, that's when you need an old pro like me. Just ask Charmain." He rolled his eyes and thought, Ha! If you only knew!

Tull pursed his lips, nodded judiciously. "Yeah, she's lucky to have good advice. It's a rare thing."

He sipped his cappuccino, then asked casually, "So...what bad move did she make?"

Kelso, suddenly alert, masked his face in a quizzical smile. Shit! That was dumb. Don't let your guard down with this guy. He's one of the best in the business.

"Oh, you know," Kelso vamped. "The usual. Staying out late partying, not getting that old beauty sleep, showing up in torn jeans for interviews, blowing off acting lessons. Ha, ha...you know Charmain, right?"

"Right," said Tull, knowing he was now hearing horseshit. He shrugged inwardly. Kelso was hiding something—and he'd let slip the direction to look in. Tull would make inquiries, ask people who'd known Charmain before she'd hit it big. But what bad move had she made? Kelso's little slip sounded intriguing. Tull had sources to check with, but wondered if any of them went far enough back to know what Kelso was referring to. He'd implied it was something that happened before Charmain's career got off the ground...

Sweat was popping on Kelso's upper lip. Goddamnit. Get under control, he chided himself. This guy's job is making people drop their guard. *Don't* let him do it to you. He shuddered. If Tull got even a whiff of what he'd meant when he'd stupidly mentioned Charmain's "bad move"—how she'd nearly killed her chance at stardom the first time she'd met Larry Buckley—Mike Kelso would end up begging for spare change on Hollywood Boulevard. Only a handful of heavies could say, "You'll never work in this town again!"—and make the threat stick. Buckley was one of them.

Tull sensed Kelso's panic. Time to chill him out. Never spook an interview subject. Not before you need to, anyway. And not before you've sucked him dry of the basic facts you need for your story. Then, and only then, do you ask the tough question, i.e., "Does the fact that you're fucking the sixteen-year-old babysitter mean there's trouble in your marriage?"

Leave the worst for last, so that if the subject slugs you, or storms off without uttering a usable quote, you still have enough to file your story.

"Mike, tell me about the first time you laid eyes on Charmain," said Tull.

Keslo's eyes softened. He sighed, settled back against the Polo Lounge banquette. That's better, thought Tull. He smiled at Kelso, waited.

"Well, I'll never forget that day, of course. It changed my life. Both of our lives. Hers and mine. It was at Frank Emmet's place in Malibu. A Sunday barbecue. You know Frank? Mr. Hula Girl? Runs the beauty contests for his tanning products...? Whoops, sorry. You know everybody, of course. Well, anyway, I was at Frank's place, practically a mansion, right on the beach. On a Sunday. And it was like most of Frank's parties. A crowd of gorgeous girls, a few high-roller guys, Frank at the barbecue, cooking ribs and chicken with a cell phone plugged into his ear. The man never stops making deals. At one point, I overheard him setting up a beauty contest in Dubai, talking to some sheik.

"I've known Frank forever. Managed some of the girls who did his contests. Did pretty well with a few of them. He likes seeing his beauty contest winners go on to bigger things. So he usually calls me when there's a party at the Malibu beach house. It's always very loose, laid back. Frank never makes a fuss or introduces you to the girls or anybody. You just grab a drink and some food and hang out.

"There's a lotta eye candy running around, of course. The Hula Girls are very young and fresh. Some of the girls who come up from Latin America are as young as fifteen, although you'd never know it. They mature early down there. But because the girls are so young, right out of the heartland, it gets a little trying to actually talk to them, you know? I mean, a lot of them have been to smalltown charm schools, or modeling schools. They're wearing too damn much makeup, especially for the beach. And they talk in these exaggerated voices, speaking very distinctly, as if you're some low-grade moron from a foreign country. They've been told that this is how you act 'poised.' Ridiculous. One of the first things I tell my clients is, knock it off and talk like a young girl. Get all breathless and silly if you feel like it. Don't hold back. Just be natural. Men love young girls and they like them to sound like young girls, not like the whisky-voiced hags they're going to become someday."

Kelso paused, aware his voice sounded loud in the late afternoon quiet of the lounge. "Sorry, I sound like I'm lecturing."

Tull shook his head earnestly. Time for some stroke-stroke.

"Oh, no," he said. "It's fascinating to hear a professional talk about what he knows best. You're famous for advising young women on how to enter a very tough business. And I guess you must develop an eye, or an instinct, for what's real...and what's not."

Kelso suppressed a modest grin. "People think it's easy, managing talent. But it's damn hard. It's not like being an agent. Those guys have got it easy, in my opinion. Just book the job, no matter what it is. Don't think about your client's long-term career goals. If there's no work, if things are looking cold, well, hell, just dump them. Find somebody else. Book the job. The agent makes the same ten percent commission, no matter who he books. Sure, a personal manager takes a higher percentage, but he works for it. He's not just booking jobs. He's advising, thinking, planning. A manager is in for the long haul, the good times and the bad. He's..."

Tull interrupted quietly. "Charmain. What made you see she had a shot?"

Kelso got a look on his face. Not reverent exactly. Sort of a goofy zealot thing, Tull decided. Like a Hare Krishna. Or Ken Starr. Kelso began to speak in hushed tones, like a man at worship.

"I walked away from the crowd on the lawn and went around the back of the house. There's a big deck that juts out over the rocks and looks down on the beach. I stood there, the sun in my eyes, and looked out at the ocean. A surf was running, so no one was swimming, or so I thought. Until I spotted this head out in the water. Man or woman, I didn't know. I looked down for a minute to blink away the glare. When I looked again, there she was, walking out of the surf, flicking her head to shake water out of her hair, which was the first thing I could make out. It looked reddish gold in the sun. I squinted. As she came up the sand, I could look down on her more, get my eyes out of the direct sunlight. I saw that dead-white skin. And a dark patch between her legs. For a minute, I thought she was naked. But no, she was wearing a tiny black thong. And a white T-shirt. It was wet and you could see her breasts, large pink nipples. Her hair, which wasn't very long, was pulled back in a tight ponytail, tied by a white ribbon.

"She walked like...I don't know, like a cat, or an athlete. Everything moved perfectly. She looked so slim and feminine, but so strong. You could see muscle move in her thighs as she walked, and her hips and ass swung in that weighted, sensual way you often see with the Latin American girls, switching one side to the other with a sort of snap. And her breasts were bouncing just enough so you could sense that they were the real thing. With lots of muscle tone.

"She ignored the stairs leading up from the beach and started climbing the rocks, moving quickly, like she had lots of balance, leaping over the gaps like a goddamn deer. She stopped on a flat rock and stood there a minute, stretching. She saw me watching her, I know, but suddenly she just stripped off that T-shirt, sat down on the rock and started wringing the water out of it. She shook it out in the wind, then put it back on and came over the rocks to the deck. She pulled herself up over the rail about twenty feet from where I was standing and flopped down in a chaise lounge shaded by a big umbrella.

"After a minute, I walked over to her..."

Kelso was talking rapidly now, his words pale translations of the vivid images flashing across his mind. The memory of that special day was still so fresh; the sunlight etching the coarse grain of the wooden planks as he walked across the deck; salty gusts whipping his sparse gray hair down over his glasses; her face turning lazily toward him; an awareness of how loudly his feet were thudding on the weathered lumber as he approached her; the sudden, weird shutter-click in his mind's-eye of Frankenstein lurching toward the village beauty. She looked up at him, waiting.

"Uh, hello...hope I wasn't, er...interfering with your sunbathing."

He'd cursed himself the moment he said it. Idiot! She'll think you're trying to start a conversation about seeing her bare-breasted.

Her eyes locked on his. God. Green eyes. For a moment, he saw nothing else. So incredibly beautiful. Magnetic.

"I never sunbathe," she said, lifting a knee and arching her back. "I'm from the sunniest place in the world, and God gave us common sense along with our pretty white skins so we wouldn't sit outside and cook. That's for lizards, snakes, and gators. Not people."

Now his gaze found her pouty mouth. Full, pink lips framing small white teeth. Jesus.

"Where are you from?"

"Florida."

"Are you an actress?"

"No."

"Well, you're going to be. If you want to."

He fished out a card, handed it to her.

"I'm a talent manager. A good one. Ask Frank. My name's Mike Kelso."

She glanced at the card, then casually slipped it down the front of her hankie-sized thong. A twang of sexual heat pulled blood out of Kelso's brain, dizzying him. She said:

"I'm Charmain...Burns."

He breathed in, tried to smile casually. "I know this is a social event," he said, "but I'd like to talk business with you, even for a few moments. May I get you a drink?"

"Maybe later for both, Mike."

She pushed up on the arms of the chaise and stood. Oh, man. Five-and-a-half feet of heaven in a ponytail. He was drowning in her aura, exultant and sad all at once; knowing she'd never be his to possess, yet certain he was destined to become part of her life, however small. From this moment on. Hers to command. Her eyes told him she knew his whole story. Had seen it in men's eyes before.

Beautiful young girls were Kelso's business, but he'd never encountered a sexual dynamo like Charmain Burns. It wasn't just her face, the body, or even the eyes. It was what it always was: the star thing. Charmain had it.

The Power.

It was invisible, but tangible; a force that reached out and captured the eyes, made you look. It coiled around the senses, made you resonate to its charisma, its strength. And it let you feel the fear, the fragile vulnerability lurking beneath the incandescence, the dark curse endlessly poised to destroy the gift.

She smiled up at him.

Face so young.

Soul so old.

"Stick close," she said. "Got to mingle with the other bitches. And the horny boys."

She turned, walked away without looking back.

He stuck close.

Kelso focused on the memory, then noticed that Tull had just jotted something on a Polo Lounge napkin. Was he telling this guy too much? Ah, what the hell. He loved reliving that magical day. He laughed sharply, shook his head, took a sip of the campari and soda.

"Man," he told Tull. "You should have seen it. Charmain walked into that crowd of two or three dozen hot-looking girls all twittering away with all these guys circling them like lions. And every eye in the place started following her. And it was the girls, not the men, who honed in on her first, I swear to God. Women just have that feline sixth sense when another available female enters the killing ground, so to speak. They want to check her out, see if she's got anything worth trying to copycat. And usually, they turn away after a minute or two, depending on how hot the new competition is.

"But with Charmain, they never stopped looking. They kept glancing over at her. And then back at the men, to see how they were reacting. And the men tried to be polite, tried not to ignore the girls they'd been talking to. But they couldn't help themselves. Their eyes just kept sliding away to Charmain as she strolled through that crowd, saying hello. Barefoot, no makeup, wet hair, as good as naked in that little thong that looked nonexistent from behind. Not even trying to look good amidst all those babes in their designer sports clothes and bathing suits, the carefully careless hair and stagey makeup.

"But the guys couldn't stop with their sneaky eyes. They'd look away, look back. I was standing, watching this whole thing, and it was almost comical. Remember, these are Hollywood types. Studio execs, agents, producers. Along with some high roller business heavies. They see the most beautiful girls in the world every day. But Charmain had that special something they all kept coming back to.

"She walked up to Frank Emmet, gave him a kiss on the cheek. She said something to him and his eyes flicked over to me. He leaned down, whispering to her, then slapped her on the fanny and went back to flipping the meat on his barbecue grill. She moved on, not stopping to talk to anybody, and went into the house. I was nervous. What had Frank said about me? Well, I'd find out soon enough. Patience really is a virtue. I went over to Frank, grabbed a plate. He threw on a piece of chicken and said, 'There's a nice piece of young breast for you, Mike, my compliments.' And he winked. That's how Frank operated. I knew then that he'd put in a word for me. I was so damn happy.

"I ate, finished my drink and headed toward the bar for a refill. Then I heard her voice cut through the chatter. 'Hey, Mike.' Not loud. It didn't have to be. She knew I'd be listening for her. I looked up to where she was standing on a second-floor terrace. She said, 'I'll take that drink now. Lemonade.' She gestured at me to come up, then disappeared back inside.

"I got the drink, took it upstairs. And I kept telling myself, 'This is the one. She's gonna go all the way. And you just got lucky, Kelso, because she's the new girl in town and nobody knows her yet. Don't blow this.' I mean, I was excited. I didn't even know if she could act yet. But who cared? Did you see Marilyn Monroe in her first movie? Or her second or third? Do you remember her acting? Of course not. It didn't matter. You couldn't take your eyes off her. She was up there on that movie screen and she just belonged there. Period. And suddenly one day, everybody noticed she could act. It was a bonus. But not a requirement. Monroe was a star. Charmain is a star. And at the end of the day, that's what makes Hollywood work."

CHAPTER 36

FRANK EMMET'S HOUSE
MALIBU

KELSO entered the Malibu house carrying Charmain's drink. He walked up the back staircase, called her name. She stepped out into the hall and beckoned him into a bedroom. He handed her the drink.

"Thanks," she said. Waved him to a chair. She was wearing a pink satin robe that looked vaguely oriental. Two suitcases were on the bed. Was she packing or unpacking? She sat on the bed, facing him. The robe slid open, exposing her legs. She sipped her drink and looked at him.

"You wanted to talk business?"

"Oh, yes. Of course. Look, I'm a personal manager, as I told you. My specialty is young actresses and I have several who work steadily in TV, sometimes in movies."

He gave her a quick rundown of his credits and his clients. Then he said, "Look, I think...no, I know...you're very special. No one has to tell you you're beautiful. You've been hearing that since you were a kid. But so far, nobody who's got the professional expertise to spot talent has seen what you've got. I don't know if you can act, but I know you're a star. You've got it. But sometimes even the people who are supposed to know need convincing. Need to see you showcased.

"That's where I come in. I want to handle your career in the worst way. I'm not giving you a Hollywood line. I want to start off with total honesty between us. I'll tell you right now that I'm not the most powerful manager in this town. But I'm good and I'm effective. I've just never had the lucky break of finding a talent like you before anybody else laid eyes on her. Believe me, I won't blow this opportunity. I've trained my whole life for it and I'm ready. I'll make you a star. I swear it. Please let me handle your career. I know you'll want to think this over, but I'd really like to conclude an agreement as soon as..."

She walked over and looked down at him, green eyes hard and cold as jade.

"I'm going to tell you this once," she said. "After that, it's your funeral. Okay?"

Confused, he said, "Okay—"

"I'm dangerous. You believe me?"

"Yes."

"I live by one rule now: nobody fucks me over. Understand?"

Jesus.

"Yes."

She thrust out her hand. He recoiled. And she laughed. A real belly laugh.

"Ohmigod, did y'all think I was gonna thump on you?"

"Uh, well..."

"Mike, I swear, when I do, you will never see it coming. Now shake hands, damnit, and help me pack."

Head swimming, he heaved himself up, shook her hand. She laughed again, kissed him on the cheek, went to the closet, and started throwing clothes on the bed.

"Uh, so we've got a deal?"

"You bet, bud. For life. Or until you screw it up. I'm hell to fuck with, but I'm loyal. That handshake's the only deal you're gonna get. No contracts or paperwork shit. Okay?"

"Yeah. I guess... Yeah, OKAY!"

He yelled it, pumped his fist in the air. So goddamn happy! She smiled at him...

The memory faded as Kelso noticed two waiters glancing over curiously as they readied the Polo Lounge for cocktail hour. Tull smiled. Kelso looked embarrassed.

"Sorry," he said. "Was I getting loud again? Forgot where I was."

"Don't blame you," said Tull.

"Goddamn! I was so happy when she said yes. It was the best deal I ever made. And it was so easy."

Tull nodded. "The best ones usually are. What happened then? I don't understand something. Was Charmain packing to leave Frank Emmet's place?"

"Yes. Turns out she'd been staying there for a couple of weeks while Frank was out of town. She'd just come to L.A. from Florida and didn't know anybody. She called Frank for advice and he told her to stay at his Malibu place until she got her bearings. He's not there more than two or three months out of the year. She had it to herself for a few weeks.

"Then when she talked to Frank at the barbecue, he said I was a good guy and she should think of signing with me. He told her I had a big house in the Valley where she could stay. So she'd made her decision and started packing before I even got upstairs with her drink. Knew she was going to sign before I even asked her. Is she a goddamn pistol, or what?"

Tull grinned. "Speaking of pistols..."

Damn, Kelso berated himself. There I go again. Poor choice of words.

"I would imagine that Charmain's violent streak must be difficult to deal with as a manager," Tull continued. "When did you first realize she had this problem?"

"Well, I don't see it as a violent streak. No, I really don't. I've never seen Charmain be anything but charming and nice to people—until someone gets in her face, as she puts it. I honestly have never seen her start trouble." He paused, leaned forward and looked at Tull earnestly.

"That's the truth," he lied. "But she doesn't shrink from confrontation, either. Someone pushes her, she pushes back."

"Or she sticks a gun in their face," Tull offered.

"Oh, a lot of the press reports about that have been exaggerated. With all due respect. I think it's been overblown. Really."

"Let me refresh your memory," said Tull, an edge in his voice now. "If you recall…"

Kelso didn't have to "recall" anything. He remembered it all. Not just the public incidents that Tull was recounting. The scary episodes that no one knew about, thank God.

Kelso's baptism under fire, so to speak, had come on that very first day. They'd put Charmain's bags in his car and started driving down the Pacific Coast Highway, turning east onto Sunset Boulevard and heading into Beverly Hills. As they came up on the first traffic light, it turned red, and as Kelso slowed, a woman in the outside lane blew her horn, darted in front of them, and slammed on her brakes. Kelso had to brake hard, stopping inches from her rear bumper.

"Damn," he said. He honked his horn in frustration. The woman, a big-haired BevHills yenta type in a Cadillac, sneered in her rearview mirror and gave them the finger.

"Fucking BITCH!" Charmain screamed. She charged out of the car, ran to the Caddy's driver-side door, yanked it open and shrieked, "Out of the car, you ugly old whore. OUT! NOW!"

Kelso blinked. He couldn't quite believe what he was seeing. Jesus! A GUN! Charmain was pointing a pistol at the woman; yanking on the door, pulling it open. The woman half-fell from the car and stumbled as Charmain jerked her out into the street and stuck the gun in her face.

"Who you think you're fucking with, you wrinkly old skank? Huh? HUH?"

The woman, crying hysterically, put her hands over her face, cowering. Charmain, laughing now, pointed at the front of the woman's skirt. A wet stain was spreading across it.

"You better pee your pants, you stupid cunt, next time you see me." It all went down so fast, Kelso had sat paralyzed. Now he moved to exit the car. Charmain looked over and shook her head, waving him back. She walked to the open door of the woman's Caddy, removed the ignition keys and tossed them on the front seat. Then she clicked the master lock button down and slammed the door.

"Hope you've got Triple-A, bitch," she laughed, then ran back to

Kelso's car and hopped in.

"Drive, man," she said.

Kelso looked up. The light had just turned green. He reversed, went back a few feet, breathing thanks that no one had pulled up behind them. He went around the Caddy. The panic-stricken woman was yanking at the locked door, sobbing.

"Have a nice day," Charmain yelled, waving and giggling.

The incident had cost him. Next day, he got a phone call from a guy who said he'd seen it all. He read Kelso's license number to him and threatened to give it to the cops unless he got paid $5,000. Kelso refused, figuring even if he did pay, the guy would keep coming back for more. A week later, two detectives showed up at his office, questioned him about the incident. Kelso was ready for them. He called his lawyer, put him on speakerphone, told the cops that the girl who'd pulled the gun was a hitch-hiker he'd picked up coming off the PCH. She'd seemed okay until the woman cut them off. Then she just went nuts. On drugs, maybe. After the incident, she'd made him drive her up Sunset to Tower Records. Hadn't threatened him exactly, but hell, she had a gun. He had no idea who she was, of course…blah, blah, blah…

The cops didn't believe him, but decided to buy it. After all, Kelso was a solid citizen. And he'd dropped the name of a deputy chief he knew pretty well. The cops left. Kelso didn't tell Charmain about their visit. He'd never even talked to her about the incident because he'd sensed that she was waiting to see if he'd give her grief. It was a test. Of their relationship. His loyalty. So he'd kept his mouth shut. But that day it happened, after they'd driven about three miles up Sunset, when the hammering in his heart had slowed, he'd said to her mildly:

"I know you're new out here, so you may not know this. But, er…guns are a much bigger deal in L.A. than where you come from. So don't tell anybody you're, um…packing."

She shrugged.

"Okay."

And that's all that was ever said about it.

CHAPTER 37

4:47 P.M.
THE POLO LOUNGE
BEVERLY HILLS

IT was nearly five o'clock when Kelso parted ways with Tull at the Polo Lounge. Driving home, he knew he'd told the columnist a lot more than he'd meant to—but a lot less than Tull had hoped to hear.

They'd talked about setting up an interview with Charmain. Kelso told him that Charmain was wary of him. A lot of her negative press had come from Tull. She thought, frankly, that the columnist hated her.

When Kelso had told him that, Tull shook his head wearily.

"That's ridiculous. And you know better, Mike. Please remind Charmain of all the positive press I've given her. Why don't stars ever remember the good stuff? You print 999 great items and the only one they can recite from memory is Number 1,000 because it stings.

"I don't cover your client any more or less relentlessly than anyone else in the press. It's just that I'm better than most—most of the time, anyway. I got the stories the others missed. That's my job. Charmain is news. Big news. And I cover what she does—the good and the bad. Just like the *Washington Post* covers politics. But I've been fair to Charmain. We don't make this stuff up, Mike. We report what she does. And I've always reported the good along with what she'd consider the not-so-good."

Kelso nodded. "I always tell her, it's not personal. It's business. The business of being a star. But it's always a shock, you know that."

"Yeah," said Tull. "First they love it, the attention, the fame. One day they're nobody and nobody cares. Then in an eyeblink, they're reading their name in the paper, watching themselves on TV, seeing their name up in lights. People are kissing their ass, offering them deals and drugs and sex. At first, they think they don't deserve it. Then, very quickly, they decide they absolutely do. Suddenly, they're golden. Demi-gods. And no one's allowed to criticize them anymore, or remind them they're still that same little nobody who got luckier than some.

"That's why so many stars end up firing the agents or managers who got their careers started. They can't stand having anyone around who still remembers when they weren't a star. They won't tolerate anyone who knew them when they were nobody. You know what I'm talking about, right?"

Oh, he knew, alright. Knew people laughed behind his back about the girls who'd fired him once they'd made it. He ignored the whispers now. It had bothered him a lot at first, but he'd finally concluded that you can't worry about what you can't control. And there was an upside to this business of managing young girls in Hollywood: there was an unending, fresh supply arriving daily.

Kelso lived in a two-story house in Encino he'd bought in the early 1970s, then gutted and modernized in the late 1980s. It was comfortable, on a decent-sized lot, with pool, jacuzzi, sauna, and workout room. He installed Charmain in one of the five bedrooms, completely private with its own bathroom and terrace.

Kelso routinely allowed young clients to stay rent-free until they got on their feet. It got awkward sometimes. Some girls acted jumpy, like he was about to hit on them, demand sex. Not that he ever would. But their watchful attitude put him on edge. Even worse were the ones who figured that putting out was the least they could do for such a nice old guy. Kelso, inarticulate when it came to sexual discussion, would say something like, "I never mix business with pleasure." Which was horseshit. He got pleasure galore from the tiny hidden video cameras he'd installed in the two bedrooms reserved for his girls. It was his secret shame, but delicious guilt was the fuel that fired the nasty thrill. That and his supreme fantasy of somehow getting caught in the act and being punished mercilessly.

Kelso's sole sexual encounter with a client had occurred one night when he'd floated up out of a deep, Ambien-induced sleep to find an achingly beautiful All-American Swede-type from Minnesota taking him in her mouth. He pretended he was still asleep. After awhile, she tried to straddle him. He wanted to open his eyes, talk to her, explain. But he couldn't. He went soft and she left. Neither of them ever said a word about it. Face-to-face sex on an equal playing field had stopped working for him long ago. Two or three times a year, when his urges overpowered him, he visited a discreet, expensive dungeon in West Hollywood.

That first night at home with Charmain had gone smoothly. After she unpacked and settled in, he took her to dinner at an unpretentious Italian place on Ventura Boulevard. They chatted easily about his plans for her career, returned to the house early. She moved about like she owned the place, poured some wine, watched TV with him for a while in the great room, then said goodnight and went off to her bedroom. No sexual tension. Just the way Mike Kelso liked it.

After a few minutes, he clicked off the TV, went upstairs to the master suite, locked the door, and entered his walk-in closet. At one end was a large painting. He ran his hand along the top edge until his fingers found a hidden latch, flicked it. The painting, which was on hinges, swung open like a door, revealing a 27-inch TV monitor. He clicked it on. Charmain had just entered the shower. Kelso settled back on a chaise lounge.

Show time…

CHAPTER 38

KELSO'S HOUSE
MALIBU

OVER the next few weeks, Mike Kelso threw himself into prepping Charmain for her first career move. His plan was audacious. He wouldn't waste time on the fringe producers and agents he ordinarily approached to get a girl her first exposure in some obscure horror flick or cheapo indie. No, he'd take her right to Larry Buckley, the biggest TV producer in town. He'd made the decision the day after Charmain moved in. He'd asked her to read for him, wanting to get an idea of how many weeks or months he'd have to invest in an acting coach. And she'd floored him.

"Where the hell did you get your experience?" he asked after they'd run through a couple of standard scenes from an audition book. She was amazing. Still needed work, of course. Who didn't? But the power was there, the fire, the honesty. And the Southern accent magically dropped away when she read.

"Oh, just high school drama class stuff," she'd lied. "We had a pretty good teacher who'd done some acting up in New York City. And I practice vocal exercises so I don't sound too much like an ignorant cracker gal. Even though I am, and proud of it."

Kelso called in a drama coach he'd used before, Arlen Trask, a, tall, mustachioed actor with unkempt white hair who'd just turned seventy. Arlen didn't get much work anymore in youth-oriented Hollywood, so he'd turned to coaching starry-eyed hopefuls. He was pretty good at it. And, because he was a certified dirty old man, Arlen gave Kelso a special rate in exchange for the joy of inhaling the heady perfume of healthy young girl flesh. He never threw heavy passes at his charges, or touched them; just ended every coaching session with a dinner invitation that was invariably refused.

After Trask's first stint with Charmain, he told Kelso: "This one's got the goods. Needs work. But I think she should do a stage showcase. Want me to ask around? My friend at the La Brea Playhouse is casting something right now."

"No. I'm going to throw her right into the big time. Nobody's seen her, so she's got no fuckups on her record. Charmain's good enough for TV right now. And she's tough enough to take the mental strain of getting thrown straight into the meat grinder. That's why I don't want her to make the rounds. I'm going to present her as something special. Take her to the right person."

Trask smiled. "Larry Buckley?"

"The man himself. What do you think?"

"It's the right move. She's perfect for that kid series he's got...what's it called?"

"*BevHills High*."

"Right. She's up to one of those roles, no question. If she's got the balls to audition without getting nervous. Buckley's an intimidating sonofabitch. But she's a tough little cookie. I think she'll do fine. Will he take the meeting?"

"I think so. I've got one girl on the show already. Larry knows I wouldn't waste his time, bring him a total dog."

"Do it. But give me a couple of weeks. I'll throw a lot of cold reads at her. The acting she can handle. I want to show her auditioning techniques. Run videotape, get her used to the camera."

"Good."

Six days later, on a Monday morning, Buckley's office answered Mike Kelso's calls. Mr. Buckley could give his client, Charmain Burns, five minutes on Thursday afternoon.

"What'll I wear?" was her first question.

"Keep it simple," Kelso told her. "Young girl shopping on Melrose, maybe headed for the beach later. That kind of thing. No sexpot stuff. You don't need it because it's there already, bubbling under. Let him discover the sex in all that youth and freshness. But don't be a goody-two-shoes, either."

Charmain gave him a dirty grin. "Don't think there's much danger of that."

Over the years, Kelso had learned that turning raw talent into gold is a mysterious alchemy, more art than science. But he had devised several strict management policies. Rule One was: never tell the girls more than they absolutely need to know. If they're smart, they don't require much advice. If they're stupid, they'll immediately forget anything you tell them anyway. If they're high-strung artistic types, information is just one more thing to obsess over.

That's why Mike Kelso never discussed the "casting couch" issue unless asked. He rarely warned his girls that they'd be negotiating a steamy jungle of sexual predators disguised in Armani, Boss, and Prada. The only time he offered a cautionary word was if he set them up to audition for one of the town's true monsters—a rutting pig on the order of, say, Don Simpson, the late and largely unlamented movie producer of macho action flicks like *Top Gun*, whose greatest joy in life had been urinating on women's heads while they told him over and over that his big cock really turned them on, baby...oh yeah, oh, oh...etc., etc.

Don Simpson's perverted misogyny was legendary even in a business where female actors were routinely brutalized and disprespected unless they managed to graduate from the anonymity of identification by body part to major star status—from, "You know, the Latin number with the fantastic ass," to "Isn't Jennifer Lopez fantastic?"

Perpetually whacked on drugs, Simpson beat women, ruined their careers if they had no power, used them if they did, and always humiliated them in the end. It was said that the truest mourners of his passing were Heidi Fleiss and two gay Japanese gentlemen in Orange County who trained large dogs to perform sexually with women. Don, like a handful of male stars, producers, directors, and studio types, occasionally enjoyed kicking back and cheering on a Neopolitan mastiff or Afghan hound as it serviced a brace of coked-out call girls.

Luckily, there were few Don Simpsons. Most of the casting couch Romeo's were garden-variety letches who copped a feel and offered you the usual quid pro quo: give it up and get the part. And it wasn't just guys you had to worry about: dykes were rampant these days, and sometimes more aggressive than the men. But, hey…girls who were gorgeous had been dealing with lechery crap since puberty—or even before, as Mike Kelso had learned after years of hearing lurid stories of sexual abuse from his nubile runaways. It was different now, what with sexual harrassment lawsuits. But even today, girls usually just handled it. Like Japanese pearl divers who know the sharks are circling somewhere out there in the murk, actresses watched their asses on casting calls. The gropers, dirty talkers, and weenie-wavers were always lurking, an occupational hazard.

There was the flip side of the coin, of course: actresses who'd eagerly pucker whichever lips you'd care to name for a decent part. One of Hollywood's A-list femme fatales was notorious for bedding producers or directors if she was hot for a choice role. She'd broken a lot of hearts and ruined several marriages.

Kelso had never advised an aspiring actress to fuck her way to success. Not in so many words. But when a girl's career needed a jumpstart, he'd arrange introductions to powerful men who wanted decorative dates for parties and premieres. Most show biz bigshots were married, but after a divorce they loved being seen out with beautiful starlets. And certain allegedly macho players masqueraded as studs to camouflage their lavender leanings.

Before sending his girls out on these "dates," Kelso would say: "It's good to be seen with this guy. He could help your career. Be friendly."

Be friendly. Get it, babe? If not, then hop a Greyhound back to fucking Peoria.

Following his rule for dealing with smart girls, Mike Kelso said nothing to Charmain about unwelcome, or unnatural, sexual attentions she might encounter in the marketplace. He did try to prep her for the meeting with Larry, but all he got out of his mouth was: "He's very businesslike... er...basically a nice guy. Don't be nervous."

She fired him a look.

It had "asshole!" written all over it.

"Duh...uh...OKAY!" she drawled, rolling her eyes and lolling her tongue out like a loony. "I won't be...duh...NERVOUS!"

Kelso nodded, accepting the rebuke. He'd blown his own rule. Smart girls you tell *nothing*! There's only one thing they need to know.

"Get the job," he said.

The next morning she rose early, ran for a mile, and worked out lightly with dumbells to pop her muscles. She stripped off her clothes and walked naked through the house to the sauna, knowing Kelso would still be asleep. Sitting on the fresh-smelling wooden bench, she cranked the heat up high and ladled water onto the rocks until her skin puffed and her pores opened, slicking her with sweat. She leaned back, closed her eyes. And thought of Patrick.

"Wish me luck, baby. You said I was a good actress. Now we're gonna find out."

She sauna-ed for twenty minutes, walked outside, still naked, and plunged into the pool, shivering at the icy shock. She walked back into the house and sprinted upstairs for a shower. Kelso was just coming down the stairs. She giggled as he averted his eyes and tried to peek all at once.

Two hours later, Mike Kelso escorted Charmain to a seat in the stridently art deco reception area of Buckley Productions and told the receptionist:

"Miss Charmain Burns to see Mr. Buckley."

"Yes, Mr. Kelso. I believe the appointment is for Miss Burns only?"

"I know. I'll be leaving for a meeting at Fox. But would you be kind enough to alert the limo driver, who'll be waiting outside, when Miss Burns is ready to leave. Here's his cell phone number."

"Of course."

He left, brushing his fingers nervously through thinning gray hair. Charmain didn't look at him.

Ten minutes later, a Buckley assistant doing a sort of gay David Spade thing bustled out, flicking long, dirty-blonde hair.

"And you are...Miss Burns?"

She hit him with the jade stare.

"Who the hell else you see sittin' out here, bubba?" she snapped.

The Spade clone pursed his lips, glanced around the deserted reception area as if he'd never seen it before, and said icily, "This way, please."

Down a glassed-in corridor bisecting a Zen garden, into a smaller but even more luxurious reception area, past a severe-looking older woman who nodded impatiently and pressed a button on her desk. The door facing them, a massive slab of marble, swung open to reveal a huge room with floor-to-ceiling windows looking out on the Zen garden and a waterfall that splashed into a pond surrounded by bonsai trees.

The Spade clone said, "Miss Charmain Burns." She took a step inside the huge, high-ceilinged room and stood absolutely still, about thirty feet away from one of Hollywood's authentic mega-moguls.

Larry Buckley was sitting behind his desk, looking at her with unfocused eyes and muttering to himself. It threw her for a moment; then she saw the tiny microphone suspended in front of his mouth and realized he was talking on some kind of cordless headset. It surprised her that he was speaking so softly. In the movies, guys like him were usually yelling.

She heard the door whoosh shut behind her. She didn't move, looking steadily at him. She saw his eyes focus, knew he was taking her in now, not missing a thing. Which was fine. She knew she looked hot.

The pleated baby blue linen miniskirt accentuated her long, bare legs. A white angora sweater and matching pumps set off her ivory paleness. She wore no jewelry, just a silver butterfly barrette in her hair, which was combed straight. No makeup, save for frosted lavender lipstick. The look was hot, but classy, teen queen. *Heathers* meets *Clueless*.

Buckley, still on the phone, beckoned her forward. Charmain did a bouncy schoolgirl walk, sat in the chair in front of his desk, primly put her knees together, then turned slightly to her right, flashing the voluptuous, toned thighs that had been killing men since elementary school. She bounced lightly as she settled in the chair, just in case he'd missed the jiggle of her bra-less breasts.

He hadn't. Judging her little performance, Buckley gave it an A-plus. He spoke into the headset briskly, saying, "Gotta jump!" He took the device off, tossed it on the desk.

"Thank you for coming by," he said. "Charmain Burns. Good name. Yours, or professional?"

"It's the one momma and daddy gave me, Mr. Buckley," she said, smiling and widening her eyes just a s'kosh.

He didn't smile back, but he didn't seem unfriendly, either. They sat for a moment, sizing each other up. Charmain decided he was one sexy-looking old guy. She'd seen him interviewed on *60 Minutes*, knew he was in his sixties, worked out seriously, entered marathons and had an amazing body. His hair was dead white—bleached, for sure—and his piercing blue eyes were so Paul Newman.

He gazed back at her, taking his time. Quite a package, he decided. Not just beautiful, but sexual. Smoky-hot under that calculated Catholic schoolgirl thing she was doing. Had presence, no question. He knew she thought she was playing the meeting understated, but he would have advised her not to push it at all. Just sit still. Let it seep out, permeate the atmosphere. Like it was doing right now. Larry Buckley had interviewed thousands of actresses in his career, could size them up fast, and usually threw them out in under five minutes. But this one...? Okay, he decided, she's made it past step one. Now let's hear her talk, loosen her up.

"So, you're a Southern lady?"

"Yes, sir," she said. "Born and bred in north Florida, just south of the Georgia line."

"And a beauty queen, I'm told. Miss Hula Girl. I've hired one or two of you in my time. Say hello to Frank Emmet next time you see him. Now, I've been told by Mike Kelso that you've had no professional experience, but don't be nervous about that. Just tell me what you have done."

"Well," she lied, "I appeared in just about every school play since I was a little girl, right through high school. And there's an itty-bitty community playhouse in the next town to ours, sort of a north Florida answer to the Burt Reynolds theater, but nowhere near as prestigious, of course. I played the lead in *Barefoot In The Park* there for a two-week run."

"You get a good review?"

Shit! She hadn't thought of that. Of course there would have been a goddamn review in the local paper.

She paused, then said quietly, "No. I got a bad review. The critic—well, he wasn't a professional critic, of course, just a man who owns a local used-car lot—he took me out for an interview over dinner after the opening night show. He...well...let's just say I had a bad experience with him...so he wrote in the paper that I'd better go back to cheerleading. It was awful, so embarrassing and unfair. And I'd never even *been* a cheerleader."

Wow, he thought. Fucking brilliant lying. Very nice. A tiny catch in her voice. Just the hint of girlish dew in the eyes. Okay. On to the next step.

"Charmain, there's a script on the table next to you. Just a page of dialogue, really. Let's read it together, okay? I'm 'Jonathan,' and you're 'Denise.' Don't push too hard. Just read naturally, the way you talk. You're playing a high school girl, but don't try to go too young, okay? You're a *modern* high school girl."

He chuckled, smiling into her eyes for the first time.

Charmain projected herself back to the house in Savannah. And she read the scene to Patrick.

DENISE: Where were you last night? You didn't even call.

JONATHAN: I was with the guys, that's all. You know, hangin' out. Man, what's wrong with that?

DENISE: Maybe you should just hang out with the guys every night.

JONATHAN: Hey, I don't like this "jealous" garbage!

DENISE: Jealous? Who said anything about jealous? Sounds like there's a girl in this equation somewhere. Is there? (BEAT) Jonathan?

JONATHAN: Hey, this is getting crazy...

DENISE: You answer me RIGHT NOW!

And on and on. The scene took less than three minutes. Larry Buckley leaned back in his chair. He had a busy day ahead, busier than usual. She wasn't right for the part. Too sexy, too knowing. This role called for a plainer type, pretty but demure; a sweet, dumbo girl-next-door who'd end up getting raped by a high school jock on steroids by the end of her first season. Second season, there'd be the trial and...he wasn't sure yet, but he knew she was going to end up dead.

He said, "Very nice. Thank you for coming in. I'll be in touch."

The moment Charmain heard those words, pure energy jolted through her. She gasped, suddenly electrified, infused with a power that felt unfamiliar. Weird...supernatural.

Patrick!

Her heart jumped. God! She felt invulnerable. She'd beat this man. Get the job. And whip this smug-ass town that thinks it's so fucking tough. This whole bullshit scene was about power. That's *all* it was about. And she knew all about taking power from whoever was using it against you, how to turn it back on your tormentor.

Charmain focused her eyes on Buckley; summoned up the hot stare that smashed men to jelly, and said sweetly:

"What you really mean is you *won't* be in touch. You think I'm not what you want? Right?"

Buckley shrugged. "You asked, I'll tell. You won't work for this role. Not your fault. I'm sorry. You did a good reading and we'll keep you in mind for the future, but..."

Charmain stood, interrupting him, holding his eyes to hers. She moved away from the chair, walked around to the side of his massive desk and stopped in a shaft of sunlight. Buckley looked suddenly nervous, like he might make a move, call someone. She held up her palm, urging him to stillness. She smiled, painting an image of demure mischief on the curve of her lips.

"Mr. Buckley, I'm perfect for *BevHills High*. Like you said, I'm a *modern* high school girl. Very knowing. Openly sexual. Athletic. And in perfect shape for wearing a thong bikini at beach parties..."

Her hand moved down her hip, popped two buttons. The pleated baby blue miniskirt rustled down her thighs and pooled at her ankles. She stepped forward, did a slow pirouette, framed in a glowing edge of sunlight that warmed her pale skin and picked out the blonde baby fuzz dusting along the spinal valley that dipped to her big, sexy ass. She stretched her arms high over her head. The white angora sweater slid up her rib cage, just beneath her breasts. Now she was facing him, sunlight illuminating her pubic tuft.

"Ohmigod!" she said. "I forgot to put on panties. Sorry."

Buckley had seen it all before, knew he was being worked. But Jesus! A pressure in his chest reminded him suddenly to breathe. He couldn't stop looking…She was so ripe, adorable, irresistible, so…very young…

He jerked back to reality. This was his office, godamnit! Larry Buckley Productions, the company he'd killed to create. He'd buried the competition to get where he was, by Christ, and he got to call the shots like few people in this town ever did. Now here was this hick teenage twat flashing him like he was some low-rent schlockmeister who couldn't keep his hands off the talent. And she had the chutzpah to demand that he cast her in the highest-rated show he'd ever put on TV, even though he'd just given her the don't-call-us-we'll-call-you-bye-bye…

"Look, I want you out of here right now, do you hear me? Now!"

Charmain laughed. "Larry—do I know you well enough to call you Larry? Listen to me. No matter what you say or do, you will never get me out of your head. You can throw me out, but that's just temporary. You are a smart man and a great producer, and you know I'm something hot, something special. And I know you've seen some really special stuff in your time, you sexy old blue-eyed man."

She turned slowly, cocking her hip.

"Now take another careful look. Especially at my ass. Isn't it big and sexy-looking? My best friend Millie always called me coon-ass. You know what that means, Larry?"

She turned again slightly. Gave him another angle.

"How do you think that'll look on camera? And you haven't even seen my tits yet. Here's a teeny peek?"

She slid the angora up over her breasts. Nipples popped out from under the fluffy wool, dusty strawberry in a bed of white. Buckley felt himself harden. Charmain looked at his lap, giggled. She pulled the sweater down.

"Now that's better. See, Larry, you can't miss with me on your show. Men get hot, but the women get all fascinated by me, too. They want to see how they can steal some of my stuff. What I am is s-e-x, mister. And that's the name of the game, y'all. You know it, and I know it. So hire me, Larry. Nobody watches *BevHills High* for its uplifting moral message. And it's not like I'm a bad actress. I'm good. I just need to work to get better. Please, tell me I've got the job."

Never, he told himself. No one beats me in a deal. I dictate the terms here. Sure, she's a hot number. But she's just talent. And you never let the talent get the upper hand. Fuck you, little girl.

"For the last time," he said. "Leave or I'm calling security."

Charmain shook her head. "Larry, you're not paying attention. I'm not some nutcase you call security to get rid of. This is business, godamnit. You've got what you've got, I've got what I've got. So let's trade. Make a deal that's good for both of us. My daddy was a salesman. He always said a deal had to be good for both sides.

"Now, I know you're a busy man, so I'll get right to the point. You give me the job, and I'll give you the best blowjob you've ever had. Right here, right now. That'll be your signing bonus. No one will ever know. And you'll never be sorry we did business. Deal?"

Buckley stared at her, genuinely dumbfounded. This little cunt had one thing right. She wasn't a nut. In fact, she must have inherited some of her daddy's salesmanship, the persistent, arrogant little bitch. He got up, walked away from his desk, away from her. He stopped, stared out through the windows. After a moment, he said:

"See that Zen garden out there? A symbol of tranquility. Supposedly. I hardly ever look at the damn thing. Everybody thinks I put it there for meditation. Well, everybody's wrong. It's there to remind me that just beyond those walls out there is one of the toughest towns in the world. An arena for killers. Where guys like me think up new ways to break your heart every day. Because it's all about putting on the show you want, and fuck anyone who gets in your way. So when I look out at that Zen garden, it's a warning for me. A reminder to stay alert, be on guard. Never, ever relax. And never forget about power. Because someone's always waiting to take it away from you. And here's the way it works: no power, no show biz."

He turned to face her. "No one comes in my office and shoves me around. Not with their brains, not with their fists, not with their cute little tits and ass. Did you really think Larry Buckley would give it up for a blowjob? How dare you? Now you leave, Miss Charmain Burns. Our business is finished."

He turned back to the window.

"Don't forget your skirt," he said.

Charmain laughed. She'd won.

Oh, this was fun.

"Don't *you* forget my skirt," she purred.

CHAPTER 39

5:20 P.M.
KELSO'S HOUSE
MALIBU

"WHAT the *fuck* were you thinking of?"

She looked at him. Laughed.

"You never say *fuck*. Not since I've known you, anyway."

Kelso was near panic. Larry Buckley's message to call immediately had been on his answering machine when he'd arrived home with Charmain a couple of hours after her interview. Kelso got Buckley on the phone and recoiled at the producer's fury.

"You'd better straighten your client out, Mike. That shit she pulled might work with a few idiots in this town, but no one comes into my office trying to trade a piece of ass for a part!"

Kelso cut in. "Larry, slow down, please. What happened?"

Buckley told him. Graphically.

"Trash like that doesn't usually make it into my office. I took the meeting with her because you've got an actress on one of my shows. Next time, I'll think twice before I do you a favor. And how the hell do I know that she won't turn this into some kind of sexual harrassment shakedown!"

"Larry, that's ridiculous. Look, I..."

Buckley clicked off.

Charmain told Kelso: "Stop worrying about it."

"Stop worrying? This man can make or break careers. And I have my client, Carla Barlow, on his show."

"So?"

"So her contract is up for renewal this season. He could drop her."

"He's not gonna do anything except offer me that part. That's why he called. He can't stop thinkin' about me."

"What?"

"Don't look at me like I'm crazy, goddamn you! Don't you EVER do that if you want to stay around me!"

"Okay, okay. But Jesus, Charmain, let's not get out of control here. I mean, you're beautiful, but—"

"Shit! You know, there's something weird about you, Mike. You gay or something?"

"What? No, I'm not gay."

She grinned lazily. "How about 'or something'?"

"No," he spluttered. "I mean…what do you mean?"

"Look, if I lay my heavy stuff on a man, he's going down. That's not bragging, that's fact. I've been doing it since I was twelve. And maybe before that, now that I think back on all those grown men on Main Street who used to watch me real good when I went to town with Momma. If you don't feel what I've got, you're either too old…or too 'something.'"

Kelso went to the bar, poured himself a campari and soda.

"Which is it, Mike?"

He walked toward the stairs, drink in hand.

"I've got some calls to make."

"Mike."

He turned to face her.

"If Buckley gives me the part, will you kiss my feet?"

He opened his mouth. Nothing emerged.

She sat down on the sofa and propped her legs up on the glass coffee table. She was still wearing the miniskirt. Now he saw what had riled Larry Buckley. She wiggled her toes.

"Want to kiss them now?"

He stood there, trying to force a smile, laugh it off.

She giggled.

"Got your number, Mister. Go make your calls."

Her mocking laughter followed him up the stairs.

Just before the day ended, Larry Buckley called, said abruptly:

"I want to see you tomorrow morning. Nine a.m. Can you do it?"

"Larry, yes, but—"

Click.

Next morning, Kelso walked into Buckley's office to face the nightmare that had plagued his sleep. But as the producer spoke, Kelso's head spun in disbelief at what he was hearing. He felt like Charmain's formidable life-force had sucked him into her deepest fantasies.

"…yes, I was pretty damn hot when I called you yesterday," Buckley was saying. "And I don't take back anything I said. But Mike, we're in the business called 'show.' Too many times we forget that! One, it's a business. And two, it's always about what's best for the show. Now I don't mind telling you that your client is arrogant, infuriating, aggressive…shit, she's even goddamn condescending. I mean, that little bitch was actually condescending to me. To ME! Parading around here like I'd never seen a pair of tits and ass before. I was goddam n angry about it.

"Then I got to thinking: why was I so…angry? Why had I reacted to this girl so strongly? Other actresses had pulled that stuff before. Not quite as dramatically, but…

"Now normally, I'd just press the buzzer and call in my secretary, and I'd say, 'Escort her off the premises.' But this young woman got to me. The realization hit me later in the day—I was still thinking about her! Why? Was I just regretting I didn't take her up on her offer? I mean, none of us are saints, Mike.

"Then I figured it out. I realized she wasn't really offering me a blowjob. She was playing a SCENE! Whether she did it instinctively, or knowingly, it didn't much matter. She wanted to show me what she had. Get my attention. She was playing out this dramatic scene in her head—and she could have looked ridiculous. But she didn't. She looked magnificent. Not just her body. The way she carried herself...the way she *played* the scene. She showed great courage, which is what the great ones have, that ability to let themselves go and fly with the moment, the passion.

"I thought, she's a four-wheel, fire-breathing bitch. She's magnificently beautiful and sexy. And that's when it hit me."

Larry Buckley paused dramatically and said:

"Charmain Burns is The Girl You Love to Hate."

Buckley paused, waiting for the obligatory "You're so right!" response. Kelso, still dazed, almost missed his cue. But like a great boxer who's just taken a hard one to the head, he instinctively fought through the daze and made the perfect move.

"You're...you're so right, Larry," he said. "You're amazing."

Buckley paced alongside the floor-to-ceiling glass wall. "If she can put on the screen what I saw in this office—and I think she can—*BevHills High* is gonna get the ratings boost I want as we go into our fourth season. It's time to juice the show, shake it up, bring in the brand-new character that I sat down and wrote last night—listen to this:

"Tara Boudreaux...the new girl with the old soul. She transfers to BevHills High from New Orleans. She's the daughter of a rich Louisiana planter. Her mother has died, and Daddy has just taken a new trophy wife who's only five years older than his daughter—and not as beautiful.

"Stepmom doesn't want Tara anywhere around, and that's just fine with our fiery little bayou bitch, who wants nothing more than a life in L.A.'s fast lane with a fat allowance from Daddy—and no bed-check!

"Right away, the *BevHills High* girls dub her 'Witchy Woman' because she's cast a spell over every male at school, teachers included. It's sex, it's voodoo, it's a location episode in New Orleans, where our bratty Beverly Hills babes take off their bras for beads thrown from Mardi Gras floats. It's boffo, Mike! That's what we used to call it in the old days, remember? BOFFO!

"Have her in here tomorrow morning at seven a.m. for makeup. I'll direct her screen test personally."

Buckley put on his phone headset and started muttering into it. The meeting was over. Kelso got up and walked out stiff-legged.

Jesus! It had all turned out exactly as Charmain had predicted. Was she a witch? Or just a powerful woman whose vision wasn't obscured by the fear that blinds? Images flashed through his mind out of control. Her pretty feet...her toes inside his mouth...his fingers caressing her silky calves...his eyes drunk on forbidden fruit beneath a baby blue skirt...

It hadn't all sunk in yet, but he knew this was the greatest moment of his life.

The Hollywood Dream.

CHAPTER 40

11:40 A.M.
BUCKLEY'S SCREENING ROOM
LOS ANGELES

CHARMAIN'S screen test sealed the deal: the camera loved her.

Larry Buckley sat alone in his screening room, watching the magic happen, watching her erase, effortlessly, the invisible barrier between the screen and the audience's heart, making you believe she was real, close enough to touch. Yet...untouchable. The dream we all dream.

It always moved him to tears, the discovery of new talent. It was why he never allowed anyone to accompany him when he viewed first tests. People might think the old man was getting soft. They might not understand that you could be tough, even vicious, as a producer, yet still preserve a soft, mushy spot in your so-called heart that appreciated, even loved, the core element that drives The Biz:

Talent.

You had to know it when you saw it. If you didn't have that inner eye, you weren't a major player. End of story.

The screen filled with a closeup of Charmain's face. Moved in on those full, mocking lips, the knowing green eyes. Her presence filled the room as surely as if she was standing right there in front of him...daring him to posess her...to touch the magic...

The image flickered, faded. Larry Buckley sat very still, sensing what he instinctively believed millions of TV viewers would feel the first moment they saw her: "Wow, who *is she*?"

He pressed a button on his armrest.

"Get Jilly. In here. Now."

The lights came up gently. Jilly Campanella bounced into the room on springy little legs. Buckley smiled. He loved this cocky New York Italian, an ex-bantamweight boxer who'd saved his money, got out of the game and into UCLA Film School. A tough cookie who'd worked his way up to a tough job as Larry Buckley's No. 2, the hands-on producer who ran all his shows day-to-day.

"Yeah, boss?"

"Watch."

Buckley pressed a button. The lights dimmed. The screen flickered and Charmain took over the room again. When it was over, Buckley said nothing, waiting.

Jilly Campanella never lied to his boss. Oh, he lied every day of his life, aggressively, creatively, loving the lies he spun to get the magic up there on the screen. Lying was what he did when he had to, to get the job done. But lie to his boss? Never. That's why he was here—to put his balls on the line, say exactly what his gut told him. That was Jilly's value to Larry Buckley. He cleared his throat and said:

"Wow!"

"Wow?"

"That's it, boss. Wow! Nothin' else to say, really."

"Exactly."

He tossed Jilly the synopsis of the new character he'd written for Charmain, plus an outline of how she'd fit into the show "bible" of plot development.

"Take a quick look at that, give me your ideas later. In the meantime, sign her up. Standard deal."

Jilly stood, tossing back thick black hair that matched his eyes. He masked his surprise, but Buckley knew it was there.

"You want me to sign her up, boss? Give her the welcoming speech, the whole nine yards?"

It was usually Buckley who signed up new stars, then gave them a fatherly speech about joining "the Buckley Productions family." The usual bullshit.

"Yeah, Jilly. You take care of this one. And watch yourself. She's a pistol."

Jilly nodded. "Okay, boss." He bounced out of the room.

Buckley sat a moment, thinking. He took a sip from a bottle of Evian, then pressed a button on the armrest.

A voice spoke softly over the speakers: "A little nap, Mr. Buckley?"

"Yeah, Sammy. Just half an hour, though."

"Yessir."

The lights dimmed to black. He pressed a button. The seat went back, a footrest rose to cushion his legs. Larry Buckley felt good, content. He closed his eyes gratefully.

By February sweeps of her first season, Charmain Burns was a star. *BevHills High*, which had started to sag after its fourth season, suddenly shot up a whopping three ratings points. And every TV critic credited Charmain with the boost. Her bad-girl character, Tara Boudreaux, inspired the show's writers, who had virtually ripped up the old storyline and thrown it away. The regular characters, torn out of their comfortable ruts in reaction to this sinfully gorgeous Southern sex bomb who had suddenly exploded in their faces, caromed into new situations and titillating revelations of nascent lusts, fears, and insecurities.

The thrust of the Tara storyline was simple: her arrival at BevHills High had the boys panting like dogs in heat, but the BevHills bitches were howling with rage.

Male TV viewership shot up twenty-two percent. Charmain was the kind of woman who made other women drag husbands and boyfriends in front of the screen to ask: "Do you think she's sexy?" And when they got the answer they'd been expecting, the ladies rushed off to hair stylists and boutiques, trying for the Tara Boudreaux "look." And the men made a mental note to tune in next week to catch this hot new number's action.

Suddenly, all America was talking about the show. Offers for cross-promotion and merchandising poured in, and the idea for a *BevHills High* clothing line was born. Buckley invited several designers in to pitch ideas, offering a profit-participation deal. One of the designers who took a meeting was Jessica Bell. She and her business partner hung out on the set during shooting, met the cast, looked at some scripts, then sat down with Buckley, Jilly Campanella, and the show's costume designer, Glenn Charles, who was awed by her presence.

"I loved your Paris show," he gushed. "Your designs just reek of no-fuss elegance!"

"Thanks," she said. "I'm just happy I made it to Paris and got out alive."

The meeting didn't go well. Buckley listened to Jessica's ideas for a line of sportswear that was young and fresh, with a sort of slouchy, sophisticated retro look. She showed him some rough sketches she'd made on the set as a point of reference.

Glenn Charles gasped when he saw them. It was obvious he liked the ideas, but he said nothing, looking up expectantly for his boss to speak.

Twenty minutes later, Charmain drove into the parking lot of Buckley Productions. She had no scenes that day, but had been called in for a wardrobe fitting and a photo session for the publicity department.

As she got out of her car, she heard two people arguing. She looked up and saw Jessica Bell walking quickly to her car a few rows over, followed by an older man. Charmain recognized Jessica immediately. She'd seen her interviewed on Elsa Klench's TV show and in the fashion mags. Charmain had sized Jessica up and knew the bitch had one thing she didn't: Class. With a capital "C."

She heard the man's voice saying, "Jessica, for Chrisssake, why didn't you hear Buckley out? My God, he's got the hottest show on TV and we could use the publicity we'd get putting out a fashion line with the *BevHills High* hype behind it. Not to mention how much money it could generate—"

Jessica, fumbling for car keys, said serenely, "Because there was absolutely no point in hearing any more. Buckley knows what he wants, and so do I. He wants a look that screams schlocky sex, *à la nymphette*! I don't want or need any association with clothes that are designed to glorify Charmain Burns' tits and ass. That doesn't mean I'd turn her into a Town & Country debutante. I'm not stupid, and I'm not anti-sex. But I'm not into sleaze, or grunge, or whatever it is Buckley's looking for."

"Jessica, *mi amore*—"

"*Basta!* I'm not a costume designer. Let Frederick's of Hollywood dress that bimbo!"

Charmain stood stock still. She felt tears welling up in her eyes. Immediately, she blinked them back. Fuck her! I'm gonna cry? Because some shit-don't-stink bitch thinks I'm trash? Well, screw you, slut! You bet I've got prime-time tits and ass! I'm a fucking star. And by the end of next season I'll be filthy rich.

"FUCK YOU, STUCK-UP GUINEA CUNT..." Charmain screamed across the parking lot, suddenly flashing on an image of herself yanking out the 9mm pistol in her purse, dropping into a combat stance and plugging the fucking whore. At the same moment, she saw Patrick's face...he was winking at her, shaking his head as if to say, "No, no, chérie."

She burst out laughing.

"EAT SHIT, JESSICA!" she yelled.

And shot the bitch the finger.

Jessica, already in her car and pulling away, didn't hear the curse or see the salute.

Charmain, giggling so hard she was suddenly desperate to pee, ran toward Buckley Productions. Her new home. Goddamn, she was so happy. Hooray for fucking Hollywood.

"I LOVE YOU, PATRICK," she shouted.

Merci, chère amie...

That first year on TV was a mad whirl of hard work. Up at 4:30 a.m., a swim, light exercise, and fifteen minutes on the treadmill, a quick breakfast, on the set by six, makeup and hair, wardrobe, quick study of today's lines, then on to the set, shoot scenes, lunch, nap in the trailer if you were lucky, back home maybe by eight, supper, some TV, into bed, an intense study of tomorrow's dialogue, maybe a quick pussy-tickle, which relaxed her more than anything, then blessed, deep sleep. God, she'd never slept like this. And then there were the acting lessons, which she worked hard at, and the photo sessions, and interviews, and the magazine covers. *Entertainment Weekly* was the first...WOW!...and seeing herself for the first time on "E.T." and MTV, and going to her first premiere, with papparazzi flashes exploding, and the A-list parties, and meeting—OHMIGOD!...Jack Nicholson and Gwyneth Paltrow and Demi Moore and Ben Affleck and Sharon Stone...and Madonna, who actually said to her, "You remind me of me, y' know?"...JESUS! She almost called Millie about that one, but wasn't sure how she'd take all this. She'd call Millie later, when things settled down a little bit, if they only would. She was getting so goddamn tired, but it was wonderful and she loved it all, just needed some time away from the L.A. whirl...

Dating? Who had time? Sex? Shit, she didn't want to *know* for the first three or four months. It was Patrick. She knew it, and knew time would take care of all that. And it did. She finally got plowed real good one night by a cute limo driver who drove her home from a screening. After it was over, she'd said, "Don't call me, I'll call you!" They both laughed. He was an aspiring actor, and he got it. A likable guy. She did call him, actually, a couple of times. Take Two and Take Three weren't quite as great, but still not bad. She finally dumped him. No time. No desire. Masturbation was quick, fun...and you didn't have to dress. The whole dating and sex thing made her sad, knowing what she'd lost, how lucky she'd been to have had it.

And she wondered if she'd ever again meet a man who came close to Patrick. No big deal—she wasn't really looking. She got a brief crush on one of her co-stars, a hunk named Brent Crawford. She gave him a blowjob in his trailer, then went to his place and fucked him. Then they sat up and talked, and that ended the crush. After the flirtation and scratching the itch, he was just another self-centered, driven actor, just like her. And not a bright one. Outside of talking about himself, he was so zero. They got it on again after that, though. Just twice, actually. Once in her trailer, once in his. An itch was an itch. But she was too focused on learning this new craft she loved to do much scratching. Fucking she could forego, if she had to. But she had no time to make friends and didn't much like any of her co-stars, outside of chatting with them at parties. She missed letting her hair down, getting pissed or pleasantly stoned on pot with a few pals. She needed someone to talk to, a girlfriend. And that turned out to be, surprisingly, Dina Buckley, daughter of Larry. Dina, not surprisingly, was a star of *BevHills High*. No great beauty, she was attractive enough—but a great chick and not a half-bad actress. Dina had cracked Charmain up one night at a bar when she'd said with a straight face:

"Of course, I'm Daddy's only little girl, but I got my job PURELY on talent...and killer looks, of course."

They giggled like fools and Charmain got into the habit of meeting up with Dina once or twice a week for drinks. Or they'd visit the pad of one of Dina's circle of friends, mostly Hollywood rich kids. It was fun and as much social life as Charmain required. One place they never went was Larry Buckley's legendary mansion in Bel Air. And Charmain figured she knew why. Ever since she'd started working on the show, and despite her huge success, Larry Buckley had avoided her assiduously. Not that he scoialized with any of the talent, but he'd occassionally call one of the cast into his office to discuss business or to congratulate them on how they'd handled a press interview. But Charmain, never. When he had anything to convey to her, Buckley did it through Mike Kelso.

It had amused Charmain at first. She ignored the snubs, then got annoyed when word of Buckley's treatment filtered out to the cast and crew. But she flew into a rage when the following item appeared in Cameron Tull's *National Revealer* column:

"Everybody loves Charmain Burns—except her producer? Tongues at *BevHills High* are wagging about why Larry Buckley snubs the star who's put the show back at No. 1. He won't talk to her—ever!—and no one knows why! Strangely enough, Charmain's new best friend is Buckley's daughter Dina. Hmmm. Does Daddy thinks sizzling Ms. Burns might corrupt his baby girl?…"

"THAT COCKSUCKER!" Charmain shrieked at Mike Kelso over breakfast when she saw the paper. "NOW I'M PISSED! DO SOMETHING, GODDAMNIT!"

"Charmain, what can I do? If he doesn't want to speak to you…"

He ducked as she swept all the dishes off the table into his lap. In the silence that followed, she looked at Kelso and said:

"Power. It's all about power. And that's something you don't know shit about."

"Charmain—"

She smiled. "I'll take care of this myself."

"Please don't. I can't afford trouble with Larry and—"

"Shut the fuck up and go make more coffee."

Toward the end of the first season, Charmain took the money she'd saved from her $17,000 a week salary and made a down payment on a house in Beverly Hills. It came furnished, although she had the bedroom redecorated by a gay designer buddy of Dina's. On the first weekend after she moved in, she invited Dina to stay over.

"It'll be my housewarming, just the two of us in our nighties," Charmain told her. "But I'm having our dinner catered by Wolfgang Puck."

"Wow! Personally?"

"Well, his flunkies, of course. But he'll drop by to supervise and cook the entrée himself. It's an arm and a leg."

"The entrée?" Dina cracked.

"No, bitch, the fucking bill. But it'll be so much fun, y'all. I just want to kick back this weekend. We'll get stoned and watch porno, or something."

"Or fuck Wolfgang's flunkies."

"Or fuck WOLFGANG!"

They collapsed laughing.

It was a great night. After Wolfgang left, they watched a very special porn film that featured several young Hollywood actresses. They'd been filmed unwittingly by a notorious young club owner and man-about-town who had taken them home and seduced them in his bedroom—which was wired for video and sound.

"Ohmigod, look at his cock! Tommy Lee, eat your heart out…"

"He needs it, to fill that over-sized pussy. Oh, look, look, she's starting to come. Shit, that's the most emotion she's ever shown on screen."

Pleasantly stoned, they drifted up to the master bedroom suite. They were drinking Cristal and toking some boss Maui Wowie. After a while, Dina went to the guest bedroom, showered, and put on a pair of wooly pajamas. When she came back, Charmain was still in the shower. Moments later, she emerged wearing a gossamer-thin silk sheath. Dina was rolling a fresh joint. She lit it, toked, then walked over and handed it to Charmain, who was standing in front of a full-length mirror, brushing her hair. As Charmain took her hit, she put the hairbrush down and one strap of the gown slipped off her shoulder, exposing a breast.

"God, you have such perfect tits," said Dina.

Charmain smiled back at Dina's image in the mirror. "You think so?"

She shrugged offf her other strap and the gown slipped to her hips.

"Oh, you've got puffy nipples. I love those. I mean, guys love those."

"You've got nice breasts, too," said Charmain.

"Well, I had a boob job."

"Really?" Charmain lied. "They look so natural. Let me see."

Behind her, Dina unbuttoned the pajama top and opened it shyly.

"Oh, what a great color. Your nipples. Like, baby pink."

Charmain turned around to face her. "Can I feel them? You know, I've never..."

"Yeah, sure," said Dina shyly. "So...how do they feel? Like rocks?"

"Uh, uh, not at all. They feel...good. Here...feel mine."

"What, are you telling me you had yours done?"

Charmain leaned forward and very deliberately and tenderly kissed Dina on the lips.

"No," she said. "I just want you to feel them."

A moment later, she breathed in Dina's ear, "You want to kiss them? Because I want to kiss yours. Here...I'll go first..."

Dina gasped as she felt Charmain take her nipple between her lips. Her head swam and she whispered, "Can we lie down before I faint?"

On Monday morning, Larry Buckley came to his office an hour before his staff arrived, as was his custom. He liked having some quiet time before the phones and the meetings started. As he went to sit, he saw an audio cassette on his chair. A note was attached. He picked it up and read it. It said: "Play immediately. Listen carefully."

Puzzled and apprehensive, he snapped the cassette into a tape deck and hit Play. It was obvious instantly that it was a recording of a woman in sexual ecstasy. For a panicky moment, he thought someone had bugged the hideaway in Century City where he met the insanely expensive and absolutely discreet call girl he had on hire twice a week.

Then it hit him. It wasn't one woman—it was two. And one kept moaning the same name...over and over...

"Charmain…Charmain…"

He recognized that breathless voice even before he heard her name spoken.

Dina.

He jabbed the Off button, sat down heavily. The silence washed over him as he fought to collect his thoughts. Minutes later, still numb, he jerked out of his reverie as the phone buzzed sharply. He picked up.

"Good morning, Larry."

Her.

"Interesting, huh?"

He said nothing.

"I offered you something special. You turned it down. But your little princess didn't. And doesn't she sound happy, Larry?"

He tried to speak, had to clear his throat. Then he said it:

"Goddamn you."

"You can damn me all you want, you sadistic prick. But I'll tell you what NOT to do. Don't ignore me in public. I'm a STAR, goddamnit. You'd better goddamn smile and kiss my ass so people notice—and so Cameron FUCKING Tull writes about it. You'd better get your head right, or Tull might just get something else to write about."

Silence.

"Are we understandin' each other, bubba? Cause if we're not…"

"I understand," he said.

Charmain chuckled softly. "Well, that 's good. Now let's get a big smile on our faces and thank our lucky stars we've got a hit show. Okay? OKAY?"

"Yes."

"Oh, that's wonderful, Larry. And you know what?"

"What?"

"For the first time, I really feel like part of the Buckley family. Dig you later, daddy-o."

CHAPTER 41

EXECUTIVE SUITE
BURFORD'S

LADDY Burford couldn't believe his good luck. After squeaking through business school and taking over a very tiny junior executive's desk at Burford's, the family department store chain that would groom him as his father's successor, the twenty-three-year-old Ivy League preppy had come to a sobering realization: he hated the retail business. The day-to-day sameness of life in the executive suite bored him to death. His fucking life bored him to death.

Lady Luck intervened. Charmain Burns, the twenty-year-old star of TV's smash series, *BevHills High*, had been booked for a personal appearance at the flagship store of the Burford's chain in Manhattan to plug a new *BevHills High* clothing line. Laddy's dad, the high-powered but aging Ransom Burford, had directed his handsome heir to make sure Charmain was happy with the company. He figured youth could speak to youth. Laddy met Charmain at the entrance to the main store on Lexington Avenue as her stretch limo pulled up in front of a cheering crowd of fans. Less than five hours later, he was buried to the hilt in her, gasping convulsively as he enjoyed this heaven-sent piece of prime-time Hollywood ass.

Over the next few months, Charmain and Laddy carried on a sporadic affair. At first, she treated him like a world-class stud. She seduced him to the point where she became an obsession. Charmain liked him a lot. And he fascinated her. He came from a class she'd never encountered: old money. The so-called "upper crust." Those who rarely had to assert themselves to demand privilege because people just naturally accorded it to them. Charmain found Laddy to be fun, sympatico, and very smart, but entirely too intimidated by his father. She gave him unfettered access to her bod—but Laddy knew he didn't command her mind, heart, or soul. She wanted him, but only on her terms. And for Laddy, that was enough. For now.

He invented more and more excuses to leave New York and work out of the Los Angeles store, terrified at first that his father would be angry. But Ransom Burford shrewdly realized the value of his son's liaison with a reigning TV star. He heartily approved when Laddy's name popped up in gossip columns coast to coast. Ransom Burford understood the arcane art of implanting images into the public mind. He valued publicity, especially good publicity.

Above all, he valued *free* publicity.

That's what Charmain and Laddy were giving him. Ransom Burford was also shrewd enough to sense that his son felt guilty about his constant absences from the New York corporate offices. That was fine with Ransom, who prided himself on being a sadistic, manipulative prick. He knew it never hurt to have an employee, or in this case, an heir/employee, feeling guilty and off-balance.

About three months after Laddy began pursuing Charmain, she embarked on an affair with sex symbol Connor O'Toole, Hollywood's flavor of the week. Connor was the latest smoldering bad-boy in the Brando/Dean/Elvis/Depp tradition. When Connor arrived in L.A. from New York, where he'd starred off-Broadway in a play, earning him rave reviews, he was ass-deep in attitude. The press gleefully reported his contemptuous remarks about Hollywood actors. "Fags" was his mildest.

One night at BuzzBuzz, the hangout *du jour*, he'd stopped by a table of young stars that included Drew Barrymore, Tori Spelling, Luke Perry, and the like—and ended up in a knock-down, drag-out fist fight with Seth Daniels, star of a faltering sitcom about a teenage CIA agent. O'Toole had knocked young Seth to the floor and was pounding the piss out of him when he suddenly felt cold metal nudging his ear—and heard the loud, metallic click of a trigger being cocked.

Connor lifted his arms in the classic, hands-up gesture, turned his head slowly—and looked into the icy-green eyes of Charmain Burns.

"Just in case you are wondering, asshole, this isn't a pussy gun," she said. "It's a Sig Sauer P226. It's cocked. If I even *think* the word 'trigger,' your head's mush. Now get off my buddy Seth right NOW!"

O'Toole twitched his famous nose. Every teenage girl in America knew it had been broken twice in street fights. He stared up at Charmain with his trademark tough-but-vulnerable stare. His lips twitched in a crooked smile, and he said:

"One of two things is gonna happen. Either you're gonna pull that trigger, or you and I are gonna redefine the word 'fuck' before sunup."

Connor's quote was on the lips of millions by morning, thanks to the ever-churning gossip mill. Cameron Tull reported that Connor and Charmain had left BuzzBuzz together in the actor's limo—and were lip-locked before the chauffeur got it into first gear.

That was a tough time for Laddy Burford. He didn't see Charmain for weeks. Like millions of other Americans, he had to read about her in the gossip columns—and there was plenty to read. Charmain and Connor were wild together: fire and gasoline. Out in the clubs every night in L.A. and New York, behaving outrageously, insulting people, getting into fights, openly imbibing booze and drugs. Connor mooned simpering girl fans. Or waved his cock at tough guys in bars, yelling, "Hey, want a suck?" Daring them into brawls. Charmain flashed tits and/or ass everywhere. Twice she pulled her gun on guys who got too close. One night, according to a Cameron Tull exclusive, she yanked every stitch of clothes off a girl who had flirted with Connor, then shoved her out onto the Sunset Strip naked.

Her wild affair with Connor burned itself out in about a month. Charmain caught him in bed with Leda Francis, a young, exquisitely beautiful British ballerina. Furious, Charmain lay in wait for Connor one evening outside his West Hollywood bachelor pad. When he pulled into the parking lot alone, Charmain pulled out her trusty gun and threatened, this time seriously, to blow his head off.

As he had done with women since he was old enough to speak, Connor charmed Charmain out of her mad. Coaxed her into his apartment for a wild night of passion.

It was their last.

The next morning, Connor had his lawyers go to court for a restraining order—to keep Charmain from coming near him. After the judge granted the order, Connor's lawyers asked the judge for more distance than the 300 feet he had set, pointing out that Charmain carried a gun and practiced with it frequently at the Beverly Hills Gun Club. The judge, a member of the same club, admitted he'd seen her shoot and made it 500 feet.

"Let me know if you see this dangerous woman around town with a rifle, and we'll see about increasing the distance," the judge cracked.

Newspapers and TV around the world picked up the judge's quote and many headlined their reports of the Connor-Leda-Charmain triangle—and the restraining order against Charmain—"A Dangerous Woman." At *The Revealer*, Cameron Tull told Mary, Queen of Scots:

"Halfway through her second TV season, Charmain has gone from star to scandal queen to—quite literally—*femme fatale*. Let's do a full court press on her. I want to send a couple of reporters back over her trail, her early life. Do one of our 'Childhood of…' features. Who is she? Where did she come from? This child-woman suddenly appears and—you'll pardon the pun—'burns' up Hollywood. Charmain didn't just suddenly become a scandalous woman. Bet your life that there's some juicy stuff in her past. We'd better dig it up before everybody, especially *The Enquirer*, beats us to it."

"Hmm—maybe," said the Queen.

"Mary, she's getting hotter by the minute. She's pulling huge ratings, the public loves her—and they love stories about 'bad' girls. You know how it works. Let me develop the best sources possible before she's big enough and rich enough to buy everybody's silence, *à la* Michael Jackson. Let's get our pipeline in place before everybody knows it's pumping champagne."

The Queen sighed. "Lovely metaphor. Reminds me of how much I'm looking forward to that first drink in about…" She glanced at her watch. "…one hour, thank God!"

"First round's on me," said Tull. "How about it?"

The Queen nodded. "Okay, but just one reporter. And no more than two weeks on it."

"I want Lulu."

"Jesus. I hate to lose her for Page One stuff for that long, but—oh, okay. And you're buying me a bottle of Cristal."

"Now it's my turn to say 'Jesus,'" said Tull. "Okay, deal."

"And don't think you've got me fooled, Cameron. You'll use everything you dig up as fodder for another best-selling book, so don't kid a kidder."

He grinned. "A book? What a wonderful idea, Mary."

She waved him out of her office. Imperiously, like a queen.

The phone rang in the new executive suite Ransom Burford had awarded his son and heir at the Los Angeles branch of Burford's.

"Laddy?"

"Charmain?"

Her voice made his heart leap. Jesus, finally! He'd hadn't talked to her —outside of a quick, "Hello, I'm crazed. Can't talk. Call me. Bye…"—in weeks. He'd been mad with jealousy and anger, but knew better than to show it. Not that it would have done him any good. Her mad fling with Conor O'Toole, that asshole James Dean wanna-be, had consumed her. While it was happening, she was blind to everything. And that included him. He'd missed her terribly. Not just the sex, but the excitement that crackled around her like hot lightning. And the intimacy. He was her best friend. Male friend, anyway. Closer to her than Dina Buckley, in some ways. After all, Laddy had the sex thing going with her and Dina didn't. Or…?

The second he had the thought, he had the doubt. *Did* she have sex with Dina? Jesus, he hadn't thought of that. And Charmain *was* bisexual! They'd talked about it. She'd teased him about his fascination with her lesbian encounters. Suggested that it might mean he was ripe for a little bi-action himself. Ridiculous. He'd done a few boarding school circle jerks at Groton, but that hardly made him homo. God, Charmain could be trying at times. But…he needed her. When they were together, the dreaded gray ennui, the boredom that had engulfed him since he'd joined Father's firm, simply disappeared. She did something to him that made him feel complete. He decided that he wanted to marry her. Not now. But someday. When she'd tired of show business, of fame. Great wealth and power were things he could give her. Father would step down soon. He couldn't last forever. And then Laddy would offer Charmain the Burford empire. He wasn't a fool. He knew she'd never fall in love with him. But she loved him, like a dear friend. Or a brother. No, that wasn't quite right. One didn't fuck one's sister. Just wasn't done. No, they were more like…

"Fuck-buddies," he said into the phone.

She laughed. "What?"

"I just defined what we are," he said. "We're fuck-buddies."

"Well, nothin' wrong with that, y'all. You are kinda like a best girlfriend with a big ol' dick."

"I was thinking we were more like a brother and sister, but—"

"Naw. Brothers and sisters fight. We never fight. And you're not really like a girlfriend because you think like a man. No, you were right the first time. We're fuck-buddies. And I feel like a nice uncomplicated fuck, buddy. So let's hop a plane this weekend for anywhere fantastic. The show's on Christmas hiatus after tomorrow. Laddy, let's go…what'd you call it…island-hopping? In the Caribbean. You've been down there a lot, and I love hearing you talk about it. Let's go there, Laddy. Please?"

"Yes. Good thought. St. Bart's is fabulous this time of year. And I have friends on Mustique."

"Great! Have your secretary arrange everything, okay?"

"Sure."

"Oh, I can hardly wait, Laddy."

"Charmain…are you…uh, okay?"

"If you mean am I pining for that self-centered asshole who fucks girls just so he can see his own precious reflection in their eyes when they start to come? No fucking WAY! It was intense, Laddy, but I wasn't in love with him. When you've had a real man, you recognize a boy when you see one. Shit, he spent more time in front of a mirror than I do. So don't worry, fuck-buddy. You won't have a weepy female on your hands. I'm in a great mood. I wanna let down my hair and fuckin' HOWL!"

It was a fabulous three weeks. In St. Bart's, they met up with one of Laddy's Ivy League pals, Granville Lodge, who'd commandeered the family's 230-foot yacht and crew while Mummy and Daddy were off in Europe somewhere. They cruised over to Mustique and fell in with more of Laddy's crowd, the idle rich, people she'd never heard of until she realized she was hearing names that were brand names—Hormel, Kellogg, Ford. Laddy introduced Charmain to Princess Margaret, Mick Jagger, and Donald Trump. The Donald hit on her immediately, and he was kind of cute. She promised to be his guest at Mar-A-Lago at Easter.

"You'll probably be married by then," she purred.

"Not on your life," grinned Trump. "Who can afford it?"

Charmain was truly surprised at how many people Laddy knew from the worlds of society, high finance, show biz, and royalty.

"It's just something I grew up with," he shrugged. "Look, there's Robin Leach."

"Oh, shit," said Charmain. "Even *I* know him."

The last week of their stay, Laddy chartered a plane and flew them down to the Grenadines, the end of the island chain that stretches from the

Florida Keys and kisses the tip of South America. They boarded a 54-foot sailboat manned by a native skipper and a cook and headed out into the open ocean, away from the protected waters of the islands. The wind freshened and white caps tipped the waves.

"Man, this is scary," said Charmain.

Laddy, who'd taken over the wheel and was sailing the ship like he'd been born to do it, grinned. "All those preppy girls you met the last couple of weeks eat up deep-ocean sailing," he teased.

"Yeah. Well, eat this."

"Come here. Stand in front of me...Now hold the wheel. Feel the wind and the water in your fingers."

Wow! She did. It was exciting, feeling all that power. The sloop-rigged boat heeled over tight to the wind.

"Look up at the sail," Laddy told her. "That's our powerplant and the wind's our fuel. Now watch what happens when I let the boat fall off the wind a bit...See? Now feel the wind on your cheek as I pull back up into it. See how we heel over and pick up speed? The closer you get to the wind, the more power you've got."

The boat, "VirginFire," plunged through the dark-blue waves. Laddy patiently showed Charmain how to sail her. He was good at it, really good. Charmain could tell from the approving way the weathered old black skipper nodded as he sucked at his pipe and stood by for Laddy's orders. An hour later, Charmain took the wheel herself.

"God, I LOVE this!" she screamed into the wind and sunlit waves. "YEAH, BABY! Go, VirginFire. GO, BITCH!"

They sailed for two days without setting foot on land. They zig-zagged down the Grenadines, anchoring off islands that looked all but deserted each night, eating delicious meals aboard or starting a barbecue fire on the beach. It was sun, fun, fabulous sex. And for the first time in her life, Charmain had a light golden tan. She felt good, rested, happy...a mood that lasted all the way back to L.A.—until her first phone call from Dina the next morning.

"WHAT?"

"Charmain, I hate to be the one to tell you this after you just got back from the islands, but you're going to find out all about it the first time you pick up *The Enquirer*, or *People*, or *The Revealer*, or even the goddamn *New York Times*—"

"He's in LOVE with that skinny, flat-chested ballerina cunt? He's actually SAYING that to the press?"

"Oh, he's being all dramatic and shit, you know how Connor is, Charmain. I don't believe he's, like, really in love with Leda Francis. I mean, why her? I think it's just him discovering that here's something new he can talk about so we'll all pay attention to him and act like nobody's ever fallen in love before—"

"WHAT? You said he's NOT in love. Now you're sounding like he IS in love and…"

"Charmain, come on, chill out. You know what I mean. Stop confusing me. And stop yelling. Fuck him, anyway. Fuck them all, right?"

Silence. Then Charmain said quietly, "You are so right, Dina. Fuck them all. That's all a girl can do. Right?"

It was Sunday morning. Charmain met Dina for lunch at The Ivy. She seemed calm. Even read a *Los Angeles Times* piece on Connor and Leda without blowing her cool.

Headline:

"Ballerina Is Wild-Child Connor's Leda-ing Lady!"

It made Charmain wild. She didn't show her anger to Dina. Outwardly, she was ice. She knew exactly what had to be done. Connor had to pay for his sins. How? Go with what you know, babe! She smiled at Dina, savoring it, wanting to tell her, but holding back.

Power. It was, as always, all about power.

A week later, Charmain attended a headline performance by Leda Francis, who was appearing with the American Ballet Theatre. Afterward, she went backstage and congratulated the young British star effusively. Leda, knowing Charmain's former relationship with Connor, and her "dangerous woman" rep, was wary. But she warmed up as Charmain turned on the charm.

"You know what, Leda. I'll admit I came because I was curious. I just wanted to see what you had. I'm just a damn woman, and that's what we do, right? Look, honey, I've had a lot of boyfriends and I know you have too, a beautiful creature like you. But the whole world doesn't revolve around men, even though they like to think so."

Leda was genuinely dazzled. "Charmain, you are the most gorgeous woman I have ever been close enough to touch, and I am such a fan. I mean that seriously, I truly do. Do you know that you have fan clubs in Great Britain? Oh, I'm sure you do, of course. But I was just back there and they adore you, truly…"

They prattled on. Charmain told Leda she'd always been interested in dance, had taken some lessons, but had recently started Tae-bo classes for conditioning and body toning. She liked it so far, but wondered if dance classes, Pilates, or yoga wouldn't be better for a woman. She asked Leda if she worked out every day. Leda said she did. They chatted for a while and Charmain left. Leda didn't mention to Connor that she'd dropped by.

A few days later, Charmain phoned Leda and invited her to come up to her home for a workout and lunch around the pool—just the two of them. Charmain told Leda she had a full-length mirror and a dancer's barre installed in her home gym, so Leda could have a normal workout. Leda hesitated, then accepted. She wondered if Connor would approve, but it didn't matter. He was out of town on a location shoot. And she really, truly was a fan of Charmain's. She thought she was just smashing. "Alright," she said. "And I'll show you some ballet exercises you can add to your daily routine."

"Oh, great. See you in a couple of hours."

Charmain hung up, smiling sweetly. Laddy Burford looked at her, shook his head, asking, "What are you doing?" Charmain got up, kissed Laddy and told him, "That's a good boy, you run along now. I'm going to be busy over the next few days. Thanks for getting those workmen up here and installing that barre."

Laddy shook his head. "I don't like this, Charmain. I don't think I like this at all. Why can't you just leave things alone?"

"Because nobody in this town craps on Charmain," she said. "Now go. And don't call me. I'll call you."

Three days later, Connor O'Toole was awakened at about one in the morning by a phone call from Leda Francis.

"Where have you been? I've been out of my mind," he snarled. "You haven't called. You haven't been at your hotel. What's going on? I've missed you, for Chrissake!"

Leda's voice was dreamy, strange. "I've been with Charmain," she said.

"What do you mean, you've been with her? What?"

Connor heard Leda gasp, then moan. "Leda, what's going on?" Then he heard Charmain's voice, some distance from the telephone, hissing, "Tell him. Tell him what I'm doing. And tell him how much you love it."

A choked gasp—or was it a sob?—from Leda.

"Please, no. Charmain, I don't want to do this. Don't make me."

"Tell him. Tell him."

"What the fuck is going on?" Connor screamed.

"Tell him!" He heard Leda cry out in pain. An image flashed in his mind: Charmain's strong hands pinching, twisting that innocent flesh. Then a whimpering of surrender and Leda whispered, "Charmain is licking me. I love her. She's, she's—" another sharp cry as Charmain twisted Leda's nipple viciously.

"SAY IT! TELL HIM!"

"She's better than you were, Connor." Leda's voice was thick with tears. Before Connor could react, he heard Charmain's purring in his ear. "This little sweetie doesn't even know you exist, Connor. See what you're missing, you asshole? And you know what she really loves better than your lame cock? Getting fisted by me. Listen to her loving it." A groan of fear rose to a high-pitched shriek of…pain…? ecstasy…?

Connor leaped up from the bed screaming and flung the phone across the room, smashing it. "You bitch. You fucking, fucking bitch." He raced through the suite in a frenzy, smashing, kicking. By the time hotel security barged in and subdued him, he'd run up damages of $7,000-plus.

CHAPTER 42

CHARMAIN'S HOUSE
BEVERLY HILLS

LEDA Francis had never had a lesbian affair before. Like most young ballerinas, she'd indulged in a few casual late night girl-gropes on the road, where the only men readily available were gay dancers. But she fell hard for Charmain. And Charmain found she'd developed quite an affection for Leda.

Charmain hadn't had a lesbian affair in her life, either. Sexual encounters, yes. Romance, never. She surprised herself when she didn't dump Leda, according to plan, after seducing her away from Connor. At first, she thought it was the sex, which was thrilling in a hot, sweet way it never was with men. Leda, as a physical type, was ultra-femme and fragile-looking, but her dancer's body was incredibly toned and amazingly strong.

"God, it's like I'm fucking a princess," Charmain exclaimed after one night of seemingly endless love. "You're Audrey Hepburn with muscles. And when you talk in that cute English accent, I start getting wet all over again. EEEWWW! Kiss me, princess. Mmmm..."

"Ooohh...Charmain...you are the sexiest girl. It must be smashing to have breasts with heft to them. And a gorgeous, womanly ass. Instead of tiny tits and no butt, like me and your beloved Audrey Hepburn. She was a dancer, by the way, did you know that?"

"No, really?"

"Yes. She started her career in ballet."

"So...uh...you've gotten it on with ballet chicks before?"

"A couple of times, but it was deadly boring, I promise you. I was interested, but not that much. They feel like boys, so what's the point? You're so incredibly female. I used to get hot all over just watching you on TV."

"Yeah?"

"And no matter where I touch you, you're female. I mean, my gawd, ballerinas don't have excess flesh anywhere. Even their cunt lips have muscles."

Charmain shrieked. "Jesus, I just love the way you say things. If I said that, it would sound filthy. But when you say it, it comes out classy and clever. 'I say, old chap, ee-a-ven they-aah caahnt lips hev muscles.' God! You're so damn adorable. I love you!"

"Charmain, I *really* love you..."

"Oh, baby. Now, be cool."

Laddy, who'd looked forward to monopolizing Charmain now that Connor was *persona non ca-ca*, got all whiny when Charmain started hanging with Leda.

"Oh, great, now I'm competing with a girl."

Charmain smacked him on his bare ass and looked up at him sharply.

"Don't ruin a good thing, bubba. We're fuck-buddies, right? Well, that's what Leda is, kinda. I don't consider myself a lesbian, but I find women very attractive. So why not enjoy them sexually? Just like I'm enjoying you right now. So shut up and fuck your buddy, buddy!"

Charmain piqued the press when she suddenly started hanging out in gay bars around Hollywood. One night she hooked up with Bonnie Farr, an in-your-face butch singer who'd had two number one hits and a smash album before publicly coming out of the closet.

Bonnie, with her short slicked-back hair and tough-boy features, was Steve McQueen after a makeover by RuPaul. But once Bonnie's clothes came off, some very feminine curves and beautiful legs were revealed. Her upper torso, which she worked intensely with free weights, was awesomely ripped. And covered with tattoos. One, nestled just at the top of her pubic hair line, spelled out the provocative message: SUCK MY DICK. A tiny arrow pointed downward.

Bonnie was nuts about Charmain. Sadly for Bonnie, however, Charmain wasn't about to play submissive lipstick lesbian; the bottom to Bonnie's top. Bonnie accepted that gracefully, so she and Charmain enjoyed sexual romps in which the two of them dominated the exquisitely feminine and willing Leda. "I'm the original bloody bicycle built for two," Leda groused good-naturedly. And one glorious night after a wild party at Charmain's house, young Laddy was allowed to join the three women for an orgy that made him realize he hadn't even scratched the surface of his sexual potential.

Now Charmain had her own gang: Laddy, Dina, Leda, Bonnie, Seth Daniels—the actor she'd saved from a bad beating by Connor—and "TinkerBell," the hot new rock singer who was built like Arnold Schwarzennegger, dressed in full fairy drag—and who kicked the ass of anyone who hassled him about it. The press dubbed them "The Burns Gang." They roamed the Sunset Strip, Melrose, and Beverly Hills every night, raising hell.

One night, a woman darted into a parking space Charmain had been waiting for outside a pizza joint on Canon Drive. In a split second, the woman found herself staring down the barrel of Charmain's trusty 9mm Kahr. The woman, terrified, backed out of the space and took off, screaming that she'd call the police. The Burns Gang grabbed a few slices of take-out pizza and hit the road, just missing the Beverly Hills cops. But the woman had recognized Charmain and wanted to press charges. Charmain was picked up, booked, fingerprinted, and mugged, then released on bail. The press flashed her mug shot around the world. A couple of weeks later, the woman dropped the charges and the DA declined to prosecute. Rumors shot around Hollywood that Larry Buckley had called in a big marker.

He had.

The next scandal occurred on the set of *BevHills High*. Linda Kole, the actual star of the series, hated Charmain for overshadowing her, and everybody knew it. Linda had always been careful to hide her feelings behind a mask of tight civility, but lost it one night as they went into overtime and Charmain flubbed a line. Linda went nuts and screamed, "You fucking amateur, you're going to keep us here all night—"

Charmain bitch-slapped Linda so hard she knocked a cap off the star's front tooth and broke her nose. That was worth a week of headlines—and more speculation about "hush money" when Linda Kole made a statement saying that she forgave Charmain; that the punch-up had just been the result of "two very tired actors—and good friends—reacting to very tough work pressures."

After that incident, Buckley called Mike Kelso and told him: "There are limits to how far I'll go to protect a star, goddamnit. You tell Charmain to play it very, very cool. Or else."

"I'll tell her, Larry," sighed Kelso, meaning, "I'll tell her. But will she listen?"

As she approached the end of her second season as a major TV star, Charmain was growing restless. She didn't have to work as hard on the show because her acting skills had improved dramatically. That should have made her happy, but it didn't. She loved working, stretching herself. But now the series was starting to bore her. She felt locked into a routine. She craved a challenge. She wanted to really ACT! Movie offers were coming her way, but nothing interesting; terrified-tits-and-ass-teens-in-trouble horror flicks, mostly. She sensed it was time for a change. But what? She was hitting the town every night now, doing more tequila and cocaine than she should. She'd just held Buckley up for a huge raise and should have been happy as hell. But she wasn't. The happy mood she'd been in after the Caribbean trip had faded. The thrill of stardom, of privilege, of being recognized everywhere she went began to pall as she realized she couldn't even go shopping at the Beverly Center without a mob forming around her. And she was getting more and more hate mail. Death threats, even. It freaked her out.

"It's not unusual, Charmain," Kelso told her. "Every star gets mail from weirdos. It's part of the price of fame. I've probably put this off too long, but you've got to hire a security expert. I strongly recommend Vidal Delaney. You've heard of him?"

"Yeah. What's that going to cost?"

"A lot. But you can afford it. And it's a business expense, a write-off."

"Shit! Why do I need this? Why can't I have privacy?"

"Charmain, we've had this conversation before. You're in the spotlight because you deserve to be—and because you want to be. It would be nice if you could say, 'Excuse me, world, but I'd like to suspend my stardom for the next few days, thank you very much.' It just doesn't work that way."

Then Charmain heard about *Medusa*. Every actress in Hollywood was buzzing about the new original screenplay written by Fergal O'Casey, the weird, reclusive Irish poet and playwright. O'Casey, acclaimed on the London and Broadway stages, had written for the silver screen only once; the staggeringly haunting *Take Down the Sun*, which had swept the Oscars two years before. He'd hand-picked the director, Clive Tinsdale, a three-time Oscar winner. He released a statement saying: "I'll leave it all to the director now. Once it's written, I'm done with it. He's a great talent—for a bloody Brit."

It was a dream role: the story of a callous young actress whose beauty, ambition, and ruthlessness turns men's hearts to stone. She ruins the lives of every director and leading man she works with—and then one day, the good roles stop coming. She looks in the mirror and she's no longer young. A hard, glitter-eyed monster stares back at her—the image of Medusa, snakes writhing in her hair. She hits the skids. But one day, there's a chance for a comeback. A role about an actress who'd literally kill to get a part. And, through a strange set of circumstances, the role can be hers—*if* she's willing to kill for it. Literally.

The script hadn't been formally offered to any star—yet. Clive Tinsdale, the director, was coming from his native Britain and had made it clear that any actress who wanted the part had better be prepared to read for it—no matter how big a star she was. Every major diva of stage, screen and TV had frantic calls in to agents, managers, power brokers, and bigshots at MGM, the studio financing and distributing the film. Kelso managed to get a copy of the script for Charmain to read. She called him in the middle of the night, just hours after he'd dropped it off.

"God, Mike, it's…it's fantastic," she said. "It made me cry, it's so wonderful. You've got to get me a reading with Tinsdale. You've GOT to!"

"Look, Charmain, it's a long shot and—"

"Don't give me your SHIT!" she screamed into the phone. "I KNOW every actress in town wants this. I KNOW I'll be up against Paltrow and Stone and Pfeiffer and Blanchett and Ryder. But Medusa calls for an actress who starts young and gets older. Well, it's a lot easier for me to age on screen than for them to get younger. This girl KILLS men because she's young and hot and dangerous—and goddamnit, that's fucking ME, Mike. I was born to play Medusa. So get off your lazy ass and get me to this guy for an audition! Earn your fucking money! What have you done for me in the last two years, huh? You're collecting twenty percent for nothing. If you want to keep collecting, GET ME THAT READING! And I mean NO fucking excuses."

Kelso knew she meant it. Like every handler of major female talent who wanted *Medusa*, Kelso was racking his brains for an "in." An edge. Leverage. Who did he know who could get Charmain to that director? He knew it would probably be tough. The guy was a Brit. And they tended to be pretentious, so he might turn up his nose at the idea of even considering a TV actress. For that matter, so would a lot of American directors. Kelso didn't know the guy. What he needed, badly, was someone who did. And then his longtime assistant, Madeline, reminded him that he had an ace in the hole.

"Mike, don't you remember Kevin Moffet, the British actor you helped out? You got him his first job in Hollywood and let him stay at your house for a couple of months until he got established."

"Yes. Kevin. Still does steady work in soap operas and so forth. Nice guy. Haven't seen him in ages. So what?"

"So what? Kevin just happens to be the asshole buddy of what's-his-name, the *Medusa* director. They both went to Bumfuck University, or whatever, in the good old United Kingdom. Roommates, drinking buddies. Probably did each other up the arse, old chap."

"What? Kevin's not gay. Is he?"

"No, Mike, but he is British." Madeline had been married to an English actor who'd dumped her for a black girl and life in a shack on some Jamaican beach. She still hung out with the Brit underground in Hollywood at pubs, attended rugby games, and watched soccer on TV. She knew her British gossip.

"Goddamn, that's great, Madeline. You have a number for Kevin?"

Five minutes later, Kevin was on the phone and promising Kelso heartily, "Not to worry, my dear fellow. I'll have a word with my mate, and Charmain's as good as in. Old school tie and all that, you know? She'll get her audition, never fear."

Mike Kelso nearly fainted with elation. He'd gotten used to being a Hollywood player. Manager of a red-hot property. But if Charmain fired him, he'd be "Mike who…?" in a nano-second. Right at this moment, life was looking peachy-keen and fabulous. Just like in the movies.

But then, as Kelso later put it delicately, "The fit hit the shan…!"

The phone call that launched them all on the road to hell came early Sunday morning. Cameron Tull had awakened later than usual. Exhausted by my exertions, he thought wryly. He slipped out of bed carefully, not wanting to disturb the sleeping beauty he'd picked up like a midnight snack at the premiere of Steven Spielberg's latest. An actress. He'd sworn to cut down, of course, but. he grinned wryly., why should he? She was a voluptuous creature. And young. Too young. Touchingly uninhibited, sweet. Adorable, really. It had been wonderful and he was sated. So why did he feel so melancholy? Why was he already thinking he'd just ease her on down the road?

He saw one new message blinking on his answering machine, started to punch it up, then ignored it. Hey, this was Sunday morning. Orange juice first, then a quiet moment with the *Times* before commencing the day's communication. But alas, it was not to be. Tull had barely seated himself on the sunlit deck when he heard her call his name. "On deck," he called. She came padding out, wrapped in a towel, and propped herself against a railing. God, what a body.

"Good morning," he said.

"Hi...wanna go for brunch somewhere?"

Somehow, he'd hoped she might be content to hang out and read the papers, take a swim. "Brunch? Wish I could," he said, "but I'm working today."

Not a lie. He was always working. News never stopped happening. He'd bet that the call blinking insistently on his machine wasn't social. Not this early on a Sunday morning in L.A.

"But let me make you breakfast," he said. "I do omelettes or eggs sunny-side up. French toast, even. I have three kinds of bagels. And I make a great cappuccino."

She shrugged, smiled. "Well, you know what? I usually meet friends every Sunday for brunch over at Lilac. On Third? So maybe I'll just go because there's still time, and you're working, so...like, I'll just take a quick shower, okay?"

"Okay, but have some cappuccino before you go. It'll be ready when you're out of the shower."

"Great," she said. She was showered and dressed in twenty minutes. He handed her the cappuccino.

"What was the name of that indie film you're appearing in?" he asked.

"Oh...it's called *Brains Like A Whore*. If you could mention it in your column, it would be so cool," she said.

"I can probably work it in. I liked that thing you told me about Matt Damon dropping by to do a cameo and treating everybody to lunch. Cute story."

She finished the cappuccino, stood up to go. "Well..."

He kissed her lightly.

"See you soon, I hope. Maybe we can do lunch. You've got my number," she said. "Or I'll call you."

She'd come up in her own car. He watched her leave, turned to the *Times*, then leaned back and stared up into the sun. Beautiful day. No one to share it with. He shook his head impatiently. Oh, let's not get all maudlin. You didn't really want her to stay. Didn't exactly want her to go, either. God, what was this? Post-coital angst? The sex had been great. Leave it at that.

What did you expect? Meaningful dialogue? Bonding? A soulmate? Well…yeah, maybe. Somebody to share this so-called life with. Tull shook his head, sighed. Jesus, was he undergoing some kind of mid-life crisis? He'd always been pretty happy being a loner until he'd hit the Big 4-0. Then something happened. Suddenly, he had vague yearnings for…what?

He walked into the kitchen, brewed another cappuccino. Why the hell was he kidding himself? His yearnings weren't vague at all. He'd been thinking a lot about having kids. He liked children. Thought he'd end up with one or two when some woman came along and coaxed him into marriage. Why hadn't that ever happened? He'd always assumed that his future wife would just magically appear someday and…well, coax him down the aisle. Isn't that what women did? So where, he'd started to wonder, was this woman? His soulmate. And suddenly…she'd materialized. Right on cue.

Jessica! The dream he'd always dreamed. The missing element that would finally balance his life. Suddenly, he was the one prepared to do the coaxing. He'd actually daydreamed about popping the question in grand, romantic style. Maybe take out a full-page ad in *Woman's Wear Daily*. Or have a couple of models bop down the runway of her next fashion show carrying a "Jessica, Marry Me!" sign. Then…he was yesterday's news. With no warning, she'd stopped taking his calls. Day after day, week after week. It hurt with a pain that amazed him. What the hell had happened? He'd felt so sure of her love. Then, she was gone. And nothing could fill the void she'd left behind. He felt cursed. Just one other woman had ruled his heart like this. He'd lost her, too: Yukiko.

Tokyo. Fifteen years ago. She was a choreographer, quite famous in Japan. He'd met her on a soundstage at Toho Film Studios. A director friend had introduced them..."and this is Yukiko Kinoshita." Tull had bowed and said in fluent, accent-less Japanese: "*Hajimemashite, yoroshiku*...Miss Snowy Underwood."

She laughed and said in English, "Yes, that is a rough translation of my name."

He grinned. "Rough? *Rambo no imi desu ka*?"

She answered in English: "No, Mr. Tull, my use of the word 'rough' would not be translated as *rambo*—a word that has the meaning of violence. Mr. Sly Stallone is 'Rambo.' No, the word would be *daitai*, meaning approximate. But I'm sure you know that and are just teasing me, because your Japanese is excellent."

"Oh, no," he said in her native tongue. "And I hope you know that I would never be rough in the presence of such delicacy."

She inclined her head, hiding a smile. "It is very clear that you are a gentleman, Tull-san," she replied demurely.

Wow! Beautiful. And smart. Yukiko: Translation: Snow child. Kinoshita: Translation: Beneath a tree. Tull's tongue-in-cheek translation:

Snowy Underwood. Bestowing a silly pet name on her had seemed somewhat uncool. He didn't care. And she laughed. He fell in love that very moment. They had eight wonderful months together, and then…

He took his cappuccino out to the sundeck, wanting to bury his thoughts. He tried to read the *Times*, but his eyes glazed and he leaned back, remembering:

Tull had been in the Far East for two years before he'd met her. He landed in Tokyo after learning the news trade on two Boston papers, then going to work for the Associated Press in New York. It was a fast-track gig for a kid barely out of his twenties. Right away, he'd started lobbying hard for an overseas job, particularly in the Orient, which had always fascinated him. But a foreign correspondent berth was a plum assignment; only newsies with seniority need apply. Then he got lucky: attending a Japanese film festival in the Village, he'd met a courtly old geezer who ran a trade paper called *Far East Film Journal* in Tokyo. His name was Glenn Firestone, and he was impressed with Tull's knowledge of Japanese film history. They struck a deal: Tull would get a one-way ticket to Tokyo and take over as editor. If he worked out in the job and lasted a year, he'd be guaranteed a return ticket and get a substantial raise. If not, he was on his own.

Tull leaped at the chance. He went to Tokyo and worked his ass off at the job. It paid him barely enough to subsist. And when old phony Firestone reneged on his promises of a return ticket and the raise—as the bastard did with every Orient-smitten, talented, young American he hired —Tull quit and stayed in Tokyo to freelance. It was rough at first, and he damn near starved. But he was stubborn, and he quickly found an edge. He had a talent for languages and picked up Japanese quickly. When other Americans and Brits living in Tokyo asked how he'd done it, he replied: "Stop speaking English."

Tull had a huge circle of Japanese friends—male and female. From the women, he learned pillow talk and gossip and the psychology of relationships in a culture totally alien to his own. From the men, he learned, first and foremost, that he was a foreigner—a *gaijin*—who'd never totally penetrate the intricate web of society. But, he formed some strong friendships, nevertheless. And he developed an obsession for the martial arts, admiring the discipline and mental focus they instilled. His passion was Iaijutsu. Unlike Kendo, this was practiced with real swords. Iaijutsu was the art of drawing a sword quickly, dispatching the enemy, and returning the weapon swiftly to its sheath in one continuous motion. He'd studied under the famed Ichitaro Kuroda after interviewing him for a story he sold to *Playboy,* "Samurai Swordsmen: Alive and Well and Living in Tokyo." *Playboy* was the one market that helped Tull prosper in the tough world of foreign freelancing; his second piece was "Unveiling the World of the Japanese Kimono," lavishly illustrated with photos of a beautiful woman gradually stripping off the many layers of brocade and silk that teasingly hid her treasures.

For two years, Tull worked assignments in Tokyo, Hong Kong, Thailand, Singapore, Taiwan, even mainland China. He worked as a stringer for high-paying publications like *Playboy, The National Enquirer, People,* and *Esquire*. He became a stringer for two U.S. newspapers and one newsmagazine. Then he started making heavy bucks doing broadcast pieces for U.S. TV networks. He became an all-around expert on the Far East, especially Japan, where he built a reputation as a *mado-guchi,* a "window-entrance" for foreign press organizations angling for entree. He had competition, of course, but, amazingly, few foreign corrrespondents spoke Japanese. Unlike Tull, they had to rely on translators.

Tull became an expert in another area—the Japanese gangs, or *yakuza*. These highly-organized groups, whose behavior was patterned after the medieval samurai warriors, had modernized into Mafia-like groups that graduated from such traditional pursuits as gambling and armed theft into more sophisticated ripoffs: manipulating stock prices by intimidating corporate officers, corrupting government officials who regulated the banking industry, etc.

Tull became friendly with high-ranking members of two gangs: the *Tosei-kai*, which controlled downtown Tokyo and the Ginza, and the *Ando-Gumi*, the quick-triggered *yakuza* from the nearby district of Shibuya. He soon attracted the attention of the FBI, which was concerned by the growing infiltration of the *yakuza* into America. He traded information he picked up in exchange for tips on major crime stories. Then the DEA and Air Force Intelligence quietly asked for his help in apprehending a ring of American servicemen using military personnel and aircraft to smuggle drugs Stateside.

Cracking that case had been no sweat, as the GIs used to say. Tull had checked with *Toseikai*, the Ginza Gang, who knew all about the operation and were furious that they weren't getting a piece of the action. There was nothing they could do because all the action was taking place on heavily-guarded U.S. military bases. The smuggling group, all U.S. Air Force members, flew heroin into Japan from the Golden Triangle, then put it aboard military aircraft headed for Stateside military bases, bypassing Customs. But lately, some low-ranking GIs in the ring had gotten stupid and greedy. Looking for good times laying over in Tokyo, they chipped small amounts of heroin from the cargo while it sat hidden in base warehouses awaiting a U.S. flight. They sold it piecemeal or exchanged it for sex in bars around the Ginza. They were about to get some fingers amputated, a typical *yakuza* warning. Tull, who hated drug traffickers, saved them from that. On his tip, they were arrested by FBI and DEA, and they fingered the ringleaders.

Like any journalist in foreign lands with great contacts and knowledge, Tull suddenly found the CIA on his doorstep. He brushed them off at first, then got a visit from a heavy: Dalton Lupo, who was described to him darkly by his FBI contact as bigger than a CIA station chief—much bigger. Think of him as a roving troubleshooter with a direct pipeline into the Director's office at Langley, he was told.

Tull did several big favors for the CIA. He was offered money, but refused. "I've got a quid pro quo, however," he told Lupo. "I want to go through agent's fieldcraft training at The Farm."

Lupo had smiled. "Where did you hear about The Farm? Ah, probably in a Charles McHarry spy novel. We have no secrets anymore. Well, this is, as they say, highly irregular. But I can arrange it. You'd have to sign an oath, of course."

Tull had the coolest time of his life undergoing the rigorous training for life as a spy. The unarmed combat and killing techniques alone were worth it. Also, the course on surveillance. He did so well, they offered him a career, but he nixed it. He'd flown secretly out of Japan aboard a CIA black flight. So his passport was never stamped in Tokyo or America, coming or going. No one could ever prove that he'd been away from Tokyo for two months.

He'd missed Yukiko terribly. When he returned, he went straight to her apartment. She held on to him like she'd never let go. The next day, they had a serious talk about their future. It was decided he'd give up his apartment to save money for their future, and move into her place. Yukiko was committed to six months of touring with the new show she'd choreographed and was headlining as lead dancer/actress. Tull had a scheduled trip to Beijing for an ABC-TV piece, plus another month in Manila and several Pacific islands for a one-hour documentary on Japanese army stragglers hiding out in jungles after World War II. When all that was finished, he and Yukiko would marry and start a family. They were ecstatic.

He was in Beijing when the telegram from her best friend, Takako, reached him. It read: "Condolences. Yukiko has died. Plane crash in Osaka. Funeral Wednesday."

He flew to Tokyo immediately. After the funeral, Yukiko's distraught mother, a prosperous widow, pressed something into his hand. "Yukiko loved you so much," she said. "Please read this later."

He didn't open the note until the next day. He hadn't slept and was almost too drunk for his eyes to focus. The message tore him open. He vomited non-stop, knowing he was on the knife-edge of alcohol poisoning. Not caring. The note had told him how truly deep his loss had been: an autopsy had shown that Yukiko was pregnant when she died.

Somewhere, as this past horror swirled through him, a phone rang insistently...His answering machine picked up.

"Tull...hey, Tull...Pick up if you're there, man...This is really important. I've got to make a move, compadre...Don't make me take these beauties to *The Enquirer*. If I don't hear from you by three today, I'll—"

Tull walked in to his study and picked up the phone. "Randy? What's up?"

"Man, where have you been? I—"

"Randy, I'm here. SPEAK, goddamit!" Fucking photographers. Hysterical and money-hungry, the whole fucking bunch of them. But oh, how we love them when they've got goodies. And Randy Cardozo was one of the best. Tull had tipped him that *The Revealer* was putting a full court press on Charmain and would pay big for newsy photos.

"Okay, man, okay," Randy said. "You know how I get excited. Sorry. Look, I've got a sequence on Charmain that's hot, man. It shows her beating the shit out of a horse with one of those short whip things?"

"A riding crop?"

"Yeah. Anyway, her face is all contorted and vicious-looking. The poor horse is fucking terrified, rearing away from her and—"

Tull cut in. "What's Charmain doing with a horse?"

"Oh, well, I was door-stepping her this weekend. Yesterday she and her little coven of dykes headed up to the ranch near Santa Barbara. Turns out butchy Bonnie Farr is going to teach her and Leda and Dina Buckley how to ride. I got up real close to them, got great quotes about how the rocking motion was firing up their pussies, stuff like that and—"

"Are any of the other celebs in your pictures?"

"Oh, yeah, especially when Charmain hits the horse. You see them all trying to stop her. And Leda Francis looks like she's crying, she's so upset. It's great stuff, man. Shall I come over and show you?"

Tull thought for a moment. "No, give this to Steve Bellini. You've got his home number?"

"Yeah, of course, but—Hey, Tull, I called you first. Don't you want the credit for this?"

"No. I want a quiet Sunday. Thanks for calling me first, Randy. I won't forget it. But give it to Steve."

"That's a hell of a favor you're doin' him, man," said Randy.

Tull laughed. "Ah, what the hell. Charmain's seen too many stories that piss her off with my name on them. Let her get pissed off at Steve for a change."

"For a hard-nosed sonofabitch, you're a good guy, Tull."

"Yeah. I'm a goddamn saint. Talk to you later."

In the days and weeks after Steve Bellini's death, Tull couldn't stop thinking about this "great favor" he'd done for the kid.

The one that had killed him.

CHAPTER 43

4:15 P.M.
CHARMAIN BURNS' MANSION
BEVERLY HILLS

CHARMAIN sits alone in the bedroom of the Beverly Hills home that fame bought her.

It's dark, save for soft light cast by candles clustered on her dressing table. A small chest of inlaid wood sits before her. She reaches under the dressing table, produces a hidden key, opens the chest. Reaching inside, she lifts out the precious images, going through them slowly, smiling at each one. The silence is broken sporadically by soft whispers.

"...I'm always here…Be strong…I'll be so proud…I can't be with you now, but someday…Just be safe…"

Charmain arranges the images around her dressing table. Looks at them intently. Closes her eyes, sees them vividly etched in her memory. She crosses her arms over her breasts and rocks gently back and forth, praying silently to the inner being she knows as her real self. Begging for the strength she must command to be The Protector.

She opens her eyes, raises them to stare into the mirror. There! There she is. Herself!

Little Charmain.

Surrounded by the tiny ones who need her strength. Her love.

Charmain's eyes fill softly with tears of absolute joy.

Finally, she gathers up the precious treasures, puts them back in the chest, locks it, and hides the key again.

She stands, flicks on the lights.

And shrieks...

"MARTA!…MARTA!…Where the fuck ARE YOU!?"

Omigod, why is she screaming? Marta raced up the stairs, into the bedroom. Charmain thrust the wooden chest at her.

"Lock this back in the safe!"

Marta recoiled from the murderous stare.

"Charmain, what...?"

"You sure you've taken care of everything?"

Marta nodded vigorously, "You know I'd never, ever forget. I know it's the most important thing. Why don't you trust me to...?"

"Just remember…you ever fuck that up, I'll kill you. Understand?"

Marta shivered. Wondered again why she didn't just walk away from all this. Sometimes Charmain really scared her. Like now. But some weird fascination held her. It was almost obsessive...but she just couldn't leave...

"Don't stand there lookin' all hurt, girlfriend. Get your ass in gear and make me a pitcher of martinis for the thermos. I'm going to a beach party, so lucky you gets the rest of today and tomorrow off. Now ain't that good news?"

An hour later, Charmain hit the freeway, headed for Mexico. She was all but unrecognizable in brunette wig, plastic hair curlers, shapeless mu-mu, the brown contact lenses she'd bought in Savannah, and granny sunglasses. She drove her own car. Renting one would defintely leave a paper trail. And she might be recognized by some clerk with a long memory.

She crossed the border just before eight p.m., stopped to call Buster from a pay phone outside a gas station.

"Hi, it's you-know-who. Look, I'm starved. Let's go right to dinner. I know a fantastic little place down the coast. Just wear jeans or something, okay? I'm in a wig and I'm wearing contacts so I won't be mobbed by fans. Don't be freaked when you see me, okay? Wait outside the hotel. I'll be there in exactly forty minutes. Bye, y'all."

Charmain hung up the phone, got the key to the restroom, stripped off the mu-mu and slipped into jeans and a light sweater. She left the brunette wig on, but removed the hair curlers. She got back on the road, made good time and pulled into the gravel driveway of the small hotel at exactly 8:45. Buster was waiting outside. He got in the car. A sleepy-looking valet parker barely glanced up as Charmain gunned it out of the driveway.

Buster grinned as she blew him a kiss. "Hey, you've got brown eyes," he said. "And I dig your wig, baby."

She winked. "Thought you might like to change your luck, my man."

"But listen," he said. "The bartender said the hotel is full. You got a reservation, or you stayin' with me?"

"We'll figure it all out later. Let's just relax, okay? We're going to have a great dinner at this really romantic little restaurant. And I want to dance. They have a great mariachi band. God, I love Mexico. I've been down here twice on location shoots."

Charmain chattered away, driving south along the Baja coast. Twenty minutes later, she pulled off the road and drove slowly through trees into a clearing. She stopped twenty feet short of a cliff that overlooked the Pacific Ocean. They got out of the car and she breathed deeply, flinging her arms up at the starry sky.

"Buster, isn't that the most gorgeous view of the ocean in the moonlight? I always stop at this spot. I love to look down at the waves. But first, we're going to have us a drink. I'm just dying for an ice-cold vodka martini. How about you?"

Buster nodded approvingly as Charmain produced the thermos. She handed him two paper cups and poured them each a drink. She raised her cup in a toast and said, "To your new acting career. May you be the next shining star."

"Alright," said Buster, taking a healthy pull at his martini. "Man, that is good. And cold." He drank again.

Charmain poured him another, filling his cup. She took his hand and led him down to the edge of the cliff, prattling on about the acting lessons he'd be taking and how Mike Kelso believed he had great potential as an action star. They stood there for a long moment, looking down at the ocean and whitecaps crashing against the rocks far below.

"Oh, look at it, Buster. Isn't it wild and beautiful? Just watch the rhythm of the waves. Imagine all that power pushing them up against the cliffs. Where does it come from, all that power? Smashing in, then falling back...Wham!...And another one...Wham!...Over and over and over again, maybe since the beginning of time...Look at them...they never stop...ever...Wham!...Wham!..."

Still holding his hand, she swayed in hypnotic rhythm, crooning her mantra to the waves. After a few moments, Buster's head suddenly rolled forward onto his chest, then snapped back as he mumbled, "Fuckin' drink's strong, man..."

Charmain patted him on the back. "Oh, you're probably just hungry," she said.

"No, man," he said groggily. "Got to sit down..."

His head lolled again. He caught himself, fighting for control. He shuffled his feet, tried to turn away from the cliff. Charmain stepped behind him, put both hands on the small of his back and shoved hard, throwing her weight into him. Buster grunted. Flew straight out, arms windmilling, legs scrabbling for one last foothold. She watched, unblinking.

He fell swiftly. Moonlight caught him as he bounced off the rocks ninety feet below. His body slid into the sea, bobbing in the roiling swells...

Wham!...Wham!

And gone.

No surprise to it. None at all. The scene had played great. Just like she'd rehearsed it in her mind. The rohypnol had worked faster than she'd estimated. Six pills must be a killer dose. And it had numbed him, she was sure. Probably hadn't known what was happening. She hoped so, anyway.

She stood still a moment, feeling nothing, really. The wind freshened. She breathed deeply, looked down at the sea, and said:

"Sorry, Buster, you punched too hard this time. No sense us both gettin' hung for it."

Charmain bent and picked up the paper cup she'd dropped. She looked around carefully for Buster's; couldn't find it. She went back to the edge of the cliff. Not there. Claimed by the restless ocean, she hoped. She went back to her car, drove a mile up the coast, stopped, got out. She walked to the edge of the cliffs, twisting the top off the thermos. She wiped both pieces carefully with a handkerchief, filled the bottom half with stones, then flung both pieces into the sea, watching as they hit the churning water and sank.

She stood there a moment, wondering if she should have taken the thermos farther from the scene before dumping it. But what if...just what if...a cop had stopped her and she'd been caught with the damn thing? A lab test would pick up the rophynol. But what if...the thermos washed up this close to the scene after they found Buster's body?

Shit! This is stupid, she thought. No one's gonna find a goddamn thing.

She walked back to the car, quick-changed back into old lady drag, and burned rubber for the California border.

She didn't see the car that pulled out behind her, headlights off.

Randak 2000 settled back for the long drive back to L.A., keeping Charmain's taillights just in view. He thought carefully about all he'd seen after tailing her into Mexico. The sudden, brutally efficient act of murder had puzzled him at first. What was her motive? The boxer had been her protector. Indeed, a lover.

He shrugged. No matter. He expected he'd discover eventually her reason for killing a supposed friend. What did matter was that she was ruthless and strong enough to kill swiftly, without mercy.

Now it is almost certain, he thought. This woman has The Power.

She is our Queen.

The Guides will be pleased.

CHAPTER 44

3:46 P.M.
NATIONAL REVEALER NEWSROOM
LOS ANGELES

IN the wake of Steve Bellini's death, *National Revealer* reporters swarmed Hollywood like fire ants, desperate for prey. And found nothing.

The day after the funeral, in late afternoon, the Queen of Scots convened a meeting of key editors and senior reporters. Barry Hale, the paper's executive editor, squirmed as Mary fixed him with her trademark stare, unwavering and relentless, not saying a word. Barry talked fast, then ran out of steam and admitted that, despite turning over every rock in Hollywood, they'd come up empty.

The Queen let the silence build, then said mildly:

"If you'd turned over every rock, Barry, I'd be authorizing that one million dollar check for some lucky person right now. Wouldn't I?"

Barry grimaced. He hated making excuses. There was no excuse, goddamnit! But he needed to catch a fucking break. The people sitting in this room had more sources than the CIA. Shit, some had sources *in* the CIA! So how come, all of a sudden, no one knew from nothing? Especially with a big reward dangling. Why? It was killing him. The mainstream press had trumpeted the news that *The Revealer* was offering a $1 million reward. Now everybody in the fucking world knew that a tip on Bellini's murder was a one-way ticket to Fat City. By rights, the newsroom phones should be ringing off the hook. But so far, nobody had gotten even a sniff of anything useful. Zero. Nada. Zipitty-doo-dah.

Mary swept the room with her eyes. A baker's dozen of men, and two women, looked back at her, carefully neutral. No one said a word. She leaned forward and said, "Please don't miss a word of what I'm saying here. Dalton Lupo prides himself on the fact that his paper pays the highest salaries in journalism. He expects your absolute best, and so do I. You know what the police say: if you don't solve a murder in the first seventy-two hours, you probably never will.

"I suggest you all eat lightly, drink not at all, and sleep, if you feel you must, with one eye open. Hound every source, call in every favor. Spend whatever needs be. But get this killer. Whatever it takes. And if it takes extraordinary measures...well, what I don't know won't hurt me."

Mary's light Scottish burr thickened. "Now, for those of you who don't appreciate a message quietly delivered, or the force behind it, let me add this:

"GET YOUR FUCKING FINGERS OUT—OR I'LL HAVE YOUR BALLS FOR BREAKFAST!"

After the meeting, Cameron Tull walked to his desk and dialed the office number of his most valuable Charmain Burns source, a real insider, who'd been ducking messages Tull had left at his home. Time to take the gloves off. He got the guy's secretary on the line and said:

"Give him this message exactly, please…Could you write it down so there's no mistake?…Thank you…Okay, the message is: 'Know you've been too busy to take calls, so why don't I drop by your office today and finally get to meet everybody?'…That's the message…My name? Oh, he'll know who it's from. I'm an old friend. Goodbye."

Three minutes later, his direct line, which bypassed Eva, rang.

"Cameron Tull."

"Jesus, man, what are you trying to do, let everyone know I talk to you?"

"Just trying to get your attention."

"Listen, I…"

"No, you listen. I need to talk to you. By phone or in person. It's your call. But it has to be now. If you refuse, I'll come straight to your office—and make sure the whole world knows I was there, so..."

"Alright, alright…Uh, I don't want to talk on the phone. Come to my place. Seven sharp. I'll watch for you and open the garage door. Drive your car right in and I'll close it behind you."

Tull chuckled. "I'm getting the impression you're ashamed to be seen with me."

"Ha, ha, very funny."

"Seven sharp," said Tull, and clicked off.

Three hours later, he rolled up the driveway of a small but classy house in Santa Monica. The garage door went up and he drove inside, cut the engine, and got out. A door leading into the house was ajar.

"Come on in," a voice called.

Tull walked in, shut the door behind him. He was in the kitchen. No one in sight.

"In here," said the voice. Tull walked out into the great room. And there, smiling behind a mahogany-topped wet bar, stood a handsome young man, stirring a beaker of liquid with a glass rod.

Tull's top-secret source. His exclusive window into the world of Charmain Burns.

"You do enjoy a Belvedere martini, as I recall?" said Laddy Burford.

Tull smiled. "Thanks for the memory."

Laddy gave the libation a final stir and poured carefully into crystal stemware.

"A twist, right?"

"Please."

Tull walked over to the bar, picked up a glass. Laddy raised his to Tull and they drank, savoring the flavor judiciously.

"Excellent," said Tull.

Laddy shrugged. "Martinis are second nature to me. My father taught me how to make them when I was eight years old. I had to have one ready for him every evening when he came home. If it wasn't perfect, he'd make me mix another, and another, until I got it right. By the time I was ten, he'd bring guests home for dinner and brag that no one made a martini like his son and heir. He never let my mother make them. Father claimed women had no feel for mixing a drink. 'The wife is barely adequate at pouring wine,' he'd say, and laugh at poor Mother, even if she was standing right there."

Amazing, Tull thought, what people reveal about themselves if you just listen; tune in to adumbrations coursing beneath words. In years of developing sources, and keeping them close, he'd learned to hear everything said, even if it had no bearing on the actual information he was trying to elicit. Picking up the nuances made you sensitive to what might be motivating someone to tell you secrets.

"Always ask yourself why a source is giving you information," Tull would remind his reporters. "If you know what ax he's grinding, it will help you evaluate how accurate the information might be. And why he's giving it up. Sometimes it's simple greed—the source wants a payoff, or a plug for his pet project or product. That's generally the best situation. Once I know I'm dealing with pure greed, I feel more comfortable. First, there's no hidden agenda to worry about. And second, the source knows there'll be no quid pro quo until you check out his story.

"And be careful of a source who feeds you info because he's looking to fuck someone: stab them in the back for revenge—business or sexual. Ex-partners, ex-spouses, ex-lovers, ex-anything are dangerous as hell. They're insiders, so they know real facts and can give you a story that's maybe ninety percent accurate. But the ten percent poison they lace it with is what kills you. Keep asking yourself: whose ox is getting gored here, and how does it benefit the source?

"The best source, usually, is the power freak. Hollywood and Washington are full of these guys. They sit in or near a position of power themselves, know a lot of shit. And they're dying to tell someone. So they'll slip you great stories, then get off on knowing they planted it with me, or Liz Smith, Cindy Adams, Page Six, *The Enquirer, Time* magazine, or whoever. Their stuff is always accurate. Otherwise, they don't get no kicks. They want to impress you and say, 'See...I told you I've got the scoop.' So it works all around. No ax-grinding, no payoff. We get a story; they get to jerk off.

"Oh, and let's not forget those rarest of birds. The sources who contact you because they actually want to do the right thing, no strings attached. Help somebody in trouble. Report a terrible crime. Expose corruption. Or child abuse. This old newsie I worked under as a kid called them 'God's messengers.' They're the ones who occasionally make us feel good about what we're doing..."

"Dry enough?" asked Laddy.

"Yeah. You're the Martha Stewart of martinis, pal," said Tull, raising his glass and taking another pull. "Now, I need some help and I hope you..."

The phone rang. "Excuse me," said Laddy. He picked up. "Hello?...Oh, Father, I wasn't expecting your call until later...What? You're on the plane now? When do you arrive?...Oh, I see. Well, what time tomorrow?...Alright, I'll be in your office at...Okay, 7:30. Fine. Have a good flight."

Laddy hung up, rolling his eyes. "Leaping Jesus. I thought tomorrow was going to be an easy day. My father's coming out from New York on one of his shake-up-the-troops visits."

And, of course, to visit the whore I know he keeps out here, thought Ransom Burford's son and heir. God, how I'd love to tell Tull; have him find out who she is, exactly. Or maybe he knows.

"Say, I've got to make one quick call to alert the serfs about this early meeting," Laddy said apologetically. "Excuse me for a minute."

Tull smiled, watched Laddy pick up the phone and dial. What would the lad's reaction be, he wondered, if he knew his old man had secured the exclusive services of an exotic British-Indian call girl who catered to his peculiar need to sit confined in a specially-made high chair, dressed in diapers and a bib, while she chastised him like a naughty infant? Just another one of those jolly kinks that, oddly, appealed to high-powered, commanding men. "Adult baby" was what they called it in the good old, repressive British Isles, where bizarre sexual perversions flourished like no place on earth.

As Laddy chatted on the phone, Tull recalled the first time they'd spoken. It was a few days after he'd broken the news in his column that Charmain Burns was dating the Burford heir in New York. Laddy had phoned, introduced himself, and said nervously, "Look...I don't know how this works, but if I tell you something you might want to print, do I remain anonymous?"

Ah, the countless times Tull had answered this question; the first baby step for a potential source. "Absolutely," he answered smoothly. "No one will ever know who you are. I'm in the business of printing secrets, but I'd never, ever, reveal the source. Think about it. If word got out on the street that I couldn't keep my mouth shut about where I get my information, I'd be out of business in five minutes. No one would trust me. And that's the only way you can cultivate, and keep, good sources in the news business. They've got to trust you. So...trust me, Laddy. Now, what've you got?"

Laddy gave Tull a terrific item about how Charmain had dragged him to the famed Hogs & Heifers, a raunchy country-western bar in New York's meat-packing district where celebrities love to mingle with the rowdy crowd for a walk on the wild side. The joint's sideshow was waitresses, dressed in hot pants and tank tops, who'd periodically hop up on the bar and shake their booties to ear-splitting music. And often, some female star like Julia Roberts or Drew Barrymore would jump up with them, wiggling T & A, and honor a Hogs & Heifers tradition by stripping off her bra, signing it, then hanging it on the ceiling for posterity.

"Charmain loved the place," Laddy told Tull. "And she wanted to get up and dance, but she wasn't wearing a bra. So I phoned security at our department store and arranged for my limo driver to go over and bring back a few bras…uh, 36-C, if that matters..."

"Details are always good," Tull told him aprovingly.

"...And, uh, she slipped on a bra in the ladies room, got up on the bar and danced…then stripped off the bra and hung it on the ceiling. The place went wild."

The *New York Post's* ever-alert gossip column, Page Six, had picked up the story about Charmain's dance, but Tull topped that in his next weekly column about Laddy sending his chauffeur to Burford's for the bra in the middle of the night. The story had everything—sex, celebrity hijinks, high society meeting low. It got picked up everywhere.

For the next few weeks, the Burns-Burford romance was all over the press, but Tull kept scoring exclusives because Laddy kept him up to date with fun stuff no one else had. Tull actually turned down a couple of items from Laddy to keep Charmain from guessing that her sweetie-pie was his source.

"It's like this, Laddy," he'd explained. "If I print something that no one but you could have known about, she'll figure that it had to come from you. I'd rather lose a good story than expose you. Believe me, I really do want to keep you anonymous."

Laddy had actually thanked him.

Tull didn't know exactly why the kid was feeding him. And he didn't ask. He knew that Laddy, like so many sources with riches or power, was more than likely motivated by the thrill of seeing his name in print, without anyone knowing he'd solicited the mention for good old quid pro quo. So, as always, Tull checked around with a few sources who knew Laddy and his father, Ransom Burford. He learned that Ransom was bragging around New York that his son was banging America's hottest young TV star and was on his way to "giving Trump a run for his money in the swordsman department."

Tull also heard that Ransom had congratulated his son on publicity-giving the old-line Burford's chain a young, sexy image. Tull shrewdly guessed that a pat on the head from that tough old bastard was worth just about anything to Laddy. It all added up to a sweet situation for Tull—and even sweeter when, suddenly, there was trouble in Laddy's love paradise.

It's usually one of the Seven Deadly Sins that sends a source rushing into a reporter's arms. Laddy's sin was white-hot jealousy. Shortly after he moved to Los Angeles to be near Charmain, she plunged head-first into her headline-making fling with wild child Connor O'Toole.

Laddy went nuts. He fed Tull a barrage of stories about their sex, drugs, and violence-drenched affair. Though he wasn't sharing Charmain's bed, he was still very much a part of her inner circle and tuned in to the gossip circulating along the Sunset Strip, from Sky Bar to Bar One, and on into the exclusive eateries and cigar bars of Beverly Hills. And even after Connor dumped Charmain, and Laddy had his bed privileges back, albeit on a strictly limited basis, he continued to feed Tull because…well, because it gave him a sense of power. He'd cruise by the newsstand on Beverly Drive on Thursday nights and grab the hot-off-the-presses edition of *The Revealer*, scrabble through the pages to Tull's column and run his eyes across its two pages—and BAM! He'd spot an item he'd planted and get a jolt, a real electric thrill. And curiously, his next thought would be of his domineering father, smiling at him. For the first time in his life, Laddy felt like he had secret influence behind the scenes.

Hell, he'd even thought about tipping Tull to his dad's visits to his West Coast whore, whoever she was. But he refrained, out of concern for his mother's feelings. Not that she'd have been surprised. Just embarrassed.

Tull looked up as Laddy finished his phone call. "I'm going to ask you a question, Laddy. I want a straight answer. If you lie to me, I'll unleash the hounds of hell all over you, your daddy, and your department stores. Sorry to get nasty, but this isn't business as usual for me or my paper. I'm talking about the death of Steve Bellini. You with me so far?"

"Yes, but what do I...?

"Here's the question, Laddy. I want it straight up. Where was Charmain when Bellini got it? Last Thursday, at about 10:45 a.m., just to refresh your memory."

"Wait a minute, you think Charmain...?"

"Answer the fucking question!"

"God, calm down…I know exactly where she was because I was with her. At her house. In fact, when I left her house…I don't know, right around noon, I heard about your colleague's death on my car radio."

"How do I check out what you're telling me, Laddy?"

"All of a sudden, you don't believe me?" he said, incredulous.

"Just because you're a source of fun-and-games gossip about Charmain doesn't mean I trust you for life, pal. I know you're in love with her and you'd ultimately protect her if you thought she had big trouble. Was anybody else there?"

"Yes, a crowd of us…Leda and Bonnie and…"

Laddy paused. "... And some others. You don't know them."

Tull noted the pause. "Come on, Laddy, who were they? TALK!"

A steely resolve suddenly stiffened Laddy. Tull was right, by God. He *was* in love with Charmain. And he would protect her. But there was no danger here. He'd been with Charmain that morning and the night before.

But some things were private. He would not surrender a word to Tull about The Ritual. But how to stop the angry beast's snapping jaws?

Why, throw him a bone, of course.

"Look here, Tull, I want this off the record. I think I deserve that after all I've done for you and..."

Tull whistled. "Whoa, listen to you. Who's been doing what for whom here? But okay, Laddy, you've got it. Off the record. Scout's honor, and all that."

"Okay...well, I was with Charmain all night. Along with Leda and Bonnie and these others, who are just beautiful people from out of town. We'd had a lovely evening that finally turned into a long night of...well, what you might call fun and games, you know...that lasted until the morning. Then we all went to the Beverly Hills Hotel pool for lunch. You can check that with Sven, the poolboy there."

"Yeah. I know Sven. All Hollywood knows Sven. The world's oldest poolboy. Been there since the 50s."

Tull looked at Laddy steadily. He sounded okay, but...Tull sensed the Burford lad was concealing a few details, and he didn't give a fuck about The Beautiful Kids and their sex orgies right now.

"Okay," he said. "So you go off to lunch with Charmain and these others. What then?"

Laddy, confused for a moment, said, "Oh, no. I didn't mean to imply Charmain left with us. She had to stay at the house for a business meeting. I guess it was with her manager. And that security fellow of hers. She was going to join us later..."

"Vidal Delaney?"

"Yes."

"And Mike Kelso was there also?"

"Right."

Bells were going off in Tull's head. So Vidal Delaney and Mike Kelso show up at Charmain's house...what?...just about an hour after Steve is killed. Coincidence? Yeah. Like a pregnancy right after the bishop visits the convent.

"You know what the meeting was about?"

Laddy shook his head. "No. But why would I?"

Tull thought for a minute.

"Did Charmain say anything about the meeting when she joined you later at the Beverly Hills Hotel?"

"Well, no," said Laddy. "Actually, she wasn't able to make it. Her assistant called over and said she had stuff to do and she'd see us later."

"And did you see her later?"

Laddy thought for a moment. "That day? No. But I saw her the next day...No, that's not right...It was the day after that, I think. Saturday. Yes, that's right. We went out for dinner at Crustacean in Beverly Hills, then over to Sky Bar."

"You have no idea where Charmain was from Thursday morning until Saturday night?"

"No. I called her at home on Saturday morning and talked to her. That's when we set up our date for that night."

"Laddy, I'm going to ask you this a different way. Do you have any knowledge that Charmain was involved in Steve Bellini's death?"

Laddy stood up. He was angry now. "Damnit, Tull, have you lost your mind? You think Charmain killed this man? It's preposterous! Why would she?"

"Maybe because Bellini published those photos of her beating a horse. That was bad publicity..."

"Oh, fucking hell, she gets bad publicity all the time. And if reporters got killed for publishing bad news, the streets of Hollywood would be littered with bodies. Please, Tull. This is ludicrous."

Tull shrugged. He'd gotten to know Laddy well over time. It took a lot to anger the kid, and the heat felt genuine. Tull was convinced he was telling the truth—as he knew it.

He rose. "Okay, Laddy. You're right, it's pretty thin. But I've got to check out every angle. Because we're getting nowhere on this and the heat's on full blast. If you hear anything, you'll let me know?"

"Of course. Look, I'm sorry your friend was killed. It's awful. But I think your paper is experiencing extreme paranoia."

"Yeah, you're probably right."

Laddy walked him into the garage. As Tull opened the door to his car, he paused. "Look, Laddy I don't want to get all heavy about it, but not a word to Charmain, okay? I don't want her thinking..."

"For God's sake, Tull, would you lighten up? I'm not going to tell her because there's no need to and it would just upset her. And as I told you, I'll swear on any Bibles you care to stack that I was with her every minute that day. She couldn't have killed this fellow."

Tull waved. "Yeah, you're right, pal. Thanks for clearing that up. And thanks for the great martini."

"My pleasure," said Laddy, hitting the garage door button and thinking, *God, I've got to call Charmain right away.*

He walked into the house, dialed her number…and then it hit him. Her first question would be, "Why are you even talking to Cameron Tull about me?" And then she'd figure it out. Just like Roseanne had discovered years ago that her then-fiancé Tom Arnold was secretly selling stories about her to the press. Roseanne had forgiven Tom, even married him. It wouldn't go like that with Charmain, Laddy knew.

All things considered, she'd probably kill him.

CHAPTER 45

1:30 P.M.
TULL'S OFFICE AT *THE REVEALER*
LOS ANGELES

FINALLY, a break.

After his talk with Laddy, Tull put word on the street that he'd pay large for Charmain items. Anything hot. Sex, drugs, fights. Or pistol-waving, his personal favorite. It just had to be new and exclusive.

In slipping the word out through his own sources and *Revealer* reporters, Tull took pains to avoid implying any connection between Charmain and the Bellini murder. That he kept to himself.

His ostensible reason for the sweep was a possible in-depth "Bad Girl" profile on the *BevHills High* star. It sounded weak, Tull knew. So he hinted that the true 411 was to dig up fresh dirt for the lawyers to throw around if Charmain sued over the horse-beating story.

A call came in. A guy claimed he'd seen Charmain nearly raped until a badass black guy busted it up.

"He sounded for real," said Eva, who'd taken the call and could usually sift out the crazies.

Tull met the caller in a sad little Irish bar over on Sweetzer. A creepy "Yo,yo,yo" white street punk in knit cap and baggies. Smelling like garbage put out a day late.

"Yo, I'll lay it down 'cause you behind some heavy bread. But see, I don't know nuthin', you know," he told Tull. "But dig, one night last week I'm comin' up this alley behind BuzzBuzz... You know BuzzBuzz, bro'?"

Tull backed off a foot as bad breath topped b.o.

"Yeah, I'm jiggy wi'd it," he said.

The punk gave him a "Whoa!" look. He shook his head, took a swallow of beer. Piggy eyes squinted, straining for memory through the perpetual mind fog of "crack" smoke.

"Uh...Okay, so dig! I'm watchin' this fine bitch come out the do' into the back alley. And then these bad mothahfuckahs start downin' the ho'! Layin' the dozens on her, man, talkin' 'bout her fine pussy, you dig? And then, these cats jump her ass, man. Yo, yo, yo, yo...they gon' get them some right NOW, you know? Fuckin' scary, man!"

"And you're just an innocent bystander to all this, right?" Tull said, not bothering to veil the sarcasm.

The punk threw him another "Whoa!" look. Like, yo, he was wounded.

"Now why you be playin' that, bro'? I was just standin' there, man. I was just walkin' in there to go to the club. Are you down wi'd dat?"

Yeah, like the BuzzBuzz bouncers would let Danny Dirtbag in the door.

Tull said, "I don't suppose you could I.D. these guys? You said there were three of them."

"No, man, it was too dark to do no eye-dee-in', no way."

"Okay," Tull sighed. "Now tell me about the black guy. You said he told you he was a pro boxer, actually gave you a name…?"

"Name be 'Buster' Brown, man," said the punk. "Mothahfuckah sho' could hit hard."

He rubbed his jaw.

Like it still hurt.

Jesus. Give this guy an Oscar, Tull thought. "How do you know he hit hard?"

The punk, suddenly conscious of his story-telling hand, jerked it down.

"Man, 'cause I saw him beat these guys' ass, you dig?"

"Yeah, I'm down wi'd it, my brother. Tell me more..."

It was a fascinating tale. Had the ring of truth all the way. Except for the punk's obvious lie that he wasn't involved. But that didn't matter; Tull now had the first solid link between Charmain and Buster Brown.

Buster. A pro boxer. A man who could hit hard. Maybe hard enough to pile-drive Steve Bellini backwards onto that wheeled cart. It could be that Buster hadn't planned to kill Steve, just bust him. And if that was so…

Goddamn! That could explain why Charmain had taunted Jessica on her answering machine. She hadn't known Steve was dead. Figured he was just nursing a sore jaw. No big deal. And no fun if you didn't share.

Jesus! Sounded right. But how to prove it, without that answering machine tape?

Find Buster. Fast.

Now that he had a name, it took Tull just fifteen minutes to get a rundown: Buster Brown, light heavyweight. Terrific punch. Glass jaw. So-so record. Coming up on his twenty-ninth birthday. In boxing years, damn near a geezer. Buster trained at "Big Blue" Gym, named after its original owner, some long-forgotten pug. An address on Olympic, just shy of downtown.

An hour later, Tull drove down an alley and pulled into a litter-strewn parking lot behind the gym. Only one other car there, next to a dumpster. Tull parked beside it, walked across the lot to a battered door with a sign that said "Enter Gym" in faded red paint. He entered.

The smell of sweat and liniment hit him first. He flashed on Tokyo: training sessions at the dojo. Urine stench jerked him back to L.A. He walked down a short hallway, walls lined with yellowing fight posters.

Past a door marked "Toilet" and a tiny, vacant office. Left turn, another door. Even before he opened it, he heard the grunts, sounds of leather slapping skin.

Tull stepped out onto the hardwood floor and stood facing two boxing rings, both in use. Ten feet to his left, a sharp-looking black kid in dreadlocks was working the speed bag so fast it strobed, looked like it was standing still. Tull watched a minute, spellbound.

"Help you?"

An old guy shuffled over, cigar clenched in his beat-up face. Tull fought a grin. Jesus, why does every white ex-pug look like Rocky Balboa's trainer?

"Yeah. Is Buster Brown around?"

The old guy looked at him through eyes squinted by scar tissue.

"You a cop?"

"No. I'm private. And that's how I'd like to keep it. Okay?"

Tull palmed a twenty, flashed it at him, then reached out to shake his hand.

"I'm Cameron Tull. Nice to meet you."

When he got his palm back, it was empty. The old guy gave him an evil grin.

"I can't tell you shit. I ain't no social secretary. Buster trains here, that's all. Sometimes you see him, sometimes you don't."

Tull stared at him, not moving.

The old guy shrugged, tilted his chin at the boxer in the nearest ring.

"He knows Buster. Should talk pretty good if you give him a taste. Hasn't had a fight in weeks." He raised his voice. "Hey, Calvin, take a breather! Someone I want you to meet."

A black man who looked forty, but was probably ten years younger, stopped shadow-boxing and climbed out of the ring. Two minutes later, he and Tull were standing in the parking lot. Calvin Turner was suspicious and close-mouthed until Tull showed him two crisp fifties. He took them, put them away carefully.

"No, man, I don't know where Buster lives," he said. "Somewhere down South Central, all's I know. Like I said, I saw him last week. Say, man, you got a cigarette?"

"No. I don't smoke. You telling me you do? A boxer?"

"Just every now and then," said Calvin Turner. "Wait a minute, okay?"

He went back inside, came out a minute later, smoking.

He grinned at Tull. "Jimmy—that's the old white guy—he keeps a pack in the bottom drawer of his desk. Thinks nobody knows."

Tull smiled, then said, "Think hard, Calvin. What day did you see Buster?"

"Oh, well now. Yeah, it might have been Thursday. Or maybe Friday. Had to be, 'cause I wasn't here Wednesday. Yeah. Thursday, for sure. All I remember is he was talkin' some jive about gettin' into the movies 'cause he did some big favor for a star."

"Buster say who the star was? A woman? Man? Movie star or TV star?"

Calvin shook his head.

"Did he say what the favor was?"

"Naw." A pause. "Well..."

"Yeah? You remember something?"

"Well, when he said he did this star a favor, he made a little punching move, y'know?"

"Like he was throwing a punch?"

"Yeah."

"What did you think that meant?"

"Shit, man, who knows?"

"Like, maybe the favor he did was to lean on somebody?"

"Who knows, man? Fighters are always throwin' punches around. Could just mean he made a big score, or he's feelin' good. Buster was real happy that day."

"Like he really believed something good had happened?"

"Oh, yeah. Buster's always braggin', but this was different. He really believed this bigshot star, whoever, was gonna help him. But who knows? He's always talkin' about bein' an actor and shit. I mean, Buster's cool. Just runs off at the mouth, that's all."

Calvin Turner ran out of words. Tull knew there was nothing else here. He shook hands with the tough-looking boxer, got in his car, and left. Calvin stood there, finishing the cigarette, looking up as a powerful-looking man stepped out from behind the dumpster and came striding across the lot.

Calvin dropped the butt, curled fingers up under his thumbs in a relaxed fist.

No question, this motherfucker was trouble.

"You a cop?" he said as the man approached.

Randak 2000 didn't answer. He stepped right into Calvin Turner's private space and smiled.

"Please listen carefully and understand. I have no time. Tell me everything you told that man. Tell me now. Quickly, please."

Calvin took a quick step back, dropped into a crouch. "Motherfucker, I ain't tellin' you shit, so—"

The first blow caught him on the side of the head, staggered him. Lights flashed across his brain. Shit! Didn't even see it.

WHAM!...WHAM!...BAM!

Fuckin' combination, man. Get your hands up, damnit, throw a punch...Do SOMETHIN'! Calvin's brain was working, talking to him, just like it did in the ring. He was a tough, experienced fighter, but this motherfucker was too fast...toyin' with him...cat on a mouse...

"Those punches hurt, boxer?" asked Randak 2000. "Tell me what I want to know, or this will get much worse very fast!"

Calvin made a bad mistake. He threw a punch.

Hell like he'd never known in a ring rained down in a shitstorm. Now the punches hurt. Bad. He went down. Out.

Randak 2000 picked the boxer up effortlessly, jogged over to the dumpster, and laid him down behind it. Time for a little privacy. He slapped Calvin Turner back to life.

"What?"

"You're still fine, my friend. No permanent damage. That's next. Now you hear me. Do you believe that I can hurt you at will? That you're way out of your class?"

Calvin nodded.

"Good. Now, I'm going to ask you again to tell me exactly what you told that man. Then I'm gone from your life. If you don't answer, I will start to inflict permanent damage. I will render you punch-drunk, to put it in boxing terms. You understand?"

Calvin's mouth moved. "Yes," he said faintly.

Then he told the white devil everything.

"Thank you," said Randak 2000. "I suggest you rest here for a few minutes before going back inside. Then I'd take the rest of the day off, if I were you."

He stepped out from behind the dumpster and walked quickly down the alley to where he'd parked. He was elated. He had it pieced together now. Buster had killed Bellini. And Charmain had ordered the execution. Why? Almost certainly because of her fury about that horse-beating story. Bellini's story.

Randak 2000 marveled again at Charmain's ruthlessness. Excitement coursed through him. She was the chosen one, the queen who would change the fate of an entire planet. He was increasingly sure of it. All was well. Except for the meddlesome Cameron Tull, who had established a link, however tenuous, between Buster and Charmain. But Charmain was in no imminent danger. The boxer could never connect her to Buster.

That's why Randak hadn't snapped his neck.

As for Tull...time would tell. Rupturing his brain stem might just be unavoidable. Randak 2000 sighed. He would truly miss reading Cameron Tull's column.

CHAPTER 46

3:51 P.M.
TULL'S OFFICE AT *THE REVEALER*
LOS ANGELES

NEXT move.

Okay, he had no next move. Tull was stymied. Instinct told him to start rattling cages. He phoned Vidal Delaney.

The conversation, brief as it was, infuriated the habitually ice-cool security guru. He was careful not to show it. When he placed the receiver back in its cradle, Vidal consciously resisted the urge to slam it down.

"Goddamnit!" he yelled at the soundproof office walls.

He took deep breaths, rose from his chair, poured a glass of Perrier. That sonofabitch Tull had shaken him up, no question. Vidal started to punch the intercom for Szabo, then paused. Calm down first, he told himself.

Jesus!

The call from the *Revealer* columnist had started off badly and gotten worse. Tull's opening statement was arrogant and patronizing. Designed to piss him off, Vidal knew.

"I think you could help us find the murderer, Vidal. You're a very resourceful man. And a smart one. *The Revealer* never forgets a favor. We'll remember who our friends are on this one."

Vidal's chuckle was genuine. "Friends? We've never pretended to be friends, Tull. People pay me to shield them from the likes of you."

"All well and good, Vidal. In ordinary times, this town is a game and we are players in it. But let's not pretend it's business as usual. This is murder."

"Tull, if there's a message here, I fail to understand it and..."

"Understand this, pal! The penalties for suppressing or destroying evidence in a capital crime are severe, as I'm sure you know."

Vidal kept his cool. "I don't know why you're telling me that."

Now Tull chuckled. "Yes, you do."

Vidal said nothing. A trickle of sweat formed at the nape of his neck.

"So," Tull said evenly, "you found Buster Brown yet?"

Panic rolled over him. Shit! How did he know about Buster? FUCK!

"Who?" he said.

"That shook your ass a little, didn't it, Vidal? You figured I didn't know about Buster. Charmain's hard-hitting pal? Look, you're a smart guy. Think about it. Protecting a client goes just so far. Then it's obstruction, maybe conspiracy. The way I see it, you're over the line already. Come on, man. Get on the right side of this thing. Get together with us; clean this mess up before it gets nasty. It's the right thing to do."

Vidal took a deep breath, managed a shaky laugh. "Tull, I don't know what you're babbling about. If you've got a story to tell, put it in your column."

"Oh, I will, Vidal. But before I do, just think over what I've said. Carefully. Then talk to your lawyer. Oh, and, uh…ask yourself who's better at finding people: your Keystone Cops, or a team of trained tabloid bloodhounds? My guess is that if we find Buster before you do, the only time you'll be seeing clients is on visiting days. Capisch?"

Vidal managed a patronizing chuckle.

"Goodbye, Tull. Please be a stranger."

Vidal took a swallow of Perrier. Goddamn. His head throbbed. He fumbled in his desk for some Aleve. How the FUCK did Cameron Tull know about Buster? This was bad. Bad!

He punched the intercom.

"Szabo! I need you right now!"

He paced a moment, then buzzed his assistant.

"Elaine, get me Mike Kelso and Charmain Burns for a conference call…No, wait. Get Kelso! Tell him it's urgent. I need to meet with him and Charmain ASAP. Urgent, got it? And tell him it's got to be here, in our offices, for security reasons."

Szabo walked in without knocking. "Vidal?"

He listened intently as his boss ran down the conversation with Tull, shaking his head just once at the revelation that Tull had somehow tied Buster to Charmain.

"Unless he was bluffing," Vidal offered.

Szabo shook his head. "He's not bluffing. Obviously, he knows. If he said the name, he knows. But he doesn't know enough. If he did, he'd be telling us what story he was going to write and be gloating about it."

Vidal nodded. "Yeah. He's on a fishing expedition. All we can count on is that he hasn't gone to the cops. He'd never tell them anything until he was ready to publish. Reporters never do."

Szabo nodded. "My guess is he hasn't told his paper anything, either, or we'd have *Revealer* reporters crawling through the AC ducts. No, Tull's trying to shake the tree. Make us sweat. It means he's at a dead-end."

"Yes, but for how long? What if he does find Buster first? Shit! How's that going, anyway? Do we have anything at all?"

Szabo shook his head. "Buster Brown has vanished off the face of the earth. We've been to his place. His stuff's there, he's not. He's got a couple of relatives, but they're not close. Say they don't see him much. He's got a few friends. We've talked to all of them. Last place he was seen was a pool hall downtown. One guy remembers he got a phone call, then said he could only play for a few minutes because someone was driving over to pick him up. He left half an hour later. Nobody saw who picked him up. Dead end."

Vidal's intercom buzzed. "Mr. Kelso on line two," said Elaine.

He snatched it up. "Mike, have you reached Charmain?...Listen, I don't give a shit if she's on the set. Have her fake a fainting spell, or whatever. Just get her here. Fast!"

An hour later, Kelso walked into Vidal's office, Charmain in tow. She was fuming.

"What's so goddamn important, Vidal, that I have to leave the set in the middle of...?"

He held up his hand abruptly, cutting her off. He nodded at Szabo, who threw the switch on a black box mounted high up on the wall behind his desk.

"Okay, we're secure," said Vidal.

"What's that?" Kelso asked.

"A white noise machine. We're soundproof in here and we sweep for bugs twice a day. But just in case, that machine would make any tape recording useless. Sounds like a shower running. So we can talk freely. Now, let me recount a very disturbing conversation I just had with Cameron Tull."

Vidal ran it down for them. Then Szabo repeated his report on the fruitless search for Buster Brown. When they'd finished, Vidal looked at Charmain and said, "This is serious. Tull has made a direct connection between you and Buster. Don't ask me how. It was bad enough that he heard your voice on that tape. Unfortunately, that's what pointed him at you in the first place. And if he had that tape, you'd be in worse trouble than you are right now. But he doesn't have it."

Kelso said, "You do?"

Vidal said, "I'm just telling you, he doesn't have it. That's all you need to know."

Szabo interjected quietly, "The question we have to deal with right now is, what if Tull and his crew find Buster before we do?"

Charmain, looking annoyed but not quite angry, rolled her eyes.

"If...if...fucking IF! If pigs could fly, bacon would be fifty bucks a pound, bubba! Tull doesn't have the tape. And he's not going to find Buster. Buster's in fucking Mexico, okay?"

It snapped Vidal's head back. "What?!"

"Mike drove him down to Mexico. I followed them in my car. Nobody recognized me. Then I talked to Buster. And everything's fine now."

Vidal looked like he'd taken a hard shot to the stomach and didn't want anyone to know it. He focused on an imaginary spot on the ceiling and said tightly, "Tell us why you think everything's fine now, Charmain?"

On a side table next to Charmain's chair was a thick copy of *Los Angeles* magazine. She threw it right at Vidal's head. Missed. Szabo quick-stepped in front of her, shielding his boss. Charmain screamed over his shoulder at Vidal:

"You look me in the eye when you talk to me, you sonofabitch! Don't you ever, EVER treat me like some little girl who's not there. You listening, boy?"

Kelso was on his feet, hovering around Charmain, trying to calm her. Vidal came out from behind the desk, making little placating gestures; cursing himself inwardly for making the one mistake he tried to avoid above all: losing his temper. In all his career, he'd never wanted to strangle anyone so badly as this hair-trigger bitch. But he'd have to kiss her ass instead. Financially, he could afford to lose Charmain Burns. After all, she was just one of many clients. But what he couldn't afford—ever!—was to have a major star walk out the door. Star clients were what lured other potential customers—the rich, but not necessarily famous.

Vidal took her hands. Smiled his best "surfer boy" smile.

"Charmain, I'm sorry, I meant no disrespect...I was just distracted, trying to focus. Please forgive me. Please."

She sat down again. Vidal pulled his chair up close, looked at her earnestly. "Look, we're all on edge. We're trying to help you. Just tell me about Buster. What happened when you saw him in Mexico?"

Vidal listened aghast as Charmain spun a tale of meeting Buster and giving him a collection of books and tapes on acting, making a deal that he'd stay in Mexico for six months and study—subsidized by ten thousand dollars in cash that she'd given him.

"I promised I'd coach him over the phone once or twice a month," she said. "When the six months are up, I'm going down there and run some scenes with him. If he's really worked hard, then I'll help him. That's the deal. I told him the next step would be to get some training in England. I'd help him with that, give him money and all, and then he'd be on his own."

Vidal looked Mike Kelso. "You knew about this?"

Kelso shrugged. "I think it's workable."

Vidal shook his head. "Well, I wish you had let me handle it. What's to stop Buster from surfacing with a blackmail demand?"

"I think he'd have done that by now," said Kelso. "I've met the guy and I think it's just like Charmain said—he wants to be an actor and he thinks she can help him. And remember, he doesn't know he accidentally killed Steve Bellini."

Charmain stood up, then walked toward the door. "Y'all can keep talking about this until you turn blue. What's done is done. Buster's having the time of his life messing with little señoritas in Mexico. And dreamin' about becoming an actor. He doesn't know anybody's dead. And he's sure not going to find out about it from Mexican newspapers, or TV, or radio. Everything is cool, Vidal. Way cool. Bye."

After the door closed behind her, Vidal thought about it for a moment. Then he said to Szabo, "You know what? She could be right. Everything might just be…real cool."

He looked at Kelso. "What's done is done. But don't leave me in the dark like that again."

"Okay," said Kelso. He paused. "Are we finished here?"

Vidal nodded. "Sure. See you soon, Mike."

Kelso bustled out after his client. Vidal looked over at Szabo, raised his eyebrows.

The ex-CIA operative shrugged.

"In the world I'm from," said Szabo, "someone would pay our liability in Mexico a visit. And reduce our risk to zero."

"The Cold War is over, Szabo. This is Hollywood, not East Berlin."

Szabo smiled thinly.

"At times, this gets almost as scary."

CHAPTER 47

8:23 P.M.
RANDAK 2000'S APARTMENT
LOS ANGELES

RANDAK 2000 clicked "Sign Off" and exited the Internet.

He'd been online with an Australian astronomer, a brilliant young renegade he'd known for years who'd been dismissed from a major university for supposedly "crackpot" ideas—one of which had been his assertion that the discovery of a new solar system was imminent. That, of course, had just come to pass in a blaze of worldwide headlines. Randak took it as another sign that the time for transference was nearing.

Now there were problems to be solved. Charmain had to be protected. Interrogating the boxer had revealed that Tull now knew of the connection between Charmain and Buster. Just a tenuous link, to be sure, but Randak knew it was enough to fire Tull's bloodhound instincts. The columnist had to be thrown off Charmain's track. Her paramount destiny was crucial to the survival of millions. Finding The Queen was his mission. If Charmain was indeed the chosen one, he had to protect her. He must not fail The Guides!

After considering options, Randak 2000 formulated a strategy: trade Buster for Charmain. Throw his lifeless body to the wolves. Even in death, Buster would come to Charmain's rescue yet again.

Randak dialed Tull's private line, a number known to few.

"Yes?"

"Mr. Tull, allow me not to introduce myself. I'll have to stay anonymous for the moment, I'm afraid. I have a proposition for you."

"How did you get this number?"

"Mr. Tull, you are a busy man and we're wasting time. Now…you and I both know—or, rather, you suspect and I know—that the boxer known as Buster Brown killed Steve Bellini."

"You seem very sure of that, pal. Look, I'd like to know who I'm talking to. How do I know you're not some hoaxer?"

"A casual hoaxer wouldn't know how to get your private number. Again, we're wasting time. Let's talk business."

"Okay. If you have information about this case, my paper is prepared to pay handsomely. What do you know?"

"I know where to find Buster Brown."

Tull tensed up. Easy does it. Don't let this guy get off the line. "Are you going to tell me right now? I mean, I want you to identify yourself so that you'll be able to collect the reward money. Or, we can meet..."

Randak 2000 cut him off. "I don't want the reward money, Mr. Tull. Let's just say that I'm a big fan of yours, and I want to help you solve this case. It will be a scoop for you. You'll hit the front pages with this story."

Tull's antennae, honed by years of experience, went up. A source who claimed not to be motivated by greed always made him nervous. Time to worry about that later. Get the info now.

"Well, sir, I really appreciate your help on this. Where is Buster Brown?"

"He's lying at the bottom of a cliff in Baja, Mexico."

"He's dead?"

"That's right, Mr. Tull."

"Was he...killed? Or..."

"I believe he slipped, but what difference does it make? Buster Brown killed Steve Bellini. Now Buster is dead. End of story."

"You seem so sure that Buster is the killer. How do you...how can we prove that?"

Randak 2000 chuckled. "There will be many ways to prove it, Mr. Tull. Once you tell the police that Buster Brown is the suspect, for instance, they'll be able to show his picture to florists and find out where he bought those unique Sonia roses."

Tull was stunned. "How the hell do you know about those roses? The cops haven't put out that information."

"I have ways of knowing things, Mr. Tull. Let's see...I also know the police scraped Bellini's chin to pick up skin samples of the assailant for DNA testing. To match against possible suspects."

"Who the hell are you?"

"I'm a warrior, Mr. Tull. Right now, I'm on a reconnaissance mission."

Tull took a shot in the dark. "Answer me this: what was Buster's motive for killing Bellini?"

Randak 2000 paused, then said evenly, "I'm not sure. Tabloid editors like Bellini have enemies. Perhaps he wrote something Buster didn't like about one of his favorite stars..."

"Like Charmain Burns?" snapped Tull.

"Yes," said Randak cooly. "Or like Madonna, Streisand, George Clooney, Alec Baldwin—any of the whiners who complain that they're maligned by the press."

"Yeah," said Tull drily. "Let's call them all in for questioning. Look, how do I know you're not some crackpot yanking my chain?"

"Here's proof that I'm not."

And Randak 2000 gave Tull the exact location of Buster's body.

"Check it out, Mr. Tull."

Tull hung up, then called the Mexican national police, the Federales. They referred him to the local cops in Baja, who sounded supremely indifferent. They'd…get back to him.

Tull grimaced. Just like L.A. Don't call us, we'll call you.

CHAPTER 48

CHARMAIN'S MANSION
BEVERLY HILLS

CHARMAIN'S obsession with *Medusa* intensified. It consumed her waking moments, invaded her deepest sleep.

She wasn't alone. Bitch heat was raging. From London to New York to Hollywood, star actresses were plotting, conniving, threatening to fire agents and managers as they maneuvered to snare the lead in Clive Tinsdale's film about an actress who'd kill for the perfect part. *The Hollywood Reporter* headlined their front-page story about the cutthroat competition:

"Diva Wars: A Role To Die For!"

One female superstar, a two-time Oscar nominee, dramatically informed her agent, a wizened old William Morris cobra:

"I'll fuck anyone I have to for this part…anyone."

She paused; added with a shiver, "Even you!"

Charmain knew it was time to rev up or shut up. Slam into high gear. Right now, she was at the back of the pack. A long shot. Mike Kelso was right. She needed buzz, high-profile headlines that screamed "Charmain Burns!!!" Yeah. Name recognition. It's what puts asses in seats. And makes studios happy.

One other problem: she had to soothe the horse-loving Tinsdale. Erase the negative image of those awful horse-whipping photos. But how?

Sweet, sweet Laddy made her realize she already had the answer.

"Give the public something new to think about," he told her. "Shock 'em out of their socks. Feed the media a story outrageous enough to make world headlines. Make them forget the horse story by feeding them a bigger story. It's all upside, babe. You'll become a household name. And a bankable one."

Charmain, reclining on her living room sofa, rolled her eyes.

"An outrageous story? Like, what? Blow a gorilla at high noon on Sunset?"

Laddy chuckled. "That wouldn't surprise anyone."

She threw a pillow at him. Laddy caught it and said, "Seriously, it has to be something that doesn't look like an obvious publicity stunt. Sex is good. It always sells. But you've got to come up with something that will put you in a sympathetic light. Look at Monica Lewinsky. Now there's a girl who really did blow a gorilla at high noon, metaphorically speaking.

But somehow she ended up a sympathetic figure. Why? Because people believed she was the victim of an older man who'd exploited her."

Bonnie Farr, sprawled in a recliner with Leda Francis on her lap, snorted.

"Exploited, my ass. That fat slut begged to get her tonsils showered with Prezzie sperm the day she flashed her thong."

Leda squirmed on Bonnie's lap. "Come on, luv, don't go all naïve on us. The Big Creep was already flirting with Monica. Seducing her with those power eyes. Probably gave her a few pats on the bum. That'll make a young girl go all wobbly, you know."

"Re-eally?" said Bonnie. She flipped Leda over, patted her pert behind.

"Gettin' all wobbly yet, duchess?"

Charmain ignored their byplay, watching Laddy intently as he ticked it off for her, like he was making points in a boardroom.

"The three key elements are: Outrageous…Sexy…Sympathetic."

Charmain swung her legs off the couch and walked over to the bar.

"Anybody need a refill?"

Getting no takers, she poured herself a glass of chilled Richemont. Leda started to sing-song as Bonnie rhythmically slapped her ass…

"Out-RAGE-ous, SEX-y, sym-pa-THETIC…out-RAGE-ous…SEX-y…"

"Ohmigod," Charmain said suddenly. They all looked up.

"I've GOT it. I've fucking got it, y'all!"

Laddy finally asked, "Got what, Charmain?"

She winked at him. "The Ritual. If that's not a shocker, what is? Maybe it's time to rattle their cages out there in TV Land."

Bonnie Farr said, "I don't get it. What…?"

Laddy got it. Almost.

"Okay," he said. "It's outrageous and it's sexy. But how do you figure it's sympathetic?"

Charmain grinned lazily and polished off her wine. "This is the 90s, babe. No one's responsible for their own actions, right? It's always someone else's fault. Or you blame it on your damn childhood. So that's how I'm gonna play it, Laddy. It'll be fucking perfect. You think I don't know how to get folks weepin' for poor little Charmain Burns? Hell, bubba…I'll have the whole damn world in tears."

Two days later, Charmain flew to New York with Leda and Mike Kelso. The girls spent an intense afternoon shopping. That night, in a penthouse suite at the Rihga Royal Hotel, Charmain and Leda dined on a sumptuous room service meal, tore through the pile of bags and boxes from designer salons, then went to bed early.

Next morning, Charmain strode into the UBS-TV network building with Leda and Mike Kelso in tow, wearing Gucci sunglasses, a long black linen duster, and thong flats.

Kowtowing production assistants met her just inside the towering brass doors and ushered her into a VIP Green Room to await her appearance on "Aspect!"—a live morning talk show that had been trying to book her for weeks. The PA's bowed and scraped, waving at a table set with gourmet delicacies and drinks, trying to usher Charmain to a leather sofa.

"I'll stand," she said.

"Great, Miss Burns, great," said one. "Uh...it will only be about ten minutes. Ha, ha...you shaved it pretty close. If there's anything you need...?"

Charmain stared past him. Kelso waved them off. "We'd like to be alone now."

The PA's bustled out, clipboards clutched to chests. Leda opened a bottle of mineral water, found a straw, and handed it to Charmain. "Don't fuck up that luscious lipstick."

"Aspect!" was a new morning show, halfway through its first season and struggling for ratings. Industry buzz had written it off as doomed. The network, refusing to acknowledge the foolish expenditure of millions on a bad idea poorly executed, fired the producer and brought in Frankie Cardiff, an ex-MTV wunderkind who was brilliant, but a wild man.

Frankie had his work cut out for him. The hosts were two forty-ish yentas remarkable for their empty, relentless smiles: Sarah Ballard and Cindy Frye. Sarah had made her name writing cookbooks and dispensing homemaking tips on a moderately successful cable TV show. Her former TV producer called her "a raving sociopath—think Sue-Anne on 'The Mary Tyler Moore Show.'" He loved telling insiders about the time her cable channel had undergone major reconstruction, and Sarah—after driving into the freshly asphalt-ed parking lot one morning to discover she'd been reassigned to a parking space fifty feet from the building—had remarked to the company chairman:

"I think parking spaces for the handicapped is a wonderful idea, but do they have to be right next to the entrance, for heaven's sake?"

Cindy Frye, an attractive but mediocre singer, had briefly blipped the charts with two minor hit records in the 80s, then steadfastly refused to slide back into the oblivion she so richly deserved. Blind to her shallow talent, driven by an obsessive need to preach holier-than-thou babble to a world she considered morally bankrupt, Cindy survived some lean years by hosting low-rent TV specials and infomercials, then wrote a self-help book called, *Start Loving Yourself!* The vaguely salacious title inspired masturbation jokes from Stern, Leno, and Letterman, which helped make it a bestseller. The book was inspired by what Cindy piously called "a life of pain that made me gain"—including a bizarre marriage to a televangelist who'd turned out to be gay. Howard Stern's oft-repeated crack was that after the preacher's honeymoon night with Cindy, he'd begged God to turn him homo.

Cindy's next marriage, to a handsome British actor alleged to have a bigger schlong than Tommy Lee's, was another disaster. He dumped her for a young sexpot—then dumped on her in a *Vanity Fair* interview with the exquisite viciousness that comes so naturally to the English, citing peeves that included "bad breath, old boy, and a bikini line heading south faster than her tits."

Cindy's fury at these setbacks fueled a burning drive to achieve stardom and wreak revenge on all who'd ever shit on her. "Aspect!" was her big chance.

The show had been dreamed up by a thirty-four-year-old network "suit" who'd hoped to mimic the success of "The View," ABC's star vehicle for Barbara Walters and her all-girl posse. He'd sold "Aspect!" to his bosses with this irresistible pitch:

"Gentlemen, think 'The View'—as hosted by the kid sisters of Kathie Lee Gifford and Martha Stewart."

The show was an instant nightmare. Lacerated by critics, derided by feminists, and totally ignored by men, "Aspect!" limped toward early death. Sarah and Cindy, propping each other up with cheery desperation, killed two hours of live TV with predictable chick-chatter and ass-kissing celebrity interviews.

Then Frankie Cardiff came on board, spitting fire. His first move was to insist on guests with an edge: controversial types like Roseanne, Jerry Springer, Joan Rivers, Bill Maher, Dennis Rodman, Charmain Burns. And he ordered Sarah and Cindy to start dishing "dirty" sex.

"I'm not talking *Cosmo* ca-ca like 'Redecorate Your Vaginal Walls,'" he'd screamed at their first meeting. "None of this 'buy a sexy negligee and light candles' shit! I'm talking cutting-edge erotica. I wanna get those ladies out there wet! I mean, look at 'The View.' Meredith Viera tries on a bustier and her tit falls out, for godsake! Maybe it was an accident, but it was GREAT television. Sex sells, girlfriends!"

In Frankie Cardiff's first week as producer, the show's log lines included:

"Get Sex Down Cold—With Ice Cubes."

"Buy a French Maid's Outfit—Then Whip Him 'Til He Wears It."

But the segment that became TV legend was:

"WOW!! He Finally Found my G-Spot!"

Amazingly, Sarah Ballard took the sex stuff in stride. She smilingly served up "Love Play with Veggies" as if it was just another household hint. Cindy Frye hated the new direction, even threatened to quit, although she calmed down fast when the Senior VP of programming pointed out that if the show tanked, she'd be labeled a loser who'd blown her shot at the bigtime. On the show the very next day, Cindy clicked two ice cubes in one hand like Captain Queeg in *Caine Mutiny* and leered to the audience:

"Gals, if you want hot sex, start your stud off COLD!"

Ladies tittered. Men winced. Ratings, like a gently tickled dick, stirred slightly.

Frankie Cardiff pushed hard. He'd forged solid relationships with many stars during his MTV days and he phoned them all, begging them to appear on "Aspect!" He'd called Charmain's PR people, but was told, "Charmain hates Cindy. Thinks she's a supercilious bitch." Phone calls to Mike Kelso went unanswered.

Then, just two days ago, he'd gotten a call from Bonnie Farr, an old pal from MTV days. Bonnie had opened the conversation by saying, "You and I never had this phone call, Frankie. Okay?"

"Okay," Frankie agreed. He listened intently. And loved what he heard...

CHAPTER 49

10:00 A.M.
"ASPECT!"
LOS ANGELES

As Charmain waited in the Green Room, the big-screen monitor suddenly came to life with a blast of music and the show's opening titles. "Aspect!" was on the air—live.

"I hate that goody-two-shoes bitch," she snapped when the camera close-upped on Cindy Frye.

Under ordinary circumstances, Charmain would never even consider an appearance on "Aspect!". She'd heard Cindy rant and rage more than once about "sexpot starlets"—after her Brit toyboy dumped her. But "Aspect!" was absolutely perfect for today's...agenda. Late morning, the kiddies in school, bored housewives still dozy after rising at dawn...

Charmain chuckled. She'd wake their asses up.

She watched Cindy tell the audience, "...and guess who's joining us in just a few minutes? Charmain Burns!"

Charmain noted that Cindy didn't crack a smile when the audience applauded. Bitch! Those old, cold eyes. Charmain flashed back to a quote from Cindy's ex-hubby in that nasty, hilarious *Vanity Fair* piece.

"Mate," he'd told the interviewer, "there isn't enough heat in Cindy's panties to warm toast."

God, he had that right! Didn't the audience see the meanness behind that sugary smile? They must, Charmain's instincts told her. Which had to mean that they tune in because the bitch makes something resonate in their souls. Something wicked.

"Charmain! This is the thrill of a lifetime for me!"

Frankie Cardiff burst into the Green Room, radiating energy, eyes darting everywhere, waving at Kelso but ignoring him; taking in her Gucci shades, the long coat, the flats.

"I just wanted to say 'Hi!' before you go on. Which is in about seven minutes. Charmain, you look breathtaking! And I'm dying to see what you're wearing underneath that duster."

They looked each other over, paused. She said, deadpan, "Yeah, I'll bet you are."

They burst out laughing. Kelso looked mystified. What was funny?

"Leda, give me the shoes, honey."

Charmain took off her dark glasses as Leda rummaged in a small leather duffel bag, knelt before her and slipped a pair of high heels on her feet. Charmain stepped back, looked at Frankie Cardiff and shrugged out of the duster. It fell to her feet, framing her truly sensational shoes. Fairytale shoes, thought Frankie. His eyes roved up Charmain's bare legs to her delicious designer dress. His imagination raced suddenly out of control.

"You're fucking magic," he said. "I'm off for the control room. Break a leg."

Moments later, in Los Angeles, Laddy Burford phoned Bonnie Farr.

"Are you watching?"

"Are you kidding?"

In a dingier part of L.A., Randak 2000 tweaked the TV volume and clicked "Record" on a VCR as Cindy launched into Charmain's intro...

"...She's gorgeous, she's controversial, she's a major TV star at age twenty-two who's suddenly dreaming of a bigger screen career...and she'll join us right after these words."

"Aspect!" went into a commercial break. High above the set, Frankie Cardiff trotted into the control room, pointed at the director facing a bank of TV monitors, and said, "Move! I'm taking over."

The guy started to protest, but Frankie cut him off. "I said, MOVE...or find yourself another gig!"

The director tossed down his headset, got up out of his chair. Frankie sat down, put on the headset.

"Okay, people, listen sharp to Frankie. We're making TV history here today—just like every other day. Let's move Sarah and Cindy over to the interview set."

He watched the bank of monitors, saw the hosts move from the desk they shared during most of the show to the interview area, where three high director stools were set up in front of a phony window that looked out on a make-believe Manhattan.

Frankie's eyes went to the monitor that showed him what Camera 3 was seeing.

"Okay, 3, listen up. You'll stay more or less where you are, giving us the audience point of view. But I'll need you for tight shots on these sensational shoes of Charmain's. Let me see a low angle, medium tight, on her stool. Yeah...a little lower. That's about it."

On the wall of monitors, Camera 3's picture waggled up and down. Everybody chuckled. Camera 3 was nodding "Yes."

"Okay, people," said Frankie. "Coming back from commercial in 5-4- 3-2...Okay...hold it there, Camera 1...stand by, 2, for the crowd shot...NOW...Camera 4, we're going on a medium two-shot of our lovely hosts...stand by for music cue...and...NOW!..."

The "Applause" sign went on. The audience clapped furiously, urged on by the stage manager.

"Hi, there, we're back," said Sarah.

"Oh, like we weren't going to come back?" quipped Cindy. "Although in TV, who knows?"

"Good heavens, such a skeptic," said Sarah with a winsome smile. "Well now, we've got a real treat for our viewers today. A gorgeous young creature who's had more honors…"

Cindy broke in. "And more tabloid headlines…"

"Now, Cindy, you stop that. Our guest is a sensational lady, in more ways than one…"

Cindy winked at the audience. "I'll say…!"

Frankie chattered intensely into the ears of his technical crew;.

"Listen close, people. When Charmain hits the stage, she'll bounce around and show off the hot dress and killer shoes she's wearing. Camera 3, track those shoes. Don't lose 'em. Music, I want it loud and sexy…Lights, I need a kaleidoscopope of color…I want excitement, goddamnit…like Rip Taylor flinging confetti…like fucking carnival time…okay, cameras, listen hard for my cues…here we go…"

Cindy was winding up the intro. "…so…let's all give a big 'Aspect!' welcome to…Charmain BURNS!!"

Music blasted and the crowd went wild. Colored spotlights caught Charmain as she emerged from the wings and crossed the stage with her best beauty queen strut. A male voice bellowed, "Charmain!"

She was a bare-legged sensation in an ultra-short white satin minidress cut square across the breasts and supported by two spaghetti-thin diamante straps. Her shoes, twinkling under the bright lights, caught every woman's eye.

"Jesus!" breathed a female producer up in control. "Bitch is wearing Cinderella's glass slippers."

"Don't you LOVE it?" screamed Frankie. "Camera 4 and 2, roll across that crowd…4, go for guy reaction…2, find me a horrified old biddy…3, you stay tight on those shoes until I need you…"

The cameras panned the crowd. Men were whooping and whistling. Women had that annoyed grin that appears when another female's kicking ass and looking hot. Camera 1 caught Cindy rolling her eyes and looking from Charmain back to the audience, as if to say, "Can you believe this outfit?"

Charmain, flashing a mischievous smile, suddenly stopped in front of the hosts, and twirled in a defiant little pirouette. The men groaned in collective sexual heat as the mini-dress, which hung straight from her hips and wasn't overly tight, flared and almost showed them heaven.

Charmain grinned coquettishly, made a mock curtsey, then hopped up onto her high stool, knees primly together, breasts angled in three-quarter profile to Camera 1.

Cindy and Sarah sat and smiled. As the audience finished applauding, Cindy said:

"Well…"

"I think you mean 'Wow!'" Sarah quipped.

"Thanks for coming, Charmain," said Cindy, trying hard to look friendly, and failing. "And thanks for giving our little morning show a big shot of glamor by dressing up. We're just not used to it."

"You think it's too much for this early in the day?" Charmain asked sweetly. "Y'all think I'm overdressed?"

Cindy couldn't resist. "'Underdressed' is the word I was thinking of, actually."

Charmain smiled. Her drawl deepened. "Well, now, that's the girl in you talkin'. Women are always so critical of how other women dress. I don't hear those boys out there complainin', though."

A big cheer from the men. Even some women applauded. A more attuned performer would have realized her bitchiness was dividing the audience, giving Charmain control. But not Cindy.

"What the fuck is that stupid sow doing?" Frankie Cardiff snarled to the control room. There was a murmur of assent. What the fuck, indeed?

Sarah's "let's have fun" smile switched to high beams. Time to change the subject. She said brightly:

"Let's take a really close look at those magnificent shoes. I love them! Can we get a closeup…?"

"Camera 3…GO!" whispered Frankie.

TV screens across America filled with the image of Charmain's slender ankles flowing into transparent glass slippers topped with tiny diamond-encrusted buckles.

"Oh, they are so, so beautiful," gushed Sarah. "Like Cinderella's slippers. But they're not glass, of course. Isn't that transparent material called 'Perspex'?"

Charmain shrugged. "I don't know. I just liked 'em. They're different."

"Cinderella slippers seem out of character for you," purred Cindy. "Getting home before midnight isn't really your thing, is it?"

Charmain gave her a devastating grin. "Oh, I don't care if my limo turns into a pumpkin. My only worry is a wicked old witch who keeps tryin' to scare me!"

The audience roared as the barb hit home. Cindy's relentless smile wavered visibly. Sarah stepped in again, determined to salvage it all.

"Now, seriously, do you think we might see a fashion trend toward see-through shoes, Charmain?"

"Maybe, Sarah. Better not have ugly toes, though."

There was a low "wwoooo-o-o" from the audience. People still remembered Cindy's ex-husband telling an interviewer she had "long, ugly toes—and corns."

Sarah, sailing on as Cindy's TV smile faded and died, said, "What's truly impressive, Charmain, is that you're so coordinated with those diamante straps on your dress and the matching diamante buckles..."

Charmain shifted in her seat and faced the audience squarely. She lifted her head and paused dramatically. The audience hushed.

In Los Angeles, Bonnie Farr—still on the phone with Laddy—said, "Oh, shit, this is it, man. She's gonna do it...!"

...Randak 2000 leaned forward. Was Charmain's legendary temper about to erupt...?

...out in Malibu, Cameron Tull, who'd tuned in late, watched impassively, wondering for the thousandth time how Cindy had survived on TV this long...

Up in control, Frankie Cardiff knew that the moment for great daring had arrived. What's the worst that could happen? Nobody fires a producer with hot numbers. So party on, Frankie Boy, he told himself. Faint heart ne'er won fat ratings. Here we go...

"Camera 4, keep the three-shot...3, let me see what a lower angle on Charmain looks like..."

He glanced at Camera 3's off-air monitor. Charmain's image was full-length on the high stool at almost a dead-on angle.

Frankie whispered into his mouthpiece. "Camera 3, go just a tad lower...that's it...and stay with those shoes. Watch for any action with the shoes, okay?...we're going to you...NOW!"

Charmain spoke. "Well, thank you, Sarah, I'm glad you noticed that my outfit is coordinated. But the straps on my dress and the buckles on my shoes are not diamante. They're genuine diamonds."

She leaned back in the high chair, lazily lifted her right leg—and cocked an ankle over her left knee. The dress slid back along her parted thighs into her lap.

Suddenly, Camera 3 was looking between her legs. And she wasn't wearing panties.

The image was vivid, detailed. The white dress reflected ambient light, just as she'd figured it would, giving her womanhood perfect exposure and revealing—on national television—the secret of The Ritual:

Charmain's clitoris was pierced.

A gold ring glinted at the apex of her sex. Dangling from it, on a tiny chain, was a glittering four-carat diamond.

In the studio, and across America, millions gasped. Charmain, smiling sweetly at Sarah and Cindy, drawled:

"Matching accessories are so important, don't you think...?"

Cindy Frye, her eyes flicking to the onstage monitor and finally seeing the image being transmitted to all her fans, lost it totally and began shrieking:

"Security...SECURITY!...Get her OUT of here! GET HER OUT!"

In the control room, Frankie Cardiff muttered happily: "Sharon Stone—eat your heart out."

Pandemonium exploded around him. Voices yelling...

"Jesus...we're live..."

"Oh, fuck, the FCC will have our balls..."

Urgent screams of, "Frankie...kill the shot...go to commercial...Frankie, switch cameras...FRANKIE...!...FRANKIE..."

He pretended confusion, paralysis, as the internal clock all good broadcasters have in their heads precisely ticked off the seconds.

...one second...two seconds...three seconds...any more and he'd be accused of deliberately holding the shot...

At precisely 3.4 seconds he yelled, "GO TO COMMERCIAL, GODAMNIT! NOW!"

The image of Charmain's decorated sex vanished.

Fabulous, Frankie exulted silently. The ratings would fucking explode after this little drama. But right now, it was time for some play-acting.

He jumped up, ripped off his headset, and said, "Ohmigod, I just froze! I just lost it. God! How long was it on?"

"Only a couple of seconds," said the director he'd displaced. "But we'll still catch hell from the brass. Thank God you were in the chair and not me, Frankie."

"Yeah, shit. Can you believe my bad luck?"

In Los Angeles, Laddy said to Bonnie Farr, "Your boy Freddie really came through for us."

"Why not?" she chortled. "Everybody in America will be watching that damn show tomorrow just to hear Miss Goody-Two-Shoes piss and moan about how she was betrayed again by a 'sexpot.' Ha! The tabloids will be calling her show 'Ass-pect!'"

Laddy laughed and hung up. Jesus! Charmain had done it. Amazing. He'd always admired her balls. But never more than now.

He remembered how she'd insisted on getting her piercing just right. She'd joked that she might just be the first star ever to reveal that she had one.

"Wouldn't it make a great *BevHills High* episode, Laddy? Ratings would go nuts."

Before undergoing "The Ritual," Charmain had persuaded Laddy to take test shots in her bedroom with a professional video setup she'd rented. Laddy had jokingly dubbed the session, "The Pudenda Chronicles." Charmain had experimented endlessly with various placements, using a clip-on gold earring.

"You're such a perfectionist," Laddy had marveled.

Her conclusion: clitoral hood piercing tested best on video.

"It's no good getting my labia pierced," Charmain says, "because if I don't move the right way when I cross my legs, the ring might get covered up by my thigh, right?"

Laddy chuckled at the memory. That's what it takes to make a star, he mused, the incessant drive to get it just right. He punched his intercom: "Get me Charmain Burns. Try her cell phone or the Rihga Royal Hotel in New York. If she doesn't answer, leave messages to call me."

Across town, Randak 2000 replayed the astounding moment of Charmain's revelation on his VCR. Now there was no doubt. The courage, the command, the ruthless scarification of her flesh...She was their queen. The time to move was at hand.

In Malibu, Cameron Tull's phones rang off the hook. Eva called on the private line. "Every TV and radio show in America has either called or is waiting on the line to ask you to explain why Charmain did it," she said. "And I'm only exaggerating a little bit."

"How the hell do I know why she did it?"

Eva chuckled. "Sorry, but you're the man who knows everything. The rest of us can plead ignorance, but you? Never. What do I tell these people?"

"I'll get back to them. Leave me alone for an hour."

"One hour. Bye."

CHAPTER 50

FROM LOS ANGELES TO NEW YORK...

THE press went mad.

Headlines screamed across America and around the world.

"Charmain Flashes 24-Karat Surprise!" howled the *New York Post.*

The spin machine whirred into high gear. Charmain's PR people protested that the exposure had been accidental, unintended.

"Charmain hopes people will understand that she didn't mean to offend," they said with straight faces.

Playboy offered Charmain $2 million for a nude spread.

Larry Flynt immediately derided the idea, saying, "What's left to show?" But he announced he'd pay $5 million if Charmain would allow *Hustler* to photograph her having a second piercing "in the general vicinity of the first one."

Jerry Falwell made dark reference to "the whore of Babylon."

Camillie Paglia and Erica Jong leaped to Charmain's defense, saying she was "a bold feminist" and "had made a striking statement about female power."

Sharon Stone was so pissed off she refused to comment and left the country for "a short vacation."

Neilsen ratings for "Aspect!" went through the roof over the next few days as folks tuned in to watch Cindy Frye nearly self-destruct in sputtering rage at "that...that...disgusting...well, I'll call her sexpot, but I'm thinking of another word that begins with 's.'"

The network got a stiff letter from the FCC. There'd be a fine, but big fucking deal. The bosses slipped Frankie Cardiff a fat bonus, told him to keep quiet about it.

Charmain fielded a ton of interview requests and finally faced the nation on Larry King's TV show. After the booking was announced, Howard Stern commented, "Larry's first question has to be, 'Are you wearing panties?'"

On the show, Charmain demurely told Larry and his worldwide audience—which had quadrupled for her interview—that she was sorry she'd shocked everybody. She broke down in tears when Larry gently brought up her wild escapades on the Hollywood night scene and suddenly blurted out:

"I was sexually abused as a child, Larry."

Once again, a mesmerized nation gasped. Charmain refused to say much more, nor would she tell Larry which parent had been guilty. People assumed she was accusing her father. Her mother, after all, was dead.

Charmain's newest sensational revelation made even bigger headlines. Now the story had "legs." And two days later it burgeoned into a full-fledged feeding frenzy for the media when Florida police reported that Charmain's father, Lawton Burns, had committed suicide by shotgun.

Stories datelined "Citrus Corners" reported that after the Larry King show, townsfolk had hissed Burns on the street, calling him "baby raper" and "filthy child molester." Rowdies in pick-up trucks had thrown bags of excrement, dead animals, and even firebombs at his house...and painted the word "PERVERT" on his car when he drove into town.

Lawton Burns left no note, so his suicide was considered de facto proof that he had, indeed, abused Charmain. Her spin doctors began to use that feel-good 90s buzzword—"closure."

When Charmain announced she would be attending her father's funeral—that no matter what, he was her father—her public approval rating shot up dramatically. There were news shots of her arriving in Citrus Corners dressed in black, but no photos of the funeral. The press and the public were barred.

Enter the Great Healer, Barbara Walters. She outmaneuvered rival grief-monger Oprah Winfrey and nailed down an "in-depth" TV interview with Charmain. It ranked as the most-viewed show of the year. Barbara failed to persuade Charmain to surrender any details of her "agonizing ordeal of sexual abuse at the hands of her father." But despite the lack of gory detail, the show was a blubbery tear-jerker that had women—even men—weeping for Charmain. Especially when Barbara showed what the world press had been denied—exclusive video of Charmain weeping at the funeral.

Charmain professed great grief over her father's suicide, and didn't challenge Barbara's statement that "perhaps it was better this way."

A subplot nobody picked up on was *BevHills High* producer Larry Buckley's attempt to exploit the situation and wreak revenge on Charmain for seducing his daughter. Invoking the morals clause in his star's contract, Larry informed the network that he wanted to fire her. The president of the network called personally to tell him, "Larry, have you been working too hard, or what? We can't fire Charmain. Why would we? Right now, she's the hottest name in the business."

When you're hot, you're hot. As proof that her star was on fire, Charmain finally got the call every actress in town was praying for—a summons by director Clive Tinsdale to audition for *Medusa.*

Charmain phoned Laddy immediately. "It worked, Laddy, it worked. Tinsdale never even mentioned the horse thing."

"I guess my old man did teach me a thing or two," he said. "The old bastard says you can always get the media to help you mold public opinion. Just give them a story that'll sell papers and jack up ratings. Outrageous, sexy, sympathetic...works every time, babe."

CHAPTER 51

CONFIDENTIAL FILE MEMO #3321B
STORY FILE #98563102
SUBJECT: POSSIBLE PAGE ONE
STORY FOR CURRENT ISSUE
REPORTER: LULU B.
EDITOR: CAMERON TULL

CAMERON:

Have taped interview with a woman named Millie Johnson, one of Charmain's girlhood cronies in Citrus Corners. Apparently her best friend. Maybe her only friend.

Background: Millie is a hot-looking country number. Only twenty-three, but starting to get that used-hard look. Makes a sporadic living as an exotic dancer. Occasionally pimped out by her biker boyfriend when the rent on the trailer comes due and he has no drug money, or his Harley's broke.

Millie's furious over what she calls Charmain's "nasty lie" about her dad. He never abused her, says Millie, who's older than Charmain. Knew her really well until she left for Hollywood and they got out of touch.

Millie says Charmain was a normal kid, liked to "play doctor" with other boys and girls, but nothing abnormal. And the usual country barnyard stuff. "I mean, just kid stuff like ticklin' a horse's pecker to see how big it'd get, watching the goats fuck, and like that," says Millie.

Now get this: we know from Charmain's press bio that her mom was murdered in a home break-in. What we didn't know was that Charmain was raped by the two men imprisoned for the crime. Charmain stayed strictly away from boys after that and considered herself a virgin—not counting the rape, of course. (I get a sense that Charmain and Millie fooled around a bit, too, but nothing serious. Kind of like Charmain does now…bi-golly!)

Millie Johnson says Lawton Burns spent most of his time on the road as a salesman, even after Charmain's mom was raped and murdered. Charmain was pretty much on her own, except for a local woman housekeeper.

Millie insists her dad was kind, even timid—although she admits Charmain told her that Mom would never give Dad sex. So every few months he'd come in off the road drunk and horny, and literally rape Mom. Then he'd beg forgiveness and Mom would treat him like shit.

Millie talked plenty. She actually admitted that she was so sorry for Charmain's dad that one weekend, while Charmain was off for a weekend in Orlando trying out for a beauty contest, she took pity on the old guy and fucked him. She was sixteen. Millie recalls she was pleasantly surprised that a man his age could ring her bells so hard. (This during an interview at a really wild place called "The Horny Toad." Tell you about that later.)

Millie says she never told Charmain about it, and still feels pretty guilty.

Millie spent some time on the road with Charmain when she was doing beauty contests. They went to Miami together, where Charmain fell in love with this hot-looking rich guy from Savannah. Turns out he was this huge behind-the-scenes drug lord and was murdered. (Research is sending you over clips from Savannah papers. It was a very bloody murder; apparently a drug hit that had nothing to do with her.)

During this period, Charmain confided to Millie in an emotional moment that her mom, not her dad, had sexually abused her when she was a little girl. And poor old Lawton knew it, according to Charmain.

Millie says there had always been mean-spirited rumors that Lawton was getting it on with his daughter after the mother was murdered. Nobody suspected that the truth was more awful, if that's possible.

Millie says that the day before he killed himself, Lawton phoned her. The abuse by the townsfolk had begun and he was devastated, crying. Millie says the conversation started with him saying:

"Millie, you know I never touched that girl."

"I told him I knew that, and I couldn't understand why Charmain would say such an evil thing if there was no truth to it."

Then Lawton said, "It was.....It was..." And then he stopped. I said, "It was what, Lawton? What are you saying."

Then he said, "Goodbye, Millie, you always were a good girl."

"After he killed himself, I started thinkin'. And you know what? Charmain is a tough girl and all. But she's never mean to people unless they mess with her first. And there was no reason to hurt her daddy after all this time.

"And that's when it hit me. What Charmain had meant, when she spoke out on TV without namin' names, was that her mom was abusing her. She just wasn't thinking that when a daughter says 'abuse,' most people think it's the dad who's guilty. They don't automatically think of the mom.

"But, hey, it happens. There was a woman in Tallahassee just two years ago who'd been having sex with both her daughters for years. Eeeeww! Awful stuff, too. Pushing things up inside 'em and all.

"You see, Charmain never thinks about how stuff she says is gonna affect people. She just hauls off and says it. So when she said she was abused as a child, she knew in her own mind she was talkin' about her momma. She wasn't thinkin' that folks would just naturally assume it was the father. I mean, it usually is, right? That's no big surprise in these parts, you know.

"I don't think she realized people would drive him to kill himself. But he was a sensitive man. Maybe that's why he was so good in the sack."

Wow!

And they say L.A. is weird.

That's the news in sleepy Citrus Corners, Cameron.

More to come.

—Lulu. . .

CHAPTER 52

2:15 P.M.
TULL'S OFFICE AT *THE REVEALER*
LOS ANGELES

TULL read the report, sat and thought about it. He called Lulu in Florida.

"It's great stuff, kiddo. It establishes that her father was innocent. And that her statement about the abuse ended up killing him. Somehow I doubt that's what she intended, but we'll never know for sure. The abuse by the mother is a sensational angle. It happens more often than people realize. But what we need is another source. This is all coming from Millie. How credible is a stripper/hooker?"

"Cameron, I have checked out everything I can. It's a fact that she and Charmain helled around together. And if a girl like Millie isn't an expert on kinky sex, who is?"

"Lulu, it's great stuff, but you've got to find another source to back up Millie. Somebody must know something. People always do in those small towns."

"Oh, come on, Cameron. Both of Charmain's parents are dead. And you can't libel a dead person."

"Don't get sloppy on me, Lulu," Tull said sharply. "I've never published a story I didn't believe. And I'm not starting now. You don't print a lie about a dead man just because he's dead. Keep digging. Get me more on that rape-murder of her mother. And remember—they're dead, but Charmain isn't. She could sue us."

"On what grounds?" Lulu persisted. "It's not defaming her to say her mom abused her as a child."

"That's what lawyers are for," said Tull. "To dream up 'grounds' that no sane, reasonable American ever could. Keep at it, kiddo. Call you later."

Later that day, a Captain Fuentes of the Mexican national police got back to Tull.

"We have found the body of Señor Brown," he said. "It was very close to where you said it would be. Your information was very accurate, Señor Tull. Where did you say you got it?"

"Anonymous tip," said Tull. "Was it foul play?"

"He looks like a man who fell off a cliff, Señor. Was he pushed? Possibly. Who can say?"

"How about footprints? Tire tracks where he went over the cliff?"

The cop, who didn't seem overly concerned about the "gringo" corpse on his hands, sighed deeply.

"If we are right about where he fell from—and we're not sure we are—it is a popular place for tourists. Tire tracks and footprints are everywhere. For all we know, Señor Brown was drinking and slipped. Or he killed himself. We have informed the LAPD. We hope they arrive soon and show us their modern detection techniques."

"Did Buster…Señor Brown…have anything in his pockets other than ID? A large amount of cash, for instance?"

The cop swallowed a chuckle.

"Why…no, Señor. We didn't find any cash at all."

Tull grimaced. It was a stupid question to ask Mexican cops. If Buster had a wad of cash, the fuzz had a fiesta.

"Look, help me out here, Captain," Tull wheedled. "Was there anything else on him? Business cards, notes, receipts, anything like that?"

Captain Fuentes hesitated. "Well, Señor…I shouldn't share information with a journalist, but…"

"Come on, Captain, I helped you out."

The cop chuckled. "Sí, you gave me a dead body and extra paperwork. *Ay, bueno*! We found one thing. It looks like a phone number on a slip of paper. It's 310-555-9206."

"Thanks, Captain. Appreciate it."

Tull hung up, called his phone technician.

"Run this number, please."

"Give me a minute."

Tull waited, drumming a paradiddle with two pencils. The tech came back.

"It's an unlisted number that was disconnected two weeks ago. It belonged to Charmain Burns."

"Bingo! What's her pattern on changing numbers? Can you see it?"

"Yeah. Stars change numbers like we change socks. But Charmain…let's see…No, not that often. Every couple of months or so. This was changed only two weeks ago. You need her new number?"

"Yeah, thanks."

Tull jotted it down, hung up. Chewed it over. Concluded it was another link. But it was a long way from being solid evidence. Buster could have gotten her number anywhere. Just like fans and stalkers do.

And reporters.

The discovery of Buster's body got a fast two paragraphs in the *L.A. Daily News*. The story called him "a local boxer," said he "drowned" in a holiday accident, was survived by a brother and sister.

That was it.

R.I.P.

Dead end. Unless I can find the missing link, thought Tull. The anonymous phone caller. He could tie Charmain to Buster.

What's my next move? Rattle Vidal's cage again? Tell him I know Buster's dead? No! Information is power. Better to keep Vidal in the dark for the time being.

Or did he already know?

CHAPTER 53

1:20 P.M.
VIDAL DELANEY'S OFFICE
LOS ANGELES

WHEN Charmain got back from New York, she and Mike Kelso met with Vidal Delaney at his office.

"Just thought we'd all get up to date," said Vidal. "So far, Tull is stymied. And I guess we'd know soon enough if *The Revealer* found Buster. Have you heard anything from Buster?"

"No," said Charmain.

"Well, I think this may turn out okay. Tull suspects you, Charmain. But I don't think he knows much. My guess is Jessica Bellini told him about hearing your message on her machine. He probably listened to it, then headed to her place to grab the tape. And we're sure he recognized your voice."

"How so?" Kelso asked.

Vidal shrugged. "You might as well know. My people got there first and removed the tape. We left a bug in her place. When Tull arrived and found the tape missing, we heard him curse me out loud. And that's because he guessed what had happened—and he knows you're my client."

"But remember this—he can't be sure it was your voice. He'd be laughed out of court if he tried to testify that he did."

Charmain rolled her eyes. "So Steve Bellini's bitch sister knows it was probably me?"

"I doubt it," said Vidal. "Tull's one of the best in his game. To him, information is power. He plays everything close to the vest. And he knows Jessica Bellini would go crazy if she knew who might have been involved. And that would definitely get messy. Screw things up.

"No, Tull plays poker. My guess is he hasn't told *The Revealer* very much, if anything. He likes to wrap the whole package before he puts it under the tree."

Charmain sighed deeply. "I'd like to kill that cocksucker."

"Chill out," said Vidal. "So far, everything's going your way. As long as Buster doesn't show up."

Kelso got up, said, "Need a quick smoke."

He opened the sliding glass doors onto a balcony outside Vidal's office and lit a cigarette. Charmain watched him go, then said to Vidal, "He only smokes when he's really stressed out."

Kelso had left the door open a crack. Charmain called out, "Don't worry, Mike. Buster will stay out of sight."

Right, thought Kelso.

When you're buried six feet under, you're truly out of sight.

He looked down at his hands. They were shaking.

He'd seen the two-paragraph story on Buster, buried in the back pages of the sports section. And knew Buster hadn't died in any accident. He began to sweat.

Charmain.

Had to be. She'd killed him.

Kelso hadn't told her he knew Buster was dead. Obviously, neither she nor Vidal had seen the story. Now Kelso was terrified. He'd thought of going to the cops. But he couldn't betray Charmain, or bear the possibility that she might be imprisoned. Life would be meaningless, empty, without her. His obsession sickened him. He knew now he was helplessly in love with her.

But even looking at it strictly as business, he knew he should keep his mouth shut. If Charmain landed the "Medusa" role, she'd be a meal ticket worth millions. Kelso wasn't getting any younger. He needed to put something away for his old age.

Fuck it! What's done is done.

As Kelso and Charmain left Vidal's office, they met Szabo on his way in. Szabo, a big smile on his face, nodded respectfully.

"First time I've ever seen that creepy fucker smile," Charmain muttered to Kelso.

Szabo was feeling good, powerful. He'd come up with a two-part plan. The first part consisted of throwing a little shit in Mr. Tull's path. If it worked out, he'd take credit with Vidal. If it didn't, no one would ever know.

Though Szabo hadn't been in the meeting with Charmain and Kelso, he'd heard everything—including Charmain's wish to see Tull dead—via a bug he'd planted in Vidal's office. Boris Szabo's nature was to know everything, and stay one step ahead of his boss. He was always careful to remove the listening device every few days before technicians carried out their office de-bugging sweeps.

Easy enough, as it was Szabo who scheduled them.

CHAPTER 54

11:07 A.M.
CHARMAIN'S MANSION
BEVERLY HILLS

NEXT morning, Charmain found an unmarked white envelope in her mail. A note inside read:

"I'm sure you'll realize this comes from a friend. How else would I have heard you say that you have a problem you need eliminated? But I can't talk to you directly. I need deniability. Here's the deal:

"I know a solid pro who can take care of the problem. He's expensive, but he's absolutely discreet and worth every penny. In a few minutes, your phone will ring twice. Then it will ring again in fifteen seconds. Pick up before the second ring, and say nothing. Have a pencil and paper ready.

"Burn this note immediately."

The phone rang twice, then stopped. She waited. It rang again. She picked up fast. A male voice that sounded weird, like it was electronically disguised, said, "Leave your house now and drive to a pay phone. Any pay phone. . ." There was the click of a hangup.

Five minutes later, Charmain got in her car and drove. Her car phone rang. It was The Voice, saying:

"You're an actress and you can memorize lines—so memorize this number—310-555-6345. . .I repeat: 310-555-6345. Get to a pay phone and call that number in exactly fifteen minutes."

She checked her watch, then drove to the Beverly Hills Hotel, just five minutes away. She slid into a phone booth outside the Polo Lounge and dialed. The Voice answered, gave her a phone number.

"The man who will answer is a hitman. He's totally reliable. Your code name is 'Carmen.' You got it?"

"How do I know I'm not calling a cop, that this isn't a set-up?"

The Voice says, "Because you know who I am. Look, ask yourself this: who heard you say you needed a problem eliminated? Only two people, right? You know who I am. But we'll never discuss this between us—ever! That keeps everything secure.

"That's why my voice is disguised. You can honestly swear you don't know who called you. Even though you do."

The Voice clicked off.

Jesus! It's got to be Kelso, thought Charmain. Vidal might bend the law to protect her, but he'd already said he wouldn't walk through fire for her. Hell, if he actually knew I killed Buster, he'd make me turn myself in. But Kelso…ah, yes, Kelso worships me. He'd do anything to save my ass.

Good old Kelso.

In his office, Szabo smiled as he hung up and disconnected the voice-altering device. Handy gadget. It had helped him convince Charmain that her faithful manager, Mike Kelso, was helping her stage the murder of Cameron Tull.

Moments later, Charmain dialed the number The Voice had given her.

"Yes."

"It's Carmen."

"Call me 'Chief.' The contract will cost $20,000. You pay when the job is done."

"How do you know I'll pay?"

"Think about it."

"You'd kill me?"

"You're a quick study."

Randak 2000 hung up. And laughed like he hadn't laughed in a long, long time.

Ten minutes later, Randak called Cameron Tull at his study in Malibu and said, "She knows you're on to her, Mr. Tull. She's furious. And now you're in danger."

"Ah! I was hoping you'd call again. What kind of danger?"

"She's taken out a contract on your life."

Tull's gut froze.

Randak 2000 chuckled. "Isn't she amazing?"

"Look," Tull said calmly, "How do I know you're not some wacko trying to shake me up? Or maybe you killed Buster."

"Why would I keep calling you if that were true?"

"I don't know. To revel, to gloat. Like a killer coming back to the scene of his crime. To glow. To bask. To relive the thrill."

Randak laughed. "I'm no thrill killer, Mr. Tull."

"No, you sound like. . .a pro of some kind."

"What I am, Mr. Tull, is a fan of your column. I enjoy your coverage of the stars, all the fascinating gossip about them. But mostly, I find your insights about them compelling and accurate. Your coverage of Charmain Burns, in particular, is excellent. And I sense that you admire her, despite her bad-girl image. Am I correct?"

"Admiration? No, that's not quite right," said Tull. "The word is 'fascination.' I am endlessly fascinated by Charmain Burns and the new breed of young actresses who suddenly started storming Hollywood in the 90s. All these bad 'girrrls'—as they've been dubbed by the Gen X-ers—starting with Roseanne and Madonna, Shannen Doherty and Sharon Stone,

Courtney Love, and Drew Barrymore the second time around. There's a whole string of women who are fiercely independent, kick-ass bad girls who've set the Hollywood old-boys club back on its ass—and are damn proud of it. Charmain embodies these women. I study her to discover what makes these ladies tick. Where did they come from? Why are they so aggressive? Is it new feminism? Or is the public falling in love with tough chicks? And what fascinates *you* about Charmain?"

Randak 2000 chuckled again. "What a seamless segue. You're always the probing reporter, aren't you, Mr. Tull? But to answer your question, Charmain Burns is—to put it exactly—a noble creature. Strong, decisive, intelligent and self-confident. And, when she has to be, ruthless. She is a leader."

Tull's intrigued. "Ruthless. What do you mean?"

"Mr. Tull, don't patronize me. Or is this another reporter's technique? Very well, I'll answer the question. First, we have her sending Buster to deliver punishment to Bellini. And she's taken out a contract on your life. But let's discuss the infamous photos of her whipping that horse. I personally observed her training sessions with that animal. It needed discipline, needed to be brought under control. The average person sees this as animal cruelty. It is actually a leader imposing her will. Just the way a drill sergeant brutalizes recruits."

Tull said, "Physical abuse isn't allowed in U.S. military training."

"Wrong, Mr. Tull. Especially in elite units."

Tull jotted a note: "Check poss. mil. background."

Then Tull said, "I wonder if we aren't forgetting another example of her ruthlessness?"

"What would that be?"

"Murdering Buster."

"She did not do that, Mr. Tull."

"No? Did you?"

"You asked that question a minute ago, Mr. Tull. And I know you're not idly repeating yourself. Good interrogation technique. Keep returning to the central issue, approaching it in various ways. Unexpectedly. Again, I assure you she could not have killed Buster. I know where she was when he died."

"Really? How do you know so much about her?"

"I have my ways, Mr. Tull."

"And how do you know Charmain has put out a contract on me?"

"Because…I'm the one she hired to kill you, Mr. Tull."

Before Tull's mouth caught up with his stunned brain, Randak 2000 said: "I know how good your phone expert is. By now, he's had plenty of time to trace this call and tell you by e-mail that I'm at a pay phone in the Beverly Center mall. Whoever you've sent will be here shortly, so I'll say goodbye now, Mr. Tull."

Tull slammed the phone down in frustration. Checked his watch.

In West Hollywood, Randak 2000 melted into the Beverly Center crowds, but stayed in sight of the pay phone he'd been using. He watched as two young men approached the phone bank, looking like they didn't want to be noticed. They weren't cops. Reporters, for sure. Tull still hadn't called in the police. Randak wasn't surprised. In his professional career, he'd learned that journalists consider their information sacred. And they know cops can bull around and screw things up. No newsie shares a story with the fuzz until it's ready to print.

In Malibu, Tull finally allowed himself to get scared. His mysterious caller sounded damned competent.

Tull wondered how long he had.

CHAPTER 55

STEVE BELLINI'S FUNERAL
LOS ANGELES

IN the days leading up to Steve Bellini's funeral, Tull kept in touch with Jessica, but their conversations were sporadic and brief. Her mourning had taken on a more oppressive dimension as she was forced to cope with a new and poignant family drama.

Her mother and father had announced that they wanted to take their son's body back to Italy for interment near the family estate in Palermo. Jessica had not opposed her parents directly, just tried gently to convince them that Stefano would have wanted to rest in the soil of his adopted land. After much agonizing, they finally agreed. The funeral was delayed to allow other Bellini family members and close friends time to travel from Europe.

Steve's send-off was well attended. The European contingent of family and friends numbered more than two dozen. About forty assorted friends and fifteen Yale classmates were on hand, along with more than 300 *National Revealer* staffers. As expected, the paper's reclusive owner, Dalton Lupo, did not attend. Just before the services, he had a note hand-delivered to Steve's parents.

It read:

> *"After all earthly things have vanished, nothing will remain but the truth. On this day of your grief, and ours, I make this solemn pledge: Justice will be served. My deepest condolences."*

After the service, *The Revealer* staff headed for their favorite bar, "Me Kangaroo," a raffish pub run by a grizzled Australian ex-journalist and ex-drunk who'd taken the pledge and challenged it every day by pouring booze for his mates. Tull sat at a back booth with Mary. He'd brought her up to date the day before, telling her about the anonymous caller.

"It's uncanny that he knows so much, Mary. Either he killed Buster, or he knows who did. He's the link between Charmain and Buster."

"Don't play this like a one-man band, Cameron. If you need help..."

"Everything's under control, Mary."

He didn't mention the contract Charmain had allegedly taken out on his life.

"What are you doing to find him?"

"All the usual. I've got our phone guy ready to trace when he calls in, but it won't come to anything. This guy's a pro of some kind. Real smart. But he's also strange. Off-kilter. His fascination with Charmain borders on obsession. If I had to shoot from the hip, I'd say he's probably a stalker. And I think that's going to work for us. Because the best way to spot a stalker, as we all know, is to doorstep the person he's after and wait for him to show up."

Mary nodded. "But if he's smart—and you say he is—he'll be looking for that."

Tull said, "Right. So I've hired the best. Dan Billings. He's been doorstepping Charmain since last night."

Mary nodded again, approvingly. Billings was a private investigator the paper used often. Expensive, but the best. An ex-cop whose specialty was tailing people. Harder to lose than belly-button lint.

The next day, Billings called Tull. "Nobody's on Charmain's tail. I'd swear to it."

"Damn. You sure? Okay, stay on it," said Tull.

He hung up, pondered. His gut told him the anonymous caller was a stalker. But if so…where was he? Stalkers stalk, for Chrissake! Why hadn't Billings spotted him?

Tull got his answer later that day. Randak 2000 called.

"That was a good idea, having your PI stake Charmain out. But, as it happens, I'm not observing her right now. I'm observing you, Mr. Tull. Remember, I've accepted a contract on your life."

Randak paused, then added, "But don't worry. I'm not going to fulfill the contract."

Tull said, "That's a relief. May I ask why?"

"Because you're not going to find out anything at all. So why kill you? It's not necessary. I'm not a serial killer, Mr. Tull. I'm a professional. I don't kill for pleasure. Only if absolutely necessary. As I told you, I am…"

"…a warrior," said Tull. "Yes, I remember. But I thought you were doing this for Charmain? The way I see it, she found out you were stalking her, bought you off somehow—for money, maybe sex, I don't know—and told you to kill me."

Randak laughed. "Is that what you think, Mr. Tull? Let me explode your theory by telling you something that will amaze you…Charmain doesn't know who she's hired for your assassination. She was referred to me anonymously and given a cutout number to call, if you follow me."

"Hard to believe," said Tull.

"It doesn't matter what you believe, Mr. Tull. None of this will matter soon. You think you know what I am, and why I'm observing Charmain. But you know nothing. Nothing. Goodbye, Mr. Tull."

Tull said, "Wait…uh…thanks. For not killing me. I owe you one. Will we speak again?"

Randak said, "Oh, yes, Mr. Tull. We'll speak again. Soon."

CHAPTER 56

12:41 P.M.
TULL'S STUDY
MALIBU

A great weight had lifted off Tull. What a glorious thing, not to be a hitman's target. Suddenly, life's mundane worries seemed petty indeed. The world looked dazzling through rose-colored glasses.

Jessica.

He was gripped by the absolute need to see her. He phoned her house, left a message. Not wanting to intrude on her mourning, he avoided calling her cell because she was with her parents every moment. An hour later, she phoned from her car.

"Cameron, I'm so glad you called. I've just put my parents on the plane. They wanted to get back for a memorial service at the villa for family members who couldn't come to America for the funeral."

"Look, Jessica, I...I've tried to respect your need to be alone with your thoughts, but..."

"I've been alone with my thoughts too long. I've missed you, Cameron. I know I'll be terrible company, but could we have dinner?"

His heart leaped. "What an appealing idea."

As dusk settled softly into the L.A. canyons, they met in the walled garden of a French bistro on Beverly Glen. God, he thought, she looks beautiful.

"Wine?"

"No," she said. "I need something with a jolt. One of those martinis you like so much."

They went inside and sat at the corner table Tull had reserved.

"Two Belvedere martinis, straight up with a twist," he told the waiter.

Looking across the table at her, he remembered Palm Beach and how mesmerized he'd been the first time he'd looked into those limpid almond eyes, so calm and confident; so mischievous with the sure knowledge of the impact she'd made. Now she gazed across the table at him as if reading his emotions. He suddenly felt awkward, wanting to blurt out something, anything; to tell her how desperately he'd missed her, his raw need for her. Say something, you goddamn fool. Get control of yourself. Make small talk. To tell her what you're feeling would be crass intrusion on her mourning. But...how long does mourning last? Or, more precisely, when does one commence living a normal life again?

"Is something wrong, Cameron?"

Yes, he wanted to say…I love you, and I thought you loved me! Why didn't you ever see me again after Palm Beach?

He smiled. "No," he said lightly. "Everything's fine. Although I did have some wacko threaten to kill me. But he phoned back to say he'd changed his mind. Just another normal day in Tabloid Land."

Her face reflected horror and he cursed his stupidity.

"Oh, God, no!" she said. Her hand reached out instinctively for his, a gesture that caught them both by surprise. There was an awkward moment, then Jessica withdrew her hand, composed herself.

"Sorry, guess I'm just emotional right now. But that's so frightening. Have you gone to the police?"

"No. It was nothing. Really. Stuff like that happens all the time. The guy was just a harmless nut. I shouldn't have mentioned it."

She hammered him with questions. He fended them off. Who had threatened him? Why? How did he know he wasn't still in danger?

"Jessica, believe me, it's nothing. Happens all the time. Are you ready to order? The food here is wonderful."

"Cameron, did this threat have anything to do with the paper's search for Steve's killer?"

"No," said Tull.

Her eyes didn't believe him.

"Cameron, I am not a fool. I know you've been putting a lot of pressure on some very important people in this town. Be careful. I don't have to tell you that some of them can be very dangerous to anyone who threatens their power."

She paused. "You've been…so kind. I'd hate for anything to happen to you."

"Please, Jessica. Let's enjoy dinner. Just forget the world for a while."

She smiled. "There's nothing I'd like better."

The meal was perfectly prepared and presented. Afterward, they ordered two cappuccinos. Tull had a snifter of Louis XIII cognac. They sat, silent. Small talk had run its course. She smiled wanly. As if to say…What's to say?

He took a deep breath.

And said it.

"Jessica, I want to be respectful of your grief. But I have to know. Why did you call off our plans to meet in New York? Why did you suddenly stop taking my calls? I thought…well, you know what I thought."

She closed her eyes for a moment. Then looked straight at him. "Yes, I know what you thought."

"Well…was I wrong?"

She sighed, cast a glance at other diners. "I can't talk about this here."

"Then where? We can't just avoid this! At least, I can't."

He motioned a waiter over.

"Would you bring our drinks out into the garden, please?"

They got up, went outside and sat on a wooden bench in a vine-covered arbor strung with tiny twinkling lights. The small, well-kept garden, dotted with tables and chairs, was empty. The waiter brought their drinks and left them alone.

Nervously, Tull quipped, "Here we are in the moonlight again."

She didn't smile.

"Well," he said, "I'll ask again. Was I wrong?"

Jessica sighed. "If you're asking whether I cared about you, the answer is yes. Very much."

"Then why…?"

She looked at him, eyes brimming with tears.

"Oh, goddamnit, this is so hard. I can't say this any easy way."

Now he reached out and took her hand. "Just say it. Straight out."

"Oh, GOD! Cameron, I—I got…pregnant. I was going to have your baby…"

"…You…what?"

"And I was so happy…so very happy. But…oh, God, Cameron…"

She stared at him, her agony hitting him like a hammer blow.

"Cameron…I…had a…a miscarriage."

The sudden rush of emotion overwhelmed him for a moment.

"Jessica…I don't understand. Oh, Jessica, why didn't you tell me? Why?"

Now she was sobbing.

"Oh, you really want to hear this? Can't you just accept that it happened, and that it…it just didn't work out?"

"What?" Totally confused now, he sputtered, "I can't even follow your logic. First of all—accept it? Of course I can't just accept it? I want answers…I want—"

"See, it's what you want! You're not thinking about me. And you say you can't follow my logic. You know why? Because you think like a goddamn man. Can you even imagine what it's like, how I felt?"

"Whoa! That's not what I mean. It's just…it doesn't make sense. I just want to know why you didn't tell me, so I could have—"

"Oh, okay, YOU want to know. Well, okay! You want me to tell you everything, right? Okay, fine. And I hope I make sense!"

She took a deep breath, tried to control the tears.

"Cameron, you think I'm sugar and spice and everything nice. Well, goddamnit, I'm not. I'm a hard-headed businesswoman. Just the way my father taught me to be. And I'm not always very nice. I come from an old European family of peasants who fought their way up into the merchant class. We are strong people. How do you think my brother was tough enough to compete on your fucking paper? To us, making and holding onto the family fortune is everything. We are pragmatists. Good people who are capable of ruthlessness. Damnit, Cameron, you don't know anything about me."

Tull felt his temper rising. Hold it, he told himself. Control. Control.

"Jessica, I don't understand. What does your business acumen have to do with our love for each other?"

"Damn you, Cameron Tull. When I miscarried our child, I knew...or I believed, maybe because of what I was going through, that if I told you about it, it would be a kind of...I don't know...a commitment..."

"Of course it's a commitment. What did you expect?"

"I don't know...or I didn't know then, anyway. And I didn't know what you expected."

"But if you'd seen me in New York, you would have! Even before I knew you were pregnant."

"Are you implying I would have forced you into a commitment because of my pregnancy? How could you say that? Oh, God, I can't do this now!"

She was devastated, spent. She's had too much, he told himself. First, her brother's death. Now this. Why hadn't he been more patient? He sensed that he was treading in the dangerous, volatile no-man's-land of visceral female emotion. He took a deep breath. Careful, he told himself. Say the right thing.

He said precisely the wrong thing.

"Don't you trust me?"

She looked at him, closed her eyes, and said, "I can't do this. I just can't talk about this now. I shouldn't have started this. Oh, Christ. I've got to go."

"No, look..."

"I'll call you. I will. Just let me go."

She turned and ran out of the garden.

"I'll NEVER let you go," he yelled after her.

Shit.

He didn't even understand what he'd done wrong.

Women.

Like speaking a foreign language.

CHAPTER 57

9:30 A.M.
TULL'S STUDY
MALIBU

TULL was in his study the next morning when radio newscasts led with a report that a guest at the Camino Rio Hotel had found a high-tech tape recorder dangling over the side of the balcony of the suite Steve Bellini had occupied. Police admitted it had been missed in the original search of the murder scene.

The tape recorder—a Sony "Scoop Man"—had been identified as Bellini's. The cops called it "important" evidence. Reliable sources reported that the machine had recorded the assault on Bellini. The killer's voice—apparently that of a black male—could be heard faintly.

One TV station had a reaction quote from Los Angeles lawyer Johnnie Cochran, who commented huffily that he stood by his assertion, made during the O.J. Simpson trial, that it's racist to say anyone can recognize a voice as being "black male."

Tull called Eva. "Do we have anything more on this report about the tape recorder than I'm hearing on radio?"

"Not yet," said Eva. She lowered her voice. "Nobody here knows it yet, but I've got a copy of the tape for you. It came from the Camino Rio Hotel dick. The guest who found it turned it over to him. He made a quick copy before he called the cops."

"What's on the damn tape, Eva?"

"You hear a knock on the door, then a voice saying, 'Gators bite hard.' Then a scuffle, some dishes breaking, a door slamming, and a big crashing noise."

"God! Okay, keep the tape buttoned up. I'm coming in."

He clicked off, stood up, and reached for his briefcase.

A man stepped through the French doors from the balcony and pointed a gun at him.

In a split second of shock, Tull thought: This is it. Final page.

-------------30-------------!

A Zen precept flashed:

"While living,

"Be a dead man.

"Be thoroughly dead...and all's well."

Tull said cooly, "I don't believe we've met. But my guess is that you're my anonymous caller."

No answer. Tull gestured at the gun in the man's hand.

"You said you'd refused the contract on my life."

Randak smiled.

And shot him.

Tull gasped at the thump of impact. He looked down in disbelief at the red stain spreading across his chest. Jesus. So this is what it's like, he thought. No pain, really. Just numbness as life drains away. His head spun with the shock of suddenly facing mortality. He heard, as from a distance, his assailant speaking.

"Ever play paintball, Mr. Tull? It's great fun. You go out in the woods on weekends and shoot at your friends, see how many you can 'kill.' You win by staying alive. It really gets the adrenaline pumping."

Randak 2000 laughed at the look on Tull's face as he slowly realized he wasn't dying, or even hurt. Randak stuck the paintball gun into his belt.

Tull looked down at his "bloodstained" sport jacket.

Randak said, "The paint is washable."

"I hope so," said Tull. "This is Armani."

He sat down at his desk, shaking but trying for control. "Can I get you anything? Coffee? Mineral water?"

"I'm here to make a point, Mr. Tull."

"I get the point. You can kill me anytime. What else do you want?"

"The tape recording the police found is a puzzle to them," Randak said. "They can't go anywhere with it unless you reveal what you know about Charmain's connection to Buster Brown. Then they'll understand Buster's statement on the tape. He says, 'Gators bite hard.' It's a warning to Bellini to pull his reporters out of Charmain's home state of Florida—the alligator state.

"If you tell the police what you know about Buster Brown, they'll have enough to pull her in as a suspect. I know you haven't told them anything yet. I'm asking you not to!"

Tull shook his head wearily. "How the hell do you know what's on that tape? Its contents haven't been reported. And how do you know whether or not I've told the police anything?"

Randak ignored the questions.

"Let me put it simply, Mr. Tull. Buster killed Bellini. Buster is dead. Justice has been served. End of story. I'm asking you to leave it alone."

Suddenly, Tull got it. "You're protecting Charmain, aren't you? You don't want her arrested for soliciting murder. But why? I know you're a fan. Or, let's be blunt, a possible stalker. But you're not like any stalker I've ever encountered. What's your stake in all this?"

Randak 2000 shrugged. "What does it matter? Let's just remember that I've spared your life, Mr. Tull. And that means you owe me. Buster killed Steve Bellini. Buster has been…executed, so to speak. So back off and leave Charmain alone."

Tull shook his head. "Look, I can't prove this, but from what I've pieced together so far, Charmain apparently set this thing in motion. So she has to answer for her part in Bellini's death, whatever it was. As for what you call the 'execution' of Buster, I'd call it murder. So would a court of law.

"So who killed Buster, pal? Did you do it? Was that part of your plan to protect Charmain? You apparently see yourself as her protector. But why? What do you want from her? You raise a lot of questions, and give very few answers. That's why I haven't gone to the cops yet. I need more answers."

Randak 2000 smiled. "You're getting closer, Mr. Tull. I know that your reporters are talking to people who stayed at the hotel on the day of the murder in hopes of finding a witness who saw anybody suspicious. So are the police. But they're at a disadvantage. They don't know about Buster. But your reporters are quietly showing people pictures of him.

"It's a big effort, Mr. Tull. That's why I admire *The Revealer*. You work harder than most other journalists. I remember that great line in the movie *Men In Black,* when Tommy Lee Jones tells Will Smith that the tabloids are 'the best damn investigative reporters on the planet.' Truer words were never spoken. Tabloids scoop the mainstream press on a regular basis. *The National Enquirer* nailed O.J. Simpson in the civil trial with those pictures of him wearing the Bruno Magli shoes he swore he never owned—and then they nailed the killer of Bill Cosby's son for the LAPD.

"Now *The Revealer* can break a big story. It can reveal that Buster Brown murdered Steve Bellini, then killed himself in a dramatic suicide. I helped you get this story, Mr. Tull. So I'm asking you again: take the glory, but leave Charmain to me."

Tull's mind raced. How did Randak know the exact statement on the tape recording found on Bellini's balcony? The cops hadn't released it. Randak had called himself "an investigator." Was he an ex-cop? With sources inside the LAPD?

Randak said, "Mr. Tull, let me make you a proposition. Don't share your information with the police for a few more days. You know they'll just go charging in and shut you out of the story if they can. If you'll give me a bit more time, I promise you that justice—even by your exacting standards—-will be served. I'll give you the Hollywood story of a lifetime—including an eyewitness report that will blow your mind."

Tull stood, walked to a window, and looked out pensively as he framed a reply. Be careful, he told himself. This guy could kill you. He swung around and looked at Randak.

"What's your name?"

"I'm not in the phone book, Mr. Tull."

"I need to call you something."

Randak inclined his head slightly. "I am Randak 2000."

Jesus, thought Tull. Sounds like a robot in *Star Wars.*

"What's your interest in Charmain?" he asked. "You're obviously a fan, but you seem to be somewhat more…uh, dedicated to her than the…average fan might be."

Randak's eyes flashed. "Don't try to figure me out, Tull. You have no idea who and what I am. Just know this: I am the instrument brought to this place to fulfill a great destiny. There is a world to be saved. My mission involves Charmain. No harm will come to any of you unless you stand in my way. But if you go to the police now, I'll be back—with this."

Randak produced another gun.

"This one makes a stain that won't wash out easily."

Christ! He's a Grade-A homicidal fruitcake, thought Tull.

"Look," he said. "I have no problem with keeping the cops out of this right now. I want to have the whole story wrapped up first. So, no problem. I'll tell them nothing."

"Turn around," Randak ordered.

Tull, confused, said, "Look, I've agreed so far…"

"Turn around. NOW!"

Tull turned, bracing for the bullet.

"Look, we've got no problem here," he said. "Why are you doing this? Why kill me now?"

No answer. No bullet. Tull put his hands up.

"Shoot if you have to, Randak, but I'm going to turn around so we can discuss this rationally. Okay?"

He turned slowly, nerve endings twitching, flinching. And…no Randak. Gone. What the hell…?

Tull edged cautiously over to the open French doors, stepped out onto the balcony. He looked down into the underbrush, where the canyon began.

A flattened bush told the tale.

Damn!

The sonofabitch had jumped two stories.

CHAPTER 58

11:25 A.M.
LAPD
LOS ANGELES

MUG shots.

After the first five minutes of plowing through photo ID books at Parker Center, headquarters of the Los Angeles Police Department, every burglar, mugger, killer, and weenie-flasher began to look like the same sullen, sneering creep. Tull had been at it more than an hour, hoping to spot the scary bastard who called himself Randak 2000. It was the only move he had. So far, it wasn't working.

Tull closed the last book, looked at his watch. He'd been here since late morning. It was after 12:45 now. He walked upstairs to the desk of Det. Sgt. Fred Payne, his primo police source. Payne was talking to someone on the phone, taking sneaky little bites of a dripping meatball sub.

Tull sat, plucked a *Daily News* out of the wastebasket, caught up on the non-Hollywood news. When Fred hung up, Tull said, "I'm getting nowhere with the mug shots. My guy's not in there."

"Hey, Tull, if you'd tell me what you're looking for..."

"I can't, Fred. Let me have a police artist for a few minutes. Okay?"

"Whoa!" said Fred. "Look, I can't just go around ordering people to drop everything and help you."

"Sure you can. This is a murder case. One of our own was killed. Help us out."

An hour later, the police artist put some finishing touches on an Identi-kit composite. Tull nodded. "That's him." He walked it upstairs to Fred, who gave it a quick glance and said, "Let's go get some coffee." They walked out the rear entrance of Parker Center into the exotic streets of Little Tokyo.

"Sushi or Starbucks?" asked Payne.

Over cappuccino, Fred Payne took another long look at the artist's rendition.

"I'm not sure," he said, "but it looks like a dead ringer for an ex-cop. Name of George Tanner. Left the force a few years ago."

"Why?"

Fred sighed. "Officially? He's on retirement for physical disability."

Tull shook his head. "Not my guy. He's a perfect physical specimen."

Fred shifted uncomfortably in his chair. "Look, all I really know is rumors."

"Okay. What's the rumor?"

"That he was was put on disability to get him out of sight."

"Again I ask, Fred. Why?"

Fred sighed. "Talk is, in the old days he was part of a special squad that put the muscle on the enemies of movie bigshots or heavyweight politicians for top brass in the department. You know, the right-wingers who got weeded out a few years back around the time Darryl Gates retired. Word has it that this guy went too far and did a hit under orders—or what he thought was orders. There was fallout, a lot of heat. That ended the special squad and the guys who ran it. It was quietly disbanded. Everybody was retired early. What I hear about this guy is, he's kind of a mental case. Scares everybody."

"That's him," said Tull. "Can you get hold of his file?"

"Tough," said Fred. "I'll let you know."

Tull went back to *The Revealer.* Eva told him one of his sources—Vita Nelson, the makeup lady at "E!" TV—had phoned in.

"She said she knows that you love items about Charmain Burns, and she's got one. Didn't sound like much to me. Said her husband, the lighting tech, was on a location shoot in Baja and saw Charmain at a gas station. That was it."

Yes, sweet mama!

"Get her for me, please."

A moment later, she was on the line.

"Hello, Vita? Tull. Listen, have I told you lately that I love you? No? Well, I do. So, what was the exact date your husband saw Charmain Burns in Baja?"

He listened, wrote it down.

"You're sure?"

She was.

"Was Charmain alone?"

She was.

"Did your husband speak to Charmain, or hear her say anything at all. Like where she'd been, where she was going?"

No.

"Vita, I'm sending you a nice, fat check."

He hung up. Now he had a witness who could place Charmain in Baja on or about the date Buster had died.

Okay. Next move?

He was still thinking it over when Jessica phoned about an hour later.

"I'm surprised you took my call," she said. "I don't know why I always end up treating you so badly. I don't mean to, but..."

"Jessica, it's not your fault—"

"No! I feel terrible about what's happened between us and I'm sorry about the other night," she said. "I know I sounded hysterical and you didn't understand half of what I said. I apologize. You have a right to answers. I'm ready to give them."

Tull sighed. "Look, I shouldn't have pressed you. You're still in mourning and I was stupid to bring it all up. Don't worry about it. You owe me nothing."

"Oh, but I do. I realize that now. You're a good man and I always treat you like a villain. Cameron, I don't like what you do for a living. And I keep using that as an excuse. Can we meet for a drink somewhere quiet?"

He looked at his watch. "How about 4:30? There's an outdoor café at Sunset Plaza called 'Brio.'"

"Fine. I'll see you there."

Tull put the phone down. He felt relieved. Optimistic. Maybe things were looking up. He started thinking carefully about his next move. He now had a tenuous connection between Charmain and Buster. But enough to arrest her? He wrote out each point on a legal pad:

#1: The punk who witnessed Buster rescuing Charmain from a mugging/rape outside BuzzBuzz.

#2: Charmain's voice on the answering machine.

#3: A reliable source spotting Charmain in Baja around the date Buster died.

Tull analyzed it, point by point:

#1 was weak. It proved Charmain knew Buster. "So what?" her attorney would say. "It also shows she had reason to be grateful to Buster, so why kill him?"

#2 was next to worthless, unless he had the actual tape. And he himself was useless as a witness, being a friend of the deceased. Tull could already hear the attorney: "Were you intimate with the deceased's sister, Mr. Tull?"

Point #3 was the strongest. It put Charmain in Baja, although not actually with Buster.

The bitch was guilty as hell.

But it wouldn't be enough for the cops. Not yet.

And he had something else to worry about: Jessica's safety.

The tape of Charmain's mocking message to Jessica had been stolen from her answering machine. It's almost certain that whoever took it—Vidal Delaney's henchman Boris Szabo, probably—would assume that Jessica had heard it. They could easily determine that the machine had played the tape after the message was left. So Jessica could be in danger. Physical danger. Not from Vidal. Tull's gut told him Vidal would go only so far to cover for a client. No, the threat to Jessica was Charmain, who was apparently capable of murder when backed against a wall.

Just before he left the office to meet Jessica, Tull got a call that underscored his fears. It was Lulu. His favorite reporter was still on the job in

Citrus Corners. Lulu sounded excited.

"How's this for a new blockbuster, boss? Millie says Charmain may have killed a guy. And not just killed—she did a whole Lorena Bobbit thing."

Lulu explained that she'd dropped by Millie's place one afternoon, and in a quiet moment—"We were sharing a joint, actually," Lulu admitted, "first one I've smoked in years"—Millie told her about a guy named Patrick Taulere, the love of Charmain's life, who was tortured, castrated, and murdered in Savannah in a mysterious, unsolved case.

"Before the murder, Millie had a short fling with a Cuban guy involved in Patrick Taulere's business—which turned out to be big-time drug smuggling, although Charmain didn't know that until after he was murdered. The Savannah cops never solved the case, but Millie's Cuban told her that a small-time Colombian drug dealer who hated Taulere ended up with his cock and balls cut off in his burned-down house in Miami a few days after Patrick Taulere got neutered. Sort of a copycat murder, right?

"And listen to this! Millie's Cuban druglord fuck-buddy, who's named Ramon Something, told Millie he's pretty sure he saw Charmain in Miami just before this Colombian was offed. It's tough to prove Charmain did it, but it sure looks that way. I'll run it down, Cameron. God, I love this story, don't you?"

Tull said, "I'll love it when we've nailed it."

He hung up. Jesus! Charmain Burns...Angel of Death! His skin tingled, like it always did when a story was about to bust wide open.

CHAPTER 59

4:30 P.M.
BRIO CAFÉ
SUNSET PLAZA

TULL arrived at "Brio" before Jessica. He picked an outside table in a corner, quiet and private. She arrived, and they ordered cold drinks.

"Please let me tell you this my own way," Jessica said. "This time, I'll try to make sense."

She smiled shyly. "I'll take questions from the floor later."

He nodded.

"I'll begin at the beginning of the end," she said. "After I left you in Palm Beach, I went to New York and couldn't stop thinking about you. Could hardly wait to see you again. Just a month, I told myself. I threw myself into my work. My fashion line was finally taking off into the big time. My business partner, Carlo Piccioli, needed me to work with him around the clock.

"It was an exciting but very stressful time. I started to feel a little off. Carlo insisted I see my doctor. I did. And got the shocking news that I was pregnant."

She looked at him solemnly.

"There was, believe me, no shadow of a doubt that you were the father."

Tull wanted to kiss her. He didn't move.

Be very quiet, he thought.

"Can you imagine how I felt, Cameron? Pregnant. By a man I'd just met? My Italian Catholic mother would have been in hysterics. But then I thought, No, I'm actually happy. I truly believe I love this man. Perhaps this can work out. I'm a thirty-one-year-old female with a ticking biological clock. I'd always wanted a child, wondered if I was leaving it until too late. Now...I had one on the way."

Jessica spread her hands in a gesture of helplessness.

"But, wait. I still had to tell you. You had a right to know. But how would you react? I knew you had feelings about me, but women always wonder how a man will feel after the thrill of new sex wears off. I tried to visualize your reaction. You, a confirmed bachelor. Would you be thrilled? Maybe. Or maybe you'd feel pressured. And that would kill whatever we had going."

Jessica made a little laugh that sounded like a sob. "It was crazy. I didn't know you well enough to guess your reaction. And yet...you were the father of my child.

"I kept putting off the decision of whether or not to tell you. I was so conflicted; under great pressure in my work. My hormones started to go crazy. I wanted to confide in someone. But who? I have girlfriends, but none that close.

"My mother? Forget it. My father? On most things, I'd go to him. But not this. He's a very old-fashioned Italian man. He wasn't happy about my brother ignoring the family business to work on a tabloid. He would hate the idea of me marrying a man who works for one.

"So how about Carlo? He's like a big brother to me. And he's a very modern Italian man. But he's still Italian, from the old country. So I told him a little bit about you, and how I thought I was falling in love.

"Carlo told me, 'Cara, usually I would say that's wonderful. But not right now. Not a serious romance. No! You don't have time. We are poised for an international breakthrough. You've got to concentrate totally, completely, on business. Not to mention the lousy publicity when it gets out—and it will—that you're ga-ga over a gossip columnist. Everyone in the business will be afraid to talk to you, thinking their little scandals might end up in the tabloids.'

"The pressure started mounting. I felt I had to make a decision. I had to tell you. Or...did I? There was one other possible solution."

Jessica paused for a long moment.

"I could...terminate the pregnancy. And not tell you. Ever."

She paused again, sipped her drink.

"The very thought of aborting my child disgusted me," she continued. "I realized I could never, never do that. Even if I could, I knew it would end our relationship. Because I could never live that lie, keep that secret. I'd hate myself. Oh, Cameron, so many times, when we talked on the phone, I tried to tell you. I said to myself, 'Just tell him! If he reacts badly, then basta! It's no good, and it's better to find that out now.' Why not just be a single mom? Everybody's doing it."

She smiled. "But I'm still an old-fashioned girl, I guess. I wanted a daddy for my baby. Not a sperm donor. Maybe a man can't understand this, but to me, by this time, the baby was real. It didn't matter that it was the size of a kidney bean. It was my baby. In my womb."

Jessica paused.

"Nonetheless...you had the right to know."

Tull sat silent.

"I'm sorry to drag this out, Cameron. I'm just trying to tell you how I felt. You can guess the rest. The pressure mounted. I felt miserable. And one night, I miscarried."

For the first time in many years, Tull felt the hot burn of tears behind his eyes. Jessica said, "Never in my life had I felt so...so empty and hopeless. Two days later, I had what the doctors called a 'collapse from nervous exhaustion.' I was in the hospital for three days.

"And still, there was this dilemma: to tell you, or not? And finally, I decided I shouldn't. Our relationship might never have worked out. And this way, before anything serious got started, we could make a clean break.

"So, rightly or wrongly, that's what I did, Cameron. And everything worked wonderfully. Jessica Bell is now a famous and successful designer. A very neat and nearly happy ending. There's just one problem.

"Jessica Bellini is still in love with you."

She looked at him, eyes bright with pain.

"Well, there. I did it! I told you. How you must hate me."

He felt paralyzed, suffocated by emotion. Tried for a smile, didn't quite make it. He took her hand and said, "Jessica, I am so sorry you went through this agony. I believe in my heart that if you had called and told me, my reaction would have been, 'Wow, I've just met the girl of my dreams and she's carrying my baby.'

"But that's easy for me to say in hindsight. Would I have reacted the way I truly believe I would have? Or, faced with the sudden reality of it, would I have acted like a jerk? What I say right at this moment probably means nothing to you because you don't know me well enough to say, 'Yes, that's what he would have done.'

"But I'll tell you one thing you can take to the bank, lady: I'm in love with you. Have never gotten you out of my head. And I suggest, now that we've been through more than most couples who've known each other for a while, let's go back to the morning after that incredible night in Palm Beach, and start all over fresh. Please, Jessica. Could we just do that?"

He pulled his chair close, looked into her eyes.

"Jessica, I guess what I'm saying is...let's have a courtship."

She blinked.

"Oops," she said, "now I'm going to cry."

Suddenly, the pain left them. Washed away. They sat happily for nearly an hour, holding hands, kissing tenderly. Talking very little, wanting to live in the moment. Finally, Tull suggested that they go out, lighten up, be around people.

"Are you asking me out on a date, sir?"

He grinned. "It's a courtship, right?"

He asked her to accompany him to a party at the Academy Theater. It would be packed with the Hollywood power elite. The occasion was a screening of Clive Tinsdale's new film. Jessica agreed. She'd go home to change, then drive over. They'd meet in the lobby at 7:30.

Caught up in the magic of finding her again, an obvious thought didn't occur to Tull. The evening was in honor of Clive Tinsdale, so it was a fair assumption that every actress scrambling for the part of "Medusa" would attend.

Including Charmain Burns.

CHAPTER 60

8:08 P.M.
ACADEMY THEATER
LOS ANGELES

KLIEG lights pierced the sky and a hundred limousines snaked down Wilshire Boulevard in Beverly Hills, slithering up to the curb in front of the Samuel Goldwyn Theater and disgorging gobs of rich and beautiful people.

The sidewalk swarmed with power. Studio chiefs, movie stars, producers, agents, and managers filed into the spacious, high-ceilinged lobby of the magnificent, art deco movie temple known in show business as the "Academy Theater," the members-only sanctum sanctorum of the Academy of Motion Picture Arts & Sciences. The atmosphere crackled as Hollywood's A-list schmoozed, boozed, and noshed a Japanese buffet catered—at $400 a head—by trendy restaurateur Nobu Matsuhisa.

"Well, Clive Tinsdale must be a hot ticket," marveled Jessica, maneuvering with Tull through the crush of beautifully-scented bodies.

"He makes money for his studio," said Tull. "They want everybody to know it."

"Do you come to these affairs often? I mean, is this where you get your news?"

Tull laughed. "Not really. I'll find out what really went down here over the phone tomorrow. Tonight, nobody will tell me a damn thing. They're afraid someone might overhear them consorting with the enemy."

Jessica had noticed how eyes in the crowd flicked to Tull. People she recognized as movie and TV heavyweights nodded and waved casually.

"The enemy? Is that what they think you are?"

He shrugged. "Not really. I'm just part of the landscape. They love me when they need me to publicize their next film, TV show, or album. They curse me when I'm exposing their little embarrassments. To them, I'm just business. Like everything else in this town."

Tull heard a loud, familiar cackle behind him. He turned. It was Roseanne. "Well, look who's here," she brayed. "Liz Smith in drag."

Everybody in the vicinity, including Tull, cracked up. "That's slander," he said, "and I'm suing."

"Ha!" huffed Roseanne. "Liz Smith's the one who should be suing. Hi, Cameron. Who's this cutie-pie? She looks familiar."

"Roseanne, this is Jessica Bell, the designer. Jessica, Roseanne."

"Ohmigod," said Roseanne, beaming. "That's right. I love your stuff. What's my discount?"

Jessica, laughing, said, "I'm so flattered. Come to our showroom anytime and ask for me. I'll take care of you."

In moments, a small crowd made them its nucleus. Tull and Jessica got involved in conversations. Then Jessica spotted a knot of fashion professionals she knew across the room. She patted his arm. "Cameron, I've just seen some friends."

He nodded. "I'll catch up with you. Look, let's have a few nibbles of Japanese hors d'ouevres, then leave here, say, in forty-five minutes and have a quiet dinner at The Grill?"

"Okay," she said. She put her lips to his ear and whispered, "I love you." His heart bounced, but she was gone before he could speak.

After about fifteen minutes with her friends, Jessica started craning her neck for Tull. When she didn't spot him, she decided to hit the ladies room and search later. He probably wouldn't want to leave before he worked the room a bit more. For all his casual air of been-there-done-that, she sensed that he loved this milieu, this landscape he moved through so easily.

In the ladies room, Jessica had just emerged from a stall when Charmain Burns came storming in. Charmain was in a fury. She hadn't been invited, so she'd crashed the event, figuring it was the perfect chance to schmooze the *Medusa* producer. Being a recognized star, she'd powered her way in with no trouble, though she'd quickly discovered, to her annoyance, that Clive Tinsdale hadn't arrived. Worse, a studio executive she knew told her it was Tinsdale's practice not to arrive at these things until the screening was almost over.

Fine, she decided. She'd stay until it ended. But then she had discovered that all the seats were reserved. She appealed to one of the organizers, but was told that the best they could do for her was a folding chair at the back of the theater.

Outraged, she snarled, "Nobody makes me sit with the peons. I have two Emmys!"

Fuck it! She'd leave. But first, she had to pee. She charged into the john and was out of the stall in moments. Jessica, still at the mirrors, was fixing her hair. If Charmain saw her, she didn't register it. Jessica, noting the star's agitation, wondered if she should say hello, or just slip out quietly.

A female attendant hired for the event hovered obsequiously around Charmain, offered her a hand towel and brushes. Jessica had gathered up her purse and started to leave when Charmain, glaring at her own reflection in the mirror, snapped at the attendant:

"Where's the damn hairspray?"

"Oh, madam, I'm so sorry. We've run out. I just sent somebody to get some. If you can wait..."

Charmain gave her a look of pure fury. She reached into her purse, took out a single dime, and held it up to the embarrassed woman's face. She flipped the coin onto the counter and purred nastily:

"How do you like your tip, bitch?"

Jessica stopped like she'd been shot. In a moment of sheer horror, she realized it was the same voice she'd heard on her answering machine, saying, with that same vicious inflection:

"How did Steve like the flowers?"

Dear God! Jessica became conscious of her heart pounding, blood roaring in her ears.

That voice! Mocking her...

"How did Steve like the flowers?"

Jessica felt like she was going to faint. She grabbed a sink for support.

Before Jessica could react, Charmain stormed out past her. Still in shock, Jessica pulled herself together and followed her out, looking around desperately for Tull. She couldn't spot him in the crowd. She saw Charmain heading for the street. She made one last scan for Tull, then rushed out after her.

Outside, Charmain yelled at attendants to get her car. A valet stepped in front of Jessica, asked for her ticket. Still shocked and confused, she rummaged in her purse, finally found it, and handed it to him. As he ran off, Charmain's car was driven up. She got in and snarled at the valet, "No tip, asshole! You took too long."

Then she yelled, "Don't you know who I am?"

Something snapped in Jessica. She ran toward Charmain's car, screaming, "I know who you are, bitch! You rotten BITCH!"

Charmain roared off, not hearing it. Jessica's car pulled up. She threw the attendant five dollars. And took off after Charmain.

CHAPTER 61

10:12 P.M.
PACIFIC COAST HIGHWAY
LOS ANGELES

CHARMAIN rocketed through Beverly Hills, heading home. Behind her, Jessica grimly kept pace, blind rage boiling her blood, gripping the steering wheel and screaming out loud, "I'll kill you, you fucking bitch...*putana*...you die tonight..."

Her cell phone rang. It was Tull.

"Jessica, where are you? Somebody said they saw you leave. Are you okay?"

Jessica, voice high-pitched, hysterical, snapped, "You knew it was Charmain on that tape. Why didn't you tell me?"

"What? Jessica, where are you? What's going on?"

He listened, horrified, as she told him what she'd heard. And that she was pursuing Charmain through Beverly Hills.

"That murdering bitch killed my brother...my Stefano. Now I'm going to kill her."

Tull raced out of the theater onto Wilshire and waved frantically for his car, speaking urgently into his cell phone.

"Jessica...pull over and wait for me. Don't confront her, whatever you do. Let me explain what's going on..."

"I can't believe you never told me it was her," Jessica sobbed angrily. "You must have known!"

"No, no...I only suspected. I've been working on it. We all have. She won't get away with it..."

Jesus, thought Tull. He prayed no one was hacking into this bombshell conversation...

"Jessica, if you confront her, you'll warn her. Believe me, we've got it under control—"

"NO!" she shrieked. "Tonight that bitch pays. If there's anything left after I'm finished with her, you can have her..."

"Jessica..."

"She's pulling into a house off Beverly Glen..."

"That's where she lives. Goddamnit, Jessica, wait...wait..."

No answer.

"Don't do it, Jessica," he yelled.

The phone went dead.

He was in his car, racing up Wilshire. At that moment, Charmain, pulling into her driveway, looked into the rearview, startled, as a strange vehicle squealed to a stop behind her. Charmain reached into her purse, opened her door, and jumped out, adrenaline pumping, as Jessica Bell confonted her shrieking, "You killed my brother. You murdering BITCH!"

Without a word, Charmain slammed the 9mm Kahr against the side of Jessica's head, knocking her cold.

Panting from the stress, Charmain's eyes darted around the quiet neighborhood, watching to see if anyone had heard. No lights flicked on. No doors opened. Goddamn, she thought, this is some bad shit. Got to get her out of here. Get rid of her. Somehow, the bitch knew. Probably Tull had told her. Or maybe not. If he had, why wasn't he here? Or maybe Jessica had just figured it out somehow and come on her own. Maybe no one knew she was here. Should I call Vidal? No, he'll freak on me. Maybe turn me in. Fuck! Got to get rid of her. And her car…

Charmain reached down and took Jessica's car keys out of her hand, then dragged her limp body down the driveway. She opened the trunk of Jessica's car, lifted her body into it, and slammed the lid shut. She caught her breath, looked around. The neighborhood was still quiet. She went into the house, threw some clothes into a bag, came back outside, and locked the house up.

With a last look around, she got into Jessica's car and drove off with her in the trunk.

Moments later, Tull braked to a stop in Charmain's driveway, right behind her car. No sign of Jessica's car. He leaped out and ran up to the front door. The house was dark. He rang the bell and pounded frantically. Goddamnit, Charmain could be killing her in there. Do something! If they were in the house, Charmain wasn't going to respond to a fucking knock! Were they inside? He had to find out. Get control, he told himself…focus without focusing…think without thinking. He knocked once again. Getting no response, he dashed over to a flower bed and dug in the dirt until he found a good-sized rock.

He got back in his car, leaving the driver's side door ajar. He started his engine, put the car in gear, and looked at his watch. In Beverly Hills, at this hour, police response time would be less than two minutes. He stepped out of the car, set himself—and hurled the rock with all his force at the huge picture window facing the street.

Glass shattered, sprayed onto Charmain's living room carpet as Tull jumped back in the car and rocketed out of the driveway, lights extinguished. Seconds later, he pulled in to the curb a block away, turned off the engine, and stretched prone on the front seat. No more than a minute later, the car's interior was lit by red and blue flashes as a patrol car whipped by, headed in the direction of Charmain's house.

Tull kept his head down. He grabbed his cell phone, quickly punched out Jessica's car phone number. Her phone rang until it rolled over to voice mail. Just in case, he said after the beep, "Jessica, call me. Please!"

He cautiously poked his head up and made sure no one was walking on the darkened street before starting his car. He made a swift U-turn and headed back toward Charmain's before switching on his headlights. He slowed as he approached Charmain's driveway.

A Beverly Hills police cruiser, lights flashing, was parked at an angle in the driveway. Tull stopped and got out. Lights went on inside the house. He saw two cops darting in and out of rooms, guns drawn. Another police car pulled up. Two cops stepped out, hands on gun butts. Tull held both hands out in front of him. In his right hand was his press pass.

"*National Revealer,* fellas," Tull said. "Just passing by when I saw the action."

One cop, nodding in recognition, said, "Hey, Cameron Tull. I'll bet you've just come from that big screening party at the Academy Theater. Seems like the whole town was there tonight."

Tull nodded.

"I see you on TV all the time," the cop added.

Tull said, "This is Charmain Burns' house, right? What's going on, a break-in?"

Two cops emerged from the house, holstering their guns.

"Nobody inside," one said to the backups. "Somebody tossed a rock through the window."

Tull said, "I saw Charmain no more than thirty minutes ago at the Academy. You're sure no one's inside?"

The cops nodded. Tull gestured toward the car in the driveway.

"Funny, that's her car there. I've seen her in it enough times."

One cop shrugged. "She could have been limo-ed to the party."

Tull said, "That's more than likely. Look, if it helps, I have the phone number of her security guy, Vidal Delaney." One of the cops took the number and reached for the radio mike to call it in.

"What do you think?" one cop asked the two who'd arrived on the scene first. They shrugged.

One said, "Probably some homeless asshole who wandered up from the park on Little Santa Monica and tried a quick smash-and-grab. It doesn't look like anything's missing, but we can't tell until she gets here and looks it over. There might be jewelry or whatnot missing. Or maybe we surprised them by getting here so quick."

Tull said, "Can I check with you guys later for an update?"

The cop who'd recognized him from TV said, "Ask for me, Jerry Smith. Hey, the wife would love an autograph…"

Tull signed, got in his car. As he turned the ignition key, his mind was racing. Okay, Charmain and Jessica aren't in the house. But where's

Jessica's car? Christ! Should he get help from the cops? There'd be so many damn questions to answer, but…

He punched out Jessica's car phone number again. This time, he got a recorded message saying the caller was not available. Goddamnit! First no answer, now the phone is switched off. Did Jessica turn off her own phone? No way. It was almost certain that Charmain had Jessica prisoner in her own car.

A chill swept over Tull. Charmain had murdered once to keep her secret safe. There was the hint of at least one other murder in her past. If Jessica had been wound up enough to confront Charmain and tell her she knew she was involved in her brother's death, then…

But did Charmain have Jessica? After all, her car wasn't here. Could she have simply gone home after a catfight with Charmain? His gut told him no. He looked at the cops. Should he tell them? Have them put out an APB on Jessica's car? He had no idea where to begin looking for her. But he had to find her before it was too late. He made his decision, started to get out of his car and talk to the cops, when his cell phone chirped sharply. He punched it on.

"Yeah?"

"You were hoping to hear your friend's voice, right? Sorry to disappoint you."

Randak 2000.

Tull snapped, "Do you have her?"

Randak laughed. "Oh, no. But I know who does. And so do you. Let's not use any names on a cell phone. Don't worry. I've got them in sight and I'm following them. You start driving north on the Pacific Coast Highway. I'll call you again soon. And don't be foolish enough to inform anyone. It will mean great danger for your friend."

"Damnit…"

"You're lucky to have me around, Mr. Tull. I'm your only chance right now."

Tull exploded. "If that bitch hurts my friend, her days on this planet are numbered, pal—and yours."

Randak laughed, truly amused.

"How ironic. You don't know how perfectly you put that, sir. Soon…you will!"

The phone clicked off.

"Goddamnit!" Tull yelled.

He slammed the Aston-Martin into gear and took off. The cops standing in the driveway looked up sharply at the squeal of burning rubber.

CHAPTER 62

10:57 P.M.
PACIFIC COAST HIGHWAY
LOS ANGELES

TULL raced up the Pacific Coast Highway with Randak 2000 somewhere ahead of him. This guy is some piece of work, Tull marveled. He was everywhere. A wraith, a dybbuk, a scary demon from some unknown hell. Knock it off, he told himself. He's no fucking superman. That's just what he wants you to believe. Randak had the two women in sight because he'd been "observing" Charmain, as usual, and saw her kidnap Jessica.

Nearly twenty minutes passed. No call from Randak. Tull pounded the steering wheel in frustration. Christ, he thought, let's hope he didn't lose them. After a moment, he calmed down. So far, this stalker, or whatever the hell he was, had proven to be ruthlessly efficient. Fruitcake or not, he was a pro. He wouldn't blow a tail.

The phone rang. Randak. After hearing Tull's location, he said, "You're only about five minutes behind me. We're coming up on an area where there are cliffs and our friend keeps slowing down, looking everything over. She's obviously scouting for a place where she can pull off the road and get out of sight."

"Shit!" said Tull. "She's going to..."

Randak cut in sharply. "Remember, you're on a cell phone!"

Tull paused, then said, "She's going to do just what she did to our friend in Mexico."

Randak said, "You don't know that."

"Oh, but I do. A source of mine reported seeing her in Mexico at about the time of the...er, accident. My theory is that you were there and observed everything from a distance."

Tull looked down at the speedometer. The needle was floating just above one-hundred.

Randak said, "Wait. I think she's turning in...Yes, she is. Where are you now?

Wait, don't say it. I'm going to start hitting my brake lights repeatedly. Now! Can you see me?"

Tull was just starting up a long slope. He strained to see ahead. Traffic was thin, not many taillights ahead...

Yes! Now he saw it. Not even three-quarters of a mile ahead, at the top of the sharp rise. Blinking red taillights.

"I see you…I see your lights."

Randak said, "Good, I've got to turn in now. I don't want to give our friends any time alone. Don't miss the turnoff. It's just before the top of the slope. Two good-sized rocks and a clump of trees. Pull in, switch off your lights, and come in quietly on foot."

"Please don't let her…"

Randak cut in. "Leave this to me. Over and out." He clicked off.

A moment later, Tull spotted the turnoff. He switched off his lights and glided in. It was a grass track bordered on both sides by high underbrush.

He parked the car, got out quietly, and headed down the track. He crouched when he saw a faint glow of light through the brush ahead, then crept forward.

CHAPTER 63

11:30 P.M.
CLEARING OFF THE PCH
LOS ANGELES

CHARMAIN drove into the clearing, stopped the car about fifty feet from the edge of the dropoff ahead, set the emergency brake. She rolled the driver's side window down, killed the engine and removed the keys. She got out, walking to the edge of the cliff. Peering over at the rock-studded beach ninety feet down, she flashed on Baja. A body, falling.

...Buster. She'd liked Buster....

She shook her head, losing the thoughts. It always came to this; she didn't know why. Always came down to being in danger...from somebody.

She walked to the back of the car, put her purse on the ground. Smiled grimly at the banging noises inside the trunk. She unlocked it, opened the lid cautiously, reached in, wrestled Jessica onto the rock-studded gravel. She wasn't dead weight, but heavy. Conscious. Still groggy. Charmain dragged her up to the driver's side door and opened it, shoving her inside.

Jessica, her mind dulled by pain, tried to struggle, limbs heavy and useless. She opened her eyes and looked at Death, staring out the eyes of this devil-child who'd killed her brother.

God, she prayed, I need strength...must fight her...hurt her...Charmain's face...there...just inches away...jab my nails at her bitch eyes...help me God, NOW!...ah, no good...no strength...like slow motion...like paralysis...

A hand gripped her hair. Slammed her head into the doorpost. She went limp.

Charmain shoved Jessica down across the front seat, then leaned down and released the emergency brake, stepping back quickly and slamming the door. She braced both hands on the front post, straining to push the car down the gentle slope. Goddamn. Tougher than she'd thought. Gravity. Soon a friend, now the enemy. Then...wheels rolled, grudgingly. She strained. The car moved now, picked up speed...

And stopped short. Suddenly. Like it had rammed a brick wall. Still shoving, she mouthed, "Shit!" Looked up.

And screamed as if she'd never stop.

Randak's face—violently contorted, eyes bulging, teeth clenched—popped up over the hood, lit from beneath in the headlight glow like some hellish jack-o-lantern. His huge arms curled around the car's bumper, straining to hold it back. He opened his mouth in a fierce, bellowing roar that echoed in basso counterpoint to Charmain's shrieks of gut terror.

Thirty feet behind the car, Tull burst out of the underbrush, running dead at Charmain. She lunged for her bag on the ground, came up with the 9mm Kahr and aimed with both hands at Tull.

He stopped dead. "Give it up, Charmain," he said. "You can't kill us all."

"Why not?!" she shrieked. Fear she'd never felt gripped her hard. She jerked her head at Randak.

"He can't let go of the car," she screamed, "And you're fucked because I have the gun."

Tull put out his hands beseechingly. Oh God, he thought. Jessica. Got to get control. Be very cool and quiet…

"Look," he said, "nothing serious has happened yet, Charmain. So put the gun away and let's just talk this out."

A strained chuckle from Randak. He had an almost engaging smile on his still-contorted face.

"Yes, let's talk," he said tightly. "My arms are killing me."

"Then let go of the car," she snapped. "Just kill the bitch. That's what you do, you fucking stalker…right? Kill people?"

"I have killed, yes. Never for sport, or expedience. I've also saved lives. I'll save hers, if possible. She's no impediment to me. And Mr. Tull kept his promise to me not to tip the police off about you. I'm grateful. You should be too."

"Oh, right, you fucking weirdo. I should be grateful you're saving me from jail. So you can fucking rape me, or kill me."

Randak, the strain showing in his knotted neck muscles as he held the car back, said, "I am here to deliver you to your destiny."

Tull said quietly, "Randak. Please. Hold on. Don't let her…go. Charmain, let me put the emergency brake on."

"Oh, how sweet," she mocked. "You think I'll let your girlfriend live, Tull? Let her help you put me in jail?"

"You won't go to jail, Charmain," he said. "This is America. We don't put celebrities in jail. For drugs, maybe. But never for murder. Look, if I've got this whole mess figured out right, you never planned to kill Steve. We can work it out. Put the gun down. What we've got here is kind of a stalemate, anyway."

"Yeah? Well, I'll fucking fix that," she snarled.

Whirling, she fired three shots at Randak. He ducked to avoid the buzzing nine-millimeter slugs, stumbled. The car inched forward.

"Tull," he shouted. "I'm losing the car. RUN AT HER!"

Charmain now turned the gun on Tull. He lunged to his left, grabbed a fist-sized rock. The ground erupted, bullets pounding dirt inches from his hand. Tull made a diving roll into the underbrush as Charmain kept firing. He kept rolling until the shooting stopped.

Goddamn. Silence. He fought to control his rasping breath. So far, so good. But he had to help Randak hold the car or Jessica was dead. Leaping up, he yelled into the sudden stillness.

"You're fucked, Charmain. You're out of bullets. I've got this rock. And I'm going to circle behind you and bash your fucking brains in, you murdering whore!"

Charmain froze. She heard the passion in his voice, knew he'd kill without a qualm. She shot a look at Randak and shivered. No fear in *his* eyes. Just a slight mocking smile—the weird calmness of supreme confidence.

The underbrush rustled behind her. Charmain whirled. Snatching up her bag, she ran flat-out back up the path toward the highway. Heart pounding faster than her feet. Running, running, running through the dark...like a little girl in a nightmare. Like the little girl *she'd* been...before conquering her fear of monsters that come in the night.

CHAPTER 64

**9:52 A.M.
TULL'S HOUSE
MALIBU**

THIRTY-SIX hours later, Tull was closeted in his study, working the phones. He glanced up at the antique Westclox on the wall. 9:52 a.m. He'd looked in on Jessica, asleep in the guest room, about an hour ago. Mrs. Gordon was keeping a sharp eye on her. She seemed fine, thank God. The doctors had told him to look for signs of concussion.

He'd rushed her to the hospital after that bizarre night on the cliffs. She'd been unconscious, but he'd revived her, kept her awake and responsive as he drove to the emergency room. Despite two blows to the head, abrasions and bruises, she was going to be okay. No apparent brain damage. They'd kept her overnight for observation, then released her to his care.

As he drove her back to Malibu the next day, she couldn't stop talking about the horror of that night.

"Who is this Randak person?" she asked.

"A stalker, I think," said Tull. "Obsessed with Charmain. And deadly. He fits the profile of stalkers who end up killing their prey."

"Randak saved my life and wants to kill that bitch? Now he's really my hero," said Jessica grimly.

The irony made Tull smile. It was no joke to Jessica. She was brooding, angry. The woman who'd murdered her brother had nearly killed her.

Jessica pumped him relentlessly. He hadn't shared what he'd known about Charmain; now she was determined to know everything. When he'd laid it all out, she said quietly, "Okay, I understand that there's not enough evidence to nail her right now. But there are other ways of dealing with a monster. Steve's death must be avenged."

He looked over at her. There were moments when she sounded so...European. Her eyes closed suddenly and she slept until they got to his house. Mrs. Gordon came out to meet them and took charge, setting her up in the guest bedroom. Jessica slept throughout the day, awoke long enough for a light meal. Tull was relieved he didn't have to face her questions right now. It gave him time to concentrate on the matter at hand: finding Charmain. She'd disappeared after running up the track from the cliffs toward the Pacific Coast Highway. Since that moment, the search he'd instituted the day before had come up zippo! No one had seen her.

She hadn't been home, used her car or credit cards.

What the hell had happened to her? She'd been on foot, having driven to the cliffs in Jessica's car. Had she hitched a ride? If so, where did she go? Or...and this thought kept buzzing at Tull's subconscious...did Randak have her?

He replayed the surreal nightmare in his mind...Charmain firing shots...his dive into the underbrush...the sound of running feet as Charmain escaped...Randak grunting as he struggled to hold the car...and his own breath loud in his chest as he raced back into the clearing and yanked on the car's emergency brake. He'd pulled Jessica out, unconscious but alive. Turned to Randak, wanting to thank him for saving Jessica's life. But—surprise, surprise—the man of mystery had disappeared. Just as he always did.

Thinking back on it, Tull figured Charmain had a good two-minute lead on Randak. Could he have caught up with her? It was possible. The man was almost superhuman. Tull could see him striding like a great cat up the path, pouncing on Charmain, knocking her cold and casually swinging her limp body over his shoulder.

He grinned. Shit! I'm making him sound like Tarzan.

Once again, he asked himself: who is Randak 2000? A stalker? Did he plan to kill Charmain? Make her his sex slave? Or was he harmless? Just an obsessed fan? After all, he hadn't harmed her. And he certainly could have, almost at will. Randak seemed to be...waiting for something. What? Wacko stuff like phases of the moon? Or did he hear voices emanating from the fillings in his teeth? Tull had dealt with a lot of loonie-tuners in his time. This guy felt different. Down deep in his bones, Tull knew that Randak 2000 was no harmless coo-coo. Yet he wasn't a garden variety stalker, either. What was his "mission," as he called it? When would he move to accomplish his objective?

The phone rang. Laddy Burford. Tull had talked to him the day before, asking him to track down Charmain.

"Tull, she's nowhere to be found," Laddy said. "I'm getting worried. It's not like her not to call. We talk practically every day. The studio keeps phoning, asking where the hell she is. I've vamped them by hinting she might be sleeping off a big hangover, but they're getting weird, talking about calling the cops. Vidal Delaney called. I gave him the same vague story. He bought it. Told me to get her sobered up and on the phone to him. Mike Kelso's going crazy, of course. Won't leave me alone."

Tull thought a minute. "Look, I asked you if you knew any friends she might visit out of town. But what about out-of-town property she might own? Maybe in Florida. Or Savannah? She have a vacation hideaway, anything like that?"

"No. I think she would have told me."

Tull sighed. "Keep trying, okay?"

He hung up. Damn! He'd done all he could think of to get a line on her whereabouts. Checked her credit cards for activity, called rental car places, had a police source check computers for any DOAs or hospital Jane Does that fit her description. He'd checked with one of his oldest, most valuable sources—an L.A. mortgage broker who could tell you who owned what property, what they'd paid, and how many times they'd mortgaged it. The broker found no property owned by Charmain, apart from the Beverly Hills house.

Tull shrugged mentally. When in doubt, light a fire under Vidal Delaney. Nothing to lose. He called him, made sure they were on a secure line, and related everything that had happened the other night—from Charmain kidnapping Jessica, to her shooting at them on the cliff. Then he trotted out his bluff.

"Jessica Bellini wants to press charges, Vidal. Assault, kidnapping, attempted murder for openers."

Vidal played it tough, just as he'd figured.

"You get crazier by the minute, Tull. A good lawyer would make mincemeat of your story. You have no direct evidence, no witnesses. And it would be Charmain's word against Jessica's."

Tull pressed it. "No evidence? Jessica's injuries didn't occur by magic. There are nine millimeter slugs to be dug out of the dirt up there on that cliff. Footprints. Tire prints. Oh, there's evidence, Vidal."

"I'm beginning to tire of this conversation, Tull."

"Let me wake you up, pal. Buster Brown's dead. He fell off a cliff in Baja. Note the key word in both incidents, by the way—'cliff.' Interesting, huh? A modus operandi. Now, I've got a witness who can tie Charmain to Buster in L.A. I've got another who spotted her in Baja the day Buster died. And there's another witness. A guy named Randak 2000. I think Randak witnessed Charmain shoving Buster off the cliffs in Baja. I think I can talk him into testifying for us. And if he won't, we'll subpoena him. Now, I think that's a shitstorm of trouble for your client—and maybe for you, depending on how much of this you've been covering up. Hell, you might even qualify as an accessory after the fact to murder.

"You awake yet, Vidal? I'd advise you to find your client and turn her in."

Vidal went silent, deeply shaken. Randak 2000 again! The stalker who'd invaded Charmain's bedroom. Whose letters, according to the shrink, fit the killer profile. This was getting heavy.

He cleared his throat. "Tull, you're not making a whole lot of sense, but why don't you let me get in contact with my client for you? I think there's a lot of confusion here and I'd like to help you clear it up. I understand your paper's passion in this matter. I'll talk to my client. Give me twenty-four hours before you do anything."

"I'll give you until tomorrow morning."

"Okay. I'll try to convince Charmain to talk to you exclusively. Give you the 'untold story,' if there is one. I believe in my client's innocence, but I want to cooperate. Believe me, Tull, it's not what you think. Truth is stranger than fiction."

Tull said wearily, "You're telling me?"

He hung up. That hadn't gone too badly. Now he had Vidal working for him. He looked again at a map of the area where the encounter with Charmain and Randak had taken place. His eyes traversed remote hills and brushy canyons. Where was she? Still on foot? Hiding out in the woods? Doubtful. A hotel? No, she's too recognizable to stay in a first-class place. Holed up in some cheap motel? No, most likely, she'd run into someone, or somewhere, familiar.

Unless Randak had her.

Suddenly, Tull had an idea. He called his mortgage broker source again. A machine answered. Tull left a detailed message that began: "It's just a hunch, but I need you to make another check for me. This time, I want you to look for something else…"

The hunch paid off fast. He got a call back in under an hour. He'd asked the broker to run a check on real estate owned by Mike Kelso and Vidal Delaney, plus Charmain's lovers and pals: Laddy, Leida, Connor, Bonnie, and Dina.

Jackpot! Bonnie Farr owned a cabin in the mountains above Carmel.

His source got him the phone number. On impulse, Tull dialed it. An answering machine came on. A female voice, not Charmain. Probably Bonnie Farr. Tull hesitated until the beep, then shrugged and thought, What the hell! He started recording a message on the machine:

"Charmain, this is Cameron Tull. Uh…I know you're there. We have to talk. If you don't pick up right now, I'm going to let the cops know your location. I haven't told them everything I know yet. But I will, unless you talk to me right now. Charmain, it's no use pretending you're not there because…"

Suddenly, a click. Yeah! It was her! Furious, spewing curses.

"You cocksucker, Tull, you fucking bastard, I hate you and your whore girlfriend, that stuck-up piece of shit, I'd like to—"

"CHARMAIN…CALM DOWN!"

He yelled, got her attention. Started talking fast and she calmed down gradually as he told her what he knew.

It shocked her how he'd put it all together. Jesus! For the first time, it hit her. Jail. She could go to jail. Prison. Lose everything. Never be a star again. Never play "Medusa." Surprising herself, she started to weep. Oh God. What do I do? Got to play for time.

Tull kept talking. "Are you hearing me, Charmain? I want to come there and talk to you. I think I can help you if you make a clean breast of everything. Tell me your story and I'll tell it to the people. They'll understand. They'll be sympathetic, understand the strain you were under. And I can help you with the authorities. *The Revealer* has a lot of clout,

Charmain. Think about it."

"Okay," she said finally. "Okay. I hear what you're sayin'...and I'll think it over. But you've got to call the cops off. You hear?"

"Charmain, I haven't told the cops anything. I did talk to Vidal and told him what's gone down. But I didn't tell him where you are. I think he'd advise you to talk to me, then turn yourself in before this gets any worse. Like I told you the other night, celebrities get off easy in America."

Suddenly, she wanted to believe him. That somehow she'd get off, not lose everything.

"Give me a few hours to think it over, Tull," she said quietly. "I'll get some advice from Vidal and Mike Kelso, maybe. I don't know what I'm going to do. God, I need time to think. So don't tell anyone where I am, you swear? Not even Vidal, okay?"

He gave her his home number. They agreed she'd call him that evening at eight o'clock sharp. Tull looked at his watch. It was 12:35.

"How do I know you won't run?" he said. "You'd have about a seven-hour headstart."

Charmain sighed wearily. "How far can I run with a face as famous as mine? And I'm too tired to run."

"Eight o'clock, Charmain. You don't call back, I blow the whistle."

He hung up. Great! He'd found her. Now I need some help. Time to tell the Queen of Scots what's going down. And the cops? Maybe...

He got up to stretch. And was suddenly aware of Jessica standing in the open doorway of the study.

"It was her you were talking to, wasn't it?" she said, a strange look in her eyes. "So you've found her. Why aren't you calling the police. WHY? Is getting a story all that matters to you?"

Her voice rose and he moved to calm her. She pulled away from him, glaring. "Jessica, if I call in the cops right now, she'll never be convicted. There's not enough solid evidence. I know you want revenge. So do I. But we've got to do this right, or believe me, she'll get off scot-free. A good lawyer would laugh us out of court.

"This has to be done carefully, Jessica. There's no really solid evidence against her. If I can get Charmain to talk to me, to confess, we'll have a much better chance of seeing her punished."

Jessica screamed, "That bitch will get away with murder because she's a star! I WON'T let that happen."

She began to sob hysterically. "Please, let me handle this the way it's done in the Old Country," she cried. "Just tell me where she is, Cameron. Please. My father knows people who can take care of this..."

Tull, shaken by the intensity of her emotion, went to her. This time, she let him enfold her in his arms. She was shaking, sobbing, pleading. He gently refused to tell her where Charmain was hiding out.

"Jessica, please trust me. And stop agitating yourself. You've had a very severe trauma and you've got to rest and recover. Please, stop thinking about this. Everything is on course, believe me."

He held her tightly. Finally, she subsided, became strangely calm.

"Cameron, I'll be fine. I'm going to take a tranquilizer, lie down. I'm so tired. Will you be here?"

"Not for a while. I've got to head into town for a meeting at *The Revealer*. Mrs. Gordon will stay with you, of course."

He kissed her and said he'd be back by eight o'clock.

CHAPTER 65

1:00 P.M.
TULL'S OFFICE AT *THE REVEALER*
LOS ANGELES

TULL arrived at *The Revealer* to find a stack of mail, e-mail, and phone messages. As was her custom, Eva verbalized what she thought was important. She was rarely wrong.

"You just got a call from CT-440," she said, using the number assigned to that particular source. It was a secure way sources could identify themselves or be identified on the phone or e-mail—and the code kept their actual names off databases or documents floating around the office. Tull had so many sources, Eva often had to tell him the name behind the code. Not this time, though.

"Good old 440," he said. "He have anything for me?"

Eva held up a document. "It just arrived by messenger. He called from a pay phone, sounded real nervous. All he said was, 'I'm sending what he wanted. It's been sanitized. If he has military or CIA sources, go there. Keep me out of this. It's too heavy.'"

She handed the package over. Tull ripped it open. It was the confidential LAPD file of ex-cop George Tanner. He looked it over and knew immediately that CT-440—aka Fred, his friendly LAPD source—was right. The record had been sanitized. None of what Fred had told him about Tanner was written anywhere in it. But an official photo proved what he'd wanted to know: George Tanner—aka Randak 2000—was his mystery man.

Go to the military or CIA, Fred had said. Tull felt a warm glow. For once, he didn't have to rack his brains. Dalton Lupo, his uber-boss, still had clout at The Company. But Tull had a great CIA source. A guy who'd been his roommate at college during senior year, Ford Massey. He'd signed up during a CIA campus recruiting drive and rose rapidly through the ranks to a top slot in the Director's Office. Massey had asked for Tull's help more than once.

Now it was payback time.

"Eva, get me CT-27." A moment later, she said, "He's on."

Tull picked up, said, "I assume we're now scrambled?"

CT-27 laughed. "What's the good of being a spook if you can't play with high-tech toys?"

"Quit calling yourself a 'spook' like you're a cloak-and-dagger guy," Tull needled. "You're a Washington bureaucrat."

"So you wouldn't believe I was just parachuted into Kashmir?"

"Would you believe I just had sex with Catherine Zeta-Jones?"

"I'm just happy somebody is. Who is, by the way?"

"I lost track after Michael Douglas," said Tull. "Look, I need some fast help. An ex-LAPD cop in his late thirties had some connection with the military and/or you guys a few years back. Name's George Tanner, T-A-N-N-E-R. I know you won't tell me a damn thing if he's active, but I think he's 'retired.' I repeat, I need this fast. Just a rundown on what he is, what makes him tick. Can do?"

"I owe you one. I'll get back."

"You owe me more than one, old buddy. And I'm talking minutes here, not hours. Okay?"

"Okay."

Two hours later, CT-27 called back on a scrambler and gave Tull a verbal synopsis of George Tanner's eye-popping profile. He'd been a U.S. Marine, then was transferred to the Navy Seals, where he became legendary for his physical prowess and daring. Tanner participated in some deep-cover insertions into unfriendly Third World countries and was decorated for bravery. But as he rose up the promotion ladder and got his first crack at command, "psychological problems" emerged. He was judged too ruthless, too daring, to make a properly cautious leader. That killed him for promotion in the SEALS—but it was a quality that greatly interested the CIA, who recruited him for "wet work."

"I can't reveal much detail here," Ford Massey told him. "But as time went on, Tanner gradually went a bit loony on us. Not unusual in the line of work he was involved in. We subject these guys to ongoing scrutiny by our in-house shrinks, who are empowered to use methods that would not be, ah...kosher, let's say, in civilian life."

Tull said, "Let me guess. Truth drugs like sodium pentothal, hallucination-inducers on the order of LSD. Sedative-hypnotics. And probably a few things we civilians have never heard of. In other words, to quote the Gestapo in World War II movies, 'Ve haff vays of making you talk.' Am I in the ballpark here, pal?"

CT-27 chuckled. "No comment. But what emerged was a weird mental picture. Very weird."

Tull sighed. "Come on, open up a little here."

"Look, all I can tell you is that in George Tanner's mind, he is a pure warrior, sent here to carry out a vital mission for his leaders."

"Sent here from where? Who's he working for? Are you saying he's a spy for a foreign nation?"

"No. Not exactly. What I'm saying is...George Tanner believes that he's from another planet."

"WHAT?"

"The planet 'Kaldan,' to be exact."

"You're serious?"

"He's very convincing. Even pointed out the location of the home planet on a map of the known universe. It's a long, long way from here. But he says they travel through space after transforming themselves into beams of light."

"Wait a minute! Are you telling me The Company believed him?"

"Hardly. What I'm trying to convey is that he's incredibly convincing. His story has amazing internal logic. He's mesmerizing when he tells it. And he totally believes it."

"Did he call himself 'Randak 2000?'"

"Ah, you do know him, then?"

"Not as well as I'd like to. What happened then?"

"We didn't consider him a security risk. In fact, our evaluation shows he's incredibly loyal and proud of his association with the Seals and The Company. So we eased him out, gave him early retirement and a modest pension. He was finished for the military and government. As often happens, he went into police work. Joined the LAPD. And attracted the attention of a weird little cell of right-wing, upper-echelon cops who financed their racist agenda with highly-paid dirty work for politicians, movie moguls, right-wing millionaires, and the like.

"Tanner was ordered to eliminate an Internal Affairs cop who was about to uncover this sinister little cabal. He was not told in advance that his target was a brother officer—not that it would have mattered. Orders were orders.

"The, ah, 'execution' was never solved. The scandal never surfaced. The heat was intense, but the department closed ranks and quietly solved the problem. Tanner was retired early on a bogus disability pension."

Massey had faxed over a photo of Tanner. It was Randak 2000. Typed below the picture was his current address and phone number.

Gotcha, Tull exulted.

He stared at the hard, flat eyes. How do I keep this beast in his cage? Rattling the bars might work. Or would it send him on a rampage?

Time to find out.

CHAPTER 66

2:23 P.M.
RANDAK 2000'S APARTMENT
LOS ANGELES

RANDAK 2000 sat at the desk in his apartment, updating his star log with a report to the higher beings he served. He was agitated; he'd lost track of Charmain. For the first time since stepping up his random surveillance of her months ago, he had no idea where she was, or how to find her. The situation had become crucial. New signs in the night skies signaled that the ascension time was imminent.

He cursed himself for letting Charmain escape that night on the cliffs. As he'd raced up the rutted path after her to the Pacific Coast Highway, the spiraling whine of an 18-wheeler accelerating up through the gears had echoed down the slope. He yelled in frustration, knowing what it meant. Charmain had been picked up by a trucker. By the time he got to his car and drove up the PCH, it was hopeless. Every brightly-lit diesel rig looked like every other.

The lapse in self-discipline was unforgivable. He'd allowed The Chosen One to disappear. Hopefully, she would surface unharmed. But there was always the outside chance that she'd been injured, even killed. If the unthinkable had occurred, his mission was a failure. And he was unworthy as a warrior of Kaldan. Like any professional military man, he conducted a post-op evaluation of the action.

Verdict: He should have allowed Charmain to kill Tull's girlfriend, while he mounted an unobtrusive rear-guard surveillance.

Randak paced the apartment. Actually, his best hope of locating Charmain was through Tull. *The Revealer* would be in full cry after her. And they were acknowledged specialists in finding hard-to-find people. If Tull got to her first, he'd more than likely turn her over to the police.

Randak couldn't let that happen. Charmain was the only hope for his planet. He had to find her. Carry out his mission.

The phone rang twice. The answering machine computer voice, not his own, asked the caller to leave a message after the beep.

Randak's skin twitched as the caller spoke:

"George?…George Tanner. Please pick up if you're there. I think you recognize my voice by now."

Tull.

Randak 2000 moved across the room swiftly, drawing a weapon.

"George—or do you still prefer Randak 2000?—I was wondering if our friend was with you, by any chance? I can't seem to locate her. If you're there, I imagine you're looking out the window right about now to see if the place is surrounded..."

Randak 2000 stepped back from the window. Smiled thinly. No question about it, Tull was a worthy adversary. A true pro. Somehow he'd penetrated CIA security. And he'd figured out that Charmain just might be here. She wasn't, of course. But now Randak knew that Tull was in the dark about her whereabouts.

Just as he was.

"...Nobody knows I'm in touch with you, George. So if you do have her, don't do anything...rash. And even if you don't have her, please call me. Perhaps we can help each other."

Pause. Tull chuckled drily.

"After all, we've been a great team in the past. So let's talk. I don't want to say my direct home line on a machine. But you know it. Call me."

The machine clicked off. Randak 2000 sat quietly for a long time, assessing the situation, measuring each bit of intelligence he'd gathered against the overall mission objective. He needed one final piece of information to make his decision. He logged onto the Web, contacting his astronomer friend in Australia. After a brief conversation, he logged off again, convinced. It was time for ascension.

He sat at his desk, wrote out his mission plan, checked it carefully. And burned it. Then he opened his star log again and carefully wrote a long entry. It took him the better part of an hour.

When he'd finished, he dialed the direct line to Tull's study.

Jessica had taken a pill and was napping on the sofa in the study when the phone woke her. She looked at her watch. Nearly four o'clock. She started to doze off again, ignoring the phone. If it's Cameron, I'll pick up, she thought drowsily.

Call screening clicked on. She sat bolt upright as she heard the caller say:

"Randak, Mr. Tull. If you are there, please respond. Otherwise, here is a number you can call at your earliest convenience. No one will answer, of course, but I will know you called and will respond quickly. It is important that we talk because I have..."

Dio mio! Randak. A voice she'd never heard. The mystery man who'd thwarted Charmain's murderous assault. Torn for a moment, she impulsively picked up the phone.

"Hello...um...he's not here right now. This is..."

"Ah, Miss Bell. I hope you're recovering from everything you went through."

"Yes...er, thank you. Thank you for saving my life."

"I was glad to help. I'm a big fan of Mr. Tull's."

"And of Charmain's?"

Randak hesitated. How much did she know?

"I have a...professional interest in Miss Burns. That's why I happened to observe her driving off with you."

Jessica shuddered involuntarily. How bizarre. A homicidal stalker who considers himself "professional." Tull believed he was dangerous, even lethal. How strange that a man who'd saved her life was a ruthless killer focused on...no, obsessed by Charmain.

A thought half-formed in Jessica's mind.

"Is Mr. Tull in contact with Miss Burns?" Randak was asking.

Jessica, who'd seen death in Charmain's eyes, heard it in Randak's voice. She paused, looked down at Tull's phone console. So...high-tech...what seemed like dozens of push-buttons. Her eyes focused sharply on one of them. And she suddenly realized, with absolute clarity, that she could win swift, sure justice for her brother simply by...pushing the right button.

So simple. So...ruthless. And why not? What justice could she expect from the kingdom of Hollywood? What La-La Land court would convict a major female TV star of killing a tabloid editor?

She stared down at the phone. Go on. Push the button on the bitch! If you don't, who will?

Ask yourself this question: IS the state of California capable of strapping a Hollywood sex symbol down into that wooden chair in the gas chamber? Of pushing the button that drops cyanide pellets into the bucket of acid beneath it?

In your dreams.

It was a compelling fantasy, nonetheless. Jessica ran the scene in her head:

Charmain writhing against the leather restraints...gasping...crying...

Choke and *die,* bitch!

"Miss Bell...?"

"I...I think I can help you," she heard herself say. "Um...he was talking to Charmain on the phone earlier. I don't know where she is. He wouldn't tell me. She said she's calling him here at eight this evening. But...I don't know the number."

A pause.

"Then...how can you help me?" asked Randak.

Jessica went back over her conversation with Tull. Yes, he'd said that he'd found Charmain's number and called her. She stared down at the phone. All those buttons...

In Mafia argot, a "button" was a cold-blooded killer.

Push a button.

The phrase was a metaphor for death by execution.

She could push a button. On Charmain.

If she had the balls.

She asked Randak, "If you had the phone number, could you get her address?"

"Yes," he said sharply. "Do you have her number?"

"No.... but isn't there a way to figure out a phone number by hearing the beeps on a touch-tone phone?"

An intake of breath from Randak.

"The re-dial button..."

"Yes," she said. "That's what I was thinking. If I push the button, it should dial her number. Because Cameron didn't make any calls after the one to her. I know because I was standing right here until he left. So..."

"Don't touch that re-dial button yet, Miss Bellini. Let me tell you exactly what to do. Hang up the phone. I will call you back in less than one minute."

"Alright."

Randak hung up, walked swiftly to a cabinet, and selected a portable micro-cassette tape recorder. He went back to the desk and punched his own re-dial button.

Tull's number rang. As Jessica picked up, Randak punched his "speakerphone" button, pressed "record" on the tape machine, and held it close to the phone receiver.

"Alright, Miss Bell," he said. "Put me on speaker phone."

"It's on," she said.

"Good. Now, being very careful not to hit any other button on the phone, push re-dial."

She hesitated, shook her head to dispel the images swirling through her mind...

Steve, plunging to his death, eyes wide and imploring...

Charmain, face twisted with rage, smashing her in the face...

Randak torturing a helpless, whimpering Charmain...

Tull's eyes, disapproving...

She heard her father's voice, speaking to her when she was a little girl. Saying, "Life is a series of events set in motion by our actions."

Such a simple thing...to push a button.

She spoke, and the words sounded to her thick and slurred and slow, as if she were on the wrong speed somehow.

"Are...you...going to...?"

His voice cut through, hard.

"Charmain killed your brother, Miss Bell."

Jessica pushed the button.

A chirpy, weirdly musical sequence of beeps filled the room. Randak said:

"Hang up the phone so the call doesn't go through."

Jessica had a sudden wild thought of letting the call connect.

Screaming a warning to Charmain.

She hung up.

Randak said, "No one will know we spoke. No one will know that I have her number. I suggest that you never speak of this, Miss Bell. Believe me, you've done the right thing. Just put it out of your mind. Goodbye."

Jessica hung up. She walked through the French doors to the balcony. She looked up into the sunlight.

Justice.

Or revenge?

No matter. The death warrant was signed.

Savage ecstasy pounded in her. She swayed, caught herself. What, she wondered, could ever match this thrilling intensity?

CHAPTER 67

11:43 P.M.
CHARMAIN'S HIDEAWAY
MOUNTAINS ABOVE CARMEL

CHARMAIN awoke drenched in sweat. A nightmare.

She'd been walking naked through a deserted theater district, carrying her head in her right hand; gripping it by the mass of writhing, hissing snakes that had replaced her hair. The eyes in her detached head brightened, looked up at a blazing theater marquee that dominated the street. The lips curved in a mischievous smile. On the marquee, spelled out in bright lights, was the dream:

"CHARMAIN BURNS IS MEDUSA!"

For a long moment after she jerked awake on the strange bed in the cabin, Charmain lay still, shivering, disoriented. Where was she? The nightmare was still playing in her head. Shit! Didn't need a $200-an-hour shrink to figure out what it meant.

She'd lost her fucking head over this "Medusa" role.

After escaping from Randak and Tull nearly forty-eight hours before, Charmain had run out onto the Pacific Coast Highway, thrown out her thumb. Immediately, an 18-wheeler had braked to a stop a hundred yards down the road. The trucker motioned her to haul ass. She climbed up into the cab, slammed the door.

"Thanks!" she said. "I need to go up the coast."

A grizzled old guy. She knew right away he didn't recognize her. Busting his ass on long hauls, he probably never watched TV. She caught him sneaking a sidelong glance at her torn, dirt-streaked dress.

"I was on a blind date," she said, not looking at him. "The jerk got angry when I wouldn't put out. So I jumped out of his car and hid until he drove away."

The trucker shrugged, checked her out. She knew he was thinking about what she'd said. The part about putting out.

He looked straight ahead at the road and said, "How far you goin'?"

Turned out he was a nice old guy. She talked him into detouring off the PCH and dropping her off on a secondary road about a half-mile from the rutted dirt track that led to the perfect haven—a remote cabin owned by Bonnie Farr. She climbed down out of the cab and walked around to the driver's side, looking up at him.

"I know you've been trying to figure what I'd look like naked, old man. Here's a taste."

She shrugged the top of her low-cut dress down to her waist. She was bra-less.

The trucker's eyes lit up like a kid at Christmas. His hand slammed the side of the cab and he hollered.

"HOOOoooooEEEEeee!"

Diesel horns split the night air with a blatting howl.

"BBBRRRAAAAWWWWWWWWW."

He waved. She did a little coochie shake. Stood there, pulling her dress back up over her tits while he wound the diesel through the gears. Watched the lights disappear around a bend. She felt very alone.

She hiked up the deserted road. Farther than she'd remembered. Nothing but woods. A half moon, so it wasn't dark. No cars passed her. This was the boonies. Nobody except Bonnie and her lesbian gang ever came up this road to what she jokingly referred to as her hunting lodge. Charmain smiled, recalling the one time she'd been up here. It was a girls-only weekend. Bonnie had passed out shotguns to a few of the diesel dykes. They'd crashed around the woods in their Doc Martens boots, shooting at panicked squirrels. After an afternoon of raucous outdoor fun, the butch babes had stripped off sweaty flannel shirts and jeans, got naked with their lipstick lesbian girlfriends—and Charmain. It had been fun.

Charmain found the turnoff, hiked up the last stretch, a rutted dirt track, to the cabin. She was exhausted. God, I hope the key is hidden in the same place. Under the white rock beside the porch. It was. She walked in, flicked on the lights, went straight to the bar and poured herself a shot of Wild Turkey. Man, it tasted good. After a bath and two more whiskies, she fell into bed and slept twelve hours straight.

Next day, she microwaved frozen bagels. Made a pot of coffee. Took a walk in the woods and pondered her situation. Stoked by rage, she wove a fantasy of killing Tull herself. She'd hunt him down in Malibu, shoot him from cover. Use one of Bonnie's rifles from the gun case. She walked quickly back to the cabin, sat down with pencil and paper, tried to plan it all out. Suddenly, she was rampaging through the cabin flinging things, frustrated and furious. Screaming, I'm so fucking STUPID! If Tull was killed, she'd be the prime suspect, goddamnit! What was wrong with her? Why couldn't she think clearly? Why had she kidnapped Jessica? She could have just called the Beverly Hills cops and had her arrested as a fucking wacko trespasser. And why hadn't the hitman she'd hired done his job on Tull? Shit, how did she even know if the guy was a hitman? He was just some voice on a phone. Why hadn't that lying prick offed Tull when he was supposed to?

She started sobbing. Hated that. God, I need to talk to someone. Not Vidal. He'd drive her nuts. Someone totally sympathetic. Someone who truly cared about her. Laddy? No, he'd never get it. She didn't need anyone judging her.

She dialed Mike Kelso's number. Got his machine.

She left her number, not saying where she was.

CHAPTER 68

3:59 P.M.
RANDAK 2000'S APARTMENT
LOS ANGELES

RANDAK 2000 hung up the phone after his conversation with Jessica. He looked around his apartment, knowing he'd never see it again, and reflected on the exquisite emotion of revenge. Its power. How mysteriously it could change a gentle soul, a Jessica Bellini, into a demon spirit capable of monstrous betrayal, savage violence, even murder. He remembered vividly the pounding exhilaration when it had first possessed him. He'd been so young. But you never forget the first blood you take. The face of his mother's friend leaped into his mind...that weak mouth, begging...

He smiled. No, Jessica, you'll never forget. You'll revisit the moment of vengeance, over and over, until memory dies forever.

Randak shrugged. Time to move. He briefly re-checked the entry he'd just finished in the large, weathered leather journal that was his star log. It was headed, "Final Report." He opened the top drawer of his desk and pulled out a FedEx envelope. He addressed it carefully, placed the journal in it. He went to a hidden floor safe, took out a bundle of cash and a large ring of keys. It was all he'd take.

He was about to leave when the phone rang again. A separate line, not the one Tull had called on. This line rang only when another phone, in a location known only to Randak, called to signal that a message had been recorded on its answering machine. Randak dialed the remote location. It rang twice, connected. An answering machine clicked on. A voice spoke. Randak 2000 actually laughed aloud. How incredibly ironic, he thought.

It was Charmain. Calling "the hitman."

"...and I just don't understand why the FUCK you haven't...you know...why you haven't done the job yet, goddamnit! It's important you do it right now...tonight...please...and listen, I've made it easy for you...I've arranged for him to be in his study later...at eight o'clock...okay?...please, don't let me down...I'll double your fee...leave a message on my home machine...just something vague so I know you got this...and that you'll do the job tonight...please?"

Randak laughed again, delighted. Alone and without resources, the Chosen One raged on, undaunted. He phoned her home machine and left a message:

"I understand...and will comply. Do not be concerned."

He hung up. So Tull hadn't been lying when he said he couldn't locate Charmain. But why had Tull called him? He knew why. A sacred rule of combat was: confuse the enemy. Tull had called to fake him out. Warn him off. Let him know that his cover was penetrated and Tull knew how to find him. The message was clear: lay off Charmain.

Time was now of the essence. He left the apartment and easily spotted the tail he knew Tull would put on him. He walked a few blocks, turned into an alley that cut through a block of buildings. Halfway down was a wire mesh gate that cut off access to the next street. Randak walked up to it, selected the key he'd had made many months ago for just such a moment, and walked through, locking it behind him. He looked back, saw the tail run up to the gate and shake it in frustration. Randak emerged from the alley, checked the street. Clear. He walked to a closed van parked in a private lot.

He drove to a grimy industrial area in downtown L.A., not far from Parker Center, his police alma mater. Pulled up to the bay he'd rented since CIA days. Leaning over to reach under the dashboard, he flipped a hidden switch, then turned on the radio to a set frequency. He listened to a pulsing tone for a moment, then turned it off. Good. Security had not been pentrated since his last visit. He got out of the van, unlocked the door, and drove in. He turned on the lights, pulled the door closed, and locked it.

The bay had been outfitted as a well-equipped workshop. It bristled with high-tech power tools, computers, TV cameras, phone equipment, surveillance gear, weapons, and explosives. Randak threw a switch. On one wall was a huge backlit projection of the stars and planets in our solar system and beyond. A dotted line was drawn through it, aimed straight at Planet Earth. Randak made entries in a computer. As he punched in data, the line on the backlit projection changed its trajectory; turned in a half-circle, as if commencing an orbit around the North Pole. Randak picked up a digital counter and entered some numbers The device began a countdown to zero hour. Ascension procedure was on track.

Randak began loading machinery into the van.

CHAPTER 69

2:36 P.M.
***National Revealer* Newsroom**
Los Angeles

A quiet ripple of curiosity swept across *The National Revealer* newsroom as seven editors, two senior reporters, and Cameron Tull left their desks and headed toward the big corner office. Mary, Queen of Scots, was convening an emergency meeting of her inner circle of courtiers—"The Heavy Mob," as they were called with sarcasm and grudging awe. This was the special team whistled into play whenever something big and secret was about to go down.

Mary snapped her compact mirror shut, tossing it and a lipstick into her top drawer as the group filed in and sat. She brought them up to speed, based on what she'd heard from Tull in an earlier meeting.

"Right, then," she said. "Cameron has traced Charmain to Bonnie Farr's little hideaway cabin. He's going to try for a sit-down interview with her. We want our own exclusive on this, obviously, but remember—this is not a normal story. We are committed to finding out who killed Steve Bellini and making sure they're punished. And even though there's circumstantial evidence that points at Charmain Burns, it's dodgy. Not solid enough. A slicky-boy lawyer would have her out of jail in five minutes, and—based on what we've seen with that murdering bastard O.J.—an L.A. jury will never convict a Hollywood star.

"Cameron's strategy will be to try to get her to confess during his interview—or at least say something that might trip her up later in the event of a trial. He might succeed in this, or he might not. At the very least, we'll get our exclusive story.

"But, the question arises: do we call in the police?"

The response came almost before she'd finished the question.

"Absolutely fucking NOT!"

It was Charlie McGurk, the paper's flinty News Editor, an ex-*New York Daily News* police reporter.

"Ah, the voice of experience speaks," said Mary softly. "And why don't we call the coppers, Charlie?"

A man of few words, Charlie kept it simple.

"Because some ham-handed dick might fuck everything up. It's our operation—period!"

Mary nodded. "I tend to agree. Any dissenters?"

Dudley Fernald, the Special Projects editor—a meticulous planner who'd earned a law degree while working nights on the *Chicago Sun-Times*—looked over at Tull.

"We can't be judge, jury, and executioner on this thing. If it blows up, we could look bad. Is there any danger to Charmain? How about this Randak character?"

Tull shrugged. "Randak wasn't with her when Charmain called. I'm almost certain he doesn't know where she is. If he did, he'd have been there. I put in the call to him to let him know his identity's blown and we're watching him. We know he's at his apartment because the reporter I have tailing him saw him go in. My phone call was a warning to back off Charmain."

Fernald raised his eyebrows. "And the answer to my question is…?"

"The answer is, I don't think she's in any immediate danger," said Tull. "However, Randak's a smart guy. I can't imagine how he'd find her, although I won't rule it out. But he knows we're on to him. I think the risk is acceptable."

Silence. Mary looked around the room, nodded.

"Right, then. Let's talk about how we'll proceed."

There was a brief free-for-all of ideas. Over the next thirty minutes, the plan was hammered out. A special team of reporters—three of them trained in high-risk driving by the famed Bondurant racing school—would proceed to a staging point off the Pacific Coast Highway about five miles from the cabin, then stand by in two cars and and a supply SUV. They'd be backed up by a radio-equipped motorcycle that would pick up the tail in case they got jammed in traffic. A helicopter manned by one reporter and two photographers would be on standby at Burbank Airport.

It was agreed that everyone would back way off until Tull gave the word. Tull would try to persuade Charmain to do a sit-down interview at the cabin—then turn herself in to the cops.

"What are the chances of this happening, Cameron?" Mary asked. "What does she gain by cooperating?"

"I've given Charmain the usual routine about telling the public her side of the story in her own way," said Tull. "A lot of it depends on the advice she gets from her advisers, if any. When I talked to Vidal a few hours ago, he didn't know where she was. I don't know if Kelso does, but I doubt it. He'd leave stuff like this to Vidal."

One of the senior reporters, Billy Duffy, piped up. "Are you going to let Vidal know where she is? Get him in on it? 'Cause if you do, he'll get a lawyer, and a lawyer will just tell her to say nothing."

Tull grinned. "Let me quote our friend Charlie McGurk: 'Absolutely fucking NOT!'"

Mary nodded. "That's it, then. We back off until Cameron advises us. No police. No Vidal Delaney. Charlie, you keep me posted."

The meeting broke up. Tull had one nugget of info he hadn't disclosed: he had Randak's cell phone number. Never know when that might come in handy. It was the one good thing that had come from a bad night for Dan Billings, the PI who prided himself on never blowing a tail.

Billings had been smarter than Tull the night of the screening bash for Clive Tinsdale at the Academy Theater. He'd realized that Charmain might show up at the event because she was vying for the "Medusa" role. And he had a hunch that Randak might be there. From past experience with star stalkers, Billings knew they loved to watch the objects of their obsession show up in fancy dress at glittering industry premieres and parties.

That night he'd parked on a side street in Beverly Hills and walked one block into Charmain's neighborhood, staying in the shadows. In less than five minutes, he'd spotted somebody sitting in a closed van. Too dark to make out who it was, but Dan treated him as a suspect. He crept up behind the vehicle, and very gently pierced the van's right rear taillight with the sharply-pointed awl of his Swiss Army knife. He held his breath, waited tensely. No movement inside the van. Good. He slipped back down the block and waited. About ten minutes later, he spotted movement in the house. Lights went off and the front door opened. It was Charmain.

Billings hot-footed it back to his car, pulled up to the end of the side-street and watched as she backed out of her driveway, then drove off in the general direction of Wilshire Boulevard. The van moved out, keeping well behind her. The minute its lights came on, it was dead easy to follow. Dan Billings grinned. Simple tricks were the best. He could spot the van easily. The tiny point of white light gleaming through the red lens of the taillight was visible at great distances or in heavy traffic. Just follow the shining white dot.

As he tailed the van, Billings switched on a high-tech piece of equipment even big-city police departments didn't have access to—an APS-104 unit. He drove up as close as he dared, switched it on. Just before they reached the theater, he lucked out. The driver made a cell phone call and the unit registered the number of the phone he was using.

That would have made it a great night for Dan, but he made one mistake. Instead of calling for backup when he saw the van park a block down Wilshire, he settled down to wait for Charmain to emerge after the event. He figured she'd be inside a couple of hours. About thirty minutes later, Dan had the powerful urge to take a leak. Anywhere else in L.A., he might have tried slipping down an alley. But the Beverly Hills cops frowned on public peeing. He went up the street to Kate Mantalini's restaurant, ordered a quick coffee, and used the john. He was back in ten minutes flat, but he'd blown it.

Charmain was gone. And so was Randak.

The day after his encounter with Randak and Charmain on the cliffs, Tull had asked Dan Billings if it was possible to track Randak's actual physical location by honing in on his cell phone.

"Not unless you're working for the CIA, FBI, or NSA," he said. "No cops or hackers have that kind of equipment."

Tull filed that fact away. In the meantime, he had Randak's cell phone number. And Randak didn't know it. He'd love to give the stalker another surprise. Phone him and say, *Hi! Thanks for saving the woman I love.*

Tull grinned. I'm getting to be quite the little stalker myself, he thought.

CHAPTER 70

6:31 P.M.
TULL'S HOUSE
MALIBU

IT was about 6:30 when Tull arrived home in Malibu. He kissed Jessica, held her a moment, and immediately sensed her tension.

"Jessica, what is it?"

"Nothing, I…I'm just tired."

"Jessica?"

She looked up at him. Strain had made her face a mask.

"Oh, God, Cameron…I've betrayed you, and even though I want that bitch dead, I shouldn't have…Oh, what is it they say about revenge? That it's a dish best eaten cold? Well, I guess I'm just not that cold. It felt good at first. Now it feels…sickening…"

"Jessica, what are you talking about?"

She told him everything. That Randak had called, that she'd given him Charmain's phone number.

Tull was appalled. She saw it in his face, and it frightened her.

"Oh, God, Cameron, I feel rotten. I just lost it when I realized she might get away with murder, and here was my chance to…"

"To execute her?" Tull snapped.

Jessica burst into tears. Tull held her in his arms.

"I'm sorry," he said.

"No, you have every right to be angry. It was so wrong…"

"Look, you did it," he said. "I wish you hadn't—and so do you—but you did. And who the hell can blame you, really? So stop worrying. Chances are, we'll get to her before Randak does. I don't think he knows where she is."

Tull looked at his watch. An hour ago, the reporter he'd put on Randak had called in to say he'd blown the tail, subject was on the move. Tull had phoned the cabin immediately. Got the answering machine, decided against leaving a message, figuring Charmain could be asleep, in the shower—or she might have split for another hideout. And was she even in danger from Randak? The stalker, if that's what he was in the classic sense, seemed anxious to protect her. If killing her was his goal, why hadn't he done it already? What was he waiting for?

After calming Jessica down, Tull left for the cabin by car. She asked to go with him, knowing it was out of the question. He just shook his head. She walked him to the car and kissed him. "I'm sorry, Cameron. Please, please be careful. If anything happens to you, I'll be to blame…"

"Stop it, Jessica, stop feeling so responsible. Remember, you wouldn't have been driven to do something so against your nature if Charmain hadn't invaded your life in the first place. Just be cool. I'll call you soon."

In the car, he phoned Bonnie Farr's cabin again. The answering machine picked up. He left a message for Charmain, asking her to call immediately, that he had something she had to know. He didn't mention Randak, figuring she'd run if she even heard his name.

Ten minutes passed. Either she was gone, or she wasn't going to answer. He phoned again. When the machine picked up, he said: "Charmain, call me now. I have news of Randak."

Tull paused, then went for it.

"Randak…if you're there, phone me immediately. Here's my cell phone number…"

He checked his watch, then kicked the Aston-Martin. The road hummed under the tires as he nudged ninety. Five minutes later, he checked his watch again. No callback. Which meant…what? The way he figured it, if Charmain was there alone, she'd have called him by now. And Randak would have responded, if only to find out what Tull was up to. Either Randak hadn't found Charmain—or he'd removed her from the cabin. Or he was too busy killing her to answer the goddamn phone. Shit!

Tull made a decision. Time to use his ace in the hole. He dialed Randak's cell phone number. Got an answer on the first ring.

"Yes?"

"George? It's Tull."

A long pause.

"Very good, Tull. You've reached me. What good do you think it'll do?"

"I just want to talk. Look—"

"Of course you want to talk. I'm sure you have someone tracing my location through a cellular district map. Goodbye, Tull."

"No! Wait…"

Randak opened the window of the van and flung his cell phone straight at the road unwinding before him.

It slammed into the Pacific Coast Highway at the equivalent speed of 118 miles per hour and shattered into dust.

Moments later, he turned onto the secondary road that would take him to the dirt track he was looking for.

At that moment, Tull reached Vidal Delaney at his office and quickly alerted him to what was going down.

"We didn't call you before this because we didn't think she was in danger," he said. "Now I think she might be and you should know."

"I'm heading up there by chopper," said Vidal. "If she calls you or me, all bets are off. She's still my client. As far as calling the cops is concerned, I think it's an overreaction at this point. First, we don't know Randak has her. She's probably safe, but if she's dead, we're too late anyway. If she's already a hostage, the cops can't get there fast enough anyway."

Tull said, "I'm not sure what to do, at this point."

In the end, they compromised. If neither of them had heard from Charmain by the time Vidal was airborne, he'd alert the cops that there might be a hostage situation.

CHAPTER 71

6:45 P.M.
CHARMAIN'S HIDEAWAY
MOUNTAINS ABOVE CARMEL

THE phone rang in the front room, which was empty. The answering machine clicked on.

Cameron Tull's voice said: "Charmain, call me immediately. You could be in danger. Randak, if you're there, you're already under surveillance. Don't do anything rash. Think about it. Call me on my cell phone number now!"

Charmain was in Bonnie Farr's shower. Rap music was pounding out of a large boombox. She turned off the faucet and stepped out of the shower. The bathroom was fabulous, she thought. And huge for such a small place. Marble. Giant roman-style bath. Eight dykes had crowded into it and played hide-the-soap last time she was here.

Charmain laughed at the memory. She was toweling off in front of a full-length mirror. She dried her hair, bent over, made the towel a turban. Straightening up, she looked in the mirror. Saw the image behind her. Recoiled. Randak!

She shrieked and started to jerk away, but he pinned her to him from behind, one arm under her naked breasts as the other arm snaked behind her neck. His fingers clamped down on her carotid artery in a chokehold that tilted her head sharply to one side. She struggled, convulsed, eyes rolled back. She went limp. Randak lifted her effortlessly, cradling her gently.

As he passed the throbbing boombox on a head-high shelf, he executed a perfect overhead kick and smashed it to pieces. The house went silent.

When Charmain regained consciousness, she was sitting upright on a high stool. Blindfolded, hands cuffed behind her, she tried to move her head, but it was totally immobilized by a massive clamp pressing in from both sides. She was still naked. She strained to push her knees together in reflexive modesty. But her ankles were chained far back on the stool's rungs, forcing her legs wide apart. She tried rocking the stool. It was immovable, bolted to the floor. Her breathing became shallow, rapid. Her ears strained, but she heard nothing.

Was he there, looking at her nakedness? Her exposed cunt? And the gold ring that adorned it? She'd never been so acutely sensitive, so aware, of her piercing. As if it was generating heat.

She screamed. "Let me go!...You bastard...Why are you doing this to me?"

No answer.

She screamed again. A door opened, closed. She cringed as soft footfalls came toward her. And stopped. She sensed him standing close. Her bladder convulsed. She wanted to whimper, but instead she shrieked, "Turn me loose, you sick motherfucker! NOW!"

The blindfold somehow made her super-sensitive to his physical presence, as if his slightest move was disturbing an electrical aura that enveloped them both. He changed position. She flinched, half expecting a blow. Or a vile caress.

He spoke, and his voice came from below her.

"My Queen!"

He said it reverently.

She recoiled as she felt his lips.

First on one foot. Then on the other.

She was confused by this bizarre homage, then felt a desperate flash of hope. Charmain wasn't truly into S&M, but she'd played sexual power games all her life, instinctively relished the role of dominatrix. Her mind raced. Maybe this creep wanted to be abused by a prime time sex symbol. She knew better than most how the power in sexual encounters can suddenly shift.

Learned it, literally, at her momma's knee.

Could she take the power? I'd goddamn better try, she thought.

"Yes, I AM your queen, slave!" she hissed. "Kiss my feet again. Worship them. NOW!"

She felt his lips on her bare feet. Her heart leapt. Shit, it's working.

Ohmigod! Be cool, now...don't go too fast...

"Tell me, slave. Are you thrilled to acknowledge my power as your queen?"

Randak's voice was low-pitched, heartfelt. "I have searched for you so long."

"Say it, slave. Say that you are in awe of my power."

"I am in awe of your power."

"And I am your queen? SAY IT!"

"You are my queen," said Randak.

Damn, she thought. It's working. Hope blazed like pure lightning.

Now. Take control now.

"Slaves are rewarded for their loyalty," she said. "But first, you must accept your punishment for not having the courage to reveal yourself as my faithful slave. And you've irritated my skin by making these ropes too tight. You must be punished."

Charmain took a deep breath. All her instincts as an actress, as a power player, told her she needed to make eye contact.

"Remove this blindfold, NOW!"

Randak laughed. Charmain tensed, sensing an off-key nuance. It hadn't been so much a laugh as…a chuckle. Not sinister, not resonating evil. Quite the opposite, almost.

Randak sounded…amused.

"You think you understand what is happening here, but you do not," he said. "But your instinct for survival, your strength, and your ability to fight on with your wits even when you are physically restrained makes me know that my planet will survive with you as our mother, our queen.

"Yes, it is time for the blindfold to come off. Time for you to see clearly for the first time. And to finally learn that nothing…not this moment, or even your own life…is what you believe it to be."

She flinched as she felt his hands. The blindfold came off. Her skin jumped at the shock of seeing him, really seeing him, for the first time. She blinked, not believing her own eyes.

"Oh, sweet Jesus," she moaned.

The horror hit her like a fist.

He was naked. And his muscular torso, from the chest down, was pierced by dozens of metal objects—rings, triangles, stars, crosses, bars, u-bolts—all in stainless steel.

Dazed, she looked up at his eyes. They burned with the zeal of a madman. Or a fire-and-brimstone preacher. Like her insane grandfather, the Reverend Galen Holcomb.

Randak spoke:

"You have been chosen for a great mission. I am a warrior from the most advanced civilization in the universe. My leaders are known as The Guides. Our planet is Kaldan, and our people are beings that, millions of years ago, looked much like you. We existed inside physical envelopes, or bodies, just like human beings.

"We became highly evolved. We shed our bodies and now exist as pure beams of light. But somehow, over time, our life-force, our inner energy, seemed to weaken. We were like…like lights that flicker in a power burn-out.

"Our scientists discovered that even though we had evolved into light, we still needed the essence of the biological life-force we sprang from. Without sacrificing our electro-magnetic aura, we needed to become corporeal beings again, regain our physical envelopes.

"Somehow, having bodies made us feel what you would call 'human.'

"Light and heat need an energy source, or they fade and cool. We, our race, needed an energy source. The seed, the life-force. The sperm of the male that combines with the egg of the female to create a physical being.

"But we no longer had the ability to mate in any physical way. So The Guides sent me to this planet and fused my aura into the egg of a human female at the time of her conception. My earth mother gave me a physical body. Now I am capable of mating.

"Yet we needed a human female to become our breeder-queen. I was put here to find a woman with heroic and queenly qualities. One who displayed the brilliance and ruthlessness of a true leader.

"You are that leader, Charmain."

Charmain drew a deep breath. Shit! Struggling to make sense of Randak's soliloquy, she had heard one theme loud and clear.

Sex.

He hadn't raped her yet, but…

"Okay, listen to me," she said. "I am not your leader. Also, there is insanity in my family. My mother did horrible things to me, abused me. Her father was the leader of a crazy backwoods bunch of religious loonies. He died handling rattlesnakes. My daddy was a weak man who killed himself.

"And me? I'm a fucking actress! You don't get much more unstable than that. Any kids I'd have should be strangled at birth. So get this really straight, goddamnit. I am not a leader! Yours or anybody fucking else's!"

Randak smiled.

"You are a leader, Charmain. I have watched you kill when necessary. You are single-minded, ruthless, and beautiful. There was a moment when I knew beyond doubt that you were my mate. It was when you fearlessly revealed to the world that you had pierced yourself in your womanhood. A taboo that you were willing to flout as a sign of self-mastery.

"Piercing the core of your sexuality proved that you, unlike other Earth primitives who pierce their flesh only through blind instinct, understand the mystical power of invading the body with pure metal.

"Millions of years ago, my race learned to gain dominance over our own bodies, to manipulate and change them."

Randak paused and spread his arms wide.

"Now comes the ultimate manipulation of physical matter. You and I will first be transformed into light and stored in a space probe hovering above the earth tonight, sent here by The Guides. Our bio-luminescence will be transported swiftly to Kaldan. Our human bodies will be regenerated from light.

"Then, I will have the honor of mating with you, my queen.

"Our race will be re-born and revitalized once my seed is transferred to you and our essences combine. Hail to The Guides, and to you, breeder-queen."

He moved toward her, arms still held wide. For the first time, Charmain looked directly at Randak's penis. Erect. And pierced. Through both the head and the shaft.

She felt hopelessness wash over her. Oh, God, he's a sick fucking lunatic and I'm going to die. First he's going to rape me and then…

"NOOO," she screamed as Randak stepped in past her spread knees and pressed himself against her.

"NOOOO...oh, help me, Jesus!"

Randak's arms went around her. He pulled her to him.

The shock was electric. Cold pinpricks of stainless steel stabbed her breasts and belly. His metal-tipped penis poked her thigh. She twisted, shrieked in absolute terror, anticipating the painful thrust inside her.

Randak shouted, "I embrace you, my queen. I yearn for the moment when I can at last transfer the seed."

He stepped back, bowed.

What the fuck...?

He isn't going to rape me?

He looked at her and shook his head, as if sensing her question.

"So much for you to understand," he said. "All will be revealed when we reach Kaldan. The Guides await our ascension."

"What are you talking about?" she wailed. "Oh God, don't you realize you're sick? This is all in your mind. There is no fucking planet. You just want there to be." Images of the Hale-Bopp Comet suicide cultists leaped into her mind. Oh, Jesus, help me, she prayed. She forced herself not to panic, to concentrate on reaching him somehow.

"Look, I can get you help. I'll...I'll take you home with me. You can live with me. I'll be your friend. We can have sex...anything..."

She looked into his eyes and heard the utter futility of every word she spoke. What was she going to offer this crazy fucker? Dancing at BuzzBuzz? Dinner at Spago? The Universal tour?

Randak had stepped out of her range of vision. Then he was back, carrying a high stool identical to the one she was sitting on. He placed it in front of her, sat. About six feet separated them.

"It is almost time and I must go first," he said. "It is necessary that I be on the planet when you arrive. If we transform into light at the same moment, my aura might mingle with your human spirit. That must not happen.

"I will become light first. Soon after, you will follow."

He looked at her and she shuddered at his mad smile.

"You may experience fear when you witness my transformation. But that is good. Fear concentrates the spirit at the moment it becomes light.

"What happens to me will happen in exactly the same way to you. Reflect on what you see. The piercing. It is the swiftest and purest way to achieve instant transformation. The aura, or spirit, is released cleanly."

He reached behind the stool and lifted a framework of metal attached to its back. He put his head in a clamp identical to the one that held her in rigid embrace. He was sitting erect, like her, head aligned with spine.

What the fuck...?

Something drew her eyes down. She looked under the seat of his stool. A blinking red light. It looked like a clock or counter of some kind. Numbers flashing. As she looked at it, the numbers stopped.

The count:

"0/0/0/0."

"Oh, shit," she said.

Randak smiled at her.

"Farewell, my queen!"

A loud metallic sound like a gunshot. His stool jerked. A gleaming steel spike shot out the top of his head, protruding six inches high. A fountain of blood welled around the shaft, spread swiftly across the skull, dripping down his face and congealing in rivulets like hot wax cooling on a candle.

His eyes, still open, lost their heat.

Randak 2000 was now light.

CHAPTER 72

8:20 P.M.
CHARMAIN'S HIDEAWAY
MOUNTAINS ABOVE CARMEL

CHARMAIN heard a weird howling. Like an animal hurting. A wild, ceaseless keening.

God! It hurts! Make it stop!

She felt raw pain in her throat and knew the shrieks were coming from her. She fought for control. Her eyes, tightly shut as the screams tore out of her, finally opened. And focused on the horror.

Randak 2000 stared at her sightlessly. The steel spike pointed up through the skull like a compass needle, tracking the path that had pierced his tortured brain and forever destroyed Kaldan—the planet that existed only in his fevered brain—in a fiery supernova.

George Tanner's world had ended. Swallowed up by a black hole in the deep space of his own mind.

Charmain's body convulsed in shuddering sobs. She twisted and strained against the ropes and head-clamp. Awareness flooded back, then terror as she remembered Randak's words:

"I will be transformed into light first. Soon after, you will follow."

Sweet Jesus. How soon? Oh God, how soon before I die?

Panic ripped through her as she looked at the bloody carcass. The husk of this evil presence that had stalked her like an avenger from hell.

The fucking Stalker From Outer Space.

Shit. It was goddamn funny, really.

Her mind, struggling desperately for escape, leaped to the future. She imagined laughing with Laddy and Bonnie and Leda. Telling them how she was going to pitch this whole story to a studio as a comedy movie. They'd giggle as she recounted her hilarious adventures with Randak the Geek.

"It's a high concept screenplay, right?" she'd say. "'Sex Goddess From Hollywood Meets the Stalker From Outer Space!' Is it way cool, or what?"

Randak's dead smile mocked her. Panic gripped her as she took in the horror of his impalement.

I'm going to die. Just like he died!

Her rectum contracted violently as her mind reeled through a video replay of her death...steel needle shooting up inside her...slow-motion of the deadly point puncturing organs...shooting up through the roof of her skull...

She screamed.

"Help, help...somebody...help me, pleeease..."

After a while she stopped, exhausted. Hopelessness washed over her. This is stupid! No one can hear me. I'm in the middle of the fucking woods, miles from anywhere. Close your eyes...stop looking at that fucking loser and think...think...think...how can I get out of this?...How much time have I got? No, don't think about that or you'll freak out again. Don't want to die...but how to escape? Is it revenge from God? For Momma...Bellini...Buster...Daddy?

Oh, Patrick. Why did you die? I'd have been safe with you...And my precious ones. What about them? I am their Protector!

The phone rang.

Her mind stopped.

It rang again.

She waited, not breathing...

The answering machine clicked on. Someone spoke. She burst into tears, weeping like a child at the sound of a human voice, knowing she couldn't answer, couldn't be heard no matter how hard she tried. Never had she felt so lonely, just hearing that voice. Choking on tears, she listened desperately, burning into her mind the last words she might ever hear.

"Uh, Charmain, this is Jessica Bell. Are you there? If you are, pick up. It's important...Hello?

"Okay...I...I don't know how to say this...and I don't really want to. Because I'd like to see you burn in hell, you evil bitch. You killed my baby brother, my little Stefano. I want you dead. Just like you want me dead. And you almost killed me, too.

"But I'm alive, thanks to that...thanks to Randak. That's why I'm calling. I know you could be in great danger from him.

"Look...after you called Cameron, he left and Randak phoned. And I...I gave him the phone number of where you are by hitting re-dial and letting him hear those little beeps. He said he could locate you through the number. I wanted revenge on you, justice for my brother. Now I realize I was wrong to do that and..."

White-hot anger burned away Charmain's tears. Now she was shrieking over Jessica's words, drowning her out. Not caring anymore about hearing the sound of a human voice. Not words from this shit-don't-stink bitch. This better-than-you-'cause-my-daddy's-rich cunt

"Fucking whore, I hate you," Charmain yelled. "I hope you die of cancer. You piece of shit, you uppity slut. YOU fucking told this MANIAC how to find me!

"I'M GOING TO DIE BECAUSE OF YOU! And now I have to listen to shit about how you're sorry you stopped being a good little girl just long enough to give this fucking monster my phone number...

"I HATE YOU...YOU WHORE...I HATE YOU...I WANT ALL YOUR FAMILY TO DIE OF CANCER...FUCKING WHORE..."

As Charmain ranted, Jessica voice continued...

"...and if you've got her, Randak, please don't harm her. That will just make things worse for you. Better to let the police have her, let the courts do their job. I believe in the system. I just went a little crazy because everybody seems to think that celebrities get away with murder, like O.J. Simpson. Now I want to do the right thing. So if you're there, Charmain, give yourself up. And if you have her, Randak, turn her in. I've told Cameron, so..."

Jessica paused.

"God, this is so weird. I don't know what else to say. If you are dead, I've done something terribly wrong."

The answering machine clicked off. Charmain, silent now, slumped against her restraints, wishing suddenly she could just close her eyes and go to sleep.

Six feet away, Randak slept forever, eyes open.

God, why do you make me sit here looking at him, seeing exactly how I'm going to die? Why do you hate me? Why did you let Momma hurt me? She stared at Randak, fighting her panic. Hating him. Taking back the control. Not fearing him.

Fucking dead piece of meat!

Taking a deep breath, she spit at him as hard as she could. A few drops spattered onto the body, six feet away. She felt good for a moment, the hate warming her.

So tired...oh Patrick, my darling Patrick, can you help me? Or is this how it's supposed to end? Will I see you soon? Oh yes...yes,...I'll be with you forever...

She dozed for what seemed like a long time. But it could have been seconds. Time. Oh shit. How much time? The clock with red numbers. Was it ticking away under her seat? How much time? Minutes? Seconds? Right NOW?

The phone rang.

Every nerve in her body twitched. Who's this? That bitch again? And in the split second between the second ring and the machine picking up, she suddenly recalled something Jessica had said, something she'd missed in her fury.

Her exact words had been, "I've told Cameron, so..."

Charmain felt faint, then wildly excited. Her first moment of hope. Oh God! If Jessica told Tull she gave Randak this number, he must be on his way here. Nothing would stop that bastard from running after a story like this. Maybe it's him on the phone, wanting to warn me!

Her ears picked up a sound from outside through the open windows. Was her mind playing tricks? Had she heard the faint sound of a car laboring up the hilly access road?

The voice on the phone filled the room.

"Charmain? You there?"

She started to weep. It was Mike Kelso! The one white knight who'd ride through hell to save her! If he knew she was in danger. Or where she was! But he didn't. He was calling back simply because she'd phoned him hours ago and left this number on his home machine.

"Okay, I guess you're out. But I can hardly wait to tell you this. I don't know what number I'm calling you at, but you said a friend's place and you're alone...so listen to this!

"YOU GOT THE PART! That's right, babe. You're gonna be Medusa. You beat out every actress in town. I just came from Tinsdale's office. Jay's still there working out the contract, and..."

Tull's headlights had just picked up the cabin up ahead when he heard Charmain's bloodcurdling scream echo through the hills. A drawn-out howling shriek that went on and on and on...

"Nnnnnoooooooooooooo...Nnnnnnoooooooooooo...!"

Christ! The son-of-a-bitch is killing her! Tull leaned on the horn and stomped the gas hard as he yelled through the open window:

"RANDAK...DON'T DO IT, YOU BASTARD...YOU CAN'T WIN THIS! LET HER GO..."

The car shot up the final stretch of road into the clearing. Tull leaped out and shouted at the cabin.

"RANDAK...COME TO THE DOOR...LET'S TALK!"

The screams stopped. In the sudden stillness, Tull heard a far-off whirring sound. A helicopter, approaching from the south. Then a yell from the cabin.

Charmain.

"TULL...HELP ME! PLEASE HELP ME!"

She was alive!

Inside the cabin, Charmain writhed and twisted in excitement, hope lighting up her soul. She heard Tull shout back:

"WHERE'S RANDAK?"

Tull, still about a hundred feet from the cabin, was approaching cautiously, ready to dive into the underbrush.

Charmain yelled, "HE'S DEAD...HE'S DEAD...BUT YOU'VE GOT TO HURRY! OH TULL, PLEASE HURRY...!"

Charmain heard him pounding up the crushed stone pathway. "Oh sweet Jesus, thank you...I'm saved," she said aloud.

Tull burst through the cabin door.

Jesus Christ!

His mind struggled to comprehend the hellish scene. The first shock was her nakedness. Then the horror of Randak's bloody, lifeless stare. He saw Charmain's eyes, alive with fear, pleading. Her mouth worked desperately. "Tull...please...help!"

He knew it was hopeless when he saw the chains, the head clamp—and the red numbers of the digital clock flashing beneath her. He grabbed the stool, tried to move it. No good. Bolted down. Jesus! Could he cut the bolt, unscrew the chains somehow? He looked under the stool. Some kind of machine. Attached to a timing device. A fucking bomb? He looked over at Randak. Saw the identical device. Not a bomb. A diabolical fucking death machine. He looked at the numbers on the clock, counting down to zero. Fuck! What was left? A minute? Think, goddamnit, think. Get in control.

"Charmain, are there any tools in here? Bolt-cutters, big wrenches?"

He fumbled with the chains holding her down. Impossible. She was tied down for keeps. Immobile. No time. NO FUCKING TIME...

He suddenly realized he was yelling.

Charmain spoke.

So quietly it stopped him cold. He looked in her eyes.

Calm as death.

"Tull! Listen...I know I'm going to die. You've got to help me. I've got to take care of my babies..."

"Your babies?"

She spoke fast, but not hysterically. "I can't explain it all to you now. Just listen. Ask Marta. My assistant. Tell her I said to give you my babies. And tell my manager, Mike Kelso, to give all my money to them. He's in charge of my money, and..."

Tull had pressed the "record" button on the tiny Olympus tape recorder he always carried.

He broke in: "Cameron Tull speaking to Charmain Burns, who is giving her last will and testament. Is that right, Charmain?"

"Yes, yes, that's right..."

"And knowing you are facing death, you are of sound mind and able to make this decision?"

"YES, goddamnit! I'm scared shitless, but I'm thinkin' just fine. Tull, quick, there's no time. Do you promise you'll take care of my babies? They need protection. Do you swear?"

He looked into her eyes, touched her cheek, nodded.

"I swear, Charmain. But who...?"

Charmain's eyes blazed. She looked...ecstatic. At last, he'd come to her.

He laughed, held out his hand, beckoning her...

Oh, Patrick, thank God! Now we can...

The flashing red light blinked for the last time:

"0/0/0/0..."

Tull flinched at the metallic clack of a trigger, saw the light flicker and die in Charmain's eyes. The steel spike exploded through body and brain, and out the top of her head. Blood misted down her forehead.

The fierce spirit of Charmain Burns faded to black.

Fighting shock and nausea, Tull moved to her slowly. He put his hand up to her face and closed her eyes.

"You were a piece of work, lady. You paid your dues, so rest in peace."

He turned and looked at Randak, recoiling at the metal piercings that studded his body.

Jesus!

Helicopter blades cut the air overhead. The sound jerked Tull out of his reverie.

Time for the news.

He reached into his jacket pocket for his trusty Olympus Stylus. Even pro photogs carried these compact jobs as backup for their fancy Nikons. He clicked the off roll fast. He wanted the shots in the camera and the film hidden before the cops arrived. You never knew when they'd try to confiscate crime scene photos.

Overall shot of the scene first. Get them both together. Now individual shots of each. Click. Click. Click. Flash is working. Good. I've got the basic shots. Now go for some angles.

Jesus! He felt creepy. But this was news. It was what he did. Tull's cell phone rang, almost drowned in the clacking roar overhead.

Floodlights washed the clearing outside the cabin. The cell phone rang again, insistently. Probably Vidal, calling from upstairs. He crouched to get an upward angle on Charmain. Off to one side so he wouldn't be shooting between her legs. The breasts were unavoidable, but they'd be obscured by a black bar in the paper.

His cell phone rang again. Okay, just one more shot and…

Then he saw it.

A tiny digital counter just below the larger one that had stopped at 0/0/0/0.

This little clock was still ticking away, numbers flashing brightly…0/0/1/7…0/0/1/6…0/0/1/5…

Of course…

Fucking Randak!

A booby trap. Just for him.

He dove through the cabin door, rolled down the steps. Picking himself up, he raced past his car and punched his still-ringing cell phone. He heard Vidal's voice and yelled into the phone:

"Fire in the hole…get some altitude fast!"

In the air, Vidal grabbed the radio mike and yelled at the cop chopper on the air-to-air channel.

"Fire in the hole…Break off NOW…Fire in—"

The cabin exploded and shot skyward on a pillar of fire that lit up the night sky. Vidal saw the police helicopter caught by the shock wave. It shook and faltered, then recovered and zipped off to the west.

On the ground, crouching by a clump of rocks, Tull saw his Aston-Martin explode in the clearing. He winced, then shrugged and punched the speed-dial on his cell phone.

"*Revealer*...Eva. That you, Cameron?"

"Yeah. Send in the troops."

"Our chopper just called in an explosion up there. You okay?"

"Yeah. Tell the Queen of Scots I've got pictures."

"Of...?"

"Of Charmain and Randak 2000...in hell together."

EPILOGUE

2:15 P.M.
TULL'S OFFICE AT *THE REVEALER*
LOS ANGELES

THE next morning, a large Federal Express package landed on Tull's desk at *The Revealer*. He'd spent hours in editorial meetings and police debriefings and didn't get back to his office until midday.

Tull was exhausted but thrilled. The rest of the press was reporting on the sensational death of a star at the hands of a stalker—but *The Revealer* would soon hit the streets with an exclusive that'd blow 'em away:

CHARMAIN BURNS: MURDERER…AND VICTIM!

Tull saw the FedEx package, looked at the sender's name:

George Tanner.

He ripped it open. Inside was a thick, leather-bound journal. A note was attached:

Tull:
For your archives.
Farewell…
R.

Tull leafed through it. Each page contained a separate entry, handwritten. Like a diary, or…

His eye fell on a heading repeated throughout the document. It read:

Kaldan Warrior Report to The Guides—from Randak 2000:
Greetings…

Tull turned back to the journal's first entry. It was written in pencil, on cheap lined paper that had yellowed with age. It appeared to have been torn from a school notebook, then pasted onto the journal's expensive-looking, gold-edged paper.

In a childish scrawl, it read:

"To The Guides:

"I am so proud I am a warior of Kaldan. When you came to the cellar last night I was scared at first. You looked like the britest light in the world. Like the sun.

"You told me I am on a special mission. I was sent here to learn about this planet from my Earth mother. I am not afraid now. Before I was scared becose my stepfather came to live with us. Now I can be strong. I will never

cry even when he hurts me. Even when he makes me bleed.

"I will never be scared of the cellar in the dark. When I am bigger I will go on my special mission you told me about and save our planet Kaldan. And my name will be Randak 2000.

"You said even a boy can be a strong warior. I will follow your comands and write reports about how strong I am getting..."

Tull lost control to the emotion surging through him. Tears stung his eyes as he realized what he was reading. He saw, pasted on the page, a penny arcade photo of a little boy of eight or nine.

Looking into the camera...

Saluting.

Tull sat very still, composing himself. Then he got up swiftly, tucked the journal under his arm, and picked up a large utility bag from his desk. He left, mumbling over his shoulder to Eva, "I'm off the clock until you hear from me. I'll check messages."

He drove to Jessica's house. She opened the door and immediately asked, "What's wrong?"

Tull showed her the journal.

Jessica wept. Bitter tears.

"Just two abused kids? Are you telling me that my brother died because that bitch and that...that monster...were tortured as children? Jesus! Now you've got me crying for them. God, how can people be so horrible? Who could hurt an innocent child?"

Tull said, "Speaking of innocent children..."

He reached into his bag, pulled out an inlaid wooden chest and placed it in front of her.

"Open it."

Jessica lifted the lid on the box Charmain's assistant Marta had turned over to Tull early that morning.

Inside were photos of six little children. Black and brown and white kids. Happy faces, solemn faces, shy faces. Wide-eyed at the magic and wonder of looking into a camera.

Jessica gasped as she laid the photos out on the table, one by one. On the back of each photo were vital statistics: Name, Age, Country of Origin, etc. And a company name: ChildHelpers, Inc.

"My God," she said. "So this is what Charmain meant when she asked you to protect her babies?"

He nodded.

"I've heard of this organization," Jessica said. "You 'adopt' a child and send money every month. And the child writes to you, tells you how they're doing in school. They're all so poor...Oh, Cameron..."

He shook his head. "Sad, huh? Marta tells me Charmain started 'adopting' them once she hit it big. She wrote each child faithfully, made sure their money was sent. Marta says it was the one thing she never dared screw up. Charmain loved these kids."

Jessica wiped her eyes. "No mystery why she wanted to protect other children, I guess. After the horrible betrayal of her childhood."

"No."

"And her request to leave all her money to them? I mean, her will…?"

"I've got an opinion from a judge. He says my tape will stand up as Charmain's last will and testament."

Jessica held up the photo of a little doe-eyed girl of about four.

"Isn't she precious?"

Tull nodded. "She's a sweetie. They're all cute."

Jessica put the pictures down. "I've got to stop looking. I'm so damned emotional. So…"

Tull looked at her, questioning....

"Well, they've got to know someone's still there for them, Cameron. Somebody's got to write to them. Who's going to do that?"

Jessica's eyes looked straight into his heart.

Tull cleared his throat and said:.

"Well…I thought maybe we could."

-------------30------------